THE STORM OF THE DARK

Shapes were forming in the sky above Quareem. Great writhing things, shot through with the grays and blacks of thunderclouds, they broke up and swirled into a host of smaller shapes, creatures that moved so quickly it was difficult to follow them. They had faces of a kind—wide, staring faces, with eyes like beams of fury and hatred. Quareem spoke to them. They listened avidly like a starving crowd promised a feast.

Quareem motioned to Zellorian. "Stand beside me. You and I will drink the power. The lives of the ten thousand will bring forward the lords of the death-storm that were locked away millennia ago. The elementals will summon them as they sate themselves on blood. And when they come, all Innasmorn will shudder!"

STAR REQUIEM

BOOK 1

MOTHER OF STORMS

ADRIAN COLE

AVON BOOKS • NEW YORK

AVON BOOKS
A division of
The Hearst Corporation
1350 Avenue of the Americas
New York, New York 10019

Copyright © 1989 by Adrian Cole
Cover illustration by Lee Gibbons
Published by arrangement with the author
Library of Congress Catalog Card Number: 92-93076
ISBN: 0-380-76767-8

First AvoNova Printing: October 1992

AVONOVA TRADEMARK REG. U.S. PAT. OFF. AND IN OTHER COUNTRIES, MARCA REGISTRADA, HECHO EN U.S.A.

Printed in the U.S.A.

RA   10   9   8   7   6   5   4   3   2   1

CONTENTS

BOOK ONE – THE SANCTUARY

BOOK TWO – ZELLORIAN

BOOK THREE – THE WARHIVE

BOOK FOUR – AMERANDABAD

BOOK FIVE – STORM CREATURES

EPILOGUE

BOOK ONE

THE SANCTUARY

1

WINDMASTER

It was early morning when word came to the village. Dawn had barely broken, the air was still crisp and the faintest of breezes stirred the trees that closed around the foot of the earthwork slopes. Winter had passed, and the season of high winds and storms was over; the land dozed under a more peaceful sky. Hounds, stretched across the thresholds of their masters' homes, cocked their ears at the sound of the far wind as if hearing it speak to them of the vanished winter. A number of them growled low in their chests.

Although the village was under no threat from any of its neighbours, there were always a number of guards set about its perimeter at night, beyond the earthworks. Most of them, like the hounds, were more asleep than awake. Occasionally they met and exchanged a brief conversation.

Two of them spoke now, leaning on their wooden javelins and gazing out across an opening in the forest where a track stretched upwards through the trees to hills in the west. The men knew someone was coming, riding quickly from the foothills, for the breeze had already warned them, whispering in the dawn light like a lover.

'He comes in haste,' said Gadrune, wondering if he could also taste panic on the air.

Decran yawned. He was getting too old to stand guard any more. But his pride wouldn't let him relinquish the authority that went with the post. 'Aye. I expect the horse is as tired as I am.'

Gadrune grunted, concentrating. He moved slowly through the low trees, and although he was aware of who was coming, he still concealed himself. 'Warn the others,' he said, not taking his eyes off the track.

Decran nodded sleepily. Gadrune was being unnecessarily fussy: if this were an enemy coming, he would hardly ride so noisily and openly upon them. But he turned back to the embankment, seeking one of the rows of tiny chimes that would wake anyone not yet out of sleep. They tinkled as he touched them lightly, the notes floating over the earth and down to the lodges beyond.

In a moment the rider burst out of the trees across the clearing and raced furiously over the open ground, the steed wide-eyed but eager. The young man riding the animal would have raced on past Gadrune, but the latter blocked his path well before he could be met. The rider pulled up, earth flying about his mount, his cloak whipping about him as if he had brought a minor gale with him.

'Gadrune!' shouted the youth, though his physique was that of a seasoned warrior. Gadrune gaped, recognising him at once. It was Tronmar, a son of this very village, who had been chosen to go westward to serve higher masters. But how the lad had changed! His eyes held a wildness, his whole bearing a military stiffness, and even his voice, speaking the single word, cut like a weapon. But what now shocked Gadrune more was the steed. As he studied it, he realised it was no ordinary horse, and though it stamped its feet and drew breath with a snort, it had something else about it, a darkness almost, as though the elements had shaped it and given it powers of its own. Its lower legs seemed lost in a haze for a moment as if the beast could be part phantom.

Gadrune felt himself stiffening with sudden fear. He tried to mask it quickly. 'What storm brings you here, Tronmar?' He could scent no fear in the youth, only excitement.

'Not ill news. But I must speak to the clan elders quickly. They must be prepared.'

'For what?'

'Vittargattus, clan chief of the Vaza, is sending out his shaman, to speak to all the Vaza clans. I bring you word of Kuraal, who will be here this very day.'

Gadrune raised his brows, looking across at the trees as if

4

he would see the renowned shaman standing there already. 'Kuraal! Why should such a powerful man visit us?'

'You will hear soon enough,' said Tronmar. He dismounted, calmed his steed and spoke to it. It turned and slipped like mist into the forest. Gadrune walked beside the youth towards the embankment. 'I know very little,' Tronmar told him. 'But Vittargattus is mobilising.' He spoke softly, as though mindful of the least breeze, thinking it might steal the words.

Gadrune felt his heart pumping. Mobilising! War? Surely the ambitions of the clan chief did not stretch further than the almost limitless lands he already had.

They came down over the earthworks to the first houses, which merged in with other trees, wisps of smoke drifting up from their thatched roofs like the last of the mist. Decran had already brought a number of the elders and senior warriors together, and though they smiled at Tronmar and gave him welcome, they could not conceal their inner qualms at the change in him. The youth was a messenger of the clan chief's men. It might mean a tax levy, or worse, a call for soldiers to go west. And Tronmar's very bearing spoke of the latter.

Above the central court of the village, crouched in the thick branches of the trees like cats, silent and invisible, a trio of young men watched the arrival of Tronmar. They, too, had reached the instant conclusion that the former son of the village had come here to fetch arms rather than tax. One of the youths, Armestor, was about to speak, when the eldest of them, Ussemitus, motioned him to be still.

The voice of Tronmar drifted up clearly on the air which had become very still, the breeze dropping to nothing. 'I can tell you very little myself. The Blue Hair will do that when he arrives. Listen carefully to what he tells you.' He looked about him, ears cocked. 'I should not say it, but he is powerful, and not to be disobeyed. I have seen what the Windmasters can do.'

'What does he mean?' said Armestor nervously, unable to keep his tongue still. 'What's a Blue Hair?'

5

'Sorcerer,' hissed the other lad, Fomond,

'The old mothers say that to scare you,' snorted Armestor, though by his face he was not convinced.

'Shut up!' said Ussemitus.

'I must ride south and let other tribes know of Kuraal's coming,' said Tronmar, his eyes for a moment scanning the trees where Ussemitus and his companions hid. But he turned back to the elders. 'Do you know anything of the mountains in the north east? Has anything been seen there?'

'Not since the night of the Falling Sky,' one of the elders answered, and there were confirming nods.

Tronmar grunted. Then he thanked them and went back swiftly to the outer embankment. In a short while he had ridden away as quickly as he had come, leaving behind him an excited murmur in the village.

Ussemitus and his companions slipped down from the trees and found another way out of the village, going to a private place of their own about a mile from it, a rocky outcrop that overlooked the path, where they could feel reasonably safe from prying eyes. A gurgling stream nearby muffled their whispers from ears that might otherwise have strained to catch their secrets.

Ussemitus was the strongest and fittest of the trio, being unusually muscular for one of his race, for the villagers of these forest clans were generally thin and wiry. Ussemitus also had a keen mind, which his friends were quick to respond to, not least because he questioned things about the world that they preferred not to, something which had brought him under the watchful eye of the elders from an early age. If there were rebels in the camp, they invariably found their way to Ussemitus. Even so, he was by no means a villain and not considered one, for he put the safety of the village before anything else, something which the elders respected in him.

He leaned back among the rocks, warmed now by the rising sun. 'Kuraal,' he murmured. 'The Blue Hair.'

Armestor had only recently attached himself to Ussemitus and his companions, and was a year or two younger. He was even thinner than most of his fellows, something which helped account for his almost perpetual nervousness. He had a pinched face and eyes that were never still, alert as a cat's. '*Is* he a sorcerer?'

Ussemitus shrugged. 'He's a shaman. Vittargattus has many, and they are ruled by an inner ring, the Windmasters. They're supposed to be able to control the storms and converse with the wind elementals.'

Fomond grinned. He enjoyed such tales, though he had always been more sceptical than wary, unlike Armestor, who was a devout believer. Fomond stroked the wooden knife that he always carried. 'They say that, no doubt, so that they can keep a grip on poor simpletons like us.'

'You ought to be more careful,' admonished Armestor. 'The wind hears everything.'

Fomond's grin widened. 'I bless the wind,' he bowed. 'But no one rules it.'

'I don't think we should dismiss the shamen too lightly,' said Ussemitus. 'I've heard some strange tales about them. Especially the Blue Hairs, though they're supposed to be a secretive lot. Kuraal is from the inner ring, and will have the ear of Vittargattus himself.'

'So he's a Windmaster?' said Armestor, impressed.

'Yes. And as such would not normally have anything to do with such a remote village as ours.'

Armestor's eyes bulged. 'Why do you think he's coming?'

Ussemitus looked across at Fomond, who nodded. 'Interesting that Tronmar asked about the north eastern mountains.'

Armestor was about to speak, but something out in the trees alerted him and he ducked down. Instantly Ussemitus and Fomond were on their bellies, listening for movement. In a while they heard soft calls and rose up, relieved. Two more of their companions were coming, Arbos and Gudrond. Arbos was a tall fellow, his face seemingly a permanent frown, though he was good-natured enough in his way, and Gudrond was shorter, as nervous at times as Armestor.

'Heard the news?' Gudrond said.

Ussemitus nodded patiently, sensing Fomond's annoyance. Fomond had no time for Gudrond and found him garrulous and crude. Ussemitus, however, guessed that Gudrond's bluster was meant to impress and was essentially harmless. 'Yes. We're to be honoured by a visit from a Blue Hair. We were just saying that we thought it might have something to do with the Falling Sky.'

'That was ages ago,' said Armestor. 'Just about forgotten.'

'Not by Vittargattus, nor his spies,' said Ussemitus.

'Maybe the Windmasters caused it,' said Fomond, though it was clear from his expression that he was being facetious.

'You think so?' said Gudrond, taken in.

Fomond snorted. 'No, you fool. They fear the mountains.'

'I think you're probably right,' said Ussemitus. 'But we'll know when Kuraal gets here.'

'When will that be?' said Armestor.

'Half a day,' said Fomond, as though he had already seen the clan chief's shaman far away.

'Well,' said Gudrond. 'I've business in the village. There's a certain wench expecting me — '

Ussemitus saw the look of derision cross Fomond's face, but said nothing. Gudrond would learn to curb his boasting in time. It may yet be a painful lesson.

Towards the middle of the afternoon the wind began to rise in pitch, tugging at the branches, spinning dust in the village. The sun slipped under a cover of racing cloud, huge grey shapes that sped like harbingers from the west. Everyone in the village had been told; they had been preparing busily since Tronmar's visit, as though Vittargattus himself was coming. Ussemitus and his companions had dutifully helped with the preparations, though they found it irksome. It seemed there was to be a feast tonight: nothing was too good for Kuraal and his party. Word had come that it was fifty strong, a guard of picked Vaza warriors. The young girls giggled and ran about excitedly; the elders shook their heads in anticipation of this visit, knowing that the clan chief must be preparing for conflict and probably on a large scale. But who was the enemy? What had the north-east to do with it?

The men of the village were inspected repeatedly, all of them decked for battle, their spears sharpened and dressed with fine plumes. They lined up to be studied until they thought the elders would never be satisfied.

A sudden gust of air heralded more cloud and shadow, until dust swirled in from the west, sent, it was said, by the shaman. When figures and horses materialised at last, they found the village ready for them, the narrow street lined with silent, reverent villagers. Among them Ussemitus and his companions waited, eyes fixed ahead of them, though Fomond glanced once at Ussemitus and upwards in mock exasperation. Armestor and Gudrond were rigid, like hares caught in the shadow of a diving hawk.

Kuraal rode at the head of his party, his horse moving at a gentle trot, its gaze haughty, so that all those who followed behind seemed to do so at its express command. Ussemitus could not keep from looking at the magnificent grey. His companions, however, were far more interested in the shaman.

He was very tall, his face unusually dark, framed in long wisps of hair that reached his waist. It was light blue in colour, carefully dyed, and looked to be the texture of silk, something which had the women gasping in amazement. Kuraal had a sharply pointed nose and eyes that were cold, lidded as though protected from a climate of sandstorms. He did not come from the northern forests, though no one doubted his loyalty to the renowned clan chief.

The Blue Hair dismounted before the village elders, his warriors following suit. A place had been prepared for the horses in one of the stockades and they were led away without fuss. Kuraal nodded silently to the elders, and after a few hushed words which no one else heard, he was escorted into the central long hut where the day's preparations had been centred.

'Now we wait, I suppose,' grunted Armestor. Only the elders and selected warriors of the village were to go in to the banquet and to hear the words of Kuraal.

'Never mind. We'll hear the rest tomorrow,' said Fomond.

'Shall we go and talk to some of the soldiers?' suggested Ussemitus. 'They must know something about the clan chief's intentions.'

The others agreed at once, and they did join other villagers in going to Kuraal's guards, most of whom had not gone in to the hall and were to be housed in another long hut. After a moment, Ussemitus slipped away from the growing chatter. It was easily achieved, for his fellows were eager to hear what news they could and no one noticed Ussemitus go to the rear of the long banqueting hut. Fomond was already there, grinning at him. He pointed upward.

'You first. I'll keep watch,' he said.

Since they had been children, they had been using this secret way in to the hall, where they had heard many an intriguing bit of news about the village and the clans of the forest lands. It was a secret they shared with no others, another link in the particular bond that had always kept them as close as brothers.

Ussemitus shinned up the wall easily, squeezing himself in through a gap he had made in the thatch earlier that afternoon. Moments after he was inside, Fomond was beside him. They pulled the thatch back into place, listening to the sounds below them. They were straddling the thick beams of the long hut, coated with dust and shadow. Slowly they edged along them, moving out to a point where they could see what transpired below clearly, and hear every word. But they were high enough up in the darkness not to be seen.

There was little conversation: the shaman had brought with him an atmosphere, as though he was not quite human. He sat at the head of the long table, guards at either side of him, and ate sparingly of the cooked meat put before him, though he seemed satisfied with it. He should, mused Ussemitus, it was the best venison, freshly killed. Kuraal's guards were less mannerly, eating with the appetites of men long on the road, though they were careful not to drink too much of the rough mead, which was notorious throughout the lands of the Vaza.

The moment came at last for Kuraal to begin speaking. Silence was instant, and Ussemitus felt it outside the thatch as well as within, a great pall of it, as if the whole of the north paused to hear this message.

Kuraal did not stand. He merely sat back, wiped his thin lips and gestured for his plates to be removed. He sipped at the mead and then looked at the anxious faces. 'Some time ago,' he began in a harsh voice, 'there was a storm, if storm it was.' Everyone knew what he was referring to. 'In the north-east. In the mountains. My brothers and I have been observing those mountains very carefully. We have spoken to the storms about them.'

No one whispered, nor moved. Fomond nudged Ussemitus, but the latter ignored him.

'Has anyone in your forest lands learned anything about the night of the Falling Sky?'

For a long time no one spoke. They had all come here in the expectation of knowledge, being given secrets, not to be asked questions. But at last one of the villagers rose. This was Scoramis, not an elder, but one of the most respected of the huntsmen.

'In my work,' he said, 'I travel to the limits of our lands with my trackers, sire. We have been far north of here. We have seen lights in the mountains. That is all, sire. Lights. But of strange hues.'

'You've seen no one?' said Kuraal coldly.

11

Scoramis shook his head, sitting down.

Kuraal nodded. 'There are intruders there.'

The company was moved by this, and even Ussemitus felt a stab of surprise. Intruders. The word cunjured up numerous meanings, but the Blue Hair had made it sound like a curse.

'They are not from our world,' went on Kuraal. 'Though we cannot say where they are from. From a darkness beyond us, and of an evil that cannot be tolerated. We have spoken to the storms, but the storms have not answered us on this. The intruders, I say again, are not of Innasmorn.'

The shaman waited until the whisperings and mutterings had died down. Now he rose, and in doing so seemed to grow abnormally in height. 'Vittargattus is already preparing for war.'

Ussemitus glanced across at Fomond, barely seeing him in the shadow. 'War?' he whispered, the word hovering like the threat of disaster.

Fomond shrugged. 'What kind of evil has come to the mountains?'

The voice of Kuraal cut through their thoughts. 'I am here to warn you all of this menace. We know little about it. Only that it will spread from the mountains and seeks to destroy us all. We must take the war to the north-east before this happens. Vittargattus mobilises in the west at Amerandabad. You must prepare to join him when he comes. Your warriors must be made ready, armed, primed.'

'Will the clans go into the mountains?' someone asked. They had never been traditional Vaza hunting grounds.

'Not at first,' said Kuraal, and his features changed as if he were about to draw on some deeper wisdom, an echo of the storms he spoke of. 'We will conjure up and send a storm upon these intruders, a scourging that will weaken them, and then our armies will close in from the west and south.'

Ussemitus and Fomond looked hard at each other. 'Whoever these intruders are,' said Ussemitus, 'they are feared.

12

Has no one communicated with these people? It is a rash war if not.'

Kuraal was gazing upwards, eyes fixed on some remote darkness. His face changed and he scowled under hooded brows. He lifted his hand and moved it gently as though stirring the air. In a moment a breeze eddied about him, quickly becoming a gust. Something moved invisibly within it, something feral and angry. It span and plates clattered off the table as if the gust spread. Kuraal pointed up into the rafters and it was as if he had flung the eddying pool of air upwards. Ussemitus suddenly found himself caught in it, the air surging around him, buffeting at him, and then there were *claws*, unseen but vicious.

Fomond leaned back, gripping the beam with his arms and legs to prevent himself from toppling. Ussemitus was less fortunate. The wind howled like an animal, tearing at his hands. He could not hold on and fell, crashing down on to the table amidst a debris of tankards and platters. There were angry shouts; weapons were pulled out, and in a moment he found himself pinned. His shoulder ached where he had landed on it, but there were no bones broken. Fomond gaped down at him helplessly, but he could do nothing.

Kuraal smiled in his cold way, gesturing for Ussemitus to be brought before him. His own guards pointed their swords at the youth and to his complete surprise he saw that they were not made of wood, but of *metal*. But such things, surely, were forbidden.

'You were saying?' Kuraal challenged him.

Ussemitus straightened up, clinging to what little dignity he had left. He cleared his throat, aware that the elders were livid. They would expect an accounting for this intrusion.

'Well?' said Kuraal. 'Something about a rash war? You seem singularly well advised.'

'I know nothing about these intruders,' said Ussemitus. 'I knew of the storm in the north east, as we all do.'

'You would rather Vittargattus sent gifts to these people?'

13

'Who are they?' Ussemitus heard himself say, as if he had been prompted by some inner voice.

'Sire,' began one of the elders, anxious for Ussemitus.

But Kuraal gestured for silence. 'Who are they?' he echoed. 'They are a danger to us. A race of beings from far beyond us. They have brought with them the ancient curse.'

This was the first allusion he had made to this and his audience reacted as though he had waved fire in their faces. Even Ussemitus felt his throat constrict.

'Oh yes,' nodded Kuraal. 'They have brought with them the kind of powers that once destroyed our ancestors, the powers which we have forbidden. Things of steel, artefacts, metals.'

Again Ussemitus looked at the drawn swords and seeing his look, the Blue Hair took one of the blades from a guard beside him. 'Metal,' he said. 'Very little is used on Innasmorn. Only certain items are made of metal, blessed by the Windmasters, protected from the dangers they once bore. These warriors are close to your clan chief. They carry the blessed metal. But not so the intruders.'

Ussemitus felt himself going dizzy. There were so many legends, so many myths, about the past, the first people on Innasmorn. And about the artefacts they had used, the dreadful weapons that had brought death to so many races of the world. But in spite of his welling fears, he found himself speaking again, unable to prevent the flow of words.

'Who has seen them? Who has spoken to them?' he called above the noise.

Kuraal gazed about him impassively until everyone was quiet. 'Spoken to them? We shall speak to them with fire and with storm. In a year we will be ready. Will we not?' He directed this last at the elders, and none of them could meet his gaze. But they nodded in silence.

'I suggest,' Kuraal told Ussemitus, 'that you look to your training. You seem a strong youth. I will forget the unfortunate circumstances of our meeting. You just remember your duty.'

Ussemitus bowed, and was led from the hall by one of the elders and two of the senior village warriors. Outside, the elder, Philotor, struck him hard across the face.

'You have brought shame to us! How *dare* you act so irresponsibly! Have you no conception of how important Kuraal is to Vittargattus?'

Ussemitus wiped his face, keeping his eyes down. There was no point in defending himself from this verbal onslaught.

'You're lucky he didn't have your head on a plate. Now get back to your tasks. If Vittargattus says it's war, then we arm ourselves and join his ranks.'

They left Ussemitus and returned to the hall. He moved away, conscious of a number of people watching him. In a moment he was joined by Fomond.

'We'd better keep well away until the Blue Hair has left,' said the latter. 'I thought they'd skin us!' He chuckled.

Ussemitus clapped him on the shoulder. 'They need us, though, eh? Our bows.' He led his friend away and up over the earthworks into the forest.

Fomond knew from his silence, however, that he was far from content. 'It still troubles you, this business?'

Ussemitus nodded. 'Kuraal? No, he could have had us flogged, but it would have been embarrassing for the village. It erodes support.'

'I mean the intruders. If they are what Kuraal says, we could be in grave danger. The Curse – '

'I am just surprised that no one has communicated with these people. I remember some years ago there was talk of a battle with the marsh clans. They were supposed to have insulted us and for a while there were rumours, insults, a few scuffles. We prepared for an invasion, and so did they. In the end, when the elders got together they decided that it was all so much hot air. A misunderstanding. There was no reason for war, and a good many lives must have been spared.'

'Surely this is different,' said Fomond.

'How do we know?'

'We can't.'

Ussemitus chuckled, for once less serious. 'Perhaps we ought to find out.'

2

THE INTRUDERS

They rode for ten days through the forests, heading northwards, screened from the sky by the thick vegetation, dwarfed by the huge trees. Mostly they followed the paths and narrow trackways of the huntsmen, as there were no villages, but now and then they had to strike out into virgin forest so that they could keep moving towards the foothills of the north eastern mountains. To the surprise of Ussemitus and to Fomond's slight misgivings, Armestor, Gudrond and Arbos had insisted on joining them on their northern quest, although Ussemitus wondered how seriously Gudrond would take it. However, they accepted Ussemitus as their leader without question, and while they were on the move, they followed his decisions, keeping quiet, knowing that although there should be no enemies here and no predators likely to molest a group of them, the sky had ears. These lands were in the main unknown.

Fomond was the most sceptical about the intruders and the so-called Curse, but Ussemitus recognised that there was a threat of some kind, however veiled. If the elders knew where the company had gone, they would extract a punishment. Kuraal, if he learned of this, would either be furious or pleased, depending on what information was brought to him. Ussemitus knew that Fomond, like himself, was bored with village life, not sure that he wanted to spend the rest of his days in thrall to it; he had said so often enough. Arbos seemed similarly dissatisfied, though he was always one to work without complaint. Armestor and Gudrond paid lip service to their own unrest, Ussemitus knew, sure that they put their sense of security first. They both enjoyed this sort of escapade, but at the end of it there was always a comfortable return to the village. This time it might not be that way.

By a clear brook they stopped, Arbos keeping watch on the forest ahead while the others drank and cut strips of dried meat they had brought, chewing in silence.

Gudrond sat back among the ferns with a loud belch. 'Think these intruders will be friendly? Will they have any women with them?' he said to no one in particular.

Fomond scowled at him but did not respond.

'Why?' said Armestor. 'Are you thinking of enslaving a couple?'

Gudrond laughed. 'There's a thought. Cause a stir in the village, eh? Derenna and Fulleen would take spears.'

'Over you?' said Armestor sceptically.

'Probably,' nodded Gudrond. 'Can't keep them out of my bed – '

Fomond said something under his breath and got up to join Arbos in the trees. Gudrond looked at them for a moment but then turned back to Armestor, a more sympathetic audience. 'And there's that young daughter of Vuldur's.' He went on to describe what he would like to do to the girl and he and Armestor began a discussion of the merits of the village girls. Ussemitus gave Gudrond a brief look of contempt, then moved away.

When Arbos and Fomond came back to the stream for a last drink, Gudrond was still describing an imagined encounter with yet another of the village girls. Ussemitus could see the anger on Fomond's face so decided to put an end to this.

'Enough of that, Gudrond,' he said crisply.

Gudrond coloured. 'It's true. She – '

'You talk about girls as if you knew their ways well,' Ussemitus went on, with a grin. 'But if you ask me, you've yet to have one. If the truth were known.'

Gudrond had gone scarlet. 'You must be mad!' he protested.

'There's no shame in being unbroken,' Ussemitus told him, enjoying his acute embarrassment. 'Now mount up and let's hear no more of these fantasies.' He turned his back and walked over to where the horses were tethered.

Armestor chuckled and Arbos nodded as though he had seen an arrow go into Gudrond, who was clearly livid. His fury was an evident testament to the truth of Ussemitus's words.

When they mounted up and rode on, Gudrond became sullen and silent, responding occasionally to some comment from Armestor, though he did not mention women again.

They found a steep valley that led up into the foothills like a natural path. Arbos went on ahead to scout its sides to see if it would take them past the first significant rock barrier. They had slept comfortably in the trees, as natural to them as beds, though they knew that it would be their last night in the forest. The open ridges and bare rock above them looked daunting: none of them had been beyond the forests before.

Armestor had been on an early hunt and returned with a small deer draped around his neck. Ussemitus and Fomond were both fine shots with a bow, but Armestor had an almost magical skill with it. They were about to compliment him, when a shout from above made them all turn. Arbos was sliding down through the bracken, his face agitated.

'Where's his horse?' grunted Fomond.

'I've seen them!' gasped Arbos, his usually calm features transformed. 'A score of them. Camped up in the hills.'

'What are they like?' said Ussemitus.

'I didn't get too close, but as far as I could tell, they're much like us. But they carry metal, and wear it about them.'

'It must be them!' said Gudrond.

'I left my horse not far,' said Arbos. 'Bring your own, though we should advance on foot when we get close. There's a ridge where we can overlook them.'

They wasted no more words, but hurried to their mounts, Armestor strapping the deer to his expertly. In a moment they followed Arbos up the narrow valley and out of the shrub on to bare rock. They followed a steep slope of stone upwards, the higher hills rising sharply, with the first of the mountains looming over them beyond like deep blue banks of cloud. No one spoke, not even to question Arbos further. In an hour they came to the place where he had tethered his horse. It looked at them calmly as though nothing could alarm it.

Arbos led them on their bellies to the crest of a stone ridge and down below they had their first view of the intruders. A fire was burning, and sitting around it were a score of warriors, dressed in light metal that gleamed as they moved. They wore scabbards that also gleamed – metal – and where their swords were exposed, they too, were of metal. There was an extravagance of it! Beside them on the rocks there were war helms, also cast in metal, and where they had stacked their javelins, the sun gleamed from the metal points that had been fixed to them, and from the ornamentation on their shields.

Most of the company had been drinking and washing in the stream that rushed through the valley. Ussemitus studied their faces, not sure what he had expected to find. The men looked similar to his own people at first glance, but they were taller, stockier and more thick-set. Where they had bared their arms, they were more muscular, so that the men seemed far heavier altogether, their faces fuller and wider. They spoke a language that Ussemitus did not recognise, but it did not seem so alien, and many of the men were laughing or talking idly in a way that any forest folk might do. Apart from their weapons there was nothing immediately sinister about them. Could they possibly be from some far part of Innasmorn?

Fomond pointed out one of them to Ussemitus, who frowned. It was a young woman, probably no older than he was. She, too, wore light armour and a sword, but her hair had been cut short like that of the men. A number of her companions consulted her and she seemed to be giving them instructions. Ussemitus felt his chest lurch. A woman in command?

'What shall we do?' whispered Armestor, his face pale. Both Fomond and Arbos were watching Ussemitus, waiting for his instructions.

'They must not see us,' he said. 'We will watch them as long as we can. But we should spread out, and watch for guards. Keep within hailing distance. At noon, meet again here, unless they move out. Then we mount up and follow.' He had no need to repeat this. In a moment his companions had melted away and he knew they would soon have taken up posts as ordered. Ordered? he repeated to himself. Already I speak as if I command a military unit. Yet I came here to question the value of war.

He wriggled downwards through the rocks and scrub, though he made no sound and did not expect to. He had been playing at doing this since he was a tiny child. If any of the party below heard him, they made no show of it.

After an hour he was some twenty feet above them. They had not started to move and seemed camped for the day, though they erected no shelters. Occasionally the woman would speak to them, asking them something, but they shook their heads. She looked up at the sky more than once, as if expecting to see something in flight and Ussemitus wondered if she thought there would be predators here. Perhaps she was aware of the dangers of the wind, the powers of Innasmorn. As far as he knew there were no dangerous birds here, at least not dangerous to him and his kind.

His attention was drawn to some banks of fern beyond the stream and he realised that something was hidden by them, something of great importance to these intruders. The young woman was receiving reports about it from the warriors, and by the expression on her face, she was concerned. Ussemitus watched her pace about in frustration, as though she were trying to weigh a major decision. Her face fascinated him. It was far less dark than the faces of her own people, and like the men, was fuller fea-

21

tured, with eyes that seemed from here to be neither blue nor brown, which he found most unusual. She had full lips, their redness highlighted by her pale skin and he found himself thinking that she was beautiful. He grinned to himself, knowing this was no way to be considering potential enemies. There was danger in these people and he should not forget it.

What did the ferns conceal? He must find out. Slowly he made his way around the ridge, confident that he would not be discovered: the intruders were relaxed. It took him another hour to find a place where he could safely look down into the fern banks. What he saw there made his heart judder.

Artefact!

A dark-metalled shape, long and sleek, gleaming. It looked hard, its angles deep green, smooth but immutable as stone. The upper part of the pod-like object seemed to have been removed, almost like a layer of thick skin. Several of the intruders were inside it, so that Ussemitus wondered if it could be a boat of some kind. He had never seen one, but he had been told of such things. Inside the strange craft there were few clues as to its true nature, for its lines were smooth, though they looked soft, as if easily punctured. There were no visible controls, just a few indentations, like hand prints. The intruders were carefully examining filaments that were as delicate as small clusters of root, using thin metal tools, though they preferred their hands, for fear of bruising the craft. Beyond them there were two openings in the earth, with heaped soil beside them, though Ussemitus could not guess what they were for. Burial? But of what? Surely no one had died in this place? There were no signs of a battle.

As Ussemitus watched, shocked by this vision of something about which he had been warned since he could first speak, the ancient curse, the young woman came through the ferns to watch the men as they worked. She shook her head sadly, but one of them gesticulated. There seemed to be a brief argument, but the girl was in control of these

22

men. The workmen got out of the craft and stood back from it. The man who had been arguing with the girl got into it. He gave her an anxious glance but she nodded to him, an unspoken command.

Ussemitus had to stifle a gasp as a sudden roar from beneath the craft shook it, like the sound of a great beast in pain. Was this thing *alive*? What sort of monster could it be? He watched in amazement as it lifted itself gently from the flattened ferns and hovered a few feet above the ground. The noise fell away to nothing. The man inside was trying to maintain his hold, like a man struggling with the reins of a horse that has to be broken, his face lined and perspiring with effort. In a moment there was another sound, a deep groan, and the craft dropped back into its fern bed.

Whatever the craft did, it was damaged, Ussemitus surmised. But could it *fly*? Was that its purpose? It had risen from the ground. Men rushed to it now, leaning over it, talking to it softly. The pilot looked stricken by grief, as if a favourite horse had broken a leg.

Ussemitus realised that these craft, animal or not, would be an extraordinary weapon in the hands of an enemy. Kuraal would have to be told of the intruders.

Shouts across the valley made him jerk up. There was a scuffle somewhere among the rocks. Three armed men were dragging Gudrond down from the rocks into the camp. The idiot must have panicked when the craft roared into life and given himself away. Ussemitus prayed that the others kept their heads and kept out of sight.

As he watched, another figure sprang from cover. It was Armestor, his wooden knife drawn. He was no seasoned warrior, no master of the knife, but the three intruders were forced to stand back from their prisoner as Armestor came at them. Ussemitus was staggered. He had never imagined Armestor acting with such bravery. But it was suicide, for the warriors drew their swords and disarmed Armestor in moments. Mercifully they did not kill him, but forced him to join Gudrond. Both were marched down into the camp.

23

Ussemitus had little time in which to make a decision. Both men were dead if he left now. Fomond and Arbos would probably get away and meet him back in the forest. What sort of pursuit could they expect? What other powers did these intruders have? Someone must get back to the village.

He was about to begin his own withdrawal, when Ussemitus saw the young woman below. She had glanced up at the sounds from above, her hand on her own weapon, and her eyes searched the trees and bushes about the valley. But as the prisoners were brought to the camp, her attention went back to the craft. Ussemitus could see then her distress, the tears that glistened on her skin. She walked around the craft, only half watching the valley, her anguish very plain. Though she gripped the haft of her sword, her free hand touched the body of the craft as though it were the flesh of someone very dear to her. She came to the place that was under the watcher, too distracted by grief to look upwards for any danger, no more than a few feet from Ussemitus.

Ussemitus put his long wooden knife in his teeth and quickly leapt, the ferns cushioning his fall. Before the girl knew what had happened, he had put an arm about her neck, his blade at her white throat. She tried to throw him, but his own skill at wrestling ensured that his grip was locked. There were cries of outrage from the men, and a dozen swords flashed, but no one dared come forward. The position was clear in any language. The girl again tried to struggle and Ussemitus marvelled at how strong she was. But he was adept enough and held his ground. He watched as Armestor and Gudrond were taken into the camp. He moved the girl forward through the ferns. The men sidled along warily, unable to get behind him. By the stream they all faced each other. Armestor and Gudrond, who had both been appalled at being captured, now saw their leader with the girl. Ussemitus jerked his head at them, indicating that they should join him, but swords barred their way.

'Tell them you'll kill her!' shouted Gudrond, his nerve giving.

'You'd be wise not to,' said the girl softly so that only Ussemitus heard. It was like a body blow to know she spoke his tongue, but he did not show it.

'If my men have to die, so be it,' he whispered back. 'But I'll not trade for you. There are others above us. An arrow points at each of your men's hearts.'

All trace of grief, of weakness was gone from her now, but he could feel her heart thumping. 'What do you want of us?'

Ussemitus eyed the intruders. They were aching to attack him, but dare not. 'I did not come to fight. Tell them to sheath their blades and you'll not be harmed.'

'And your archers?'

'They'll not attack without provocation. They'll drop their bows when your men do as I ask. They have my strict orders and will not disobey them.'

The girl nodded, barking something at her men, and although they were evidently reluctant to do as she ordered, they put away their swords, watching the forest about them. Armestor and Gudrond leapt across the stream like startled cats and stood close to Ussemitus, though neither of them spoke.

'What do you want?' said the girl again.

It was only now that Ussemitus realised he had been pressed close to her, the light metal she wore. He released her, but held on to her wrist so that she could not pull away. Armestor and Gudrond had heard her speak their tongue and were wide-eyed in surprise.

'I have been sent to question you,' said Ussemitus. 'Do your warriors all speak my language?'

She shook her head. 'A few of them only. But they are all learning. It is our hope that your people will traffic with us.'

'In what?' said Ussemitus, his voice thick with suspicion.

'Knowledge. Release me and there will be no conflict here. You are free to go as you wish.'

Ussemitus nodded thoughtfully. His concern now was for his men. He turned to them. 'Go back up to the ridge. No one is to leave it. Is that absolutely clear? No one.' He looked at Gudrond, knowing he would want to race back to the village without another thought. But both he and Armestor were too afraid to disobey.

They went back across the stream. Some of the warriors looked as if they might bar the retreat, but the girl called out to them. Ussemitus watched his men go back up the ridge, pleased that Arbos and Fomond had remained under cover. He could not be sure that the girl was to be trusted, but if four of them got away there would be more chance of the village being warned. He had to take a risk of some kind with the girl. He released her hand and dropped his knife arm.

She turned to him and smiled, for a moment taken aback by his face. Like the few people of this world that she had observed, he was slender by her own race's standards. His features were thin, almost sharp, yet handsome, his eyes a startling brown, his hair long but fine, covering most of his ears, which seemed large in proportion to his face, yet in no way ugly. When he moved, it was with the peculiar lightness and grace of his kind, as though he might lift into the air and she remembered that she had heard that Innasmornians were one with the elements.

There was a movement behind her, but she called out an imperious command, her eyes not leaving those of Ussemitus. 'My name is Aru,' she told him. 'Of the family Casruel.'

'You are not of Innasmorn,' he said simply. Beneath her gaze he felt suddenly very vulnerable.

'No. But I hope that my people and I can live here. We have not come to make war.'

'You seem well armed.'

'You would not begrudge us precautions?'

'You carry much metal. You wear it.'

She had seen that his knife was made of wood, primitive,

26

though his bow looked more expertly crafted. 'We are in a strange world. We have to protect ourselves.'

Ussemitus managed a smile. 'Perhaps.'

'Am I to know your name?'

'In a while. First I must talk about other things.' He nodded back at the ferns, which again concealed the craft.

'Your people fear such things?' She said it in such a way that he knew she understood the answer. How long had her kind been studying his?

'What do you know of our history?' he asked her.

'Almost nothing. Will you teach me?'

'Perhaps.'

One of her warriors came to her and spoke sharply. He was a tall man, twice her age, his face lined, his eyes angry, as though he was not used to peaceful missions, but conflict. Though Ussemitus did not understand his words, he knew that the man resented him and could feel the hot impatience. Aru was far calmer and spoke soothingly. The man muttered and waited, staring at Ussemitus in clear mistrust.

'He is angry with you for threatening my life,' said Aru, smiling. 'But I told him you acted as he would have done.'

Ussemitus had no wish to be patronised. 'Where are you from? How did you come here?'

'We have made our home in the mountains to the north. We came here by three of the craft you have seen.'

He was about to protest that the mountains were not their true home, but the question of the craft intrigued him more. 'How could you come in such craft?'

She looked saddened for a moment, her eyes turning. 'If they had not been hurt, I would show you. They move above the ground.'

'As a bird can?' he said, his worst fears realised.

She laughed softly and he felt himself drawn by the sound. 'Not quite like a bird. They glide on the air, a little like a ship on a lake, or the sea.'

'And do the wind gods help you?'

'In a way,' she said, though something about his question disturbed her.

'My people have a long history. It is said that such things once did great harm to us. They angered the storm gods and brought destruction to Innasmorn. Since your craft are now damaged, the wind gods must have struck them down.'

She attempted to cover the hurt his words had given her, though he saw it in her eyes. 'If you say so. But we meant no harm, no sacrilege. Please believe me.'

Ussemitus wanted to do so, but how could he be certain these warriors meant no harm? 'Why are you here?'

'To find peace. We are alien to your world. Our own is – ' She hesitated. 'Destroyed. Lost to us.'

His eyes narrowed. 'Destroyed? How?'

'There was a war. For many, many years. We sought sanctuary and found Innasmorn. We have not come here to fight, but to recover. If you take me back to your rulers, I will show them – '

Ussemitus frowned. If this could be true! If the intruders did not mean harm, then there was no need for war. Vittargattus might be mobilising without cause. Yet the intruders, the metal-bearers, had fought a war that had destroyed a world. With artefacts? 'If you are what you say,' he told her, 'then it is pleasing news. But I have only your word, and you are a total stranger to me.'

'Yes. What would you suggest? If you wish it, I will come alone to your people.'

His heart cried out that yes, this would be a perfect solution. But he dare not let his heart rule him in this. 'I cannot take such a risk,' he said eventually. 'I do not mean this as an insult to you, but you would be in danger.'

'Could you not protect me?'

'You don't understand the way my people think. There are those who would see you as a threat. Whether you intended us harm or not, they would never trust you and your kind. Metal – '

'They have an aversion to it?'

'The history is long. Yes. I have little power of persuasion.'

For a moment she looked away as though at a scenario from her own past. 'There are those who seek only war among my own kind, I fear.' She looked at him again. 'Then if you will not take me to your people, will you come to mine?'

'To the mountains?'

'Yes. Bring your entire company. You will be made welcome. We will share what we can with you. Whatever you seek to learn about us.'

At this the man beside her coughed and leaned over to speak.

Ussemitus snorted. 'He pretends not to speak my language, but I think he knows it well enough.'

Aru laughed at this, and to Ussemitus's surprise the burly warrior also laughed. He came forward and although Ussemitus stepped back, held out his hand.

'Here, lad, take my hand. It's offered in peace. I'm Denandys, captain under the Casruel banner. I'm a soldier, but I'm not here to make war.'

Ussemitus thought it prudent to take the man's hand. He felt the strength in it. 'My name is Ussemitus.'

'Well met, Ussemitus. Will you and your men be guests in our mountain home? The Casruel knights will be your surety of safety. Aru's words caused me some anxiety as you might expect a soldier to blanch at the thought of any secrets being shared. But if your people and mine are to get together, we have to talk.'

Ussemitus felt himself warming in spite of himself. Surely these people did not mean harm. They had done nothing but protect themselves. And in their world, metal must be part of normal life. They could not have known it would be considered evil on Innasmorn.

'I am not an elder of my village,' he said. 'Those who are with me are, like me, fledglings – '

'I cannot believe that,' said Denandys, his use of Innasmornian a little clumsy. 'You handled yourself with skill. Have you seen battle?'

Ussemitus did not answer. 'I have not been vested with any rank. For me to go with you to your home might not be acceptable to my people.' And if we all go, he thought, we could be killed off easily. I must remain cautious. There is so much to lose if I do not.

Aru intervened, perhaps sensing Denandys's growing exasperation. 'I understand, Ussemitus. We both have cause for care. But somehow we must bring our peoples together. If we cannot, there may be conflict. But it would be one of ignorance.'

'Yes, I see that. What do you suggest?'

'Go back to your elders. Tell them that you've met us and that we seek a meeting, on whatever terms your people wish.' She looked at Denandys. 'We have to do this,' she told him in Innasmornian, but he was nodding.

'Very well, Aru. No arms. No artefacts.'

'Yes,' she agreed. 'Since we are the intruders, we must make the sacrifices. Ussemitus, I will go back to my own people. There are those among them who lack the patience and understanding of Denandys. But I am sure that between us we can arrange for proper communication to begin.'

Ussemitus smiled. He took her hand and shook it awkwardly, a gesture which seemed to please her. 'Very well. How are we to know when we are ready to begin?'

'It will take us two weeks to reach our mountain home on foot.' Aru told him. 'Let us meet here a month from today.'

'Very well.'

They watched from the ridge as the strangers began the steep climb up into the mountains. Aru and Denandys gave a last wave an hour later, then they were gone from sight. They had buried three of their strange craft, beating the earth solid over the graves, and Ussemitus had watched as they spoke words over them as though they had lost comrades, friends. Aru herself had wiped at a tear, and Ussemitus was left to ponder on this new aspect of the mystery.

Gudrond turned to Armestor, saying softly, 'You saw him touch her by the hand? The look in his eyes? Is she a witch, Armestor?'

'Don't be a fool,' Armestor hissed, afraid that the others would hear.

'You saw their arms. Their metal artefacts. Why would they carry such forbidden things? Ussemitus is a fool if he's been taken in by this girl and any promises she has made. He may think himself above lust – '

'Lust? Why do you say that?'

'Perhaps desire clouds his judgement. All I'm saying is, we'd better look after ourselves, that's all.'

Armestor glanced sharply at him. But Gudrond looked away. 'I don't think they're here for war,' said Armestor. But he wondered. The girl had not been without beauty.

Beyond him, Ussemitus was wondering about war as well. He had made a dangerous agreement, and yet, deep inside, he felt right in his judgement. He looked up at the skies for a sign, but the vaults of heaven were blue. That in itself seemed propitious.

3

IMPERATOR ELECT

The view from the gardens, he thought, was superb. Quite apart from the beautifully arranged shrubs with their exotic blooms and stunning range of colours, there was the vista itself, which looked out over a lake dotted with rich green islands to the mountains beyond. These rose majestically, invitingly, alien yet enchanting, a foreign world that promised still further wonders. The Imperator Elect breathed in deeply, delighted at the fragrance of the flowers, the mist of perfume. His architects were to be praised for this miracle of engineering. How far away the wars all seemed, and how perfect a sanctuary Innasmorn was. He shuddered briefly as he thought of the bloody battles, the slaughter, the Csendook. The way they had swarmed across an Empire that had lasted a millenium. The war had seemed to last as long. Was it really over?

'Your pardon, sire,' said a voice, breaking in to his darkening thoughts.

He turned to see Gannatyne, one of the principals of his Consulate, whom he had magnanimously agreed to meet here in the gardens. Gannatyne was less tall than the Imperator, a man who, though middle aged, looked far older, not wearing the mantle of his office well. His face was lined, pale, as if he should spend more time out in this marvellous air instead of being cooped up in the narrow confines of the Sculpted City. His eyes looked tired and he spoke with something of an effort.

The Imperator Elect saw a momentary image of Gannatyne as he had been before the Empire had begun to collapse, before the fury of Csendook aggression. The endless days of the withdrawal from the Empire to this sheltered world had taken their toll on his subjects, and where once men like Gannatyne had been strong, dedicated, they were now tired, their spirits worn away, pained at the loss. Yet what have *I* lost! he told himself. I am like a parent robbed of its family!

'Thank you for permitting me this private audience.'

The Imperator inclined his head. 'You look troubled, Gannatyne. You should learn to relax. Your people have made an extraordinary job of the gardens. And one would have thought they had scooped out the lake bed and constructed the entire thing. It looks so perfect. Can't you find time to take a little more pleasure in such things? One would think a Csendook Swarm about to descend upon us.'

Gannatyne managed a thin smile. 'The Csendook are never far from my thoughts, sire. It seems a miracle that we have evaded them.'

'They'll not find Innasmorn. Not in another millenium.'

I wish I shared his confidence, Gannatyne thought to himself. But he sees what he wishes to see, hears only what suits him.

'You are right, sire. The war has made me edgy.' Gannatyne followed the Imperator along the winding pathways of the gardens, knowing he would not have long to speak to him privately. His mind would not focus on affairs of government for long.

As they made their way to an even more secluded place, the Consul's thoughts strayed back over the wars. How they had raged, in world after world, and how many millions had died? The Csendook were intent on genocide, their superior strength battering back Mankind, squashing resistance, wiping out cities, worlds, an empire. In the end it was decided to seek a place where the Imperator Elect, symbol of resistance to the enemy, could be hidden away out of reach of his conquerors with his Consulate and the fittest of his defenders. But it had been a long and difficult search for a door out of the cycle of worlds that made up the empire. Zellorian, Prime Consul and a man of great knowledge, had spared no efforts to find such a door. And at last he had found this haven, this strange world of

Innasmorn. Even now Gannatyne was not sure how it had been done, or where Innasmorn actually was. If it were truly in another dimension, or a world parallel to those of the empire, then perhaps they had escaped their enemies after all.

The Imperator Elect yawned, though he could not be tired, for he rose long after dawn every morning. He pointed lazily through a gap in the trees, trees which had been geometrically planted and artificially nurtured to reach maturity in a period of months, to the buildings below. 'I can hardly believe my eyes when I see how fast the city has risen up. And it is a true city.'

'Yes, sire. It has grown very quickly out of the bowels of the mountain. Our people have slaved over it. ' Unlike yourself, who think only of pleasure, and who do nothing but amuse yourself here in the palace we built with our pain.

'Has it taken their minds off pursuit? I trust it has, Gannatyne. We must look to the future. It is why we came here, is it not?'

There's not an ounce of guilt in him, Gannatyne thought. How few we left behind, a number of crippled worlds, barely surviving. Yet he cares nothing for them. Only that he is here, his own bed soft, his table full. 'Of course, sire. And it is of the future that I wish to speak.'

The Imperator nodded, though his interest still seemed focused on the plants. In spite of his excesses, he was a lean man, not yet forty, his complexion darkened by the sun of this world, his hair thick, not flecked with grey, his face as smooth as that of any boy. There was a darkness around his eyes, but otherwise he looked like a man who led a simple, carefree life, and who had never seen war or killing, or streets running with the blood of his people.

'Ah, the future,' he nodded. 'The city must be finished by now. What is it to be? Another?'

'I wanted to discuss the people of Innasmorn, sire. The inhabitants.'

The Imperator studied the erratic flight of a bee, grinning

as it swerved clumsily to avoid him. 'Oh yes. What about them?'

'I have, as you know, had a number of our knights sent out to study them. Civilisation exists here, though it is not advanced – '

The Imperator grunted. 'Quite so. Zellorian also has his sources of information, and he tells me these people are primitives. I gather he has studied their language.'

Gannatyne cursed inwardly as he had done many times before at the mention of Zellorian, whose power over the Imperator was considerable. 'Indeed, sire. There has been contact with a few Innasmornians who dwell beyond the lakes on the shores of the northern sea. But they seem a remote race. I'm not sure that all Innasmornians are primitives. It is true they seem to have no technology – '

'None at all?'

'No, sire. But as you know, our own technology cannot sustain itself as it once did – '

'But Innasmorn must have resources beyond dreams – '

'Perhaps, sire. But we were able to bring such a pitiful amount of our own with us. We are very limited in what we can achieve. I am convinced that our technology will have to undergo drastic change.'

The Imperator at last showed signs of being interested in the conversation. 'Change? What sort of change?'

'If Innasmorn is to be our future, and we are to have no contact with the worlds we have left, then we must adapt – '

'And sink into barbarism?'

Gannatyne felt himself shudder at the ludicrous comment. But he held himself in check, drawing on his reserve of patience. 'Not at all, sire. But we will have to learn new skills. How to harness the powers of this world. At the moment our knowledge is sketchy. I am convinced that we should do everything we can to foster relations with the inhabitants.'

'But surely, Gannatyne, we cannot expect to *learn* from primitives? An inferior species? According to Zellorian's research, these people are one step removed from cattle!

What could they possibly teach us? Besides, they seem to look upon us as aliens, intruders. They may even think about taking up arms against us, although it would be quite ridiculous of them to do so.'

Gannatyne smothered his fury. Zellorian had already poisoned the Imperator's brain. 'I know very little about their religions, sire, but they live in a different way to us. They are not cattle, sire. They have built their own empires, they have their own network of nations, and they are numerous. And this is their world.'

The Imperator Elect turned to him, brows raised. 'Then are you saying that I should have sought their permission to bring us here?'

Gannatyne tried to be patient. 'I did not mean that, sire. You know that I would not wish to be impertinent to you. But surely we could offer them some of the benefits of our knowledge in exchange for theirs?'

The Imperator smiled condescendingly. 'Gannatyne, I know that you and a good many of your fellow Consuls think me dull-witted. But I'm not entirely a fool, you know. I've studied history.'

Gannatyne would have laughed aloud had he not known what the consequences of such an act would mean. He did not reply.

'Consider the Csendook. I know we would rather put them from our minds altogether, but we can learn from them, in spite of their savagery. They bred carefully, selectively. They became the strongest and most powerful race in the Empire. Quite extreme in their methods, but it's in their nature to be utterly ruthless. Man, however, was far less severe. We spread out, world by world. Our moderation undid us.'

Gannatyne felt his blood running cold. This was Zellorian talking.

'And here we are. Beyond our rightful empire in some other region. We will begin again, following the dictates of life itself.'

'Sire, you think we should be more like the Csendook? Crush those life forms we consider to be inferior?'

The Imperator took a deep breath. He was offended. 'You misunderstand me, Consul. Look at this garden. Have you ever seen anything more beautiful? There is not a weed in sight. The trees, shrubs, flowers, all grow without a blight. Do you see a seared leaf?'

'No, sire.'

'No.' The Imperator gazed about him with an air of hauteur. 'This is how Innasmorn will become. We will make it so. We will teach the lower orders true beauty.'

Gannatyne felt he must try once more. 'We would all wish for a better world, sire. But surely the people of this world would be only too glad to see such a thing. They would help us – '

'But would they accept us? Do you think they would accept me?'

'As their ruler?'

'Well, of course. I could hardly share power with them. Would it not seem incongruous to you that I, Imperator Elect, who once ruled the numerous worlds of Empire, should share power with fishermen?'

I should have known, thought Gannatyne. Even now he thinks only of himself and his power. His people mean nothing to him. 'Perhaps, sire, they would welcome you as a new leader. With our knowledge, we could teach them much. We could hardly fail to win their respect.'

'Yes, but what could they teach us that we couldn't find out for ourselves, Gannatyne? Zellorian's power has bridged a dimension!'

'I don't dispute that, sire. We are all in Zellorian's debt. But we know nothing of Innasmorn. The inhabitants have been here for centuries.'

The Imperator turned away, bending to attend to a large purple bloom. Gannatyne knew then that he had lost. Zellorian had already determined the future. 'We'll talk about this again,' said the Imperator.

Gannatyne considered making a final effort, but he heard

soft laughter from beyond the shrubs. He straightened, again hiding his ire. The Imperator had also heard the laughter and smiled to himself. 'In the meantime I have other business.'

Two of his harlots came into view, clad as always in thin, transparent silks that hid nothing of their bodies. They had been chosen for their voluptuous beauty. There were many about the upper courts of the palace, the Imperator's principal diversion. He went to the two girls with outspread arms and they laughed again, pressing themselves to him.

Gannatyne tried to close his mind to them. He turned and walked briskly back up the path, knowing that he was already forgotten.

However, there was someone else in the gardens who took far more interest in what he had had to say to the Imperator Elect. Leaning backwards, obscured by the tall shrubs, a figure held its breath while Gannatyne passed within a few feet of it. It waited until the Consul had gone and then crept from cover, making sure that it was not seen. It listened for a moment, hearing the giggles of the two courtesans and the laughter of their ruler by the lakeside. Then it slipped away through the gardens to a small gate and left.

The man pulled his robes about him as he went, his throat dry, his heart thundering. He loathed this duty that Zellorian had put upon him, but he had little choice in the matter. He knew the price of failure only too well.

Carefully he entered the palace, going along lesser corridors where he was least likely to be seen. He was not a full member of the Consulate, but as the head of one of the principal families, he was a servant of inner government and was rarely challenged. He preferred to be unseen.

In the lower buildings, set within the rock of the mountain, he made his way to rooms he knew to be occupied by guards controlled by the Prime Consul and knocked on one of the doors. A young man answered, pulling the door wide. He wore the harness of a soldier on duty, and carried at his side the thin-bladed sword of his office. It was Vymark, a hard-faced man whose eyes lit with scorn when he saw Mannaston standing before him.

'What do you want, you old drunkard?'

Mannaston smarted. How dare a mere soldier speak to him like this! But he could not meet the steel gaze. 'Zellorian is expecting me – '

'I don't think so.'

'It's all right, Vymark, let him in. Close the door.' It was Zellorian himself who spoke, rising as he did so from a bare table where he had been scribbling on a sheet of vellum.

Mannaston had to pull himself together before he could meet the gaze of the Prime Consulate. He could never come before him without a feeling of dread, and worse than that, shame at his own weaknesses. Weaknesses that Zellorian had used just as he used them in all those he manipulated. The smile of the Prime Consul was cold, serpentine, his eyes grey, his hair the colour of steel, cut short to his skull. His mouth was firm but the lips seemed almost bloodless, his skin pale. There seemed to be a hint of malice, bitterness, in his eyes, and Mannaston knew that the man had been incensed by the collapse of empire. What humanity he had ever had had been crushed out of him by the wars, along with his soul, if he had ever possessed one.

'You've been in the gardens, I take it?' he said softly. They might have been discussing the climate.

'Do you wish me to leave, eminence?' asked Vymark.

'No need.' Zellorian waved him to one of the wooden seats. The room was purely functional. No attempt had been made to soften its hard stone lines. Zellorian enjoyed his luxuries elsewhere.

'I've come from there,' began Mannaston, clearing his throat.

'Get our guest a drink,' Zellorian told Vymark.

'No,' said Mannaston, grasping at his dignity, but he could not hold so slender a thing. 'Well – '

Vymark grinned, as if enjoying the torments of the older

man. He went into a chamber beyond and came back with a small earthenware vessel. Mannaston knew that it had been brought especially for this meeting. Zellorian left nothing to chance.

Mannaston took the vessel in shaking hands and uncorked it. Zellorian watched him expressionlessly as he gulped at the fiery contents. He evinced no pleasure at seeing his servant humiliating himself before him, waiting patiently. Vymark, he noted, did seem to enjoy the pathetic spectacle. He had weighed the officer well.

'Well, did you overhear them?'

'Yes,' said Mannaston, sinking on to another chair. 'Gannatyne met the Imperator Elect as you told me he would.'

Zellorian nodded, turning his steel gaze on Vymark. 'I knew he would attempt this. Gannatyne is for some reason determined to set the Imperator against me.'

'But why?' said the younger man.

Zellorian turned back to Mannaston, gaze hardening. 'What did they say?'

'I heard every word. Gannatyne said that our future on Innasmorn will be better secured if we go out to the people who dwell here and share knowledge with them. If we teach them our ways, they will teach us the secrets of Innasmorn.'

'Secrets? Did he use that word? Secrets?'

Mannaston frowned. 'I can't swear that he actually said "Secrets" – '

'*Think!* What were Gannatyne's exact words?' snapped Zellorian, eyes suddenly ablaze.

'He meant that in his view, we would learn far more about Innasmorn if we lived more closely with her peoples. He spoke of building together – '

Zellorian's fire subsided. 'I cannot understand the man's obsession with unification. The people of this world are primitive, backward, a thousand years and more behind us. Ruled by superstition.'

'I'm sure you're right, eminence,' said Vymark. 'From what I've heard of them, they have no technology. They believe that the air is god, and worship the wind. To them

40

a storm is the voice of their god. Consul Gannatyne must be a fool if he thinks we should ally ourselves to such rabble.'

'How much easier to control them if we don't educate them,' said Zellorian. He turned abruptly back to Mannaston. 'How were Gannatyne's views received?'

'Not well.' Mannaston repeated what he had heard. Zellorian nodded to himself, pleased to think that the Imperator had swallowed wholesale the things he had been taught.

'It is as I expected,' said Zellorian. 'Very well. You can go.'

Mannaston lifted the vessel, which was now empty, and looked pitifully at his tormentor. Zellorian turned away, hardly bothering to conceal his disgust. 'There's another vessel in the chamber beyond. Take it and get out. Say nothing of this, Mannaston, do you understand me?'

Mannaston stood up shakily and went to fetch the vessel. 'Not a word. Not a word.' He found what he sought and hurried out of the door.

'Forgive me, eminence,' said Vymark, 'but if the Imperator knew – '

'He won't hear it from that drunken buffoon. Mannaston knows that if he says one word to upset me, I'll see he doesn't get another drink. Not of that.' He indicated the empty vessel.

Vymark went to it and picked it up, sniffing at it. He wrinkled his nose at the sickly sweet smell. 'What is it?'

Zellorian smiled unpleasantly.'*Keroueen.*'

Vymark nodded, putting the vessel down as though it contained a dangerous animal. *Keroueen* was particularly strong wine, highly addictive. It was not common, but it seemed perfectly usual for Zellorian to have access to it. If Mannaston was an addict, he was entirely dependent on the Prime Consulate for his supply.

'You must get used to using such methods of control. They are the tools of government, Vymark.'

Vymark bowed. 'As you say, sir.'

'I don't like the thought of our people going out from the mountains and involving themselves with the clans. It interferes with my own intentions.' Zellorian moved softly to the door and slid the bolts.

Vymark waited. He knew that he and a few other warriors had been granted particular confidence by Zellorian for reasons they had yet to learn. Vymark was thankful for the opportunity. He knew, as all the city knew, that Zellorian controlled the Imperator Elect and had done for many years. He was the real power behind the throne. No one moved up or received honours without the express approval of the Prime Consul. Most of the Consulate supported him, some from ambition, most through fear. Those who did not, and Gannatyne was the first of them, Zellorian had marked and would systematically destroy, as surely as he was destroying Mannaston.

'You've not questioned me too deeply on such things,' Zellorian said to the warrior. 'Perhaps you should.'

'You've no reason to doubt my loyalty, eminence.'

'Oh? You express it well enough. But I'm a cautious man, Vymark. I pick my servants very carefully. If you are loyal, you'll do very well. If not – '

'I understand your position, your power,' Vymark replied. 'No one else matches you. Even the Csendook feared you – '

Zellorian's face did not change. 'They are physically more powerful than us. Faster. But their minds are not superior. And limited by their own devotion to the physical. They have no gods, but substitute for them another kind of power: the strength of the body, its speed. Just as the people of Innasmorn worship the natural elements, the Csendook revere physical power. They utterly abjure what they call supernatural powers. But it is to our advantage, because they could never understand that we came here by using such power. Thus their lack of belief will prevent them ever from finding Innasmorn.'

Vymark felt the hairs on his nape stiffen. There were numerous tales among the soldiers about the dark powers

Zellorian wielded: no one knew what rituals he had undertaken to break down the barrier between the known realms and the unknown. Some called it sorcery, some science. Some suggested it was evil, calling on powers best left untapped. But it was outside the understanding of most men, and only those closest to Zellorian were permitted to share the knowledge. These men were said to dwell away from the rest of the court, privately housed, but it was also said that they enjoyed unimaginable luxury.

Zellorian was still speaking, almost to himself, his face white, his lips taut. 'It is their narrow-mindedness that will one day bring the Csendook to heel. They will be crushed, just as they have crushed us.'

Vymark nodded, surprised at the intensity in Zellorian's voice, the sheer, livid hatred. 'Yes, you are right, sir. Someone – '

'Someone? It will be us, Vymark. Make no mistake. It will be *us*.'

Vymark was stunned. Was Zellorian mad? Rebel against the Csendook, who had already won the Empire and who were even now exterminating Man wherever they found him?

Zellorian read the soldier's amazement and his face changed. He smiled and put an arm round the young man's shoulder. 'No, Vymark. I'm not insane. There's none more cautious than myself. But the Csendook have a weakness. And it will be exploited.'

'But how?'

Zellorian dropped his arm but walked on through the chambers to a less formal one, where there were plants and a small pool. 'Innasmorn has the answer, I'm sure of it. We sneer at the customs of the primitives who live here, their worship of storms. Do you know what the name Innasmorn means?'

Vymark shook his head.

'Mother of Storms. I've heard a few of the legends already. There's something here, Vymark. I shall find it. And

43

when I do, I will forge it into a power that will make the Csendook shudder.'

Vymark gazed down at the pool. He could feel the power of the man beside him, the fanaticism that almost glowed.

In a moment Zellorian was smiling again. 'But enough of this boasting! Tell me, are you prepared to commit yourself?'

Vymark nodded automatically. 'I did not realise – '

'No. Guard your tongue. Others would think me dangerous. But know this. I will let nothing, absolutely nothing, stand between me and the goal. It can be reached, believe me, Vymark. I will show you things that will convince you of that. But I tell you now, our path will be a bloody one.'

'I'm a soldier, eminence. I've never been disturbed by the sight of blood.'

4

GANNATYNE

Gannatyne sat in his chamber alone, looking out over the roofs of the Sculpted City but seeing nothing. He felt old, far too old to be continuing this long struggle. But he could not give it up now. What a fool they had for an Imperator! he said to himself for the dozenth time. A man who could speak eloquently enough when he had to, a self-styled poet, but whose grasp of the real dangers threatening his race was poor. We have sunk so low, Gannatyne thought. We who once controlled so many worlds, peacefully, sensitively, if history is accurate. And yet here we are in this darkness, a lost realm, our powers dwindling. We think of conquest, of putting ourselves above all life here. He thought of the palace, its decadence, and saw again those harlots, the corruption rife, the grasping officials, the structure of government that rotted from within. There were far too many sycophants, and the Consuls used the pleasure gardens too freely and thought of little else but their own amusement. The people would be appalled if they knew half of the things that went on at court. Or would they? Would they merely envy their rulers? Ah, Mankind, you have come to the last days. The tiredness crept over him anew and he shook his head, too tired for the moment to be angry.

There was a gentle knock on one of the doors and he called out for whoever it was to enter. One of his servants came in, bowing. 'A messenger, lord. She is anxious to see you.'

Gannatyne nodded, and in a moment the servant had returned with a girl. It was Aru. Gannatyne went to her and hugged her as he would have done a daughter of his own.

'You look well,' he told her, suddenly younger, his eyes lighting up.

'And you look tired,' she told him, concern in her own eyes. She could see at once that he looked exhausted, the affairs of the Consulate weighing on him like stone.

He nodded. 'This city ages me. I've not long come back from seeing the Imperator.'

'How is he?' she said, frowning.

'He does not change. He is the puppet of Zellorian. More than ever, I think. Since Zellorian pulled him away from under the talons of the Csendook, the Imperator thinks of him as some kind of god.'

Aru screwed up her face in distaste, nodding. 'What did you see him about?' Whatever it was, she knew, it had caused him grave concern.

'I managed to see him alone, so I had some hope of turning him away from this stupid idea of treating the inhabitants of Innasmorn like animals. But his mind is fixed. They are cattle, he insists. Not worthy of equality with us. But if they would accept him as their ruler – '

Aru groaned. 'The fool! If you can't make him see sense, who can?'

He took a deep breath, seemingly trying to pull his strength together. 'I wonder if we ought to gather our allies and leave this city. Form a state of our own.' There was little conviction in his words.

'But it would lead to further divisions, probably a war among us. You said that yourself.'

'I know, I know. But while we are here, Zellorian controls us.' They moved across the room and sat on one of the long divans, looking out at the sparkle of sunlight on distant sea. 'But what have you been doing these last few weeks? What have your knights discovered?'

Aru grinned and he felt the warmth in her smile, a welcome relief from his oppressive thoughts. She was a credit to her family, the Casruels, one of the few families of repute left in the city. What had happened to the Djorganists? The Ekubals, the Philastrons? Great houses, who

46

had kept Man in control of his destiny for so many generations? But Gannatyne bit his lip. No use getting maudlin
about them. They were no more. Vanished like the Empire.

'I've met some of the inhabitants,' Aru told him and her
young face lit up. There was no doubting her beauty. It
was time she found a partner. 'I don't mean those poor
people who dwell in the north. These were foresters. We
flew to the south and had crossed the last of the mountains,
when all three of our gliderboats began to fail.' A cloud
crossed her face.

'Oh?' Gannatyne arched his brows.

'It was curious. The gliderboats could not understand it.
They communicated their distress to us, but in spite of all
our efforts, we could not soothe them. We put down, but
within an hour two of them were lifeless. The third survived, but the pilot could not get it to rise. It succumbed
soon afterwards. What does it mean?'

He was thinking hurriedly. Gliderboats dying? 'Several
of our knights have reported similar problems beyond the
mountains in the east. There must be something in the air
that disrupts the system.'

'A virus?'

'Possibly, but not one we have been able to detect. The
internal system of a gliderboat is not quite like our own
nervous system, but the air on Innasmorn has not proved
harmful to us.'

'Perhaps Innasmorn objects to our gliderboats.'

But he did not smile. 'There may be something in what
you say. A number of our machines below the city have
fallen into disrepair. At first it was thought to be some
magnetic turbulence, or an electrical charge in the atmosphere, but the tests reveal nothing. It is just a slow drift
down into inertness, as if a man were developing lassitude
and falling into a coma.'

'It is how the gliderboats perished,' said Aru. 'As if their
energy was slowly bled from them. They did not complain
of pain, but were powerless to rouse themselves.'

He turned away with a snort. 'Like this Empire, eh? Drifting into oblivion.'

She could see that he would have to be jerked out of his mood. His session with the Imperator had seriously upset him. She could not remember when his spirits had been so low. 'Beyond the mountains,' she said, trying to sound enthusiastic, 'the forest lands spread in all directions. While we were trying to help the gliderboat, a group of foresters came upon us.' She described Ussemitus and his companions. 'Ussemitus was not much older than myself, and he led the group.' She talked of the exchange, her smile widening as she told how Ussemitus had caught her unawares and put a wooden knife to her throat.

'But I felt no danger,' she told him, for he had looked stunned.

'With a knife at your throat?'

'Ussemitus was surprisingly strong. I say that because his people are not as we are. They are of a slighter build, almost as if they were hollow boned! And they have an elemental look about them, as if they are truly a part of the forest, or of the air. Yes, that's it, the air! I kept thinking they would fly, or drift on the wind. And Ussemitus was strangely gentle, as if he was anxious not to hurt me even though he had a knife at my throat.'

'You found him attractive?' Gannatyne grinned.

She blushed prettily but smiled. 'If I'm honest, yes. He was no primitive, Gannatyne, nor were his men. They were intelligent. Far more so than the fishermen of the north.'

'You've picked up the rudiments of their language, so you already know that.'

'Yes, but having met them, I understand so much more about them. I tried to persuade Ussemitus to come here –'

Gannatyne drew in his breath sharply. 'No. That would be a mistake. Zellorian would find a way of killing them.'

She looked horrified.

'They must not come. Not yet.'

'Ussemitus said he dared not. I think he guessed that he and his friends would be trapped. I asked him if he would

48

take me to his village, to his elders, but again he was reluctant to trust me. I think he was worried that his elders might want *me* killed. It was an impasse.'

'But your exchange was amicable?'

'Yes, it was. We both wanted to discuss peace. Denandys was excellent. A bit gruff to begin with, though that's his military way. But in the end I think Ussemitus liked him. And he was certainly impressed by the young Innasmornian.'

Gannatyne nodded thoughtfully. 'So how did you leave things?'

'I'm to go back in a month to meet Ussemitus again. We are to discuss things further. Try to bring our peoples together. Gannatyne, it's an opportunity we cannot afford to miss. Can't you speak to the Imperator again?'

But he shook his head. 'No. A waste of time.'

'Then what must be done?'

Again he warmed to her eagerness, her determination, and he patted her arm in a fatherly way. 'I think you should go back, have further meetings. But you may have to go in secret. I hear word that Zellorian's elite are watching the ships leave and noting them. He is not in favour of gliderboats full of knights going across Innasmorn without his express sanction. But it is a risk you should take.'

'I think Ussemitus was concerned that his own people might see us as a threat. It was as if he feared war. I could read that in him.'

'Of course. And it would take so little for the Innasmornians to be drawn into a war. Think of the havoc we could wreak! But we have *nothing* to gain by conflict. How could we even begin to think of such a thing!'

'I will go back. But with only a handful of family knights. I mean to go to the villages of the foresters. If they have cities, I'll go there. I'll tell them what we are. And of the problems we have in our own city.'

He looked out at the buildings. 'Of Zellorian?'

'They should be warned. Don't you think?'

'If you can win the confidence of the Innasmornians, make them see our own dilemma – '

'I have to. Gannatyne, you spoke of leaving, of forming a separate state – '

'It may come to that.'

She shook her head. 'How long before Zellorian had it discredited? Then razed?'

He could not meet her gaze. She was right, of course. Zellorian would not permit such a thing. But while Gannatyne was here in the Sculpted City, he would be controlled.

'But if I become an ally of the Innasmornians,' Aru went on, 'I could pave the way for those who defy Zellorian. In time they could leave here and go to them.'

'I understand you perfectly, my dear. But it would be extremely dangerous. Zellorian would have the perfect reason for embroiling them in war. And he would brand us as traitors.'

'Then if it's war, let it be war!' she snapped suddenly, getting up.

Her vehemence surprised him. He smiled thinly. 'You don't mean that. My dear, think coldly, as our enemies do. Zellorian would welcome such a war. He'd destroy all of us who were against him and he'd subjugate the Innasmornians and force them to kiss the boots of that puppet we call Imperator. No, war is to be avoided at all costs. Peace is our goal.'

She emitted a great sigh. 'I'm sorry, Gannatyne. I get so furious. It's as though our every move puts us against a wall.'

'He's the most difficult opponent we could have.'

She thought for a moment. 'What does he really want? Surely he can't be interested in Innasmorn or its people? Why would he take delight in ruling them if he really thinks of them as savages? There were worlds in the Empire where he would never think to set foot. Innasmorn would be the same if it were a part of that Empire.'

Gannatyne felt the familiar coldness creeping into him at her words. He sat back, the weight of his tiredness again

50

assailing him. 'I am sure he did not choose this world at random. There is something here that he wants.'

Aru looked puzzled. 'But what could it be? Minerals?'

'I don't think so. Innasmorn doesn't appear to be richer in minerals than many of the other worlds we have known. But Zellorian has gone down another path in recent years. There are many whispered stories about him and his methods.'

Aru sat down beside him again, lowering her own voice. 'That he uses sorcery? Has revived long-forgotten magical powers?'

Gannatyne shrugged. 'Such rumours exist. No one really knows how he opened the Pathway here. We are in a realm beyond that of the circle of worlds of empire. And who can say what power is invested in this world? Our gliderboats cannot fly here, and other machines are dying. Some of the scientists are already saying that in a few years our technology will be useless, paralysed.'

'But how will we survive?'

'As the Innasmornians do. They have no love of artefacts. They see metal as a curse. And all who carry them.'

She nodded. 'Ussemitus was most concerned about the metal we carried. Our gliderboats must have been like demons to him.'

'We must learn new ways. I fear that Zellorian has already begun a deep study of such things.'

'But if there is a war, and we have no artefacts – '

'Then the balance would be evened, eh? And there are many more Innasmornians than there are Men. In such a war, we would be wiped out. Unless Zellorian has found some other dark power to tap.'

'Sorcery.'

'Innasmorn has something he seeks. Power. Power is his goal, his only god. There may be something in the worshipping of the elements. Did you learn anything from Ussemitus? His people think of the storms as the voice of their gods. They see the wind as an army of elementals which rules Innasmorn, with thunder as its weapon.'

51

'But these are like myths – '

Gannatyne chuckled. 'This is another realm, Aru. Who knows what is here? Who is to say that our gliderboats have not offended the sky gods?' He sat back, running his hands through his hair. 'There, I've alarmed you. But discard nothing. Not here.'

Aru had suddenly gone stiff, her eyes opening wide on some remote scenario. 'If Zellorian seeks power, supernatural power that does not exist in the old worlds, what is his intention? What would he do with such power?'

'It's not so hard to guess,' Gannatyne said hollowly.

She drew in a sharp breath. 'He would not be so stupid – '

'No one hates the Csendook more passionately than Zellorian. They took an Empire from him. He ruled it, through his puppet. And we have already said he would never be content to rule a speck of dust like Innasmorn.'

'You think he would go *back*? To that hell?'

'If he found power enough to challenge them, oh yes. Yes, indeed.'

Aru stood up. 'Then he must be stopped. No matter what it costs.'

'I've thought of assassins, you know,' he said, eyes cast down at the carpet. 'But he's too well protected. He knows there are a few of us who would have his head tomorrow if we could.' He stood up abruptly, as if annoyed by his own ramblings. She took his arm.

'There will be a way. We'll find it,' she said.

'Yes,' he nodded. 'But you'd better leave me now. I still have a few allies, but I'm always ill at ease when they visit me, for their sake. And I would dread your being overheard. Zellorian is as eager to bring me to ruin as I am to see his rule ended.'

He hugged her once more and she left him, saddened to think that a man of such vision should be so ignored by the Imperator Elect.

She made her way through a maze of corridors that ran down from Gannatyne's apartments, careful to ensure that she was observed only by staff loyal to him. She passed through a part of the city that was cut from within the mountain and went back outside to a level area beyond, where the daylight above made her eyes smart. She made for the house of her father. She felt no guilt at visiting him only now, after she had reported to Gannatyne. Sometimes she almost wished Gannatyne had been her father, for she had little love for her own, who like many of his fellows seemed to have fallen under the shadow of Zellorian. She rarely saw him, and kept her movements a secret from him. But for now, she knew, she ought to make a token appearance at least.

She entered the house, not surprised to see that the servants had made little effort to keep it tidy. There were carpets thick with dust, tables littered with plates in one room and hounds running freely in the inner courtyard. Aru bellowed and servants appeared sluggishly, as though they had been sleeping instead of working.

'Now that I'm back,' she told them through her teeth, 'I want this pigsty cleaned up. At once, do you hear me? Otherwise you'll be out on your ears.'

She turned her back on them and they began work immediately, seeing the mood she was in. They could expect little mercy from her, whereas their master cared little about what they did or how well.

Aru found him in a small chamber, slumped across a desk. In his hand was a jar, the last contents pooling on the papers before him. She took the jar and sniffed at it, wrinkling her nose in disgust as she flung it at the wall. It shattered noisily and the figure before her stirred.

'Father. Wake up. It's your daughter. I've returned.'

He gazed at her vaguely, then smiled, flopping backwards with a belch. 'Aru! Good to see you my child.' A look of exaggerated happiness spread over his features and he waved his arm before subsiding.

'Stinking drunk,' she hissed, disgusted. He was getting worse, the drink in complete control of him these days. He had made no attempt to clean himself up, his shirt front soiled, his beard matted. Head of the family of Casruel, he was an utter disgrace, another victim of the collapse of the empire that had once been so powerful. She looked around for a pail, but there were none. Again she bellowed for the servants. One of them came scurrying in within moments.

'Fetch a pail. Cold water. To the brim.'

Her father giggled helplessly as if she had said something hilarious. Aru waited. In the background she could hear the sound of water being piped into the pail. A moment later the servant returned and held it out, hands shaking. Aru took the bucket and without a word emptied the freezing contents over her father. He gasped, spluttering for breath, toppling from the chair. The servant grinned but one cold look from Aru turned her to stone. She meekly took the bucket and left.

Aru went over to her father, who flopped about like a landed fish in a pathetic attempt to rise, though he still giggled. Aru knew it would take more than water to revive him. What had he been drinking?

'Can you understand what I'm saying?' she asked him. She could not bring herself to touch him and watched as he laboured to his knees, using the table to force himself up. Gannatyne had told her that once he had been one of the most highly regarded family heads in court. Seeing him as he was now, it was hard to imagine.

At last he sank back on to the stool. 'Yes, yes. I hear you, daughter.'

'I'm staying for a day or two. Then I'm going to move out to the barracks. I won't be coming back here, father, do you understand me?' She dare not tell him she was leaving for the forest lands.

He nodded. 'Won't be coming back.'

'So you'd better pull yourself together or the servants will walk out on you. The house will fall down about you. There'll be no one here to look after you. Do you hear me!' She could feel the tears at the back of her eyes, but fought them back.

He took a deep breath. 'Yes. No need to shout, Aru. I

hear you. But it's all right. I'm looked after,' he winked stupidly, tapping his nose as if he had access to some great secret.

'By whom? Your friends? They deserted you long ago.'

'Oh no, no, no. Got to look after me. I'm useful. Zellorian says so.'

She straightened as if he had spat at her. '*Zellorian*. What have you to do with him?'

'I give him what he wants, and he gives me what I want.' He groped around for the vessel.

'*He* provides you with drink? In exchange for what?' A fresh wave of horror assaulted her. Her father had been drinking for many years, though it had only become a serious problem in the last year. Surely Zellorian was not using him. Why should he?

'Keep him informed of all sorts of things. Zellorian'll not let old Mannaston down. Too valuable.'

Aru knew it would be pointless chastising him in his present state. But the old fool might say things while drunk he would otherwise keep to himself. She closed the door and bolted it. 'So you share the confidence of the great Zellorian?'

'Absolutely right,' he nodded.

Aru's mind was going back to her conversation with Gannatyne, his fears that Zellorian sought a particular power here on Innasmorn. Could her father know anything of this? 'The Imperator would be most impressed, father. I suppose you must know things that even he wouldn't be party to.'

'You cannot imagine, my dear,' he belched, his lids drooping.

'Really, father? Such as what?'

'Like the temple.'

Aru felt herself going cold. *Temple*? Temples were a thing of the remote past, a throwback to the days when primitive Man worshipped gods. 'Temple, father? How interesting. You've seen it?'

'Yes, though secretly. I'm not supposed to, but I keep

55

myself informed.' Mannaston was talking now almost as though he had been drugged, his eyes closed, a smile on his lips. He folded his hands over his robes and grinned. 'Down below, in the bedrock. Zellorian had it cut out.'

'And what is it for?'

'The rituals.'

Aru tried not to let her face betray her emotions, even though her father would not have noticed. 'Rituals,' she repeated softly, the word somehow appalling in the images it brought to mind.

'He's searching, you see. Using the ancient powers to look for what he wants. Takes life to do it. There's blood on the stones.' Mannaston's voice dropped, his hands tightening. 'And other things.'

Aru felt her throat constrict. 'Whose blood?'

Mannaston frowned. 'Don't know.'

'Sacrifice?'

'Don't know.'

'Why? What's it for?'

'Searching. For the lost place.'

Aru wanted to shake him, to drag the knowledge out of him, but she knew she had to step with care. If she lost him now, he might never speak of this nightmare again. 'The lost place?'

He sagged back. 'Somewhere on Innasmorn, there is a lost region. Lost in the haze of the past. But he wants its power. Sorcery, demons, control – ' He began to mutter.

Aru shook her head. This was bizarre. What did he mean by demons? These were legends so old that they were hardly remembered.

'Science dies,' said Mannaston, belching loudly. 'No good here. The Mother crushes it as we kill flies.'

The Mother? Of Storms?

'Other powers live here,' Mannaston went on. 'And he'll find them. In the west. Far west.' He seemed then to shrink, his head dropping on to his chest, his eyes closed tightly.

Aru knew she would get no more from him. She unlocked the door and called to the servants. Again they appeared.

'Clean him up and get him to bed. If he wakes up and calls for drink, deny him, is that clear?' She was less angry now, a little more patient.

'Yes, mistress,' said Olvara, the senior serving girl.

Aru went to the broken shards of the jar and took one. Outside, she summoned Mazzu, a shifty eyed fellow who had been with the family for some years. Aru would have dismissed him, but Mannaston seemed to favour him for some reason. Mazzu bowed as he came, but she could sense his disapproval of her.

'You know something about wine, Mazzu,' she said to him.

'Only a little, mistress,' he said in his hard voice.

She smiled patiently. 'Do you know what this is?' She held out the shard.

Mazzu blinked at it, scratching his unshaven chin. 'It's not from one of our vessels, mistress. Most of ours are of glass.'

She nodded. 'But what did it contain?'

Mazzu sniffed at it, his eyes widening. 'Very strong wine.'

'How strong?' He'd recognised it, she knew. 'And how rare?'

'I'm no expert, mistress – '

'If you can tell me what it is, I'll make it worth your while.'

'You may not like what I tell you, mistress.'

'I'm sure it will be bad news. But I need to know, Mazzu. Don't disappoint me. If you know what it is, tell me.'

Mazzu looked about him nervously. 'I've never tasted it, you understand. But the smell suggests that it's a royal potion. It's named *keroueen*. It is dangerous to drink much of it.'

'Why?'

'It has addictive qualities. And it kills from within. Slowly.'

'And where does it come from? How can it be obtained?'

'You cannot want it, mistress – '

'No. But my father has been drinking it. For how long I don't know. But I want to know *where he got it*.'

Mazzu could see the bridled fury in the girl. 'It must be from the palace, mistress. Only there. Even the smugglers do not get hold of it. Not pure *keroueen*. One jar would be worth a ransom.'

Aru nodded, dismissing him. So her father had been trapped by his own stupidity. Caught like a fly in Zellorian's web, where he would slowly die, drained of use by the Prime Consul. He did not deserve this. Once he had been a man of estimation, they said. A man unlucky enough to be brought low by the sudden death of his wife, whom he had adored. No one could have foreseen how his life would be thrown out of joint by her demise, how it would almost unseat his reason. Aru controlled her welling pity. Pity was a luxury: she could not afford it, not in the face of the evil that threatened to choke them all.

5

KURAAL

On the evening before their last ride to the village, Ussemitus called them all together. 'I want to be sure we are
resolved on this,' he told them. 'Fomond?'

'I'm with you. A war with these people would be a
mistake.'

Arbos nodded. 'Yes, we should have our elders talk to
them.'

'Armestor, Gudrond? You've had time to think it over
as we've come back. I need to know what you will say.'

Armestor nodded. 'If we all keep to the same story, the
elders will have to take note.'

Gudrond also nodded, but made no further comment.

The following mid-morning they rode into their village,
the noise of their coming deliberately loud. By the time
they had crossed over the earthworks to the houses, a small
crowd had gathered. Ussemitus could see some of the elders
among it, their faces creased with annoyance rather than
concern.

He leapt down from his mount and grinned. 'My apologies for this rude arrival, but we bring important news.
From the mountains.'

One of the elders, Hippractus, faced him. He had been
one of Ussemitus's principal teachers and usually had more
patience with youths than his fellows. But his face was
drawn, his eyes full of anxiety. 'You have been to the
mountains?'

'To their edge. There we–' Ussemitus paused. He had
seen the soldiers pushing their way through the crowd.
Warriors of Vittargattus. Had some of them remained here?
He waited until they stood beside the elders.

'You're the youth who made a fool of himself at the

59

banquet,' said their captain, his thumbs tucked inside his belt. 'Where did you run off to?'

'I didn't run off anywhere,' snapped Ussemitus. 'I've nothing to run from.'

'Mind your tongue!' said Hippractus sharply, more than a hint of warning in his voice.

'That's all right,' said the soldier with a sneer. 'The boy's big enough to speak for himself. Or he thinks he is.'

'What I have to say,' said Ussemitus, 'I'll say to the elders.'

'What you have to say,' corrected the captain, 'you'll say to my master.'

Ussemitus would have protested, but something in Hippractus's face told him to be quiet. 'Kuraal is still here,' said the elder. 'You had better come with us, all of you.'

Ussemitus had not been expecting this, but decided it may be for the best. He glanced back at his companions, all of whom had dismounted and whose horses were being led away. Fomond winked at him, but Arbos's expression was perfectly unreadable. Armestor and Gudrond, however, were both visibly nervous, faces beaded with perspiration.

The soldiers led the way to the large hall, which Kuraal had apparently decided to use as a base. Inside, its cool shadows did little to alleviate the anxieties of Armestor and Gudrond as the elders and soldiers gathered. At the head of the table, with maps spread before him, sat Kuraal. He did not look up but went on discussing the maps with two of his officers.

Eventually he lifted his gaze to Ussemitus, staring directly at him. 'Ah, the runaway returns.'

Ussemitus was about to reply indignantly, but he felt the hand of Hippractus on his arm, and though the elder looked elsewhere, his concern transmitted itself. He was right. The situation called for tact.

'Well?' said Kuraal. 'What have you to say?'

'My companions and I rode northwards, through the

forests beyond our usual trails. To the edge of the mountains.'

Ussemitus was aware that every eye in the hall was turned on him.

Kuraal nodded. 'A dangerous journey, one would have thought. In view of what was said here several days ago.'

'Not as it turned out, sire. Though we did meet strangers.' Ussemitus was determined to drop the use of the word 'intruders'.

The soldiers straightened as if they had already scented a battle. Kuraal's interest was clear, his eyes narrowing. 'Men of Innasmorn?'

Ussemitus shook his head. 'No. They were those who you said had arrived from – elsewhere.'

Kuraal got up slowly, his gaze never wavering. Ussemitus could sense the dormant powers in the man, and remembered well the quick summoning he had made in this very hall. 'Go on,' said the Windmaster.

'They are like us in some ways, but are more heavily built, both the men and the women–'

'They had women with them?'

'One, sire, and she led them. She said her name was Aru Casruel–'

Kuraal stiffened. 'She spoke *our* tongue?'

'Yes, sire.'

There were gasps among the soldiers as well as the elders. Ussemitus tried to stifle their unease by expanding on his report. But each new revelation seemed to give rise to further fears. 'Apart from the metals they wore, seemingly without fear–'

'With utter disregard for our laws,' cut in Kuraal.

'They had certain artefacts with them. Craft that moved through the air, though I did not see that happen. They were crippled somehow. The men were trying to repair them. It is how I managed to get the better of the woman.' He went on to describe how he had dropped down upon Aru and had put his knife to her throat, and the conversation that had followed.

'These artefacts,' said Kuraal, whose expression was like ice. 'Can you describe them more fully?'

'They were like elongated pods, split open to reveal their inner works, though they seemed more flesh than metal, sire.'

'Flesh? What else? What sound did they make? What was their colour? How large? As long as three men, four?' Kuraal asked question after question, seemingly obsessed with the craft. He was interested in nothing else, so Ussemitus thought as he struggled to answer clearly. But his mind was confused, his memory not sharp.

'And they were crippled you say?' Kuraal went on, his searching eyes almost willing an image from Ussemitus's mind.

'Yes. The strangers confirmed that. They buried them.'

'Ritual burial.' Kuraal nodded thoughtfully. 'Then these things were imbued with life. Life that Innasmorn saw fit to strike down. And the intruders have learned to speak our language,' he mused. 'They are every bit as dangerous as we supposed.'

'I think not, sire,' said Ussemitus. He could feel a knot of unease uncoiling in his gut.

Kuraal raised his brows. 'You think not? What do you, a simple youth, know of these matters?'

'Aru and Denandys are here on a mission of peace. They wanted to come here—'

'I'm sure they did.'

'I would not bring them—'

'It is good to know that you did something correctly.'

'But I have arranged a further meeting.'

Kuraal's hands clenched, but he spoke calmly. 'Where?'

'In the foothills. A month from the day we met. Aru wishes to speak to us all. Of many things. Of bringing our peoples together.'

Philotor coughed into the silent pause that followed Ussemitus's words. As a senior elder he was held in much respect by the villagers, but Kuraal turned to him with an almost dismissive gaze.

'Sir,' said Philotor, 'perhaps we should view this as an encouraging sign. Perhaps we were mistaken in thinking these strangers warmongers.'

Kuraal's coldness showed no sign of thawing. He waited for the elder to say his piece.

'We have assumed that the strangers came here with the express purpose of conquest. That may not be so. If they have offered to talk peace—'

'And would you not offer peace if someone held a knife at your throat?'

Ussemitus started. Kuraal, he knew then, was not going to listen to reason. 'You misunderstand me—' he began.

'And you misunderstand me, boy. I came here to tell you to prepare. This enemy is dangerous, cunning. How easy for him to lull us into thinking him peaceful, arrange a meeting so that his front lines can move straight into our heart, assessing our strengths and weaknesses. You were the perfect opportunity, boy. You and your sympathy. You should have killed this woman when you had a knife at her throat.'

Ussemitus felt his cheeks flaring. 'I cannot believe you will not listen to reason.'

There were gasps at this. No one dared speak in such a way to a Blue Hair. Was the youth mad?

Kuraal walked slowly down the hall. He pointed at Fomond. 'And you. What have you to say about this affair?'

'I can add nothing to what Ussemitus has said, sir. I believe the strangers have come here to sue for peace. A war would be unnecessary.'

Kuraal twisted his mouth in a sneer. 'Have your elders taught you nothing about our past? About the dangers of artefacts? About how they almost destroyed us all and Innasmorn with us?'

Fomond met his gaze, but said nothing.

Kuraal moved on to Armestor, sensing the youth's terror. 'And you? What have you to say about the lessons of the past?'

Armestor felt his mouth drying up. 'Sir—' he began, but

could say no more. He avoided the gaze of the Windmaster, who mercifully moved on to Arbos. But the tall youth looked straight ahead of him, saying nothing.

Kuraal passed on to Gudrond, knowing that the fear was rooted deepest here. He stopped, his eyes fixed on those of the quaking youth. 'And you?'

'I – I – know of the Curse, sir,' Gudrond stammered.

'You do? Your companions seem to have forgotten it. And what did you make of these intruders?' He stressed the word to show that he would not consider any other.

'Well, sir, they, they seemed to be – friendly.'

'Seemed to be? Did you speak to them?'

'No, sir. Ussemitus spoke for us.'

'For all of you? None of you talked and shared a joke with these friendly intruders? With whom you got on so well?'

No one answered, though Ussemitus looked angered by the clear taunt.

'And which of you was caught? Yes, caught! Ussemitus told us that the only reason he leapt upon the woman was because someone was foolish enough to be discovered. Who was it?' But Kuraal had already guessed. He looked again at Gudrond. 'Was it you?'

Gudrond nodded violently. 'I couldn't help it–'

'Are you so poor a woodsman?'

'No, sir, I–'

'Or perhaps you were tricked, your mind clouded?'

'I think so, sir. I don't remember–'

'I told you the enemy was clever. Some sort of spell, perhaps?'

'It could have been. I'm a good woodsman, sir, and I must admit I didn't expect to be so easily caught. I–'

'I'm sure,' said Kuraal, turning away for a moment, as though he had made his point. But he turned back to Gudrond, unwilling to release him from his own particular spell. 'Tell me about this woman. Was she attractive?'

Gudrond swallowed, his hair matted with sweat. 'I suppose so–'

'You suppose so? Don't you know? How did she compare to the girls of your village? Would you consider having her in your bed?'

'I protest!' said Ussemitus, but again felt the hand on his arm as Hippractus tried to restrain him.

Kuraal ignored him and kept on looking directly at Gudrond. 'Your spokesman seems to have had a better opinion of the woman than you did. Did he speak to her for long?'

Gudrond nodded. 'Quite long, sir.'

'Did he, perhaps, touch the girl?'

Ussemitus felt himself seething with fury. It would have been easy for him to put his fist in the face of this infuriating Blue Hair. But still the elder held him, gently shaking his head, knowing what was in the youth's mind.

'I didn't see, sir,' said Gudrond softly.

'You mean you can't be sure that there was not some kind of physical contact?'

'What are you trying to say?' snarled Ussemitus. 'That this woman bewitched me?'

Still Kuraal studied Gudrond. 'Were they left alone together?'

'Gudrond, tell the truth!' said Ussemitus. One of the soldiers suddenly gripped him by the chin, the fingers like steel.

'Hold your tongue!' he hissed.

Ussemitus brought his knee up hard, aiming for the groin, but the soldier knew enough about brawling to be ready for such a move. He dug with the fingers of his free hand into Ussemitus's stomach and the youth doubled up. Kuraal turned for a moment but then drew closer to Gudrond. The youth blinked away tears of perspiration mingled with fresher tears.

'We seem to be touching on a nerve here,' said the shaman with an unpleasant smile. 'What was there between Ussemitus and this woman? The truth, now, otherwise I will have to be more ruthless in my pursuit of it.'

Gudrond felt his legs going numb. Beside him another

65

of the soldiers gripped him, holding him up. Arbos and Armestor were very still, but Fomond suddenly reached out and struck the soldier who had winded Ussemitus. It was very fast, a blow to the side of the head that sent the man staggering. Swords rang as they were drawn, and within moments the hall was erupting as the elders moved back and the soldiers crowded in. Fomond stood guard beside Ussemitus, his own short wooden knife held before him.

Neither Arbos nor Armestor were able to join him, their own backs covered by other warriors. Gudrond shook, hardly able to stand up. The man who Fomond had felled got up groggily. He pulled out his own blade, his face murderous, but a single glance from Kuraal kept him at bay.

'I suggest everyone keep very still,' said the shaman, seemingly unmoved. 'It would be a pity to shed blood in this hall.' Once again he turned to Gudrond. 'You were about to say something?'

Gudrond's eyes were full of tears, his whole torso shaking. 'I, I, can't remember—'

'You were telling us how Ussemitus spent time alone with this woman, and how you and your companions heard very little of what passed between them. How you could not possibly know what bargains were struck in exchange for what. As far as you know, Ussemitus might have agreed on a further meeting at which—'

'Sir,' cut in Hippractus, and Kuraal turned to him, angered at being interrupted. 'Sire, this seems unreasonable. These young men have acted in good faith.'

For a moment Ussemitus thought Kuraal would actually strike the elder for his effrontery. But instead the shaman suddenly smiled. 'It is touching to see your loyalty. But I am a cautious man. I have seen more than enough evidence to know that Ussemitus is a youth ruled by his emotions. By sentiment. And regrettably, by lust, no doubt.' He put his hand softly on Gudrond's shoulder. 'Would you say that was a fair judgement, boy?'

'I – I –'

'Oh, come, come. Speak up. You foresters are lusty youths, are you not? And is Ussemitus not as lusty as the next man? I see nothing unusual in that. Or are you yet untested?'

Gudrond felt himself flush at this taunt. 'Of course not, sir.'

'No doubt you and your friends have shared a tale or two on such matters? Ussemitus also.'

Gudrond looked angrily at Ussemitus, remembering the mocking he had received in the camp on the journey north. 'I lack his experience in such matters, sir.'

'Oh, he is one for the women, is he?'

'He likes to think so,' muttered Gudrond.

Kuraal nodded, apparently satisfied. 'Yes, I'm sure. Though I doubt that Ussemitus has the wit to appreciate when he's being used by a woman, especially one experienced in such matters.' He turned from Gudrond to where Fomond and Ussemitus had backed away. 'Well, since you've arranged a meeting, Ussemitus, we'd better honour it.'

'What do you intend?' said the youth, his loathing of the Blue Hair obvious to everyone.

'How many of them will come?' said Kuraal.

'Don't answer him,' said Fomond.

Ussemitus grinned. 'Several thousand, I should imagine. All armed.'

Kuraal smiled coldly. 'Your humour is wasted on me, boy. How many?'

But neither Ussemitus nor Fomond answered.

'Give me an hour with them, sire,' said the soldier Fomond had cuffed. 'I'll have all you need.'

Kuraal drew in a breath slowly, stroking his face. 'No. No need.' He walked back to Gudrond. 'Our young friend here will find the place for us, I'm sure.'

Gudrond could not look at his friends, so he did not see their looks of contempt for his weakness.

Kuraal leaned over to him and whispered very softly,

though the words were as clear as the wind, 'And there will be rewards for such help, my boy. Whatever delights you most.'

Ussemitus and Fomond were locked in a room below one of the larger huts with Arbos and Armestor, given no opportunity to resist. Fomond chuckled, in spite of their position 'If it hadn't been for the elders, I reckon Kuraal would have had us skinned.'

'The elders believed us,' said Ussemitus. 'If only that cursed Blue Hair hadn't still been here. Why is he so determined to take war to Aru's people?'

'What will happen to us?' said Armestor.

'Nothing,' said Fomond. 'We'll be left to sweat in here for a few days, then released. By then it will be over.'

'We can't let Aru and the others fall into the trap,' said Ussemitus. 'She won't come with many of them. To show her desire for peace. And they'll be up against an army.'

They had heard the preparations overhead. Kuraal had drawn up his troops and the village was assembling as many men as it could afford. In the morning there would be more coming from other villages which had received the shaman's summons. Gudrond would be leading a large force northward in the dawn light.

Ussemitus could not sleep, though Armestor snored, exhausted by his fear. Fomond and Arbos dozed beside him.

In the middle of the night, Ussemitus heard something above him. A beam of light wavered and he saw a face limned by the glow of a torch. Someone called his voice gently. It was Hippractus.

Ussemitus stood up, his face inches from that of the elder. 'What is it?'

'Quickly, wake your companions.'

Ussemitus did so at once, cautioning silence. The elder helped them out of the pit and they all stood like ghosts in the silence of the hut.

'You must go north and warn the strangers,' said Hippractus. 'No time to talk to me. But some of the elders have talked privately. Kuraal is wrong. Go to the north edge of the woods. There are horses there. Lead them well away from the village before you mount, and then ride hard.'

Ussemitus clapped an arm around the old man. 'Innasmorn bless you for this,' he told him. 'You have saved much bloodshed, I swear it.'

'So we calculate. Now go!' Hippractus hissed.

They needed no second bidding, threading silently through the village until they came to the place they had been told of. Two young lads nervously kept the horses under control, jumping out of their skins when Ussemitus and the others appeared like spectres. But Ussemitus calmed them and in a short while he and his companions were moving beyond into the forest, silently leading the horses.

'What about supplies?' whispered Armestor.

'The elders have thought of that,' said Fomond, tapping a saddlebag. 'And these bows look well made.'

'Do we ride directly north?' said Arbos.

Until this moment, Ussemitus had taken for granted that the others were in favour of going straight to Aru's people. 'What else?'

'We should not go too obviously to them,' Arbos suggested. 'We would arrive too soon, for one thing. And we'll be pursued. Kuraal will track us.'

'Unless he thinks we're still in the pit,' chuckled Fomond.

'We must assume he'll learn that in the morning,' said Ussemitus. 'He would leave nothing to chance.'

'All right,' said Arbos. 'I'll ride westwards a little and make tracks clearly. Then I'll swerve back and meet up with you later. It will win us valuable time.'

Ussemitus was not keen to break up the company, but Arbos's suggestion was sensible. He nodded.

'Take care,' called Armestor, but Arbos swung up on to his horse and waved, his face a white blur in the dim light of the forest. Moments later he was gone.

The others walked their mounts another half mile, mounting up and using a stream to cover their tracks as they rode on. There was moonlight to pick out the way for them, and they moved on swiftly.

Hippractus returned to his own hut. He put out his torch and reached for his pelts. As he did so, a grip of iron took hold of his wrist. He cried out and a torch flared, swinging towards him. There were warriors here.

From the dark interior of the hut stepped another figure, its hair trailing behind it like a cloud. It was Kuraal. 'Not yet asleep, elder? After such a busy day, one would have thought you exhausted.'

Hippractus stared at the shaman, but there was no mercy in his gaze. 'My bladder is not what it was,' mumbled the elder.

'And the youths? Are they away safely?'

'Who?'

Kuraal snorted. 'You were observed. Releasing the prisoners.'

Hippractus frowned. 'Then why didn't you prevent me?'

'I was curious. I imagine they will go north to their new-found allies. I am surprised, I must say, that the entire village is a party to this conspiracy. What prize have the intruders offered you for this betrayal?'

'You are mistaken, Kuraal. The village is innocent.'

'Really?' The shaman laughed unpleasantly.

'The decision to free the youths was mine, and mine alone.'

'Then I am surprised that you betray Vittargattus.'

The elder shook his head. 'I am no traitor. I could not accept your judgement. I know that boy Ussemitus well. He is a loyal youth. He would rather die than betray his village.'

'I am delighted to hear it,' said Kuraal coldly. He walked past the elder to the door. 'Bring him,' he said curtly to the warriors, who took hold of Hippractus.

70

Outside, there were still several hours to go before dawn and the air was cool. Kuraal led the way through the trees, going over the earthwork wall. If any of the villagers saw, they did not interfere. In a glade that was well out of hearing of the village, Hippractus was released.

'What will you do?' he asked Kuraal as he stumbled out into the middle of the glade.

'Traitors are not tolerated,' said Kuraal simply.

The elder gasped. It had been a trap. He had been allowed to release the youths, playing into the hands of the Blue Hair in doing so. 'You meant them to escape!'

Kuraal smiled. 'If I'd executed them in the village, the elders would, like you, have found my decision harsh. But since they have fled and thus compounded their sins, well, I have no choice. I cannot take chances, can I? Vittargattus and my fellow Blue Hairs would have my head on a pole if they knew I had let our enemies have an advantage.'

'What will you do?'

'Keep still and watch. See the judgement of the great Mother.'

Kuraal opened his arms to the night sky, and around the glade his warriors looked on eagerly, like dogs sensing the gathering of power. The shaman began to speak words, directing them up at the night, and in a moment there were eddies of wind that lifted fallen leaves and rustled the branches. Where there had been no breeze there was now a wind. It began to gather in strength, uncoiling like a serpent, until the trees shook and the hair of the watchers whipped back from their faces.

Hippractus felt the coldness closing round his heart. Kuraal was calling on the wind elementals to help him bring Ussemitus to heel. Kuraal was weaving his arms, light flickering around him out of nothing as he made the wind dance. His hair flared about him, a wild cloak, and in it danced more lights, sounds crackling. The air screamed, soaring in and about the trees, as though a pack of aerial hounds had been let loose. It was a sound of hunger, of angry need.

71

Kuraal pointed with both forefingers into the north, and the air funneled itself through the tossing treetops there and tore away, gradually dying to nothing. Kuraal dropped his arms, his chest heaving. His warriors came forward.

'You are well, sir?' one of them asked.

Kuraal grunted. 'I have sent windwraiths. In an hour the runaways will be overtaken.'

Hippractus rushed forward, falling to his knees before the exhausted shaman. 'No! There is no need—'

'There is every need!' snarled Kuraal, face as white as death. 'This is war, old fool. It has already begun.' He turned away and nodded abruptly to one of his soldiers.

The elder did not even hear the hiss of metal as the blade bit deep into his neck. He was dead before he hit the ground.

Somewhere to the north of the village the swirling windwraiths howled, tearing through the high branches, seeking out their foe, eager to rip it asunder.

BOOK TWO

ZELLORIAN

6

BETRAYAL

The figure blended well with the shadows that clung to the narrow alley as if it were a habitual frequenter of the place, a spider in its lair. Few of the city dwellers came here often as it led to a doorway that opened into a remote part of the palace. There were no guards, but the door was always locked and no one would have been foolish enough to have forced it. The figure glanced furtively over its shoulder, anxious that it should not be seen. Satisfied, it knocked on the door and hung back, waiting. After a second knocking, the door creaked open to reveal a guardsman. He peered into the dark of the alley, saw the figure's face and nodded for it to enter. The door closed and silence reclaimed its domain.

The figure disappeared into the maze of corridors beyond the door, knowing its way along this particular route, ducking down to avoid the heavy beams above it, kicking at the rats that scuttled by even more furtively than it did. The guard had not bothered to follow.

At another door it paused, listening, then knocked. Rusty hinges creaked; the door opened wide, swung back almost in annoyance by the man who stood there. His face was hard, the eyes merciless in their appraisal of this intruder. The figure recognised him as Vymark, one of the guards who was very close to the Prime Consul.

'You're in the wrong place,' he said bluntly.

Behind him another guard stepped into view. 'It's all right, Vymark. He's expected. Let him in.'

Vymark raised his brows. The man in the doorway was a particularly unkempt specimen, his beard grizzled, his hair unwashed. Why should Urtbrand want to entertain him? But Vymark stood aside and the figure entered with a low bow.

Urtbrand went to a cupboard and opened it, bringing out an earthenware vessel and Vymark recognised it at once. 'What's in there?' he said.

Urtbrand chuckled, his huge chest heaving. 'Poison. Of a kind.' He gave it to the man who had come. 'Ever heard of *keroueen*?'

Vymark nodded slowly. 'Who's it for? It wouldn't be Mannaston, would it?'

Both Urtbrand and the intruder looked startled. 'What do you know about this?' said Urtbrand, his humour dissolving.

But Vymark grinned. 'I was with the Prime Consul when Mannaston arrived for his last supply. So this is how it's given to him. And who is this creature?'

'He is Mazzu, one of Mannaston's servants. But we reward you very well, don't we, Mazzu?'

The man grinned, showing his uneven teeth. Vymark scowled at him.

'And I suppose you expect something for your trouble,' said Urtbrand.

Mazzu's eyes widened and a new expression crossed his face. Vymark wondered it it could be lust. Mazzu was nodding. 'If it is not too much trouble, master.'

'Nothing is a trouble to one who serves the Prime Consul well. You know where to find the room. She is ready for you.'

Mazzu took the vessel but paused. 'Master, there is one other thing.'

Urtbrand had turned away. He glanced back, not really interested.

'Mannaston's daughter has returned from the forests.'

'Aru?'

'Aye, master. She has visited her father, but I have spoken to friends of mine in the city. She visited another first.'

Vymark looked askance at Urtbrand. What did all this

mean? One of Zellorian's networks? How was it that Urtbrand was a party to it and not himself? Was Urtbrand, perhaps, even more deeply involved with the Prime Consul than he was?

Urtbrand looked intrigued by the news. 'Oh. You have something of interest to report? Is it valuable?'

Mazzu licked his lips as if in anticipation of some greater reward than the one he had already been promised. 'Yes, master. I think so. You know that Aru Casruel commands a unit of her family knights. They went to the forests beyond the mountains. They took three gliderboats.'

Urtbrand frowned but Vymark was nodding. 'I knew about that. So?'

'One of the knights, master, has a brother who works in the lower city and whose friends are known to me. Gossip about the outside spreads very quickly.'

Both Vymark and Urtbrand knew this to be true. Everyone listened out for news of the outside world, although rumours could be dangerous, falsely corrupted and inaccurate. 'Go on,' said Vymark.

'Aru's gliderboats all failed. While the knights were trying to repair them, they were ambushed.'

'Ambushed?' said Vymark incredulously. 'A party of knights *ambushed?*'

Mazzu explained how it had happened.

'You say this peasant was called Ussemitus?'

'Aye, master. Aru made a pact with him. She is to return to him and he is to begin negotiations for peace on his people's behalf.'

'Peace!' snorted Urtbrand. 'This is a pretty tale! If it's true, Vymark, Aru has committed treason against the Imperator Elect. Isn't it so?'

Mazzu did not smile, but his heart leapt within him. All the slights he had taken from the hated family of Casruel would be repaid soon. He would exact a full revenge and see them all damned for their abuse of him.

Vymark nodded thoughtfully. 'Sounds like it. But tell

me, you said she visited someone else before her father. Who was it?'

Mazzu prepared to push home his knife of treachery. 'I have it on very good authority, master. It was the Consul, Gannatyne.'

Vymark thumped the table. 'Gannatyne!'

'But this fits the puzzle perfectly,' said Urtbrand. 'Zellorian is bent on Gannatyne's downfall. It is known that Gannatyne favours peace with these stinking Innasmornians.'

'Zellorian must be told of this,' said Vymark. 'You say nothing to anyone,' he told Mazzu. 'Keep your ears open. If you hear anything more, come to Urtbrand at once.'

'Rest assured, master, I will.'

'You have no love for the Casruel family, I see,' observed Vymark.

Mazzu shook his head but said nothing.

'Go and claim your prize,' said Urtbrand. 'There'll be others after this day's work.'

Mazzu bowed low. 'Master.' He left quickly by another door.

'And what do we give the roach for his treachery?' said Vymark, curious to know why Mazzu should have left so eagerly.

Urtbrand chuckled. 'It's rather amusing. Mazzu, like most of the lower orders of the city, has never known a woman of any beauty. So we make use of his lust. Zellorian weighs these things perfectly, my friend, as I'm sure you know. And his power reaches deep into our system.'

Vymark's face twisted in a wry grin. 'His mind has more mazes than the palace.' He reached for a ewer and poured himself a goblet of wine.

'Mazzu was offered his heart's desire. And he chose one of the court harlots.'

'Which one?'

'Oh, any one, I suppose. They hear such stories about them, down in the lower city. Zellorian told him he would choose the best for him if he did his work well. Which he has. Mannaston is slave to the *keroueen*. Zellorian, as you know, is not a man to offend.'

'Not if you want to remain alive and sane.'

'Well, apparently one of the harlots offended him in some way. I know nothing of the details. My own work keeps me far from that part of the palace—'

'Just as well,' laughed Vymark. 'I wouldn't want anything to do with the harlots.'

'Quite. Anyway, Zellorian wanted to teach this harlot a lesson, so the rumours go. Her name's Suzeral.'

'That she-cat! I wouldn't bed that if I were alone with her on a moon.'

'Nor I from what I've heard. Apparently Zellorian told her that he wanted her to service a rather unsavoury specimen from the lower city. You can imagine how appalled she was. But she dared not argue.'

Vymark sipped at the wine. It was very good. Urtbrand had remarkable contacts in the palace. 'And what did Zellorian offer Suzeral for this task?'

'He simply told her that when Mazzu was of no further use to him, she could have him to do with as she pleases.'

Vymark coughed, spilling his wine. 'Then Mazzu's days are limited!'

Urtbrand roared with laughter. 'Yes! Zellorian does have a way of tying things together, don't you think.'

Vymark's laughter fused with his friend's. 'And they say the Prime Consul has no sense of humour.'

Mannaston sat stiffly in the ornate chair. He was sober, his mind for once clear. He looked straight ahead of him, not really seeing the room. Like all the others he was summoned to under the palace, it was almost bare. It was the last place the officials would expect a member of the Consulate to come to. No one knew how Zellorian operated, how he used those around him, though many had guessed. Fear stalked through the palace hungrily, one of its masters. It was useless trying to resist Zellorian, his brutal methods.

But what did it matter? Mannaston mused. Mankind had had its day. The slow spiral down to oblivion had begun long ago. This world would hear the last strains of man's requiem.

The door behind him opened. He recognised the erect soldier who came in and stood with folded arms by the wall, watching him but saying nothing. It was Vymark, one of Zellorian's growing personal bodyguard, an ambitious man with the hunger of youth, who would undoubtedly go far in Zellorian's scheme of things. But for what? Mannaston mused. What use was there in the pursuit of a dream long dead?

Zellorian himself entered, going around the table and sitting oposite Mannaston. He studied him closely, looking for signs that he was breaking, succumbing to the terrible *keroueen*. 'I fear I have more work for you,' he said.

Mannaston nodded resignedly.

'There is unfortunate news.'

Suddenly Mannaston looked as if he might come to life. He leaned forward, an expression of anguish on his face. 'My wife—?'

Zellorian shook his head. 'It is your daughter who concerns me.'

'Aru? Yes, she is back. I seem to recall speaking to her.' Mannaston looked dazed, as though the discussion with Aru had been a vision, part of his fragmented drunken imaginings.

'I'm afraid she is involved in something that she is not equipped to deal with in the proper manner. I think she is being manipulated.'

Mannaston shook himself. He did not understand any of this. 'Aru? By whom?'

'We think Gannatyne has some hold over her.'

'She is her own woman.'

'But you recall Gannatyne's talk with the Imperator Elect. His desire to convert him to peaceful policies here on Innasmorn? It's deceit, Mannaston. I know too much. Gannatyne plots the Imperator's destruction, and he intends to use the Innasmornians to achieve it. And now he has involved your daughter.' Zellorian leaned across the table, his knuckles whitening where his hands clasped themselves. 'Look, I don't think she realises what he's doing. I bear no malice towards her. But we have to be careful. These are dangerous times.'

Mannaston found himself reeling. Perhaps a drink would help. But no, he had steeled himself to stay sober before Zellorian this time. Yet all this talk of rebellion. Zellorian had spoken so quickly, he could not follow.

'You'll have to watch your daugher very closely for me.'

'But I can't. She's gone—'

'No. She's in the city. Preparing to go south again. She has friends here. People she talks to. I want to know everything, Mannaston. Every word. Who she knows, what she tells them. This is important. It concerns the Imperator Elect.' Zellorian knew that he had only Mannaston's cravings to play on, but he forced home his point by tapping the table as he spoke. 'This is for the good of your own daughter.'

'What will happen to her?'

'I'll see she is protected. If Gannatyne is brought to justice, I'll see that you and your daughter are removed to a place of safety, further north. You'll not be troubled again.'

Mannaston seemed to be struggling with some inner vision, his arms shaking. He looked imploringly at the Prime Consul. Vymark was surprised at the depth of despair in the man. But it did not move him to pity, only disgust.

'And my wife?' said Mannaston, the words barely audible.

'I will do everything in my power, as I have promised. But if you are instrumental in bringing about Gannatyne's defeat, I will use all my influence. Be assured.' Zellorian patted Mannaston on the shoulder and Vymark felt himself go cold. Mannaston was no more than a husk, about to collapse in upon himself.

'Very well.' Mannaston struggled to his feet. Vymark opened the door for him and watched him shuffle away like a man in a dream.

'Sir, is his mind capable—'

Zellorian nodded. 'I hold it by a thread.'

'He spoke of his wife. Who is she?'

'It is a pitiful affair. Not one I take any pleasure in,' said Zellorian, scowling. 'She was not satisfied with Mannaston's position, even though the Casruels are, or once were, a major family of Empire. Her own ambitions went far beyond it. Some time ago she became entangled with one of the higher court officials. The name is not important. There was a minor scandal and she was reprimanded. But she was a restless woman and enjoyed the frivolities of court. Mannaston tried to keep her away from such things, but lacked the strength of character to control her. Before long she was sharing the beds of a number of officials. Clearly she sought to win the couch of the Imperator himself. She was accomplished enough to draw his eye, and he made her one of his harlots.'

Vymark was surprised. 'But did Mannaston not object?'

'Another man might have, and might have won his case, for the Consulate can overrule the Imperator Elect in certain matters. But Mannaston is weak. He whined and he protested to the wrong people, never having the nerve to bring the whole thing out into the open, threatening the Imperator with a scandal. And he was besotted with the woman. He didn't want it made open that she was as cheap as a lower city whore. These things have happened before, but the men concerned were usually glad to be rid of their wives. Yet you see how it torments Mannaston still. The woman has affected him as wine does.'

'Does the daughter know?'

Zellorian shook his head. 'She has far more mettle than her father. She is much more like the Casruels of old. No, she believes her mother to be dead. She has no idea that she is here on Innasmorn. Mannaston would never tell her the truth.'

Vymark nodded. 'Then he will do as you ask and betray Aru into your hands in exchange for the release of his wife?'

Zellorian looked away. 'That is his hope. As long as he clings to it, he is my puppet.'

In his house, Mannaston felt weighed down, overburdened. Even the thought that Zellorian might free his wife for him could not give him the strength he needed. His hands shook, his stomach ached. But if he gave in to the craving—

A shadow crossed his door. He looked up. It was Mazzu. In his hands was the familiar vessel. No, not now—

'I heard you come in, master,' said the oily voice. 'Is there anything you want?'

'Bring it here.'

Mazzu smiled, handing the vessel to his master. Mannaston pulled the cork from its spout and drank eagerly.

Soon afterwards he left the house, lurching down the street towards the lower city, his head ringing, his mind dancing with countless images. Among them his wife laughed.

The tavern was noisy, full of shouting soldiers and city workmen. Here they rubbed shoulders, swapped yarns and drank the common beer by the barrel, often until late at night. Although the soldiers did not have the busy tasks of the stonemasons and carpenters to wear them down by day, they were kept busy in the exercise yards, working off their boredom as best they could. Their officers had been told to allow them more license than usual at night: they needed relief from the monotony of their daily round. When, they constantly asked, were they going to be able to go out and colonise this damned world?

Among the soldiers in the tavern was Denandys, though he was far more careful with his drink than most of his contemporaries. Even the knights were a little too boisterous for his liking. He sat in a booth with some of his friends, talking idly about the future, and how the city had become a place of wonders in such a short span of time.

It was here that Aru joined him, ignoring the coarse comments flung her way by those who did not know her. She would be more than a match for most of them in a fight with a sword. Most of the other women in this tavern had been brought here to amuse the men. Aru expected to be taunted, but she knew she was under the protection of her knights.

'When's it to be?' he asked her.

'It will have to be soon. I've heard things that frighten me. Tomorrow would not be soon enough.'

He raised his brows. 'We are not due to meet Ussemitus again for some time. Should we leave the Sculpted City early?'

'Denandys, I think we have to make the decision to break away from this city altogether.' She went on to explain what she had heard from Gannatyne, and what had disturbed her more, the things her father had told her.

Denandys pursed his lips, his mind racing. 'You're right, Aru. We dare not stay. The Casruels are not welcome here any longer. And Zellorian has other families marked down. I have a dozen men who are loyal to me whatever I ask of them. They'll come at once. We'll take one gliderboat—'

'But will it survive?' she asked, her face lined with worry.

He smiled reassuringly. 'The gliderboats seem to be unharmed in the mountains. We can land before we reach the forest lands. But if we take one, we may have to kill to get it.'

'They're watched? Yes, I thought the net had tightened. And we are also watched, I'm sure of that.'

'Zellorian?'

She looked about her. 'The people of Innasmorn are in grave danger,' she said abruptly.

'Very well. I'll have my men together in half an hour.' He gave her instructions, telling her where to meet him. Minutes later she had left and Denandys was speaking to the closest of his friends.

Outside, as Aru left the tavern, she did not see the shadow in the street beyond her. It moved away more slowly than she had, staggering as it went, muttering to itself.

Denandys came out of the tavern, pretending to be drunk and shouting noisily that he would go home to bed, making his goodbyes to other colleagues who came with him. He, too, was watched, and another figure slipped away down an alleyway to another nearby tavern.

Inside it, at the gaming table, Vymark stiffened as he saw Mazzu enter by a side door. The little man looked around and catching sight of the soldier, nodded to him. At once Vymark excused himself and joined Mazzu.

'What have you heard?' he asked him.

'The knights who went south with Aru. She has spoken to them just now. They have all left the tavern.'

Vymark smiled grimly. 'Then they're leaving,' he nodded. 'Very well. Go back to your master's house. Where's the girl?'

'She left first, alone.'

'Find her and watch her. Mannaston is supposed to be doing as much, but we cannot depend on the old fool.'

Mazzu was gone within moments. Vymark nodded to certain of his men who were scattered about the drinking hall. He had picked the best for this job, and though they had been making a pretence at drinking heavily, they had been careful.

They met in the alley, twenty strong. 'You know what to do,' Vymark told them, but briefly went over it. He nodded and they moved away with great stealth, their hands gripping their sword hafts.

Mazzu had given Vymark careful instructions. He knew where to find Denandys and his men, and had guessed already that the gliderboat yards would be the target. At night the craft were locked away and no one had access to them, even those officers who were in charge of the glider-boats during daylight hours. Each of the families owned gliderboats, but they were all subject to the same restrictions. There were very few guards put on the pens, as no one expected anyone to attempt to get in. No one usually had a reason to steal a gliderboat: anyone who took one up for amusement could expect to be stripped of rank if caught.

Vymark and his men came upon Denandys and his own knights a short while later. Denandys was watching the street while his companions were using their weapons to force a way into the gliderboat yard. Vymark grinned. There were a dozen of the Casruel knights. This should not be too difficult. He stepped out into the moonlight. His men were already fanning out like ghosts.

'You there!' he called.

Denandys swung towards him at once, cursing. He understood immediately that he and his knights had been watched in the tavern. 'Ready yourselves,' he whispered. 'They don't mean to take prisoners.'

'It's Vymark,' one of the knights said. 'Zellorian's man.'

Vymark moved forward comfortably, his men with him, tightening their semi-circle. Denandys knew that if he were to survive, he must cut his way out of this. His men lifted their blades, knowing the same.

'Throw down your blades and come peacably,' shouted Vymark.

'Hold your swords,' hissed Denandys, but he had no need. His men had fanned out, linking to form the best wedge of defence they could.

Vymark nodded to his own men and they moved in quickly, steel ringing as the first blows were exchanged. Sparks danced in the night air, leaving trails as they fell. Both groups of warriors were well trained and would have been a match for anyone. Only the weight of numbers swayed the balance. Denandys's men knew this was to the death, but they did not complain. Defeat meant death anyway – Zellorian wanted none of the Casruel knights to survive this.

Denandys heard the first of his men die. He gasped, not crying out, sinking down. Denandys tried to get to Vymark, but he was shielded by his men. Swords darted in and out like snake tongues. Thank the stars that Aru was not here! Would they have struck her down, too?

Vymark watched as the Casruels fell, angry that some of his own men died, but those of Denandys fell more quickly, for all their skill. There had been no witnesses to this butchery, but now there were cries from beyond the pens.

'Who goes there!' shouted someone, holding up a light.

'The Imperator's guard,' called Vymark. 'Has anyone entered the yards?'

'No,' came the reply, though Vymark knew they could not be certain.

Moments later the work was done. Only Denandys stood against them, his knights cut down, sprawled in the pooling blood.

'Finish it, you barbarians,' said Denandys, his chest heaving with effort, his face corpse-white in the moonlight.

Vymark gave him a look of contempt. 'You chose the wrong side,' he said, nodding to his men. Quickly they stepped in, three blades driving unopposed into the chest of Denandys. They had given him a clean death.

The guards pressed up against the fence. 'What is this?' called one of them, horrified by the carnage.

'Spies,' said Vymark. 'Lucky we were passing. If they'd broken in, you'd be the ones lying in your own guts.'

Three streets away, hiding in a neglected doorway, Aru waited. Where was Denandys? Surely he had freed a glider-boat by now. Was that distant shouting she had heard? Had they been discovered? But if they had, they would have overpowered the guards easily.

She peered down the street. Was that movement at its end? Cautiously she moved along the wall, drawing a long knife in case there were other dangers here. Something moved in the shadows and she caught up with it, twisting

87

the figure around. It was not one of the knights as she had hoped.

'Spare me!' gasped the man, cowering, and in horror she saw that it was Mannaston.

'Father!'

'Quickly. We must get away from here. There's death all around us.'

'What are you talking about?' She could smell the stink of strong wine.

'Soldiers. Killing. Men have died. I saw—'

'*Who?*' she almost snarled, her hands digging into his flesh so that he cried out.

'By the gliderboat yard—'

She felt herself teetering on the brink of a pit. Denandys—

'Quickly,' Mannaston urged. 'Away, away.' He pushed her, ignoring the knife and scrambled up the alley. She was too dazed to stop him.

Further down the alley, Mazzu watched them from the darkness, gloating on their misery.

7

THE GLORY PATH

At the heart of the palace a pleasure area had been constructed for the Imperator Elect. Overhead a curved dome of crystal sparkled under the sun of Innasmorn, and from the upper reaches of the dome trailed long fronds and plants, the air heavy with the perfume of the exotic flowers that bloomed in profusion. In the centre of this extravagant playground there was an oval pool, tiny waves set in perpetual motion about it, and around the sides of the pool there were groves and bowers, seats and hammocks. A score of the court harlots draped themselves about these seats or walked languorously about the gardens, others swimming or floating in the warm water as though events outside had no meaning.

Zellorian entered the area, but its atmosphere had no effect on him. He was one of the very few men allowed to enter without the express invitation of the Imperator, and ironically one of the few who cared nothing for its pleasures. The harlots who saw him pouted, but he ignored them, searching for the man who ruled the Sculpted City. He found him in one of the bowers, a goblet in one hand and a brace of naked harlots on the couch beside him. One of them, Zellorian saw with some surprise, was the wife of Mannaston. Her glance lingered on him, but he pretended not to have noticed her. It was talented of her to have kept close to the Imperator for so long. Of course, she had used drugs to keep herself looking younger than she was, and although her skin and her body were beautiful, her eyes had the look of one who had paid for her pleasures, barely glossing over the despair that dwelt there. In her glance, Zellorian had seen the plea for pity.

Annoyed with himself for even noticing such a thing, he spoke sharply. 'May I speak to you privately, sire?'

'Zellorian! Come and sit down,' grinned the Imperator. Zellorian was relieved to see that he was not drunk, apparently coherent. 'Thank you, sire. Send the girls away for a short while, if you would.'

'If I must.' The Imperator waved at the two harlots and they grimaced but slipped into the pool, swimming away as naturally as fish. 'Perhaps later you'll enjoy them with me?'

'If time permits, sire.'

'Time, time,' the Imperator sighed dramatically. 'Now that we're here on Innasmorn, away from the terrors of the Empire, I should have thought we could afford to relax.'

'It's why I've come,' said Zellorian, glad of the opening.

'Oh dear, not trouble?'

'A small matter. I am a little concerned that some of your subjects seem to be entertaining the wrong ideas about the inhabitants of Innasmorn.'

'In what way wrong?'

'Subversive, perhaps.'

The Imperator raised his brows and sat up. 'You intrigue me. Do go on.'

'We have given ourselves certain goals. If we are to rebuild, we must take a very hard line. You understand these things, sire.'

'It will take time, Zellorian. I am beginning to think we try to do things too quickly. Why, we have an entire world to utilise.'

'Of course, sire. But there are certain paths to follow. I would be the last one to foster a war–'

The Imperator looked taken aback. 'A war? What do you mean?'

'If we are not careful, we may find ourselves embroiled in a war with the Innasmornians.'

'How?'

'I cannot see how our two cultures can mix. The people

of Innasmorn are so barbaric. They have no technology. They—'

'Forgive me, Zellorian, but we have walked over this ground several times already. I appreciate your judgement and concern, but I have already agreed with you on this.'

'Even so, sire, there are those who seem to think that our future lies in the fusing of our two races. That strength would come from union. In a way this is laudable. But to me such a thing could only mean genetic suicide.'

'Who is in favour of this principle?'

'I have so little proof, but I do know that contact has been established with the Innasmornians.'

'Contact?' The Imperator drank his wine. 'Against your will?'

'The position is difficult. As you know, some contact had to be made. I myself had Innasmornians brought here so that we could learn their language.'

'Yes, so you said. What happened to them?'

'They are still here, sire. I did not think it prudent to let them go back to their own people.'

'No. Keep them entertained here.'

'We have also had certain parties of knights studying the mountains and the lands beyond them in preparation for more ambitious journeys. These have been controlled, although I am not sure that they are as controlled as they should be.'

'The Consulate controls such matters, doesn't it?'

'In principle, sire. But if you'll forgive me, it's an area where our government sometimes falls down.'

'Oh?'

'Obviously I can only applaud our democracy, and you are fortunate to have such a devoted body of men to run it, but there are times when the dispersal of power can be unwise.'

'In what way?'

'Take the matter of exploration. To me it would seem prudent, no, essential, that all journeys are controlled centrally by a single body within the Consulate. At the moment there are too many of the Consuls investing in small forays. The houses have their own gliderboats, their personal Controllers. Knowledge is becoming scattered, as is opinion. Before long something could go awry. Hency my anxiety about a possible conflict.'

The Imperator was nodding. There was nothing he feared more than the threat of another war. 'A valid point. So what do you suggest? Take the matter to the Consulate?'

'Much as they would prefer that, I think you should issue an edict. Only those journeys approved by yourself may be undertaken. All requests should come before you. I can easily set up a committee to look into the detail.'

'I have to be careful with the Consulate. They may see me as being a little dictatorial—'

'It would be for our safety, sire. And it would ensure that the wrong kind of fraternisation did not take place. It is not just the potential conflict that worries me.'

The Imperator looked even more concerned. 'Go on.'

'I have a strong feeling that some of the Consulate themselves are actively encouraging contact with Innasmornians. I believe that this could be the first step to rebellion, or something very much like it.'

'Rebellion?' The Imperator sounded appalled.

'Perhaps not in direct terms, sire. I don't think anyone would be stupid enough to rise up against you, or the Consulate. But Innasmorn is a large world. It is quite possible that someone might wish to leave us and create a state of his own. A state which would actively welcome the natives. There would be in-breeding. A new race would be born, a diluted race. And how long before it saw us as an enemy?'

'It staggers me to think that anyone should want to do this. We have everything here. The Csendook have become a shadow in the past. Why?'

Zellorian sighed. 'I have no hard proof, of course.'

'No, no. I'm sure you must be right, Zellorian. You've kept your head better than any other through all this change. As a matter of fact—'

Zellorian leaned closer, knowing that the seeds he had sewn were at last taking root in that sluggish pool of a mind. 'Sire?'

'Do you have any reason to suspect Gannatyne?'

'Why do you ask?'

'It's just that he came to see me not long ago. He was most persuasive, too. I found myself thinking, privately, that his arguments had some merit. But I put them down, quite firmly.'

Zellorian frowned as if baffled. 'I don't follow, sire.'

'Gannatyne told me he thought it vital that we integrate with the Innasmornians. That our future should be inter-linked with theirs. We should *share* our technology with them. I told him that it was quite out of the question. If anything, they must bow to me. There can only be one Imperator.'

Zellorian sighed and sat back as if stunned by these words. 'You see, it is as I feared, sire. Gannatyne is a clever man. Yes, remarkable. I am afraid this all ties in too well with other events.'

The Imperator studied him anxiously. 'Gannatyne?'

'These journeys. There was another recently. Led by one of the Casruel family and her knights. The daughter of one of our leading families. Her father is Mannaston.'

'Do I know him?'

'There's no reason you should, sire.'

'What of his daughter?'

'I have no idea who authorised her journey, but certain information has come to me about it. She met and talked to Innasmornians, having been taught their tongue. Many of the officers have been so schooled. We thought it a wise precaution.'

'To whom did she report back?'

'I have no clear proof—'

'But you suspect Gannatyne?'

'I do. And last night there was an incident at the glider-boat pens.'

The Imperator was beginning to look even more

93

uncomfortable, as though assassins were already at his back.

'Some of the Casruel knights who were with the woman on the journey attempted to break into the pens and prepare a gliderboat. The girl is known to be a Controller. The craft was being freed for her, so it seems.'

'Ah, she can fly the craft?'

'She has the special talent, yes. Quite obviously the Casruels intended to take the craft southward, in search of their allies.'

'Allies?'

'The Innasmornians. I am certain.'

'Then have these knights brought before me at once!'

Zellorian feigned discomfort. 'Sire, I am sorry to say that it is not possible. Some of the night guards discovered the Casruels and hailed them. There was a skirmish. My men are not inexperienced, but there were not many of them. Even so, they fought well. Some of them were killed, as were the guards in the pens.'

The Imperator had gone white. '*Killed!* And the Casruels?'

'All dead. We thought we had saved one for interrogation. But he died.'

'So you cannot be sure who was behind it?'

'I can prove nothing. But they were knights who served under Aru, Mannaston's daughter. She was not with them, and I feel sure if we tried to interrogate her, she would have an alibi prepared.'

The Imperator grunted. 'This is terrible news. In this very city!'

'I am having the girl watched.'

'Would it not be better to have her held on some charge? To ensure that she causes us no more problems?'

'If you'll allow me, sire, I think there is a better way.'

'Oh? What is it?'

'She is a small fish. I would rather net the larger one. If, as I am sure, she is the servant of Gannatyne, then

94

sooner or later she will lead us to him. Once he is connected to her and her actions, we will have him.'

The Imperator nodded. 'Yes, I see. Gannatyne is a clever man. He would have covered himself very well.' He stood up and paced along the side of the pool, for once ignoring the harlots who postured for him.

Zellorian did not smile, though he knew that he had tightened his hold on this fool. Soon the trap would be nicely baited.

The Imperator turned back as though a thought of great moment had just occurred to him. 'Very well, Zellorian, I will issue a royal edict. There are to be no further journeys from the city without my approval. Call your committee. You'll chair it, of course?'

'If that is your wish, sire.'

'It is.'

Vymark stood before his master, showing no sign of tiredness or that he had been involved in a bloody battle the previous night. Zellorian admired him for that. He would unquestionably fulfill his promise.

'You did well,' he told the warrior. 'Your men acted exactly as you told them? No qualms?'

'There's not one of them that doesn't want my job, sir.'

Zellorian laughed harshly. 'That's good in a warrior. But you'd better see to your back.'

'We decided we could not trust the guards of the pens.'

'Witnesses?'

'My men, sir. But they can be trusted.'

Zellorian was about to say something when there came a knock on the door. Vymark looked annoyed, but Zellorian gestured for him to open it.

The wretched figure of Mannaston stood outside, and after a pause, shuffled in.

'Sit down, Mannaston,' Zellorian told him. 'I've work for you.' He nodded for Vymark to remain.

Mannaston nodded. He seemed even more exhausted

than normal, his eyes swollen, his face like dough. But he was sober.

'I saw the Imperator Elect today,' said Zellorian. 'And one other.

Mannaston looked up, for a moment hope on his face.

Zellorian nodded. 'She was there. But he is tired of her. Soon he will allow me to replace her. I will bring her out from the inner palace.'

Mannaston gasped. 'Can this be true? You deceive me—'

'No, I promise you. She will be freed. But as I said, there is work for you.'

'What must I do? Spy on my own daughter? She has done nothing!'

'I'm sure you are right. She is being used.'

'Last night there was fighting,' 'Mannaston said hurriedly. 'But she was not part of that—'

'They were her own knights,' said Zellorian mildly. 'But I was mistaken about her. It was they who intended treason. Your daughter is not part of Gannatyne's deceits. I will protect you both.'

Mannaston suddenly swung his gaze on Vymark. 'You! You were there. I saw you.'

Vymark looked down at him arrogantly. He bowed.

'Vymark is loyal to me,' said Zellorian. 'And we both serve the Imperator Elect. As you must. However much personal harm he has done you. We have our people to think of.'

Mannaston felt the cloud of confusion enveloping him. It was so difficult to think properly. But Aru was safe? Not implicated? Yet why had she been in that part of the city? And what were the supplies he had found? There had been enough for a dozen men, hidden in the wide gardens beyond the house. A good place to land a gliderboat.

Zellorian was talking to him again, snapping him out of his dark thoughts. 'I want you to go to Gannatyne,' the Prime Consul told him.

'Gannatyne? Why should he see me?'

'He will. You tell him you have an important message

for him that only he must hear. It concerns myself. Do you understand?'

Mannaston repeated the words, nodding.

'When he admits you to his apartments, you tell him you have learned something about me, about my work, that you are afraid to speak of.'

Mannaston digested this, again repeating it.

'He may not believe you, but he cannot afford to take the chance that you are lying. Tell him you have evidence that I am plotting against the Imperator.'

Mannaston looked aghast and Vymark kept his own feelings under control with difficulty. What new moves had Zellorian set for himself?

'Gannatyne knows your daughter,' Zellorian was saying. 'He may not be using her as I thought, but he respects her. He knows you are her father.'

'He shows me nothing but contempt.'

'He has no reason to suspect you of lying to him. Tell him you can prove me a traitor. Then arrange a meeting with him.'

'Where?'

'I will tell you. Memorise the address very carefully. I want no errors, Mannaston, otherwise you will lose your wife and your daughter with her.'

'There'll be no error.'

'And keep away from drink. Afterwards you will have all you wish.'

'And my *wife?*' he said, his voice like a knife.

'Do as I bid and she can be with you in days.'

'Give me the address.'

Vymark watched, fascinated, as Mannaston learned the address, forced over and over again to repeat it and the directions. It was in a part of the lower city where there were mostly warehouses and stores, not often frequented by anyone. To Vymark's surprise, Mannaston learned its location expertly.

When he had at last gone, Zellorian was satisfied that he knew it by heart.

'As long as drink does not rob him of his senses,' observed Vymark.

'He'll hold off long enough.'

'He must desire his wife very much. Is she that beautiful?'

'Past her best. It would be very easy to have the Imperator release her. He has many others. Apart from his poetry, Vymark, it is all he really cares about. That and his cowardly hide.'

'It puzzles me, sir.'

'How such a weak-willed man could rule us?'

Vymark looked down, suddenly aware that he was talking to the Prime Consul. This was dangerous talk.

'You can speak plainly to me now. I told you, serve me well enough and you'll prosper. The Imperator is a fool. But we need him. He is our shield: The Consulate needs him and so do the people. He is a symbol of our resistance to defeat. When the Csendook Swarms tore into us and threatened to destroy us utterly, the Imperator became the symbol of man's last hope. Imagine that! That pathetic man, our last hope!'

Vymark had never heard Zellorian speak so openly. But it filled him with an even greater ambition to serve him.

'The illusion has to be maintained. The Consulate know he is weak. But the people don't. They never see him. And those that still survive back in the Empire, in pockets, on crippled worlds, they never see him. But they know he lives. And fight on.'

'And the Csendook?'

'They wouldn't care. Not now. They have won, as they imagine. Soon they will grow fat, with no one to kill, as all conquerors do. So we will hold on to our fickle Imperator. He is my toy, Vymark. One day you will see how I play with him. But show all respect. Do everything in his name. Let the Consulate see what a loyal warrior you are. And teach your men the same.'

Vymark smiled. 'We are honoured.'

'To you will go the glory. I have chosen you for that.'

Vymark thought for a moment that Zellorian would say

no more on the matter, but after a brief reflection, the Prime Consul nodded to himself as though he had come to a private decision. 'Come with me,' he said softly.

He led the way beyond the chamber through yet more of the confusing corridors and rooms of this part of the citadel until he came to a narrow stairwell. Two guards that Vymark was not familiar with challenged them, weapons drawn, but they stiffened in salute when they saw Zellorian. He exchanged brief, soft words with them and then nodded for Vymark to follow him down into the semi-dark.

The descent took time, but far below there was a circular chamber lit by firebrands and guarded by two more of Zellorian's picked men. They unlocked a door for him. Beyond was a huge chamber, a cavern, deep below the heart of the Sculpted City. Vymark drew in his breath as he saw its dimensions, though shadows clung to them jealously. The cavern was scooped like a rough sphere from the rock, its tilted floor curved and dusty. Columns rose up from it, thick as tree boles, some of them daubed with pictographs as if this place belonged to some forgotten history, a remote aeon of the world. And the atmosphere was thick, like the smell of a battlefield after the carnage.

'What is this place?' said Vymark, his voice almost lost in the immense void.

'The beginning and the ending of the Pathway,' said Zellorian. 'This is where we first set foot on Innasmorn. Where we walked from the dream of our rebirth.'

From somewhere in the distance there came a cry, the sound of someone in torment. In spite of himself, Vymark shuddered.

'A place of great power,' said Zellorian. 'Very few are permitted to come here. It is our key to the future.'

Somehow Vymark could sense in the clogging air about him a dreadful suffering, as though these walls and columns had been hewn from agony, the misery of countless scores of people. What force did Zellorian draw on to fuel the power of this place? How had he achieved the leap between worlds, the journey down the forbidden path?

The Prime Consul pointed and in the odd haze of light and smoke Vymark thought he imagined an immense tunnel, like the inside of a titanic worm, stretching out into the distance.

'Like a womb,' said Zellorian, a whisper in his ear. 'And just as a woman gives birth, so the Pathway laboured to release us, through pain and with blood. Power, Vymark. Unimaginable. Life.'

The image winked out and Vymark felt the air thicken about him. Life?

'I'll teach you the secrets of this place,' Zellorian told him. 'And you'll taste its power. But for the moment we have to deal with more modest matters.' He drew the warrior away, back to the door. 'You heard me arrange for Mannaston to bring Gannatyne to ùs.'

'To us?'

Zellorian smiled. 'I want him destroyed, but not by the sword. And I want the girl, Aru. You must get a message to her. She is Gannatyne's servant.'

Vymark's eyes hardened. 'Am I to tell her he wishes to see her urgently? At a certain address? I have memorised it better than Mannaston.'

Zellorian closed the door with a low chuckle. He nodded and began to explain what other arrangements he wanted made.

8

IN THE WEB

Gannatyne frowned.

'Shall I tell him you cannot see him, sir?' said the servant.

Gannatyne shook his head. He thought for a moment. 'No. You had better admit him.'

The servant bowed and left. Gannatyne rose and went to the open window, looking down at the streets below. He was some distance from the palace, preferring a home in the heart of the city where he could watch its people at work and hear their noise. They had settled well on Innasmorn. Perhaps he should be more positive about the future, he told himself. But they could not be expected to be content here in the mountains forever.

A cough behind him made him turn. Mannaston stood before him. He had made some attempt to tidy himself, his beard combed, his robe unexpectedly immaculate.

'Your pardon, sire,' he bowed.

'Sit down.'

Mannaston did as asked. He knew that the Consul had no love for him, and that there were few among the government who had any time for him these days. He had become an embarrassment to them all. Well, none of them had made any attempt to help him when he needed it, something which he still found puzzling, so why should he think of sparing them from the fate that Zellorian had planned for them?

'I am told you wanted to see me on a matter of some urgency,' said Gannatyne, himself sitting, though he did not look directly at his guest.

'Yes, sire. It is difficult to speak, however.'

Gannatyne glanced up from his papers. 'Why is that?'

'It concerns the Prime Consul.'

Gannatyne leaned back. He masked his interest. 'Yes?'

'There are things you should know, and the Consulate.'

'Who sent you to me?'

Mannaston was almost taken off guard by the bluntness of the question. He looked away nervously. 'I am capable of making decisions for myself,' he blurted. 'You are high in authority.'

Gannatyne fidgeted. He always felt uncomfortable with this wretched man. If only he had kept his head through his personal crisis, he could have gone on to become a fine administrator. Such a waste. 'Very well.'

'There is a great evil at work in this city,' Mannaston went on, using the words he had been taught. 'And I believe the Prime Consul is at the heart of it. He plans the downfall of the Imperator.'

Gannatyne's eyes narrowed. 'How do you know this?'

'I have seen certain things.'

Gannatyne rose and went to the louvred shutters, closing them so that the hubbub of the city became muffled. Light slatted across him as he returned to the table.

'What things?'

'He has made prisoners of Innasmornians. Those whom he brought here to teach us their language. Sire, he has abused them and used power on them.'

'Power?' nodded Gannatyne. He knew only too well that Zellorian tapped things none of his fellows would have dared consider. 'Where was this?'

'It is not for me to get involved in such matters, sire, but my daughter tells me we should be more considerate to the Innasmornians. She says that they are not a primitive people, but should be encouraged to trade with us. I know nothing of that, but when I saw the torment of the prisoners—'

Gannatyne's knuckles whitened as he gripped his chair. 'You are saying they were *tortured?*'

'I did not stay long in the place. I came upon it by pure chance. I had been visiting that part of the city on a private matter—'

102

Gannatyne studied him suspiciously, prompted by contempt.

Mannaston looked down, but Gannatyne was reacting precisely as Zellorian had predicted. 'I am a slave to certain habits. I get what I need from a man in that part of the city. By chance I went below.'

'Where?'

'I can direct you.'

Gannatyne pushed a sheet of vellum across to him and a pen. 'Show me.'

'I know the area. But I would need to go there if I were to retrace my steps. Tonight–'

'Who else knows of this?'

'I have told no one else. Not even my daughter. I was too frightened.'

'Very well. I'll arrange for my knights–'

Mannaston's eyes widened. 'Sire, it would be dangerous. A conflict would expose you and your men–'

'If we go immediately–'

'It will be deserted. But if we go tonight, Zellorian will be there. You will catch him as he performs his black arts.'

Gannatyne tried to suppress a stab of elation. 'What do you suggest?'

'If we go alone, we can be unobserved, and can come away easily.' Mannaston scribbled on the vellum, his writing large and scrawled, but his instructions were readable. 'Meet me at the junction of these streets an hour after sunset. From there I'll take you below.'

Gannatyne picked up the sheet and studied it. He turned away into the light. 'You've done well, Mannaston. But mark this – you are not to succumb to your weakness today, do you hear me? If I smell wine on you when we meet, I'll have you imprisoned.'

'So be it, sire.'

After Mannaston had gone, Gannatyne studied the instructions for long moments before calling his servant. He would need an escort for this business, in spite of what Mannaston had said. If they were truly to discover Zellorian performing some ritual, they had better be armed. Ah, but if they could take him in the act! How this could change things.

It had begun to rain when Mannaston set out for the night rendezvous. By the time he had reached the appointed place, his robes were heavy, his hood soaked. He saw no one in this neglected part of the city, the streets empty, slippery and treacherous. He found a doorway and sheltered, watching the thickening shadows, wondering if Gannatyne would bother to come.

Some time later, sure enough, cloaked figures coalesced in the darkness and in a moment the first of them came abreast of Mannaston's hiding place. He leaned out and hailed them softly. Their leader was beside him in an instant, face hidden in the deep cowl.

'Mannaston?' he called.

'Is Gannatyne with you?' said Mannaston, beginning to panic. Zellorian had guessed the Consul would not risk coming alone, but if he had not come himself, Zellorian would exact a cruel punishment.

'He's with us—'

'Show me his face,' insisted Mannaston. 'I'll not take you below until I see him.'

One of the others was consulted and he came forward. It was as Mannaston had prayed: Gannatyne stared at him from under his hood. 'Hasten!' he hissed.

Mannaston nodded and led the way along the street as he had been told to. He found the door that had been described to him, a thick wooden one with crossed iron bands. It was not locked and he went within to a thick darkness. No one spoke, but behind him Mannaston could feel the tension of this company of ghosts. There were steps and he led the party down, the air cold and unpleasant. Somewhere below there were lights flickering, brands stirred by a current of air.

At the foot of the stairs there was a wider chamber,

barely lit, its walls draped with cobwebs, long neglected. By the pale glow, Mannaston found another door and went through it into a narrow passageway, ducking his head. The others followed, though Mannaston could hear the ring of steel as they slipped their short blades from their scabbards. Did Zellorian intend to kill them? Surely he would not dare.

Beyond the long passageway there was a door that led out into an open courtyard, though it was very dark, walled in by high buildings. Gannatyne came close to Mannaston's side. 'You told me the place was beneath us. How much further?'

'Across this court. There is a chamber with a winding stair. It leads to the place.'

Gannatyne scowled but nodded. He was surprised at the extent of these slums in a relatively new city. How had they become so neglected? They spoke of age and decay, which seemed incongruous.

Mannaston walked on. He had been told nothing more. If there was a chamber beyond, it was all he knew. Zellorian had given him no further instructions.

Abruptly there were lights above them. Torches flared in a dozen places around the courtyard. Staring up at them, Mannaston could see no one, only the guttering light. The air suddenly hummed and someone gasped, falling. Mannaston yelped and rushed across to one of the walls, trying to find enough darkness to shelter him. There were curses behind him and more cries of pain. Somewhere above, archers were sending a steady stream of arrows down into the party below. Did they mean to kill them all, including Gannatyne? But even as Mannaston wondered, the arrows ceased. Several men were stretched out on the ground, some writhing, groaning.

Those who had not been felled, about six of them Mannaston saw, were grouped about a central figure. It had to be Gannatyne. The archers had not bargained for rain. As the knights below them were hooded, they could not see which one was Gannatyne. Mannaston wanted to warn the defenders: scatter! Gannatyne's anonymity will keep him safe! But they grouped around him protectively, thus proclaiming his identity.

Other arrows sped to their targets, and three more knights fell. A fourth. The three remaining figures circled. Mannaston shrank back, hoping they would not see him, knowing they would cut him to pieces in revenge for this treachery.

Something else fell through the air, and in a moment the three men in the courtyard were writhing against it. Like a huge web, a thin mesh had been cast over them. Moments later figures were dropping into the courtyard, their heads completely masked, their uniforms black, so that they blended perfectly with the night. A score of them went to the net, tightening it. Mannaston's terror prevented him from seeing clearly as they closed in, but he guessed they did not want Gannatyne dead after all. He shrank back as much as he could and to his horror heard something snap behind him. He fell back, wood disintegrating around him, hitting the ground and rolling to one side. There was barely enough light to see by, but he dragged himself into the doorway and the abandoned store beyond. There were heaped boxes here and the stink of rotting wood. Quickly he got to his feet and wriggled between two stacked mounds. He was certain that the assassins would think nothing of killing him. For a moment he thought he heard voices outside the room, but they passed and he shrivelled back into the dark, praying the daylight would come quickly. In the silence he thought of his family: this was the blackest hour yet for the Casruel house.

Outside the three survivors had been secured. The cowls were ripped back from their robes. Gannatyne was revealed and hauled away by his captors. The other two knights died swiftly and cleanly.

Vymark watched his men gathering the corpses. It had been superbly efficient. Zellorian would be more than pleased with this performance.

The bodies were taken into the chamber beyond the

106

court with the spiral steps. Some distance below, in yet another chamber, there were ovens. It was not long before the slain were shut away. By morning there would be nothing left of them but ash. And the rain would wipe any blood from the courtyard.

Gannatyne was gagged, Vymark's men kept their swords pressed into his back and force-marched him along yet more corridors. Behind them all trace of the night's events was being removed.

Eventually the party came to another dusty chamber. Vymark tapped on its door and was admitted by two more black-clad assassins. There was a chair in here and an old table. Gannatyne was roped to the chair so tightly that he could not move, but his captors were very careful not to mark his skin.

Vymark went to the table and lifted a goblet that had been set there. He walked over to Gannatyne.

The Consul tried to struggle. Poison? But why such an elaborate trap? He was gripped, his nose held tightly, and he had to swallow the contents of the goblet. His head swam at once. Drugged? That must be it. But why, why? His mind raced, but the confusion had already begun. He looked up into the eyes of his tormentor, the only part of Vymark that was visible through the mask. But the eyes were indifferent, cold and untroubled.

In minutes Gannatyne had slumped and they cut him loose, checking again to see they had not marked him. Satisfied, they lifted him and began another march.

Aru watched the rain as it dripped from the eaves. She had spent many hours thinking about her next moves. How had Denandys and his knights been betrayed? But it was so difficult to fathom. Their journey out of the mountains had been no secret. A number of such journeys were being undertaken by different parties as the Consulate began a steady move towards expansion. But Zellorian watched everything. He must have known the officers of every party, and been given details of everyone who served under them. But how had he known that Denandys was about to flee the city with his knights? And why had she been spared? Did Zellorian know that she had been a party to the planned flight? He must have – he knew she was a Controller. She shook her head, confused. Her father? But he was too much the drunkard. How could he follow any pattern, serve anyone? Yet he relied on someone to get him *keroueen*.

She heard a movement behind her, turning like a cat.

It was her father, bedraggled and haggard, his face white as if he had been mingling with ghosts. Her mother, perhaps? How she must have haunted him.

'What is it?' she said, annoyed but too tired to begin a fresh fight with him. 'Where have you been?' The question seemed pointless.

He tried to speak, his mouth opening and closing. At first she assumed he was drunk, but now saw that he was not. But he was afraid, his body shaking. For a moment she almost put her arms about him to comfort him, recalling the man he had once been, but she could not bring herself to do it.

He looked at her, almost through her. 'I'm sorry,' he blurted, unable to say more.

Behind him there was movement. A number of figures appeared, dripping with rain. They held swords.

Aru reached for her own, but before she could grasp it, an arm took hold of her and flung her away from it with terrible force. She toppled over a chair, her feet caught up in it as it fell with her. Seconds later there were three assailants standing over her, swords aimed at her belly.

'Come without a struggle,' said one of them. Garbed almost completely in black, only their eyes showing, they were anonymous. But she knew whose pay they must be in.

'Aru, I am not to blame,' gasped her father, his eyes pleading. 'They followed me. They waited for me to unlock the door–'

'Up, girl!' snapped the leading intruder.

She did so, knowing that there was little point in struggling. Did they want her alive? Or was she to suffer the same fate as Denandys?

One of the men pointed to Mannaston. 'You, old man. You get to bed. You've done your work. Keep silent. You know nothing. Out!'

'He said nothing of this,' protested Mannaston. 'Not my daughter—'

'Get out!' snarled the warrior, raising his blade.

Mannaston cowered back, shaking his head.

'Who is behind this, Father?' said Aru icily. 'Zellorian?'

Two of the men gripped her arms and forced her out through the door. If her father had answered her, she had not heard him. But she already knew the answer.

Outside in the rain there were horses and she was thrown over one, her hands tied. It was unlikely that anyone would see this abduction, not on a night like this. She bit her lips against the terror that was threatening to consume her. The ride began.

By the time the party had reached its destination, Aru felt sick, buffeted by the wild ride, her head dizzy. She tottered as they pulled her to her feet, bundling her through a low doorway and up some stairs. In the poorly lit room beyond, her hands were untied. She massaged them, wincing as the blood rushed back into pinched veins.

There were other abductors here, all dressed in black, but none of them spoke. They had been given clear instructions.

The room itself was in surprisingly good order. It was carpeted, its walls pleasantly though not lavishly draped. There were a number of small statues and carvings, tasteful and she guessed valuable. But whose room was this? The lights were subdued, carefully chosen to show the room off to its best advantage, and it was clean, carefully tended. And yet the streets through which she had been brought were narrow, suggesting that this was a more remote part of the city.

Another man entered the room, his face also masked. He carried in his hand a small goblet. He nodded at Aru's

109

captors and one of them held her around the neck, his hand closing over her nose. In horror she realised what they meant to do to her. As the contents of the goblet entered her mouth, she tried to spit them out, but in the end she was forced to drink them.

The men let her go, laughing softly at her anger. She swung at them, but already the drug was working. She stumbled and one of the men kicked at her legs, bringing her down. They lifted her, holding her up while another of them began undoing the cord of her shirt.

She swore. They meant to rape her, and the thought made her fight harder to keep from succumbing to the drug. But her movements became slow, her arms waving uselessly. Her legs failed her and the men had to hold her up while they pulled her boots and then her breeches from her. They did not stop until she was entirely naked, grinning as they held her.

The man with the goblet, whose eyes remained on her all the while, put it down and collected her clothes carefully. He nodded to his men and they carried her, limp now, through a doorway into the room beyond.

Aru vaguely saw its ceiling, felt the warmth of the room. A low fire smouldered in its hearth. There was a bed, its sheets of silk. Knowing what the men intended, she allowed the drug to claim her, sinking mercifully into its oblivion.

Vymark put down the clothes beside the bed, then kicked them gently, scattering them. He pulled back the expensive sheets to reveal the naked body of a man. It was Gannatyne. Vymark again nodded to his men and they lowered the unconscious Aru on to the bed, arranging her arms so that they were wrapped around Gannatyne, who did not murmur. Vymark draped the sheet partially over them, pausing to take a last admiring look at the girl's breasts, wishing that Zellorian had not been so specific about the arrangements. The Prime Consul had forbidden any interference.

Vymark could see the lust in the eyes of his men. 'Go

on, you dogs. There are enough whores in the city to keep you amused. The work here's done.'

Without another word they left. Vymark went about the room, making certain that it looked to be a natural place of assignation. He took the goblet and placed it in a small bag with one other, tying the bag slowly. From the small room he brought other goblets, half filling them with wine. Some of this he spilled carefully on the bed, before placing both goblets on the floor.

It looked perfect. The drug would not wear off for some hours yet.

Vymark closed the door to the chamber and went down the stairs. One of his men was waiting. 'It's ready,' Vymark told him. 'Keep watch here. It is unlikely that the couple will stir. But keep your ears open, as a precaution. Do not go up unless you hear them.'

The man nodded. Vymark knew he could be trusted. He had removed his black garb and mask, and Vymark did the same, tucking the clothes away in another bag for disposal. He clung to the shadows as he went to the place where his horse had been stabled. Mounting it he rode quietly back into the city. At his own house, a modest apartment, he filled his bath with water, heating it to a point which made it steam. He plunged himself under it, gasping, scrubbing himself, his hair, using the unguents he had bought as a rare treat. He did not normally care for such things, but tonight he luxuriated in them. He thought of the girl, her fine body, tempted to slip out for an hour to find a whore, but he washed himself down with icy water, laughing at his own libido. In time he would possess a dozen women far more beautiful than Mannaston's daughter. He went to bed and slept lightly for an hour.

At the appointed time he rose, dressed himself and went out to find a fresh horse. He rode swiftly to the house of the man chosen by Zellorian. It was some time before the servants came to the door.

'Have you any idea of the hour, fellow?' groaned the retainer.

'I am Vymark of the Imperator Elect's guard. I am here on urgent business. You must wake your master instantly.'

'My lord Pyramors won't take kindly to this—'

'He won't have to. But if you don't get him up, he'll have your head on a plate tomorrow morning when he finds out I've been.'

Grumbling, the servant admitted Vymark. He took him up into the splendid portico of the house, waiting in the lamplight while his master, the youngest member of the Consulate, was woken.

Pyramors arrived dressed in white robes, his hair tousled, his eyes bleary. 'The explanation had better be good, soldier,' he snapped.

Vymark saw that here was a man unlike many of his fellow Consulate. Pyramors looked a soldier himself, the eyes steel grey, the arms those of a man used to using a sword, even if it was only on a practice field these days. But he had known war: such things left their mark on a man, even one as relatively young as Pyramors.

'Your pardon, sire,' said Vymark, feigning shock with complete conviction. 'I know you are a friend of the Consul, Gannatyne.'

Pyramors was alert at once, as though he had never slept. 'Is there something wrong?'

'I am ashamed to speak, sire. But I think you should come with me. At once.'

'Is he harmed?' said Pyramors, gripping Vymark's arm. Vymark was surprised by the strength of the young man.

'No, sire, Will you come?'

'Very well.' Pyramors turned to his scowling servants. 'Get a horse ready. And summon a guard. How many?' he asked Vymark.

'You'll not require swords, sire. There is no danger.'

'Six men,' Pyramors told his servants, who rushed off quickly.

A short while later, Vymark found himself at the head of a small party of horsemen. Pyramors had dressed quickly, arming himself in spite of the warrior's words. His personal bodyguards were also armed. Again, Vymark found himself impressed by the young man's efficiency. It was a pity he was a potential enemy.

At the house in the city where Aru and Gannatyne yet slept, the lone soldier waited, saluting as Vymark rode up, with a company of men as he had promised. The Consul Pyramors dismounted and stood beside Vymark.

'Perhaps,' he said irritably, 'you'll be good enough to give me an explanation *now*.' He was plainly angry at still being uninformed.

'Allow me to lead the way, sire,' said Vymark.

Pyramors nodded, his men close behind him, swords drawn. Vymark climbed the stairs. He opened the first door and motioned for Pyramors to go in, but the Consul had drawn a short sword of his own. 'After you.'

Vymark went in, opening the door to the bed chamber. Aru and Gannatyne had not stirred, her arms about him as before.

Pyramors drew in his breath as he saw them. He realised at once that Gannatyne's enemies had arranged for him to be discovered like this in order to discredit him. Pyramors had had no idea that Gannatyne had a mistress, much less the Casruel girl, whose family had once been highly favoured in the Empire. But Gannatyne had a wife who honoured him and supported him tirelessly in his efforts to bring sanity to this corrupt city. It distressed Pyramors to see Gannatyne like this. And the foolish Casruel girl had placed the last of her own family honour in jeopardy. Many things tore through Pyramors' mind, but he must try to remove any advantage Gannatyne's enemies might gain from this discovery.

He turned to Vymark, his course decided. 'Why have you dared to bring me here?' he hissed, his face suddenly suffusing with fury. He gestured for Vymark to go out, closing the door behind them.

'Forgive me, sire, but I thought you should know,' protested Vymark.

'Know! Know what? That Gannatyne has a mistress?

113

That this is their private meeting place? Have you no shame?

'Sire, forgive me. Did you not see the girl's face?'

For a moment Pyramors was taken aback. Had he missed something? It had been the Casruel girl, but where was the significance in that? 'What does it matter?' he snapped, making his way down the stairs. 'Go back to your posts quietly. Mount up,' he told his men. 'We are not staying here.'

At the foot of the stairs, Vymark was very close behind him. He spoke softly and evenly. 'I think you misunderstand me, sire–'

'And you misunderstand me–'

'The girl is Aru, daughter of Mannaston.'

'What does it matter who she is!'

'We have reason to believe she is in collusion with the Innasmornians.'

For the first time Pyramors wavered. 'What are you talking about?'

'She has been watched, sire. She is an agent of the Innasmornians. We knew that she was reporting to someone in the Sculpted City. But we did not know who it was until tonight.'

Pyramors lost some of his colour. 'You have proof of this?'

Before Vymark could answer, there was a commotion outside. Pyramors turned and pushed his way to the street. Another group of horsemen had arrived, and by their torches, the Consul could see that they were also the Imperator's guards. Two of them were holding up a man who appeared to be injured.

Vymark watched impassively as Pyramors went to investigate. The injured man was clad in thin clothing, his hair matted.

'Who is this?' said Pyramors.

'We caught him hiding in one of the rooms below the house, sire,' said one of the guards. Blood ran from his sword.

'Will he live?' said Pyramors, but already he could see that it was too late. He lifted the dead man's face, gasping. It was thin and angular, the hair fine, unlike that of Pyramors's race. 'Stars! This is an Innasmornian'

'We did not mean to kill him, sire, but he almost killed one of us.' The soldier nodded to where another soldier nursed a wounded arm.

Vymark's face showed no sign of his elation. His men had staged this perfectly.

The sound of hooves turned all heads and a further group of horsemen pulled up in the street. Pyramors cursed under his breath: he would rather have covered up the embarrassment of finding Gannatyne in bed with his mistress. Perhaps it was not too late for that.

But as he saw the first of the figures dismount, his heart sank.

It was the Prime Consul.

Zellorian stood before his fellow Consul, brows raised quizzically. 'Word reached me of this tryst,' he said.

Pyramors shot a glance at Vymark, but the fellow's face was a mask.

'What have you found?' said Zellorian.

Pyramors looked away, controlling his fury. This entire business reeked of treachery. 'You'd better go up and see. I for one have seen enough.'

Zellorian bowed slightly. 'As you wish, Consul. No doubt we will have a fuller opportunity to discuss this in the morning.'

Pyramors did not grace him with another look, walking to his horse. 'No doubt.'

9

A JUDGEMENT

Aru heard the keys rattle in the door, but she was too tired to leap up and challenge whoever it was that had come for her. She had spent too much energy trying to attract attention to herself after she had woken up in this cell, only to be totally ignored. At least they had had the decency to leave her her clothes. There was no window and only the faintest of light seeping under the door. As her mind had focused, shrugging off the remaining effects of the drug, she had relived her last waking moments in the bedchamber where the masked guards had taken her. She had not slept here. Throughout the night she had tried to understand what was happening. There could be only one conclusion. Zellorian had found a way to discredit her.

The door opened. As expected, a guard stood there. He had drawn his sword. Beyond him there were other men. The guard motioned her out, but did not speak. She knew instinctively she was in the palace.

Outside the cell there was a corridor, its floor scrubbed, its walls clean, which surprised her. The guards took her along and up a flight of stone stairs. Soon they were in the palace proper, and she could hear the sound of many voices coming from a large chamber beyond. She would have asked what was happening, but she guessed the guards would remain absolutely silent. They paused before a set of high, ornate doors, their leader speaking briefly to other guards there. In a moment the party was admitted.

All was noise and colour beyond. It was one of the main audience chambers of the Consulate, and today it had been filled with both members of that august body and its administrators, so much so that Aru wondered if the entire government had assembled. They talked animatedly, pre-

116

paratory to going into session, and many of them turned to look on Aru, shaking their heads or making comments that were clearly about her. Before her, beyond the seats, were the benches of office, raised up so that the Consulate could gaze down on their subjects, and on them sat the many officials of court. Aru scanned the faces for a sight of Gannatyne, but in vain. Pyramors, one of his closest confidants, was thankfully there. She tried to catch his eye, but he looked elsewhere and she could not be sure if he was avoiding her gaze deliberately.

Two of the guards led her to a small dais and took up post on either side of her. There seemed to be hardly a friendly face here. Was this, then, to be her trial? But even Zellorian had nothing with which to charge her. Unless he had linked her with the attempt of Denandys to steal the gliderboat. But even that would not have led to an affair such as this. This, clearly, was to be a major hearing.

To her horror she saw another figure being brought into the arena. It was Gannatyne. His head was bowed as he walked slowly between two more guards. He was dressed in a single grey robe, and he was barefoot, as if he had been pulled from his bed and given no opportunity to dress himself. He was made to stand on a dais opposite her, but he did not resist, his eyes fixed on the floor. Aru longed to speak to him, but it was impossible. And, like Pyramors, he would not look at her. She gazed around her and was certain that many of the administrators were studying her, noting her reaction to Gannatyne's misery.

At last a party of guards entered from one of the grand doorways and to Aru's amazement, the Imperator Elect was with them, his robes of office flowing out ostentatiously behind him, a wad of scrolls under one arm. He took his place at the head of the benches of office and stared about him loftily. Silence had fallen at once, broken only by the movement of those who came with him to the table. One of them was Zellorian. For a brief moment Aru almost laughed, taking in the spectacle of their pomposity, the walls lined with coats of arms, the murals depicting glorious

117

victories of past decades. How absurd it seemed now, here in this remote place, deep in the mountains of a world far removed from the Empire they had once been so proud of.

'Be seated,' called the Imperator Elect, though no one moved until he himself had sat down. He flicked through the scrolls he had set down in front of him. Again no one moved or spoke. Zellorian's face was like stone. His part in this was yet a mystery.

'We have before us today,' went on the Imperator at last, 'a most serious matter. I have summoned you all — and I see that we do have a full complement — as this matter affects every one of us. The well being of our city, our future, is threatened.' He paused to allow the dramatic effect of his words to sink in, looking about him to ensure that everyone was suitably impressed. There were nods and a few exaggerated gasps: the administrators had long since learned how to act according to protocol. Their leading player reacted best if his audience showed clear appreciation of his talents.

Aru felt herself growing colder. There was something terribly wrong here, but she could not grasp it fully. Perhaps her mind was still clouded by the drug.

'Certain matters were brought to the attention of the Prime Consul last night,' the Imperator was saying. 'Matters which bring us here in such haste.' He turned to Zellorian. 'Be good enough to make your report, Prime Consul.'

Zellorian stood slowly and bowed. 'Of course, sire.'

The Imperator sat down. He had not as much as acknowledged the presence of either Gannatyne or Aru.

'My lords,' Zellorian began, his voice level, assured. 'I have to report that I was summoned from my chambers late last night by a number of guards serving under Vymark, who last night happened to be the officer in charge of the city night watch. Vymark had sent the men to me following an incident in a certain part of the city. In view of the seriousness of this incident, of which you shall hear, Vymark had the foresight to go personally to the house of

118

Consul Pyramors,' and he inclined his head towards the young Consul who sat further along the bench to his right.

Aru saw Pyramors flinch, his face cold, but he did not acknowledge Zellorian's gesture.

'I was escorted by the guard to a certain house, where I found that Consul Pyramors had already preceded me. What I discovered I shall relate in due course, but with the Imperator's indulgence I would ask that other witnesses are asked to give their own reports before me.

Aru knew then that the trap had been prepared infinitely carefully. Zellorian did not make errors. But what did Pyramors have to do with this? Surely he could not possibly be involved in a betrayal, either of Gannatyne or the Casruel house?

'As you wish, Prime Consul,' said the Imperator. 'Who would you like to hear first?'

'As it was the officer Vymark who discovered the incident, sire, could we have his report?'

'Agreed.'

A moment later Vymark entered the court. He went before the Imperator and bowed, then turned to the audience of administrators. 'During the course of my duties as officer of the night watch,' he began, and immediately Pyramors stood up.

'Might I ask a question, sire?' he said to the Imperator. Aru wondered if this could possibly be pre-planned. But Pyramors was perfectly within his rights to question anything Vymark, or any other witness, said.

'You may.'

'Thank you, sire. Officer Vymark, could you outline for us, briefly, what your actual duties were last night?'

Zellorian coughed, and all eyes turned to him. 'Consul Pyramors, I am sure we are all familiar with the duties of an officer of the watch – '

'I would not wish to insult my colleagues by suggesting otherwise, Prime Consul, but I wondered if officer Vymark had been given any specific duties last night.'

Vymark glanced at Zellorian, but before he could

answer, the Prime Consul stopped him with a signal that no one else in the chamber would have recognised.

'Perhaps I should answer that question, sire,' said Zellorian, with a trace of a smile. 'In view of the fact that I myself issued Vymark with his duties.'

'That would seem appropriate,' nodded the Imperator.

'Vymark acted on my instructions. He was indeed carrying out specific orders related to the security of the throne.'

There were genuine murmurs at this and Aru felt another stab of cold. Then it had been Vymark who had drugged her. And Gannatyne was the prey.

'May we know the exact nature of these orders?' said Pyramors. 'I assume they must have a bearing on this hearing.'

Zellorian did not seem to take too kindly to this and Aru wondered if she had been wrong to suspect Pyramors. He seemed intent on upsetting whatever scheme Zellorian was planning.

'Officer Vymark,' said Zellorian, his voice hardening, 'had been asked to monitor the movements of certain persons.'

'Who were these persons?'

'Sire,' said Zellorian, turning to the Imperator, 'I intend to include the details of this matter in my own report.'

'In that case, Vymark may continue. Do you agree?' the Imperator asked Pyramors, though his tone made it clear it was an instruction.

It seemed, however, that Pyramors was not content. 'Yes, sire. But could I ask who told Vymark to monitor the movements of these people, and for what reason?'

The Imperator frowned, but Zellorian spoke before he could answer. 'Again, sire, I will detail this in my own report. It does not seem to me to be necessary to discuss it at this time.'

'I apologise,' persisted Pyramors, though there was no apology in his tone. 'It is just that I wanted to ascertain whether officer Vymark came upon the incident we have heard mentioned by pure acident, or whether his discovery of it was a direct result of instructions he had received to follow, uh, certain people.'

The Imperator had not grasped the implications of what the young Consul was saying. He coughed irritably. 'If you'd allow the man to speak, Consul, perhaps we could get somewhere in the matter! Now do sit down. Officer Vymark, will you continue?'

Vymark bowed. 'Certain of my guards were in the western end of the city, an area that is comprised mainly of storage houses, most of which were constructed hastily in the first days of the city. Normally they would not have expected to find anything of note in such an empty part of the city. Last night, however, my men became aware of activities in one of the buildings, formerly a dwelling house connected to what had once been a grain warehouse.'

'How did they become aware of these activities?' one of the Consulate asked.

'While patrolling the streets in that area, they saw a man and followed him.'

'Then it was a chance meeting?' said Pyramors.

'No, sire. He had been under surveillance.'

The Imperator was drumming his fingers on the table before him, but he did not interrupt. Pyramors ignored him.

'He entered the house and for a while my men waited,' said Vymark. 'Shortly afterwards a woman came to the house — '

'This is monstrous!' Aru shouted abruptly, shocking them all. One of the guards made to grip her arm, but she shrugged him off. 'My lords, hear me! I was forcibly abducted — '

'Be silent!' shouted the Imperator. 'How dare you interrupt this session! You will be given every opportunity to speak in due course. Assuming you can conduct yourself in a proper manner.'

Aru bit her lip and nodded. She could see at last what had been prepared for her. And Pyramors, somehow, was trying to help her and Gannatyne.

121

Vymark continued, unruffled. 'The woman went into the house, and it was then that my men summoned me from another part of the city. When I reached the house, my men had surrounded it. There were two doors, one which was at the front of the house, by which the man and woman had entered, and one at the rear which led through a yard to the warehouse, which itself had a number of doors.

'I entered the house as quietly as I could, hoping not to disturb the occupants. I thought perhaps I might hear their conversation.'

'Why should it be significant?' asked Pyramors.

'It was not idle curiosity, sire. I had my duty.'

'Quite so,' snorted Pyramors. 'Had you been told to record the words?'

'I don't follow you, sire,' said Vymark calmly.

'As you'd been having these people watched, you must have had a reason for recording their conversations?'

'I – well, yes.' Vymark looked mildly unsure of himself.

'So you'd been following the woman as well as the man?'

'Yes.'

Pyramors nodded. Zellorian did not look at him, but the Imperator did not seem at all pleased.

'But I heard nothing,' said Vymark. 'When I reached the upper room, I found the inner one to be a bedroom. It was surprisingly furbished for a house of that kind. I had expected the place to be neglected, but clearly the rooms upstairs were used frequently and had been decorated in a manner that seemed to me to be very tasteful.'

'And why do you think that was?' Zellorian asked him.

'Sire, the couple were on the bed. They were naked and had presumably been engaged in intercourse. They were asleep when I discovered them. The room was, I am sure, their regular meeting place.'

'You are not certain?' said Pyramors.

'It seemed most likely, sire.'

'Then this was the first night you had been asked to follow these people?'

'Consul,' interrupted the Imperator, 'forgive my naïvety, but why must you persist–'

'Sire, if this was the first time that the night watch had been asked to follow these people,' said Pyramors, 'I could understand officer Vymark's hastily drawn conclusions. His assumption that the people he saw met in the house regularly – '

'It was the first night that the watch had been set up,' said Zellorian.

'Then why?' said Pyramors, rounding on him. 'How is it that this house had not been observed before? Who knew that it would be used? If the couple had not been followed before, who knew that they were worthy of pursuit?'

Zellorian took this without moving, his face calm. 'No one knew about the house until the couple led Vymark's guards to it.'

The Imperator nodded to Vymark. 'Continue, please. And Consul Pyramors, that will be enough questions for a while.'

'There was wine in the room,' said Vymark. 'And evidence that the couple had been drinking freely. They were in a deep sleep.'

Aru's mind cried out in protest. So this was what was behind it. They wanted Gannatyne's head and had stooped to this to be rid of him. She controlled her fury with effort, her hands tightening. But she had to remain calm if she were to outwit them. Zellorian had been careful, and that cold-blooded reptile Vymark was his perfect tool. Stars, but he would have graced the court of a Csendook!

'Shortly afterwards,' Vymark went on, 'I fetched Consul Pyramors.'

'Does that conclude your report?' Zellorian asked him.

'Not quite, sire. There was a further incident. At the rear of the house, my men discovered another person. One whom, we believe, had been in the lower part of the house some time before the man and woman appeared. My men were not aware of him at first. Indeed, he surprised them when he rushed from his place of concealment, injuring

123

one of them with his knife. A curious object, sire. It was made of wood. In the confusion, another of my men struck at the intruder. He died before we could question him. On bringing him to the light, we discovered that he was a native of Innasmorn.'

The administrators could not hold back their amazement, and the hall echoed to their cries and shouts. However, the Imperator waved them all to silence, restoring it eventually.

Zellorian was nodding. 'An Innasmornian. Their weapons are made of wood. And who were the couple that you found on the bed?'

'Sire, the man was Consul Gannatyne, and the woman was Aru, of the family Casruel.'

The audience had already gathered this by the presence of the accused, but again there was a loud murmur. This time it settled quickly. Vymark bowed and left the centre of the hall, standing to one side, his face calm, expressionless.

'Perhaps you'd be good enough to let us have your own report, Consul Pyramors?' said the Imperator.

Pyramors nodded grimly and stood up. He confirmed briefly that he had been taken by Vymark to the house and that he had seen the couple on the bed.

'You made no attempt to wake them?' said Zellorian. 'To question them about their behaviour?'

Pyramors looked furious. 'If my lord Gannatyne and Aru wished to sleep with each other, I had no business to interfere. Especially as they had had the sense to do so privately, away from the affairs of state. I saw no crime in what they had done. In fact, I have to say that I was ashamed that I had been summoned to witness the scene.'

'It did not surprise you?' asked Zellorian.

Pyramors paused before answering. He had known from the beginning that this whole business was a trap, but he could not see yet how it could be sprung. Every question Zellorian asked would be the thrust of a sword. 'What do you mean?'

'That they should be lovers?'

'Gannatyne is a man of power. Aru a young woman of beauty – '

'Then you are implying that she was attracted to Gannatyne's power, his position in the Consulate?'

'I have no idea. This is speculation.'

'Quite,' agreed Zellorian unexpectedly. 'But you would agree that there is no reason why Gannatyne and Aru should not be lovers, and indeed, you felt embarrassed at having discovered them naked together. That seems to me to be a perfectly normal reaction, sire,' Zellorian ended, turning to the Imperator.

Pyramors felt a gnawing anxiety. Somehow he had played into the Prime Consul's hands. But what had he missed?

'I was shown the corpse of the Innasmornian,' Pyramors said. 'Though I did not see from where he was brought. And no one was able to question him as to why he was there. There was no reason to suppose he had been connected to either Gannatyne or Aru – '

'By which you mean,' said Zellorian remorselessly, 'that you think it was pure coincidence that he chose that same building from so many in which to hide?'

Pyramors looked at him coldly. 'In much the same way that it was pure coincidence that Gannatyne and Aru were found together in bed the very night they were followed for the first time.'

The Imperator banged his fist down on the table, his cheeks a bright red. 'You are not here to make judgements!' he told Pyramors, but the latter sat down, staring ahead of him. The Imperator turned to Zellorian. 'Could we have your own report now, Prime Consul?'

Zellorian bowed. 'I have very little to add to what has been said about the man and woman in the house. I was summoned and I witnessed exactly that which has been reported by officer Vymark and Consul Pyramors. But perhaps I should clarify the events leading up to the arrests.'

'If you would be so kind,' said Pyramors, and there

were several gusts of laughter in the hall. The Imperator, however, had not regained his sense of humour.

Zellorian inclined his head, confident in every muscle. He would not have called this hearing if he had expected to be deprived of success. 'For some time now,' he began, 'I have been greatly concerned about the movements of the Innasmornians. There have been reports from beyond the mountains that they grow increasingly unsettled. They see us, my lords, as intruders, enemies.'

At once there were shouts of protest, for the Consulate were yet divided on the issue. But the voices of anger were not as loud as they had once been, Aru could tell.

Zellorian waved the protests aside. 'Yes, yes. We cannot be sure of our ground. But there are so many dangers. Even here in the Sculpted City there are dangers. I have long had my suspicions, especially about infiltration. And collusion.'

'What proof do you have?' someone called.

Zellorian waited. 'Alow me to finish my report.

'Get to the point,' someone else called, but Zellorian could not see who it was.

'Collaboration is dangerous. We have too much to lose. That is my opinion and I know that some of you dismiss it. It is a matter for another day's debate. But I have the throne to consider. While I hold office, it is my duty, is it not, to uphold our laws? We have signed no treaties with the Innasmornians. We have not opened our gates to them. We know little enough about them. Those who traffic with them secretly do so at their own pleasure and not at the Imperator's. Therefore I am watchful. Where I find fraternisation and collusion, *I will cut it out.*

'I hear many rumours. We all do. Whispers and hints, most of them fantasies. But some of them I am forced to follow up. Which is why I was forced to look into the matter that ended up with the incident you have heard reported today. The movements of the Casruel girl, Aru, have become of particular interest to me of late. And of her knights. She has been beyond the mountains and met with

Innasmornians. Knights under her personal command attempted to take a gliderboat from the pens one night. For what purpose? Why should they feel it necessary to go secretly and illegally from the city? What do secret meetings with the Innasmornians mean?

'I found it difficult to believe that the Casruel girl acted on her own behalf. She is intelligent as well as beautiful, but for whom did she work? I think, my lords, we may have discovered that much.' Zellorian sat down while another burst of noise shook the hall.

As it died down, Pyramors stood up, receiving approval from the Imperator to question Zellorian. 'Your concern for the Empire has always done you credit, Prime Consul,' he said.

Zellorian inclined his head.

'But I wonder if it has clouded your judgement on this occasion.'

'I trust you will substantiate that remark,' said the Imperator.

'I meant no offence,' said Pyramors. 'But I have spoken from the outset of this hearing about the nature of officer Vymark's duties. He was told to watch Consul Gannatyne and Aru Casruel. Why? Why should Consul Gannatyne be watched? Was this sanctioned by yourself, sire?'

Zellorian was quick to answer, his smile cold. 'You cannot expect the Imperator to sanction every decision of his Consulate. And you could hardly expect me to take pleasure in such a duty, Consul. But no one is above suspicion, or the law.'

'Who did you discuss this "decision" with?' said Pyramors.

'I am under no obligation to discuss my decisions with anyone. Not when the security of the throne is in question,' said Zellorian.

Pyramors looked out at the sea of faces. 'Perhaps we should dismiss this gathering, then. We seem to be wasting time consulting our colleagues.'

'Consul Pyramors,' said the Imperator through gritted

teeth, 'either you phrase your words very carefully, or I will instruct you to leave this hall at once.'

Pyramors bowed. 'Very good, sire. Isn't it true,' he said, turning to Zellorian, 'that you will not accept the opinions of certain of the Consulate? In particular, as you have already stated, that it would be better for Mankind if we were to seek the friendship of the Innasmornians?'

'An opinion to which you subscribe, I imagine?'

'Answer my question, if you would.'

'My opinion is already spoken, although I have also pointed out that our law does not permit such an alliance. And our law comes before mere opinion.'

'Isn't it true, Prime Consul, that you would prefer to eliminate those who do not follow your opinions about the future of Innasmorn? That it would suit you very well to see Consul Gannatyne disgraced – '

The Imperator stood up with an angry roar. There was silence in the hall, everyone watching him. 'Explain yourself!' he snarled at Pyramors, on the point of completely losing his temper with the young Consul.

'I am saying that far too much has been read into this incident, sire. That the Prime Consul's determination to undermine confidence in Consul Gannatyne has led him to use this incident against him. There is nothing to show that he and Aru Casruel were collaborating with the Innasmornians. If they are lovers, what of it? It proves nothing. Indiscretion, no more. Zellorian is trying to use it to discredit one of our most esteemed Consulate.'

'Sire,' said Zellorian so calmly that Pyramors felt a shiver along his spine. The Prime Consul was still very sure of his victory.

'Well?' said the Imperator, sitting down, though he looked far from comfortable.

'I think it should be made clear to everyone here that my concerns about Consul Gannatyne are not idle ones. I think certain confidential conversations that you and I have had should, perhaps, be taken into consideration.' No one else would have dared to prompt the Imperator Elect in this way, but Zellorian knew his own value too well.

The Imperator seemed visibly relieved that he had been given an opportunity to resolve the situation. 'I share the Prime Consul's concern. I am not in favour of opening relationships with the Innasmornians. And mark my words, I said this very thing to Consul Gannatyne recently. He had been to me in private, with a plea.'

Zellorian tried not to enjoy Pyramors's discomfort. The audience had become very quiet.

'Yes,' the Imperator went on. 'He had begged me to consider an alliance with the Innasmornians. I refused. I did more than that. I gave the Prime Consul strict instructions to have him watched. I did not want an open scandal at that time, and I thought it wiser not to convene the Consulate to discuss the matter.'

'Indeed, sire,' nodded Zellorian. 'And I have hardly had time to draft the edict that you asked me to announce on your behalf.'

The Imperator frowned, but then nodded. 'Yes, yes, of course. The edict. It has not been pronounced officially yet, but it will have a bearing on this incident. No further journeys beyond the mountains are to be undertaken without my express consent. It's far too dangerous allowing journeys that are not properly authorised.'

'I had been curious,' said Zellorian, after the hubbub had died down, 'as to why an officer of the Casruel knights should attempt to steal a gliderboat. The man, Denandys, must have had word of the edict in advance. I confess, it is not something I have been secretive about. Presumably Aru told her man that he would be refused a gliderboat.'

'And Aru would have heard this from Gannatyne?' said the Imperator.

Zellorian shrugged. 'Possibly, sire. Though this is conjecture.'

'Let her speak for herself,' suggested Pyramors. 'And let Consul Gannatyne speak in his own defence.'

Gannatyne had not raised his eyes from the floor, nor

did he now. He remained motionless, almost as if he were still drugged. But Aru was eager to receive the opportunity to speak. She was led by the guards to the front of the audience. She did not face Zellorian, but looked directly at the Imperator.

'Well, girl,' he said. 'What have you to say about this business?'

She shook her head. 'Sire, this has been an elaborate trap. You have all been taken in by it.'

'You had better clarify that,' said the Imperator tersely.

'It is true that I have met with Innasmornians. On my last journey. I do not deny that. But I do deny that I am fraternising with them in an attempt to undermine your authority. Gannatyne has had no part in my meeting with them. He and I are not and never have been lovers.'

Again the audience had to be quelled. 'The evidence against you seems to contradict you,' said the Imperator, with more than a hint of scorn.

Aru explained how she had been taken to the house and drugged, and how the same thing must have happened to Gannatyne. As she spoke, Pyramors felt himself shaken, horrified. She was telling the truth, he knew it! And he had made the mistake of thinking she and Gannatyne had been lovers. If he had taken more trouble when he had found her, or waited to question her – But he had jumped to the wrong conclusions. Just as Zellorian had known he would! *He* had been summoned by Vymark, not some other, indifferent Consul, because Zellorian knew he would be too embarrassed to stay.

No one believed Aru. It was evident. Even Pyramors's allies, he could sense, wavered.

'I imagine,' sneered the Imperator, 'that the Innasmornian skulking in the rooms under you was also a figment of the imagination.'

Aru stiffened. 'I can prove I was abducted. There was a witness to it.'

Zellorian leaned forward and she felt pinned by his gaze, as helpless as a lizard pinned to a tree. 'Then perhaps they can ratify this bizarre tale of yours. Bring this person before us at once.'

'He is my father,' Aru breathed, but Zellorian heard.

'Sire,' he said to the Imperator, perfectly coolly. 'Let us have Mannaston brought here.'

When Mannaston was ushered in, he looked dreadful, his face blotched, his hair and beard unkempt. There were muttered suggestions that he was in no fit state to speak here, but the Imperator was adamant that he should do so.

Zellorian looked at Mannaston and the man withered under that gaze. He had been told what he must do, the choice he must make.

'Last night,' said the Imperator, 'you saw your daughter?'

'Last night?' echoed Mannaston. 'I don't think so —'

'Father!' cried Aru. What had they done to him? Had they filled him with that poison again? 'At the house. The guards followed you.'

'Guards?' said Mannaston. 'To our home? No.' He could feel Zellorian's eyes blazing into him. Hear his words of fire. *You can have your wife, old man. The Imperator has agreed her release. But not your daughter. Choose.*

'Tell them!' cried Aru.

But Mannaston would not confirm her story. After a while he was led away. Aru felt as though an abyss had opened up before her. Her last hope of defence had been removed, unless Gannatyne would speak.

She watched, appalled by his silence, his apparent shock, as he was ordered to stand before his accusers and account for his actions.

Zellorian was merciless, though he assumed the role of dispassionate, unbiased administrator.

'You have heard the words of Aru Casruel, who has denied all charges and made charges herself against the throne. Charges which her own father has not substantiated.'

Gannatyne moved slowly, at last raising his head. His

eyes were dull; they focused on Zellorian, as though he saw him only momentarily. Then he looked away, far beyond the walls that surrounded the hearing.

Like a tide, he thought. Sometimes it pounds in, at others it laps gently. But remorseless. And so the Empire is eroded away, and what little soul is left is dark, so dark.

'I have nothing to say,' he told them, again lowering his head.

Aru could see the crumbling of his spirit, the chafing of her own.

10

SUZERAL

In the half-light, Aru contemplated the wall before her, painting upon it images from her recent past. Strangely it was the image of the young Innasmornian which had come to take precedence there and she saw Ussemitus constantly. He would go to the place at the appointed time, his companions with him, possibly even some of the elders, and she would not be there. How would the Innasmornians react? With anger? Would they be affronted? Or would they merely accuse Ussemitus of having imagined the entire affair? A score of possibilities crossed her mind, none of them pleasant, and in each she pictured Ussemitus's distress, and worse, his sense of betrayal. This pained her more than anything, but she tried to force it to the back of her mind.

The nightmare of the court and the hearing plagued her over and over again. It had been disastrous for her and Gannatyne. She had still not got over the shock of hearing her father's denial. He had become the complete puppet of Zellorian, and it was easy now to see that the Prime Consul was providing him with *keroueen*, the means by which he controlled him. She should have been quicker to follow that up, she kept telling herself, but it was far too late.

The verdict had come quickly: they knew the Imperator Elect wanted no arguments. His own views were obvious. Both Aru and Gannatyne were found guilty of collusion, and worse, of treason. Pyramors had spoken for them both, saying that it was not treason, merely the following of beliefs they held that would strengthen the Empire and not weaken it, and it was his plea for leniency and the support of Gannatyne's followers that spared them the axe.

'The crimes committed,' the Imperator had said, 'must

be punished. But in some ways the accused acted in what they thought to be my best interests. Execution would be unreasonable. Gannatyne, you will be stripped of all official titles. You may retain your house and land, but your movements will be restricted, and you will be observed, reports written regularly. The detail of this will be worked out in due course.

'Aru is young and impressionable. She will be imprisoned for a minimum period of two years. After that time I will consider her future.'

She stared at the wall. Two years! In this cell? Surely they could not be that hard on her.

As she thought of this, the door opened and one of the guards came in, carrying a tray. The food was excellent, and there was even wine if she wanted it, though she refused it.

'Who is your officer?' she asked the guard. She could see another outside, a drawn blade catching the torchlight.

The guard, a burly fellow, grinned. 'No questions. Eat your food.'

She gripped his arm. 'Come on, you can answer a few simple questions – '

He eyed her with appreciation and she felt herself shrink under the lust in his eyes. 'Save your breath. Neither I nor my men are open to trade.'

She recoiled at the crude meaning in his words.

He chuckled obscenely. 'My lads and me have got all we need. We're well provided for. You, lady, are stuck here.'

'But you can't keep me here for two years! Not in this cell.'

He picked up an empty tray and mug. 'No more questions,' he grunted, locking the door behind him.

Mannaston stood at the foot of the spiral stairway, gripping the rail that curled up into the shadows. His head rang, though not with *keroueen* or other rich wine. At last! his mind cried. Zellorian has given me what I have begged him for. She is up there somewhere, as promised.

This tower was remote, at the edge of the palace in an area kept for servants and certain of the royal harlots. Mannaston had come here as quickly as he could, his tongue thick, his mind racing. The Imperator Elect had agreed to release his wife: she no longer interested him. Zellorian had achieved it, and in exchange for Gannatyne's downfall he had arranged for her to be at Mannaston's disposal. Mannaston had used what money he could raise to have his house put in order. There were horses in the courtyard below. And she was above.

He climbed the stone spiral, which seemed to go on for ever. His legs ached but he forced himself to go on, stumbling more than once. At last he came to the round gallery at the top with its single door. He paused outside it and as he did so, he heard laughter. A woman, chuckling to herself, amused by something.

Not a man! his mind roared. Surely Zellorian would not do that to me now, not after all I have endured.

Mannaston twisted the ring of the door and pushed gently. The door was not locked and swung in on oiled hinges. Light streamed into the room from a window that had been flung wide. The day was brilliant beyond. Bathed in the light was a woman. She wore the harlot's silk, scarlet, her body revealed beneath it. Mannaston felt giddy at the sight of her. Age had done little to impair her miraculous beauty. He had always been a slave to it.

She turned and saw him, her brows arching. 'Well, well. A ghost from my past.' She did not seem surprised to see him.

'It's all right,' he whispered, finding it difficult to speak. 'I have come with Zellorian's blessing.'

This did puzzle her. 'Zellorian? He sent you? Why?'

He was about to explain, when he saw that there was blood on her hands. On a table near her there was a long blade. It may have been the light, but he thought it looked slick.

'Speak up, you old fool, have you some message?'

'You're free,' he croaked. 'Free.'

Again she echoed him. 'Free? But I'm not a prisoner. I never have been. What are you talking about?'

'The Imperator has agreed to your release. You can come home.'

She laughed softly. 'With *you?* Who put you up to this?'

He came forward and as he did so he saw beyond her for the first time. His head reeled at what he saw, and she laughed again at his reaction.

'It's a present from my lover,' she said, as though she were talking of a jewel or a ewer filled with blooms. But Mannaston stared in horror at the object.

It was a severed head.

'You should know him,' his wife whispered. 'He was a servant of yours.'

Mannaston felt his guts churn. It was Mazzu. The dead eyes stared horribly, the tongue hanging out of the mouth, bloated and grey.

'How did you come by this abomination?' Mannaston gasped.

She turned to it with a grin, as though it were a pet. 'Zellorian let me have it. I couldn't perform the beheading myself, but I took my pleasures with Mazzu before the headsman dealt his blow.'

'I don't understand,' gasped Mannaston, unable to take his eyes from the hideous stare of his former servant.

She suddenly became impatient with him, her mood darkening. 'So what do you want here? What is all this nonsense about home? This is my home.'

'No, no. You are no longer a prisoner – '

'I've never been a prisoner. Even now you haven't understood that! You cannot think I left you under duress?'

'The Imperator – '

'He had nothing to do with it. It was Zellorian.'

'What do you mean?' He felt a sudden rush of panic surging up from within him. This confusion was a whirlpool, his mind veering away from truth but sucked down to it.

'It was always Zellorian I wanted. I did everything in

my power to win his attention. *He* it is who rules this sorry Empire! Not that pathetic fool who calls himself Imperator. Zellorian rules. And he took me. Oh yes, he wanted me. And he put me in the royal seraglio. It was convenient, a cover for his own desires. And I have amused the Imperator. How else was I to make myself available to my lover? It has worked admirably.' But as she spoke, tears formed in her eyes, tears of anger. She clenched her fists.

Mannaston wanted to interrupt, trying to untangle this new web of deceit. Zellorian?

'But he soon grew tired of me. No one can control him, have any hold on him. He uses us all, administrators, lovers, even the Imperator. We are all of us disposable. Yes, he saw that I was well provided for as a harlot. But it has been a long time since he took me to his bed. Not long ago I caused him some embarrassment, thinking I might again force him to acknowledge me, take me back. But you see the result of that before you. She held up her hands, where the blood had dried.

Mannaston shook his head, dizzied by her revelations. 'Suzeral – '

'Mazzu performed some service for Zellorian. I have no idea what it was. But Zellorian wanted Mazzu paid for the service. He offered him whatever he most desired. Do you know what the vermin asked him for?'

Mannaston drew back from the heat in her gaze.

'He had always watched me with something vile in his eyes. As he went about the house you and I shared, I caught Mazzu looking at me many times, thinking to catch me unawares. I asked you to dismiss him, but you were too busy, Mannaston. You thought him harmless.'

'Zellorian *gave* you to Mazzu?'

She nodded. 'I was ordered – ordered – to service him. Like a common whore. Zellorian did it to punish me for upsetting him.'

'What had Mazzu done to earn you?'

'I told you, I don't know – '

'The *keroueen*,' whispered Mannaston, something falling

137

into place in front of him, a tapestry completing itself. 'He brought it to me in exchange for *that*?'

'Zellorian told me that if I did as instructed, I could have Mazzu once it was done, this business. To do with him as I saw fit.' She turned and pointed with a long nail at the head. 'So you see, I have not gone unavenged for the abuse I suffered! That excrement used me, Mannaston. You cannot imagine how.' Her voice dropped, her frame shaking.

Mannaston made a move to comfort her, but she struck his arm aside. 'Don't touch me! You'll not punish me for this. Zellorian protects his own.'

'Punish you?' said Mannaston. 'But I have come to take you away, back to our home. Later we can sell it and go into the mountains, make a new home. Away from the corruption that festers in this city.'

She barked a laugh, throwing back her head. 'Are you mad? Do you think I would come with you?'

He looked stunned, as though she had rocked him with a punch. 'You cannot stay here – '

'Why not? I have all I need.'

'You cannot still love Zellorian – ?

She sneered, turning away.

'You do? Is that it? You love him in spite of this horror – '

'Oh, get out, Mannaston! Go back to your wine. Look to that brat of a child of ours. How you ever sired her will always be a mystery to me.'

Mannaston gasped. It was a double blow, knowing that even now Aru was in some cell below the palace. How could he have sold her into that for this woman? How could he have been so ridiculous? Anger, humiliation, shame, all welled in him now. Fury at Zellorian's power. And utter loathing for his own failings. His self disgust took a hold of him and gripped him, shaking him.

He emitted a howl, animal-like, and his fingers reached out for his wife. They took hold of her throat, closing on the soft flesh and tightening. He swore at her, again and again, twisting, shaking, blind to her face, her pleading eyes.

She reached back and grabbed the knife from the table, trying to swing it at him, but he flung her down and straddled her. She was not a strong woman, having been softened by the idle days at court, while he had his fury, a volcano that had been simmering for years. It gave vent to all its heat now as he snatched the knife from her and drove it into her body a dozen times.

When at last his anger had spent itself, he sobbed over her.

It was a long time before he stood up. He tried to clean the blade on her silks, which were heavy with her blood. His own robe was smeared, but a brief search of the room's closet revealed other clothes. He selected a robe and put it on, washing himself and concealing the knife inside his robe.

The act of murder had cleared his mind miraculously. It was no longer fogged. Already he had formed a precise idea of what he wanted to do, what he must do. The weariness left him, and he took strength from his new resolve.

He left the death chamber, locking the door with a key he had found. He doubted that anyone would discover the body of Suzeral for many hours, possibly days. Anyway, it would be long enough. He went down the spiral stairway, drawing on fresh energy that he did not think he possessed any more. He kept his fury before him.

As he went back into the main maze of the palace, he was met by a number of guards and officials, but he used his office to talk his way past them. It was only when he came to the unauthorised lower zone that he was questioned.

The guard here was adamant. He could go no further.

'But I have papers I must deliver to one of the prisoners. Zellorian himself wants them signed.'

'My orders are strict, sire. Zellorian himself sends such things to me, through his officers. No one else.'

139

'Zellorian wouldn't give these papers to a guard,' protested Mannaston, keeping his voice low. 'They implicate members of the Consulate. Which is why I was sent. I'm an old man. Do you think I could be a danger to you and your men? You could beat me senseless with one arm.'

The guard stared at him, and in a moment one of his companions emerged from the room behind him. 'What's the fuss?' He saw Mannaston and grinned. 'You're Mannaston, are you not?'

'He claims he's from Zellorian, Urtbrand,' said the first guard.

'He works for him, don't you, old man?'

Mannaston nodded. He had seen this man before, but he could not place him.

'What do you want here?'

'I have papers that must be signed by one of the prisoners.'

Urtbrand scowled. 'Papers? For whom?'

'You are holding Aru Casruel. She is my daughter.'

Urtbrand nodded. 'It's all right, Kregar, I'll deal with this.' The other guard withdrew. 'What about her?'

'She's to be moved, but there are papers she must sign. Confessions to other crimes. Zellorian has agreed to move her for me, if I persuade her to incriminate others who are enemies of Zellorian. You understand me? Only I can persuade her to do this. And the papers are confidential.'

'Let me see them,' said Urtbrand suspiciously.

Mannaston pulled a roll of them partly from his robe. 'I cannot allow you to read them.'

Urtbrand's unease was plain, but he had no wish to stand in the way of Zellorian. Vymark had told him there would be rich rewards if he served him well. And this old fool was undeniably the tool of the Prime Consul, as he well knew.

'Very well. I'll take you to her. But pull up your hood. Let no one see you.' Urtbrand spoke briefly to Kregar in the room beyond, then took a torch and led Mannaston down into the lower regions. He said no more until he reached a particular cell.

Mannaston hid his disgust at seeing the place where Aru was being kept. Urtbrand unlocked the heavy door and motioned Mannaston in. The door closed behind him, but he spoke through the grille. 'I'll wait here until you are done. Be swift.'

Aru had been half asleep on the cot. When the hooded figure came into the room, she gazed at it as if it were merely another of her nightmares. When it pulled back its hood, she gasped, seeing her father's face. He leaned towards her as she struggled to get up.

'Not a word,' he breathed, finger to his lips. Something in his eyes kept her silent. From inside his cloak he pulled out a long knife and she shrank back. This must indeed be a nightmare.

'Lie down and keep very still,' said Mannaston, and she understood then that he had not come here to kill her. He went to the grille.

'Quickly,' he hissed to the waiting Urtbrand.

His face appeared. 'What is it?'

'The girl. She is dead.'

'What!' came the howl of anger. At once the door creaked open and Urtbrand came in, rushing to the inert form of Aru. As he bent over it, Mannaston put an arm around his neck and drove the knife up under his ribs in a killing strike he had been taught many years ago. He had not forgotten it.

Urtbrand sucked in a long breath as if he had dived into freezing water. Aru watched his face screw up in agony. Mannaston released him and he thumped into a wall, dropping down, clutching his ribs. He could not speak, gasping for air. Mannaston looked on, unsure how to finish this, but Aru leapt up and took the blade from him. She was about to deliver a final blow, when Urtbrand slid down.

Aru turned to her father, who stood shaking before her. 'He's dead, Father. Your thrust was perfect to the inch.'

He could not look at her face. 'We have to get out of

here,' he said, suddenly feeling his years. 'I have no time to explain my actions. But I have wronged you. I haven't come here to ask forgiveness. But you must get away. Keep close to me, and say nothing.'

She had many things to ask him, but knew they must all wait. She could see the urgency in him, the need to unburden himself of so much, but time was against them. Instead she took Urtbrand's sword and allowed him to usher her quickly out of the cell. He pulled up his hood and they went as swiftly as caution would permit along the passageways. There was only one way out of the maze, and it led past the other guard. Near to the room where he sat, Mannaston turned.

'Wait here in the shadows.'

'What will you do?'

'Wait here,' he repeated, and she flinched at the unexpected steel in his voice. What had happened to him? Years ago he might have been like this. But now – had his mind turned?

Mannaston reached the door to the guardroom. The guard was leaning back, his feet on the table, polishing a sword. He looked up as Mannaston entered. 'All done?' he asked.

'Yes. It was easier than I imagined.'

'Where's Urtbrand?'

'Who? Oh yes. He's back there. Seeing to one of the others.'

Kregar got up, sword in his hand. 'Is he?' He came forward slowly. 'What's wrong?'

'Nothing. I must get back.'

'Wait.' Kregar reached out for Mannaston's shoulder, but the old man swung round, digging upwards with the long knife. He felt it tear through leather and flesh, glancing off bone and missing its target area. Kregar swore in pain and thrust with the cutting edge of his blade. Mannaston felt his own skin part as the blade cut him, and he tumbled to one side of his opponent. The breath whooshed from his body as Kregar twisted in mid-air, Mannaston landing underneath. He could not use the knife.

Kregar was far stronger than Mannaston and in a moment was over him, his sword point raised for the killing thrust. But before he could stab downward, his head jerked back. Aru had hold of his hair with one hand. With the other she had driven her own blade into his neck. He toppled sideways and Mannaston wriggled free.

'Are you hurt?' Aru whispered.

He nodded, wincing as the blood leaked from his side. 'I'm all right.'

'Where are we going?'

'Up. To the roofs.'

She did not question him, having little choice but to obey. He had killed for her: this was not Zellorian's doing. Unless it could be some other trap. But she could not believe that. It would be far too elaborate.

They crept from the prison area and went up into the lower palace levels. Mannaston found a chamber and clothes for his daughter. She washed his wound, an ugly slice in his side that needed attention from a surgeon if he was to survive.

'Later,' was all he said. 'Get to the roofs.'

She found an outfit that fitted her, robes that were meant for officials of the palace, men, though she would have preferred a warrior's trappings. There was no time to disguise herself properly and she let Mannaston draw her on up more stairways.

By a miracle they reached the higher levels of the palace without meeting anyone. It was early evening and many of the officials were having their meals. There were few guards here, as there was little need for them.

As they came to the final upper landing, they almost walked right in to one of the Consulate, a man called Diamatas. Mannaston knew that he was Zellorian's lackey. He scowled at Mannaston, then turned his gaze on Aru.

'This is the Casruel girl. What is she doing here?'

'I'm taking her to Zellorian,' said Mannaston quickly.

143

'He's not up here, you fool,' snorted Diamatas. 'Why should he be here? These are the archives –'

'Nevertheless,' said Mannaston, 'It is where I am to meet Zellorian. With my daughter.'

Aru was looking round to see if anyone had noticed them. No one was in sight, but she could hear muted voices from beyond an open doorway.

'I think you had better –' began Diamatas, but Aru delivered a sudden punch to his midriff. Her hand sank into soft flesh and the man doubled, his face scarlet. Aru grabbed him by the neck and swung him round into a doorway.

'Pray no one's in there,' she said to her father, for the first time grinning.

He pushed the door open. Beyond there were rows of rolled parchment in darkness. Aru used the flat of her sword and brought it down hard on the back of Diamatas's skull. He slumped as she pushed him into the room, slamming the door.

'Quickly,' Mannaston hissed, his face pale. They ran down the corridor. Behind them they heard a shout and in a moment three robed figures had emerged from the open doorway. They were calling after them.

Another narrow flight of stairs led upwards, and they reached a last doorway. It was locked, but Aru used her sword haft to splinter the lock. Outside, the sun was slipping down into the pointed embrace of the mountains beyond the city. The roof area was flat.

'Now where?' Aru asked.

Mannaston looked about him with an air of desperation. 'Sometimes there are gliderboats here –'

'Sometimes?'

'It was the only place I could think of,' he said helplessly. The roof was bare. As he stood there, his face haggard, his guilt wrapped about him like a cloak, Aru suddenly felt an overwhelming sense of pity. She put her arms about him and hugged him, the warm tears stinging her eyes.

144

'Aru, Aru, what have I done?' he gasped, his body heaving.

'They're coming,' she said, disentangling herself. Quickly they moved across the bare roof to its edge. Another flat roof stretched before them, a little lower. They crossed on to it. They could hear shouts behind them, but ran for the cover of an observation tower, sheltering under its shadow.

While Aru looked out for signs of pursuit, Mannaston slipped around the tower, searching for an escape route. He came back to her, his eyes wide. 'There's a gliderboat,' he said. 'For the guards in the tower. Two of them are with it. We can kill them – '

She scowled. They would be prepared this time. Two trained guards, on the alert. She shook her head. 'When they've gone.'

Mannaston nodded back at the way they had come. 'Those others will be here in a while. We have no time.'

'We can't fight them in the open – '

'You always were a stubborn child.'

'Father!' But he had gone. She went to follow him, but saw his intention. He was using himself as a decoy, running along the edge of the roof, ducking down, but intending to be seen. Aru was caught in two minds. If she ran after him, they were both dead. If she got to the gliderboat, she could perhaps save them both.

Easing round the tower, she heard shouts from above. Men were directing the attention of the guards by the gliderboat. She could see them, some twenty yards away. As one they looked up and caught sight of Mannaston as he weaved along the edge of the roof. Drawing their swords they ran after him, leaving the gliderboat unattended. Behind them there were other guards coming from the archive area.

Aru sprinted across the flat roof for the gliderboat. At once there were cries from the tower behind her, but the guards were intent on catching Mannaston and did not hear. Aru reached the gliderboat, praying that she could control it. She spoke to it softly, gently probing its delicate controls. It responded, but was reluctant to obey a foreign Controller. But she forced her will upon it and at last took it up from the roof, swinging its blunt nose around, aiming for the guards. It protested, but she gritted her teeth.

Mannaston was already fending off the first of the guards, but all he had was the long knife. They closed in, a ring of five of them.

Aru forced the gliderboat to aim at them, and they saw her coming, scattering and dropping flat. Mannaston shouted something that was lost, waving her away.

Again she swung the objecting craft around, meaning to use it as a weapon on the guards. She must get her father aboard. But she saw his anger as she passed. He went to the very lip of the roof.

'Escape!' he howled. 'Escape!' The wind tore the tears from his eyes as suddenly he leapt out into the void.

His body was a blur as Aru turned back, trying to see what he had done. Then he was gone from sight. The gliderboat wrenched itself free of her control and swooped upwards. Her own eyes stung as the craft accelerated, moving towards the mountain. She knew that the little time her father had bought her was already ebbing away. Angrily she took control of the craft again, and the darkness of twilight beyond the city swallowed her.

BOOK THREE

THE WARHIVE

11

THE GARAZENDA

Light pulsed in the high chamber, its symmetrically curved ceiling suffused with colour and warmth, an artificial womb. The temperature was perfectly controlled, the furniture exquisitely carved, moulded to the forms of the beings who had gathered here. They sat in precise ranks in ascending order of command, the principals at the head of the assembly, facing their subordinates, who looked up at them, attention fixed, not a single head turning, intent, obedient. All wore full battle dress, immaculately prepared, their weapons at their sides, their war helms on their laps. This was a gathering of the Marozul, the high command of the Csendook military machine, a score of the Garazenda, the generals who ruled the Csendook nation, and below them the upper ranks of the Zaru, their commanders, beyond them the principal Zolutars, their captains.

Once the Marozul had assembled, silence fell for a few moments, broken only by the gentle hum of the walls that betokened the immaculate environmental conditioners that worked invisibly behind them. The Csendook were a hardy race, capable of withstanding enormous physical discomfort and conditional variation, but on their artificial home, the Warhive, they spared no effort to create their concept of ideal comfort.

At last the central figure lifted his head and spoke to the assembled military might before him, aware that he addressed every important Zaru of the Csendook peoples. Such gatherings were rare, for the war spread them over many worlds, but the business to be conducted today would effect the entire nation, every one of those disparate worlds.

'Warriors,' he said in the deep, guttural voice of his kind, 'at last we are able to enjoy a respite from our labours and come together. I trust that the Warhive is providing you with everything you require.' He did not wait for a reply. As you are aware, I am Zuldamar, and on my left is Vulkormar, with Horzumar on my right. We are your principals, your voice, and with your agreement, we shall chair today's historical proceedings. We have received fully detailed reports from all of you and from a number of Zaru who are unable to be here, but rest assured that we are able to deliver to you an accurate and complete picture of the state of the war.

'I believe I am not speaking out of order when I tell you this, but in summary, the war is as good as over.'

There were nods from some of the assembled, who had been expecting as much. But there was no sound. None of the gathered would as much as murmur until asked to speak.

Zuldamar lifted his chin as he made his announcement, pausing as if to let it take effect. He was a large being even by Csendook standards, standing over seven feet tall with wide shoulders that were emphasised by the war gear of light armour that he wore. To a Man he would have been huge, his arms and legs almost twice as thick and muscular as a Man's, his neck bull-like. His head was broad, with very little hair: it covered the top of his skull like a dark down. The ears were flat to the sides of his head, his nose wide but similarly flattish, the mouth large, the teeth sharp, almost canine. The eyes were slanted, the irises were dark, and in the Csendook expression there was, to a Man, always a hint of animal, of cunning. Strength combined with relentless power and speed seemed to be epitomised by the Csendook warrior, and Zuldamar was the perfect example. His hands, resting on the table before him, were huge, like weapons, capable not only of appalling destruction but also of intricate workmanship, an extraordinary duality of purpose.

'Mankind is not exterminated, I grant you,' he went on. 'But in the last Warhive year we have almost achieved that goal. Man's Empire, which once ruled supreme, is dust.

We have taken it from him and levelled it. There are a few pockets of resistance left, none of them open, down forgotten Paths to worlds we do not covet, gates that we need not fear. Like worms, Men have burrowed themselves away, out of sight of us.' He nodded in the direction of a number of the assembled Garazenda as well as at the Marozul alongside him. 'All reports concur. Resistance is minimal. Our Crusade is at an end.'

One of the Garazenda leaned forward, holding out a gloved fist in the gesture of request.

'You wish to comment, Zurmagar?'

The latter nodded. 'With deepest respect, we have yet to agree on whether or not the Crusade is ended.'

Zuldamar gazed at him coldly, though the look on Zurmagar's face in return was equally as cold. 'You are correct, of course. I move on too swiftly. We are here to debate the issue.'

Beside him Vulkormar nodded. He was almost as large as Zuldamar, his face as wide, but harsher. 'The matter for discussion is a simple one. Either we put an end to the war or go on with it until we are sure that Man no longer exists.'

'There are arguments for and against the issue,' said Zuldamar, although no one in the huge chamber had the slightest doubt about his feelings. For one of the Marozul to think of peace was food for thought. Many of the assembled were fervent supporters of Zuldamar.

He again looked at Zurmagar. 'Perhaps you would like to give us your views on the matter? I know that you were, until recently, involved in heavy fighting.'

Zurmagar nodded and got to his feet, turning to the multitude. 'We've fought this Crusade for a long time. Although the Csendook have always had the upper hand, always threatened to overwhelm our opponents, it has been difficult, and we've lost a good few comrades. But we are now in a position to remove the blight of Man for all time. We are within a stroke of doing this. Once we have administered the death blow, we can rest, build. If we do not take the opportunity to do this now, we can never be sure that Man will not grow in numbers and again threaten us, in some small way, in the future. But why put the life of a single Csendook at risk? Why not remove the blight? We seek to eradicate plague, famine, disease in our crops. Why should we not ensure the removal of our greatest foe?'

Zuldamar could not judge the reaction of the assembled Csendook, though he knew it was their nature to fight, to worry out and kill any threat. It would have been very easy to whip them up and have them agree to Zurmagar's suggestions. His speech was well-worn, a typical rallying battle cry.

Horzumar was given permission to speak. 'In theory, what Zurmagar says is perfectly sound. Man is a plague to us, and our medicine does seek to destroy disease. Why should Man be any different? But it is the practicalities we have to consider. The expense, for example. Not just in Csendook lives, although perhaps we could achieve the ultimate goal now with minimal losses, our superiority being so great. But we should consider some of the worlds we have fought on: those we have reduced to rubble, some of them being no more than wasteland now. Csendook cannot populate them for millennia.

'We must also consider our resources. We have, it would seem, unlimited resources. But should we squander them in hunting down the last dregs of Man? As we reduce our enemy, so we will find him harder to locate. In terms of resources and effort, the hunt becomes more costly. To the state. You would not take an axe to an apple.'

Zuldamar nodded slowly. 'That is my own feeling, I have to say. Man is not dead, but he is crippled. He has hidden himself so far from our eyes that I ask myself, is he worthy of our attention any more?'

Another of the Garazenda, a ferocious warrior known to have been in the front ranks of the war all his life, Xeltagar, banged his fist down on the table. 'I cannot believe the words of the Marozul!' he stormed. 'Give up the war! When we are within an inch of our goal? Zurmagar is right. We should go on. Man must be cleared away.' He sat back, a look of disgust curling his lips.

Zuldamar acknowledged his few angry words with a patient nod. This was the raw emotion of the Csendook speaking, he knew. The natural way of the warrior was in all their hearts, however much some of them suppressed it.

'I would not wish Man to go his own way,' said Horzumar. 'I am as anxious as Zurmagar and Xeltagar to see that no single Csendook life is endangered again. But I wonder if there might be a better way of dealing with the problem.'

'You have suggestions?' asked another of the Garazenda.

'It is true that I have given the matter some thought. As Zurmagar correctly says, the most obvious way of dealing with the matter is to continue the Crusade until Man is wiped out. Every last one. But that is a task that would take millennia. No, before you shout me down, Xeltagar, let me say this: the fewer Men there are to kill, the harder it will become to find them. There are many gates, many hiding places. If we could limit Man to one world, then it would be the simple task you speak of.'

'That is sound thinking,' said Vulkormar.

'Man hides on more worlds than we know,' went on Horzumar. 'But my proposal would be neither to dismiss him, nor ignore him.'

'What then?' said Zuldamar.

'Control him,' said Horzumar.

'How?' said several of the Garazenda.

'Introduce a system of enslavement. We already use Man in our Games and in the Hunt. I suggest we consider ways in which a fuller system could be developed. Let us make use of our enemy. Let us bend him to our will.'

'But you are sidestepping the problem!' snorted Zurmagar. 'We would still have to hunt him down. Man would hardly come willingly.'

Horzumar smiled calmly. 'You misunderstand me. I would not expect Man to rush to our service. But Man can be used. If we were to develop a significantly tiered gladiatorial system, with, shall we say, certain rewards built in to it, we might find that Man would respond admirably. Certain of his species would adapt to such a system very well. I have studied such things. And I have come to the conclusion that Man, suitably trained, could be used to *find* those who elude us.'

'They would serve *us*?' said Zurmagar. 'Betray their fellows?'

'Provided with the right kind of rewards, I am certain of it.'

Zuldamar looked to Xeltagar. 'How does my colleague react to this?'

Xeltagar snorted. 'With contempt. You suggest we trust Man?'

'Not at all,' said Horzumar. 'Those we enslave either serve us or die. They have a simple choice. They have no scope for negotiation. All I am saying is that if we choose the right kind of Man, he will put himself first, before his fellows, and serve us. It is in his nature to be selfish.'

'A Csendook would rather kill himself than do such a thing,' growled Xeltagar.

'Of course he would,' agreed Horzumar. 'He would be unworthy of our race if he did not. But we are talking about an inferior species. Man thinks of survival at any cost. Which is why I say it will be hard to exterminate him.'

'If we cannot kill the wild beast,' said Zuldamar, 'we can remove its legs.'

Horzumar inclined his head. 'Aptly put.'

Zurmagar raised his fist again and was acknowledged. 'I am prepared to recognise the merits of Horzumar's scheme. It is a pretty theory. But allow me to test a few of its weaknesses.'

'I welcome your opinions,' said Horzumar with a wolfish grin.

'Are we assuming that Man is scattered, spread into every remote crack and bolthole of his Empire, dispersed and leaderless? There must be leaders, just as we have our Garazenda. We know from bitter experience that Man

154

organises himself well. Although we have smashed his armies, they were not without merit. And they had their champions, their heroes.'

'I presume,' said Zuldamar, 'that you are referring to their Imperator Elect, their supreme ruler?'

'Is there news of him?' said Zurmagar. 'I have heard as many rumours as a cat has fleas.'

'The latest report I have,' said Zuldamar, 'is fairly conclusive.'

Everyone in the chamber looked at him, their attention riveted. They all knew that the Imperator Elect was the one figurehead, the one focal point of all resistance. His death had never been confirmed.

'If he's dead,' said Zurmagar, 'then I would reconsider my suggestions. To Man he is a kind of deity. Without him, Man's will is broken. You would have removed the bones in his body.'

'The report,' said Zuldamar, 'is that the Imperator Elect and his Consulate, his principal warriors, including Zellorian, the most talented of his advisers, were pursued through gates to a remote part of the Empire, at its rim. In a desperate bid to avoid our Swarm, Zellorian attempted to use scientific methods that relied heavily on speculation and experiment. He acted blindly, grasping at straws, trying to operate techniques that were beyond him. Whatever it was he attempted, it was his last act. He failed, and in failing brought about the annihilation of the Imperator Elect and all the company.'

'Is there proof of this?' said Zurmagar.

'Witnesses to the destruction, the violence of the explosions, the devastation on Eannor, their world of refuge,' said Zuldamar. 'They can be brought here, but I have the reports. No one could have survived such a disaster. It was, apparently, an attempt to break through the Circle of Worlds that binds us, an act of desperate madness.'

The company considered his words in silence for a long moment.

Eventually Zurmagar spoke again. 'It will be a crushing

blow to Man. Across the ruins of his Empire, word will spread.'

'Man will not be able to regroup, to choose another supreme leader,' said Horzumar. 'His spine is broken.'

'Warriors,' said Zuldamar, 'I think we should discuss these matters for a while among ourselves. There are chambers here for that purpose. In two hours we will come back and plan the way forward.'

It was customary procedure at these debates for the assembly to air its views informally, and the meeting broke up, grouping itself again in the various ante-chambers. Zuldamar and Horzumar found a private room, sipping at the wine that was brought to them.

'Can we do it?' said Zuldamar.

'Two things,' said Horzumar. 'One is that we have to replace the Crusade with something just as stirring to Csendook blood. You and I consider ourselves to be civilised, Zuldamar, and less quick to resort to arms than we once were. But our race likes nothing better than the scent of blood, human blood at that. We cannot remove that.'

'So you think your organised system of slavery and gladiatorial combat can replace war?'

'Properly handled, it can refine it. We have an entire Empire as our hunting ground. Without the insecurity of a war. Those who hunt, hunt. Those who wish to pursue other matters, such as the rebuilding of shattered worlds, can do so without being disturbed.'

'That is good. And the second thing?'

'We must convince our people that the Imperator Elect and his Consulate are dead.'

'But we cannot be sure.'

'No. But we must convince our people that we are sure. If they think he's alive, Man will find out. And we'll never subdue him.'

When they returned to the assembly, they had fixed firmly on their own particular resolve. A further debate followed and it went on for many hours, though the Csendook were tireless when it came to such matters. In the end it came down to a simple division between the militants under Xeltagar, who would accept no other course than the genocide of Mankind, and the moderates under Horzumar, who saw a more constructive future for their race in the rebuilding of the war-torn Empire. At last, the matter came to a vote.

Horzumar, now supported by Zurmagar, who had shown a deepening interest in the proposed gladiatorial system, won the debate. It took a while for the assembly to realise that they had probably made the most momentous decision in Csendook history. The Crusade was at an end.

For a while there was an unprecedented hubbub in the chamber as those real implications sank home to them all. A thousand years of war at an end! This was the day of victory.

In a while they began to devise the means by which their nations would be told, and how the news must be celebrated.

Zuldamar brought this subsequent discussion to an end, aware that Xeltagar and his supporters were becoming restless and anxious to leave the chamber. 'Warriors,' called Zuldamar, now standing, 'we have many things to plan. But I do not think it is possible for us to detail everything ourselves. I do, however, offer up a proposal to you, which I think would assist greatly in the despatch of our new resolutions.' He turned to Xeltagar. 'New duties mean new responsibilities, new posts.'

Xeltagar straightened. Defeat here meant dishonour to him. He was incapable of seeing this any other way. The ending of the Crusade was not, in his eyes, a victory, but a defeat. He saw all that he had striven for fading.

'Since we are to organise the enslavement of Man,' went on Zuldamar, 'we will need someone to oversee the operation.'

Xeltagar's eyes betrayed a fresh interest. He stood up at once. 'May I put myself forward? Who better to do this?' His chin jutted out like a rock at the assembled Csendook before him. Many were nodding. Who better indeed than the Csendook who had undoubtedly been responsible for more destruction among Man than any other?

'Your devotion to duty is legendary,' said Zuldamar. 'But we have to consider the ramifications of government. As one of our principal Garazenda, Xeltagar, I would submit that the post would be beneath you, as it would be subordinate to the post of Garazenda. What I was going to propose was a post that would be immediately responsible to the entire Garazenda, although directly under the supervision of an appropriate one.' So that we can control him, Zuldamar mused. He knew that if Xeltagar held the new post, he would merely use it to continue the Crusade in his own way.

Xeltagar scowled, but said nothing, waiting.

'A Supreme Sanguinary,' suggested Horzumar. 'Responsible to all the Garazenda, through Xeltagar. Can we put this to the vote?'

The response was instant, the motion carried. It took the sting out of Xeltagar's anger, and he had to bow to the assembly's will. When he left, it was with a curt nod to Zuldamar and the others, and a number of his followers went with him. Shortly afterwards the long debate ended and the Garazenda went their various ways into the Warhive to begin their own preparations.

Zuldamar and Horzumar looked for Xeltagar, who was preparing to leave for another part of the Warhive where he had his own private lands.

'Before you leave us,' said Zuldamar, 'we had hoped to discuss the matter of the new post further.'

Xeltagar's chamber was luxurious, but he had not taken advantage of it, preferring the simplicity of battle quarters. He waved the two Marozul to seats, calling out to servants for something to eat.

'I am opposed to the ending of the war, you know that,' he said gruffly. 'But you've carried the day. It's a mistake.'

'You think us soft?' said Horzumar.

'You are Csendook. Underneath, warriors. Man is

dangerous. You know that. You've spent time in the front line.'

'Neither of us has any intention of promoting mercy,' said Zuldamar. 'But we want the best for our inheritance. Man became soft. Perhaps if he had been more like us, more single-minded, he would have held on to his empire.'

'Precisely!' snapped Xeltagar, taking a long pull at his wine. 'And now you want to change that –'

'No,' said Zuldamar. 'We want tighter control. True domination. As long as Man persists in fighting us, we cannot utterly dominate him. But through the new way, we shall.'

'Tell us,' said Horzumar, 'who do you think should fill the new post?'

'I could name you a dozen brilliant Zolutars, even some of our best warriors, our Zemoks.'

'The post demands someone exceptional,' said Zuldamar. 'Your warriors are the elite, Xeltagar. I do not say this to patronise or flatter you. It is a simple fact. They are the backbone of our Swarms.'

Xeltagar stiffened at the compliment. 'They are. A few more years and they would have settled this issue –'

'And then what?' said Horzumar. 'If they had wiped out Mankind?'

Xeltagar shrugged. He had never considered life without war.

'Who have you got?' asked Zuldamar.

'There is one of them who would be perfect,' said Xeltagar after some thought. 'A Csendook who is devoted to the cause. If I tell him he cannot eliminate Man, but must enslave him, he will do it. And he will do everything in his power to see that the law is carried out with utter precision.'

'That is what we need,' said Zuldamar. 'And not, as you suggested earlier, someone who has gone soft. His task will not be an easy one.'

Xeltagar smiled, but it was the smile of a hunting animal. He drank more of his wine. 'You may know him. A fine Zaru. Auganzar.'

159

Zuldamar nodded slowly. 'Yes, I know the name. Something of a legend among your Swarm, is he not?'

'In single combat, no one is faster, stronger. Even I would be hard put to get the better of him.'

'Obedient?' said Horzumar.

'Absolutely.'

'To you first, or to the Garazenda?' said Zuldamar.

Xeltagar scowled. 'There is no difference.'

'I imagine,' said Horzumar, 'that it would be excellent for the morale of your Swarm if we promoted him to this new post?'

'Every fighting Csendook admires him,' nodded Xeltagar. 'They would be obedient.'

'Then I think we should do our best to persuade the rest of the Marozul that Auganzar is the Csendook we want,' said Zuldamar.

Xeltagar bowed slightly, wondering if there was something he had missed. To him war was war: politics were something else and this whole business stank of politics. He was still musing on this after the two Marozul had gone.

Zuldamar and Horzumar went back into their own private sector of the Warhive, glad at last to relax in a steaming bath.

'You probably know more about this Auganzar than I do,' said Horzumar. 'If he is Xeltagar's personal favourite – '

'We should cover our backs? I don't think so. For all his fury, Xeltagar is a Csendook to the bone. He's been given a task he sees as contrary to his beliefs in many ways, but he won't cross the Garazenda. And he'll relish being in control of the Supreme Sanguinary, or thinking that he is. It makes far more sense to have the post responsible to all of us, which will limit its own power considerably.'

'Limited powers of control?'

'Certainly. Auganzar is the perfect choice. He's ambitious. Loyal to Xeltagar because it has been the best way for him to gain favour and status. Once he becomes

Supreme Sanguinary, he'll seek ways to become a Gara-zenda, rest assured.'

Horzumar frowned. 'And you think this is a wise move! Surely there are dangers.'

Zuldamar laughed, a sound somewhere between a deep chuckle and a growl. 'Ah, but Auganzar's desire to become one of us will ensure that he does as we require of him. Xeltagar may encourage him secretly to wipe out as many Men as he can find, which he may do, I don't know. Xeltagar is a fanatic, but Auganzar will do as the Gara-zenda wants. Once he's had his brief, he'll be our servant, not Xeltagar's. Make no mistake, old friend, Auganzar is a superb warrior, quite terrifying, but he is far more than simply a military machine. He has a good mind. This will be an opportunity for him that he will celebrate.'

Horzumar sighed, leaning back in the scalding water. 'So the Crusade is truly at an end.'

'I think so. And there are so many other pleasures to pursue.'

12

AUGANZAR

The arena was small, a perfect circle of stone, sunk down into the ground, the central feature of the extravagant house. On the balcony overlooking the arena, a number of figures gazed down in silence, watching the two warriors who faced each other across the sand. One of the warriors carried a short broad sword and a rounded shield, while the other carried a stabbing spear and a longer sword. They circled each other in ritual fashion, thrusting and jabbing, seeking an opening. Both wore light armour, thinly beaten metal that was far stronger than it looked, as was presently demonstrated when the short sword of the one opponent found a gap in the other's defence and struck at him. The point of his blade rang as it hit the armour and a small shower of sparks fizzed.

Above, the watchers nodded to themselves. The fight continued, with both warriors displaying tremendous skill and speed; several killer blows and cuts were parried by the armour which seemed unmarked by them.

'I'd like to examine the armour after the display, if I may be so bold as to ask,' said Vorenzar. He himself was a renowned Csendook warrior, a Zaru, a commander who had made a name for himself both in gladiatorial combat and in the battlefield. He was one of the Zaru particularly favoured by the new Supreme Sanguinary, Auganzar, whose house this was. Favoured because he preferred the more traditional way of fighting when possible, the way of the sword. The Csendook had far more sophisticated weapons these days, but to Vorenzar's mind none of them had the dignity of the sword, nor its soul.

Beside him, leaning over the balcony to watch another thrust and parry directly below, Gannorzol grunted, lost in concentration. The armour had impressed him, too. 'It does not appear to be marked, Zaru.'

Auganzar, the largest of them, who had not spoken since the combat began, nodded. 'I've had it used three times now,' he told them. 'But there's something else.' He called out to the Zemoks below, and for a moment the warriors ceased their circling, looking up through their war helms.

They bowed, and the one with the shield held it up. Auganzar nodded to him. For a moment there was a faint hum, then the fight began anew. Both Vorenzar and Gannorzol were fascinated by it, though Vorenzar masked his interest better.

Abruptly the swordsman cut into the body of his opponent, but the shield swung round quickly, receiving the blow on its curve. The sword clanged, held fast as though caught in wood.

'Magnetic,' said Vorenzar, though his opinion on the matter remained hidden.

Gannorzol was more openly enthusiastic. He watched as the Zemok below tried in vain to free his sword. He was forced to release it, and once he had stepped back, the field was turned off and the blade fell to the sand. Now the shield-bearer moved forward and it was only a short time before he had trapped the other blade, leaving his opponent without any defence.

Auganzar waved them to a halt, dismissing the Zemoks and telling them to have the armour and shield brought up later.

'You don't approve,' he said to Vorenzar, ignoring Gannorzol.

Vorenzar avoided the steely gaze of his master, knowing that it would not be possible to fathom his thinking. There was no one in whom the Supreme Sanguinary confided, and the word was that he told his superiors only what he wanted them to know. In the past attempts had been made to learn his thoughts, by direct means and indirect, but all had failed. Auganzar was the complete warrior. Even dressed as he now was, in informal regalia, a light cloth uniform, he looked daunting, his girth massive, his arms corded with muscle, their length scarred where exposed, testament to the innumerable battles he had fought. And like Vorenzar, he was a champion of the games.

Vorenzar knew that he was probably the only Csendook who could speak his mind to Auganzar without fear, as near to a friend as the Supreme Sanguinary had. 'It is not the sort of weapon you would use, I think,' he told him. Nor was it, for it unquestionably broke many rules of warrior discipline and tradition.

Auganzar smiled, and to Gannorzol's surprise there was a degree of warmth in it. He always felt uncomfortable when the Supreme Sanguinary was near, as if in the presence of an unpredictable reptile, although he told himself he had no reason to fear him that he was aware of.

'Useful in an emergency,' said Auganzar. 'It could deflect an assassin's blow. But you are quite correct, Vorenzar. I would rather fight bare-chested with a single blade. I'm not sure the Garazenda would approve of that these days. Not quite fitting for the Supreme Sanguinary.'

'May I ask if you are thinking of issuing these to our Zemoks?' said Vorenzar. 'Or are they to be used in the games and the hunt?'

'Well, apart from the Games and the Hunt, what is there?' smiled Auganzar, looking directly at Gannorzol. There was little to choose between the Zolutar and Vorenzar: they were heavily built, though light on their feet, both tested warriors, and in their eyes was the unmistakable gleam of a warrior who had tasted conflict, known it all his days. But in Vorenzar there was, Auganzar sensed, something else, an additional touch of cruelty, possibly, a streak of hardness, something that would not flinch if the brand was placed threateningly before it. It was why he had picked him from so many who were keen to serve him.

Auganzar's question had unnerved Gannorzol, though he managed a thin smile. 'Have all our battle corps been withdrawn, Zaru?' He addressed Auganzar as a commander, as did all his kind, though none of them had any doubts as to his power as Supreme Sanguinary.

Auganzar was nodding. 'At the express command of the Garazenda. The Crusade, as you know, is over. But I have managed to convince our betters that there are still frontiers, as it were.'

'We wage a different war now,' said Vorenzar.

He spoke with a confidence, an inner knowledge, that worried Gannorzol. He sensed there was something beneath this conversation that yet had to surface. He had not previously been granted particular favour in the new regime established under Auganzar, who had been in his new post for a month. Could there be a promotion here for him? He had been considered most worthy by the Garàzenda, and even Xeltagar had once remarked on his efficiency. And Auganzar reported direct to the fighting Xeltagar.

The Supreme Sanguinary was nodding again. 'We no longer speak of war. Peace has come. An unfamiliar state.'

Gannorzol waited. He would comment when he was more sure he would not cause offence.

'And so,' Auganzar went on, 'I develop what weapons I can with a view to making the games more interesting. It will amuse those who are not satisfied with more basic combat. Those who enjoy real battle, governed by the correct traditions, the true spirit of combat, will be disappointed.'

'It is remarkable to think that it is over, Zaru,' said Gannorzol.

'As you say, Zolutar. I sometimes wonder if the Garàzenda have been a little premature in bringing the Crusade to an end.'

Gannorzol felt a stab of alarm at this. It was coming: whatever the Supreme Sanguinary had in mind, it was coming. He did not approve of the Garazenda ruling? Of this peace?

'You are shocked, doubtless, to hear me say such a thing,'

smiled Auganzar. 'But this is a private place. I merely express my concern for our people. I am cautious.'

'May I presume, Zaru,' said Gannorzol carefully, 'you think there may still be organised rebellion among Mankind? That Man is not so dispersed as the Garazenda think?'

Auganzar glanced at Vorenzar and Gannorzol wondered how much they had spoken together on this matter. He felt suddenly very isolated. The ground beneath him had become a tissue, and one wrong step would send him through it. This was a test.

'The Imperator Elect is dead,' said Vorenzar. 'And Zellorian, his brilliant scientist. Without them, humanity is a rabble. Wouldn't you agree?'

Gannorzol felt the sweat dripping down his back, soaking into his shirt. His being here was no accident, he knew it now. 'I suppose it is possible Man will find other heroes, Zaru. Other leaders. But on a small scale only. Man's Royal Houses were symbols of his power. But in destroying them we have cut off their heads. Taken away their sword arms. You think otherwise, Zaru?'

'Possibly,' said Auganzar, almost dismissively, though it was no comfort to Gannorzol. Auganzar turned as one of the warriors from the arena entered, bowed and set down the armour and the magnetic shield. He left as quickly as he had come.

Auganzar picked up the breast plate and tossed it across to Gannorzol, who caught it deftly and examined it. It was polished, unblemished, as if new.

'Try the shield,' said Auganzar, this time handing it to Gannorzol.

The latter took it, surprised at its lightness. He found the stud that activated its magnetic field, listening to its hum as he pressed it. Yet the real significance of this shield still eluded him.

Auganzar crossed the room silently to a large chest, which he opened. From this he took yet another sword, pulling it from its priceless, ornate scabbard and weighing

166

it as gently as he would have weighed a fragile ornament. He made several passes in the air with it, simple, basic movements which flowed with the twists of his arm and wrist in a fashion that made an art of what he did. He walked across to Gannorzol, whose face had become a sheen of sweat. Surprisingly, worryingly, neither Auganzar nor Vorenzar had commented on this.

'A simple demonstration,' said Auganzar. He waited for Gannorzol to stand clear of the table.

Surely he has not brought me here to kill me, Gannorzol thought. Not here in the privacy of his own home!

'Defend yourself,' said Auganzar, smiling.

Moments later the sword was stabbing out, then cutting, twisting and coming back at Gannorzol in a blur of movement. But he was an excellent warrior himself and in a while his instincts took over and he used the shield to good effect.

'Turn the shield on,' said Vorenzar. 'Otherwise he will draw blood, Zolutar.'

Gannorzol did so, weaving to avoid his opponent. Then the inevitable occurred: the sword was caught fast by the magnetic field and locked with the shield. Gannorzol wrenched it free of Auganzar's grip, and the latter stood back, nodding with approval.

'Effective, is it not?' he said.

'Indeed,' said Gannorzol, relieved. Perhaps he had been too cautious. It had, after all, been a simple demonstration.

Auganzar reached for the sword haft, and Gannorzol was about to relinquish it, but the sword came free of the shield grip. He had not switched off the field and looked at the weapon in surprise.

'This particular sword,' said Auganzar, 'counters the effects of the shield. And it has other interesting properties.' Before Gannorzol knew what was happening, the sword point reached out and touched him on the side of the face. He felt an instant stab of excruciating pain and staggered sideways as if he had been dealt a blow. He dropped into one of the chairs, gazing up, his mouth open.

Vorenzar was looking at him curiously, but he had not moved.

'But – what is it?' gasped Gannorzol.

'An electrical charge,' said Auganzar. 'Quite painful, I believe.'

Gannorzol rubbed at his cheek. 'That is so, Zaru.'

Auganzar carefully resheathed his blade and set it down before him, unmoved by the discomfort of his guest. 'Such a weapon has many uses. It would be possible to inflict a long and exceptionally agonising death on an opponent with it, if one so chose to do.'

'Torture, Zaru?' said Gannorzol. 'But surely a Csendook warrior would not use such a device, either in battle, or in the games.'

'It is interesting, Zolutar,' said Vorenzar, 'that you keep mentioning battle. The Crusade being over. Surely there are to be no more battles.'

'Unless you know something that I do not, Zolutar,' said Auganzar, laughing softly.

The words were like the icy stab of steel in Gannorzol's gut. At last he realised the full extent of his predicament. His life hung in the balance here, he understood that now.

'However,' Auganzar went on, in a seemingly friendly way, though Gannorzol knew that he was twisting that cold steel in his belly, 'you are probably a party to all manner of knowledge.'

'Zaru,' Gannorzol protested modestly, 'I am merely a Zolutar, little better than a Zemok.'

Vorenzar reached over to a small table and picked up a sheaf of documents there. 'You may be a mere Zolutar, Gannorzol, but you are an extremely highly paid one.'

'Zaru, I like to think that I have earned my rewards in battle – '

'I am certain that you did,' said Auganzar. 'But that is not what the noble Zaru had in mind.'

'No,' said Vorenzar. 'I was just looking through your assets, Zaru. You do seem to have acquired a remarkable amount of land here in the Warhive. In fact, forgive me, but your wealth barely falls short of that of the Garazenda.'

'With great respect, Zaru, you exaggerate,' said Gannorzol, his stomach twisting. They could not know! *They could not.*

Vorenzar dropped the report on the table between them, but Gannorzol made no move to pick it up. It was bluff. It must be. They could not have had access to his private affairs, his wealth. The Garazenda would have been far more careful. They would have covered their tracks. Even someone as powerful as the Supreme Sanguinary could not have uncovered them. After all, he was their servant!

'You must have performed a remarkable service to have earned such wealth, Zolutar,' said Vorenzar.

'Which again begs the question, what is it that you know, Gannorzol, that I do not?' Auganzar repeated, leaning forward, his face hardening, the deadly chill of his anger barely concealed behind its mask.

Gannorzol tore his gaze away. 'I have nothing to say.'

Auganzar did not move for several moments. Then he drew back. 'No. I quite understand. You have your loyalty to think of, as I would expect of a good Csendook. Your military record is excellent. One to be proud of, Zolutar.'

Gannorzol glanced at him. 'I can say nothing, Zaru.'

Auganzar rose and walked calmly across the room as though the conversation had never taken place. Beyond him was a curved expanse of glass and through it he could see a stretch of land that had been meticulously landscaped, rich in shrubs and trees, one of his few pleasures in life. He opened the window section and walked out on to the balcony that overlooked his estate. In the distance he could hear voices, children at play, and the laughter of the women who tended them. They were in one of the gardens on a lawn.

'I am a warrior,' he said, his voice carrying back to them. 'Thus I can appreciate peace. What could be more peaceful than these estates? No one could be unhappy in such a place.'

169

Vorenzar rose and indicated that Gannorzol should go with him out on to the balcony. He did so, his throat constricting. His ordeal had not even begun, he was sure of it.

Auganzar pointed to the garden, its rich hues and banks of bloom. 'Those people are enjoying my hospitality. They reward me with their great pleasure. Could anything be more satisfying? I am not, as you may know, mated myself, although I have a number of offspring. But it pleases me to see the families of others appreciating the beauty of my gardens, the joy of their simple blooms.'

Gannorzol's look of puzzlement suddenly fell from his face to be replaced by one of horror. It was his own mate out there, his children.

'Quite a family occasion,' said Vorenzar. 'Three generations at least.'

Gannorzol shuddered as the coldness of complete terror took him. His *entire* family. 'How did you get them here?' he said, his voice a rasp.

'Most Csendook consider it an honour to be invited to the estate of the Supreme Sanguinary. Your own family was no exception, particularly as they were all told you would be here to meet them later, having been honoured yet again for your excellent services.' Auganzar did not look at him as he spoke, smiling instead at the people in the distance.

After a while he turned his back and went indoors, waiting for Vorenzar and Gannorzol to join him. He closed the window, shutting out the distant happy screams and laughter, which had somehow become that much more acute. By the table he stopped, picking up the scabbard and returning it to its chest. He closed the lid.

'I don't expect to have to use such a weapon again, not here,' he said, sitting down. He seemed again to be without emotion.

Gannorzol remained standing. What did Auganzar already know? If he knew the truth and wanted it confirmed, he dare not speak. But if Auganzar had only a part of it,

170

then the real truth could yet be hidden, as the Garazenda wished.

'What do you want of me, Zaru?' he asked.

'Sit down.'

Gannorzol did so, though Vorenzar remained on his feet, intimidating.

'I think we can be sensible about this,' Auganzar went on. 'Vorenzar, would you be good enough to ask my servants to provide us with some food and perhaps something to drink.'

'Of course, Zaru,' nodded Vorenzar, in a moment gone.

'I have a particular duty to perform,' said Auganzar, interlocking his fingers, his elbows on the table. 'Man is still an embarrassment to us. The Garazenda are not in favour of continuing the war, which would, I agree, be a guerrilla war. It has been like that for five years anyway, and such wars are not good for morale. And such wars never end.'

Gannorzol nodded, waiting.

'Enslaving Man, turning him into a stock-pen animal, breeding him for the Games and for the Hunt, that is all very well. It has been going on unofficially for many years. I have my own human slaves and gladiators, and I've no doubt that's one of the reasons why I was chosen as Supreme Sanguinary. But it is not a post that many of my colleagues envy.'

Again Gannorzol was not drawn to reply.

'I think that, given time, the enslavement of Man will be the answer. There may be a spirit of rebellion in him, but as a subjugated race, that will wither. With a new purpose, Man can be an excellent servant.'

Gannorzol nodded slowly. If Auganzar accepted all this, why should he have arranged the events of the day?

'But all this relies on one thing. The successful subjugation of Man. The destruction of his leaders.' Auganzar sat back. He looked up at the curved ceiling, for a moment appearing to study the dramatic reliefs there, the bright battle scenes. 'Tell me,' he said almost casually, 'you were

171

involved, were you not, in the pursuit of the Imperator Elect?'

'I was.'

'You had a particular role?'

'I was, as you are surely aware, Zaru, Zolutar in command of the main pursuit Swarm.'

'Yes, I've read the reports with great interest. I have them all. You understand my keen interest in the Imperator Elect. As a potential rallying point for Mankind, he could hinder my work.'

'But, Zaru, he is dead.'

'So the reports say. You yourself have been most specific.'

'I have provided the Garazenda with every detail available to me,' nodded Gannorzol. 'There are no secrets. The conclusions are public knowledge.'

'And yet you seem uneasy,' Auganzar smiled.

'Why should I be, Zaru?'

'Quite. Tell me about it again. What happened to the Imperator Elect?'

'My Swarm had pursued him through a number of Paths and gates until we had him and his principals closed in, in the world of Eannor. There was no way they could have escaped us. Their armies had been reduced, and they had little technology to sustain them.'

'Were their forces vast?'

'Vast, Zaru?'

'I find it strange that such an important gathering should be so poorly protected. Had it been a Garazenda of the Csendook defending a world, I would have expected the human equivalent of a dozen Swarms, a huge force. But the Imperator Elect, or rather his Prime Consul, had seen fit to provide him with a minimum of defenders. Why do you think that was?'

Gannorzol frowned. 'Zaru, I did not think too much of it at the time. The war raged in several places, through many gates. I assumed it was poor organisation.'

'Not typical of our enemies,' said Auganzar coolly. 'And

172

not at all typical of Zellorian. He is no fool. He had a reason, I am sure.'

'Then it was of no use to him, Zaru. It did not save him.'

'What happened?'

'There were reports that Zellorian used sorcery and evil powers. But it was quite clear to me and my warriors that this was a pathetic attempt by the defenders of Eannor to scare us away.'

'You do not believe in this kind of power?'

Gannorzol was genuinely shocked by the question. 'But of course not, Zaru. How could such a thing exist? Sorcery? No sane Csendook would – '

'Accept such a thing? I agree. An abhorrent idea to us. But there was a release of energy, a discharge of power?'

'Whatever Zellorian attempted to do, it fell about his ears, Zaru. Eannor was ripped asunder by it and a good many of our Zemoks lost their lives.'

'A total disaster? With the Imperator Elect and all his most valuable servants destroyed.'

'Exactly, Zaru. We were lucky to escape. Had we been closer in, the entire Swarm would have been annihilated.'

'You saw the devastation?'

'I never got too close to it. Even now Eannor is dangerous. But we saw enough evidence to show us that nothing could have lived through it. Not only had they destroyed themselves, but Eannor is uninhabitable, the gateway to it closed.'

'The reports are interesting. I notice that all the reports on Eannor have been channelled through yourself.'

'I have been charged by the Garazenda to coordinate them.'

'And to vet them?'

Gannorzol frowned more deeply. The terror was still within him: he heard in his mind the laughter of his family. It was with difficulty that he kept his eyes from the windows. 'I suppose so, yes, Zaru.'

'Do you have copies of all reports?'

'No, Zaru, they go straight to the Garazenda.'

'You do not find it necessary to revise any and forward fresh ones?'

'No, Zaru, I do not.'

'I see. But all reports comply? Eannor is dead, uninhabitable?'

'Yes, Zaru. As I have said, the gate is closed. No one goes there. It is effectively removed from the Circle of worlds. Whatever Zellorian did, it released unprecedented power.'

Vorenzar returned, taking his seat with a nod to Auganzar that again made Gannorzol's blood run cold.

'Ah,' said Auganzar. 'A little food, I think.'

Vorenzar tapped on a small gong that rested beside him and it sounded musically. Moments later a Zemok arrived, bearing a silver tray and some dishes. He set it down on the table and stood stiffly to attention.

'Thank you,' Auganzar told him, and the Zemok left expressionlessly. Auganzar bent forward and lifted the curved lid of one of the dishes. Something steamed beneath it. 'Please, help yourself.'

Gannorzol gaped at what was revealed, unable to speak. Vorenzar watched his face, fascinated by the sheer horror there. On the platter there was a heart, neatly sliced from within its living chest, the blood thick about it as though it had been used to baste this delicacy.

Auganzar closed the lid of the dish, shutting the repulsive object from view as if it offended him.

Gannorzol shrank back, the shadows closing in. He dare not ask whose heart it was. But it had been Csendook, larger than a Man's. He had seen enough of both to know.

'What really happened on Eannor?' said Auganzar, all humour gone from his eyes. There was no mercy there now, only the driving, relentless will that his warriors knew and feared.

'They'll kill me,' Gannorzol breathed helplessly.

'They won't know,' said Vorenzar, leaning forward as if in sympathy.

'What happened?' repeated Auganzar.

174

Something broke within Gannorzol. He straightened up, closing his eyes. 'I do not believe in sorcery. But Zellorian must have performed some kind of ritual of power. Of sacrifice. Call it sorcery, what you will. And there was a release of power. It was as though a vortex had opened up in the very fabric of the sky. A nightmare.'

'A vortex?' repeated Auganzar.

'Yes, Zaru. Like a vent. A cyclone. Such a storm!'

'A gate?' said Vorenzar.

'Not as we know them. Not like the Pathways.'

'Go on,' prompted Auganzar.

'The winds rose up such as we had never seen them. They wrought havoc. Many died. A rain of blood. Eannor plunged into darkness and we thought it would burst asunder.'

'But you survived,' said Vorenzar.

'Some of us,' said Gannorzol, shaking his head. 'A few.'

'And?'

'I've been there since. I've seen the so-called uninhabitable world.'

'So have I,' said Vorenzar.

Gannorzol stared at him incredulously. 'You have?'

'As you say, it's a wasteland,' said Vorenzar. 'But habitable. And suitable for cultivating. Quite unlike the world you describe in your reports.' He tapped the papers.

Auganzar stood up. 'So where are they?' he asked, though the question was directed at no one in particular.

'They could not have survived,' said Gannorzol.

Auganzar swung round to him. 'That is the official line. It suits the Garazenda to perpetuate this myth in order that the Crusade remains at an end. And it is a mistake, Zolutar. The Imperator Elect is alive. But where?'

'We have scoured Eannor for a year,' said Gannorzol. 'But there is no trace, and no Pathway.'

Auganzar nodded. 'Alive,' he murmured, striding to the window. 'Then I will find him. And Zellorian. And I will put *their* hearts on a platter for the Garazenda who have denied his existence.'

Gannorzol stared wretchedly at the platter containing the heart. 'Whose?' Vorenzar heard him whisper.

The Zaru smiled unpleasantly. 'It belonged to a Zemok who died in the arena earlier today. Unfortunately he left himself unguarded. He met an opponent who was quite ruthless, quite without mercy.' And he glanced meaningfully at Auganzar, who appeared to be preoccupied with his thoughts, the other Csendook in the chamber forgotten.

13

THE WINDWRAITHS

Armestor was the first to hear it. He was bringing up the rear of the trio as they wound through a narrow cleft at the upper reaches of one of the tributaries of the river that had been their night guide northwards. Armestor hissed for them to halt and they pulled up, their anxious faces peering back at him.

'What is it?' called Ussemitus softly. The forest was deeply silent, the only sound he could hear the splash of the stream on the rocks.

'I can't hear a thing,' murmured Fomond.

'Then something's wrong,' said Ussemitus. 'The forest is never this silent. What did you hear, Armestor?'

'The wind. Listen.' Armestor stretched up on his horse, cocking an ear back towards the direction from which they had come. 'Yes!'

Now they all caught the strains of distant sound, like wild music or the whining of animals, though distorted.

'Beasts of the storm?' said Fomond.

Armestor looked appalled. 'You imagine things.'

Ussemitus waited for only a moment, then, his own face pale, turned his steed to the north again. 'We'd better move on quickly. We need shelter, and this is no place to be caught.'

They moved on as swiftly as they dared, afraid that their mounts would snap a leg in this difficult terrain, but Ussemitus's warning goaded them on. Behind them they could hear the wind intensifying in power, its moan and whine mocking their efforts to escape it. No natural storm moved as fast, nor did it speak with such a rasping voice.

Up through the defile they went. To their right was an open slope that led up to a number of rocky outcrops, the last place they would find shelter. To their left the ground dropped away steeply into the trees, and they dismounted and pulled their horses down with them, sliding and almost tumbling in their haste. The horses were aware of the oncoming wind, their eyes wide, their flanks shaking as if they knew more than their masters, their fear obvious.

'A sending,' said Fomond. 'Kuraal has discovered our escape.'

Ussemitus nodded, but said nothing. Under the trees again, they moved on, the darkness closing around them. The undergrowth was minimal so they were able to press on quickly, though it was almost impossible to see what was ahead of them. This part of the forest was strange to them, its paths unknown.

When they stopped, in another dip, the trees were all about them, looming like giants, their canopy thicker than the night, shielding them as though they were in a cave. They tied up their horses, soothing them as best they could, though the beasts looked as if some strange power had already whispered to them of dire things to come. The youths then pressed themselves up against a large tree bole, moulding themselves to its contours, hardly able to see each other. A wall of darkness spread before them.

'We can't go north until this storm passes,' whispered Ussemitus, as if he feared the trees were listening.

'We'd better wait until morning if we want to move on through the forest,' suggested Fomond.

They knew the forest land well enough, but equally they knew the dangers of trying to travel through the trees by night. In silence they waited for the storm, none of them wishing to speak aloud his fears. Ussemitus wondered about Arbos. Was he, too, holed up safely?

The storm came with frightening speed. High above them the tree tops shook, the wind howling. The listeners felt the trunk of the tree shudder as though alive, touched by something repugnant to it.

'Pray to the forest,' said Ussemitus. 'It may protect us.'

Overhead the wind roared, the sound of a hundred

shrieking voices, winged beings trying to beat away through the thick foliage. It shook, rustling, boughs snapping, larger ones creaking as if trying to repel an army. The noise grew horribly in volume, the wind racing through the forest, whipping up fallen twigs and leaves, eddying and swirling. Ussemitus and the others pressed their hands tight to their ears, trying to shut out the sounds of fury, but they persisted.

The darkness was alive, as if the wind had taken on material form. But the full anger of the storm could not breach the canopy of the branches above, which formed a determined barrier, as if the gods of the forest objected to this violent intrusion. The gusts that shrieked around the trunks, buffeting the three runaways, were strong but nothing to what tore across the heavens above them, clawing with grim power at the trees beneath.

Armestor shrank down, making a ball of himself, looking through his fingers into the dark madness before him, seeing in it twisted forms, raking hands, wild faces pulled out of shape by screaming mouths, though he told himself it was illusion, the power of the wind. Was it a live thing? Could the Windmaster really conjure demons from it? In this cold place, it seemed so, and he began to cry out.

Ussemitus felt the weight of the power above, hearing the rage of its frustration, and he could imagine the lunatic faces, the talons trying to tear aside the trees. But they held. If the forest gods had heard his prayers, they were merciful. His reason told him that Kuraal's sending was evil, an abuse of his powers. Innasmorn did not treat her children this way. And the forest was also affronted by such perversion of power.

Ussemitus tugged at Fomond's arm. 'We can't stay here,' he shouted. 'It'll mean madness.'

Fomond nodded, bending down to pull Armestor to his feet. Their eyes were almost closed against the stinging wind and the danger of being blinded by one of the many sticks whipping past.

As they moved from the safety of the tree trunk towards

the horses, bent over by their efforts, the first of the steeds reared up, hooves flying, and ripped its rein from the branch that had secured it. With another whinny of terror, the horse bolted back towards the slopes that led out of the trees. Then the other horses had pulled themselves free, their terror sheer. It was too late to stop them. As Fomond groped for a trailing rein, the wind caught him and punched him over.

They could hear the tearing sounds overhead as if great claws were intent on smashing their way down to them. Somewhere beyond them they heard a tree groan, toppling and crashing through its fellows like a warrior felled in battle. Others were falling deeper in the forest.

Ussemitus pointed beyond into the darkness and together they hunched up and moved as quickly as they could. They struggled on for a long time, almost blind, and still the wind whipped about them, their hands torn and bleeding, clothes ripped. They could hear a distinct snarling now, a wild, demonic sound, the heart of the storm, the unleashing of aerial hounds, which redoubled their efforts to plunge down into the trees to fasten on their prey.

Although the youths' strength began to ebb, worn away by the constant buffeting, the power of the storm did not diminish. If anything it grew, mounting as it sucked more and more of the raw elements into it. The three figures moved very slowly, and now there was a new element to their dilemma: the cold. It was seeping into them, dragging at their strength, sapping it.

Armestor was the first of them to fall, collapsing, burying his head in his hands, curling up like a child. Fomond and Ussemitus tugged at him, pulling him along, though they all felt exhausted. Usemitus could barely see. He was trying to find a suitable tree at which to make a stand. He turned, the ground abruptly moving like a live thing, and toppled forward, hands flinging out, groping uselessly at leaves. He hit something soft and earthy, rolled over and landed on his back. In a moment he caught a glimpse of something dark above him, then he was struck in the face and chest as the dark closed in.

It was a while before he opened his eyes again. The darkness seemed to have congealed. Overhead he could still hear the persistence of the storm, howling, raving, beating frantically at the trees, its rage murderous. He rolled over, straight into one of his companions.

'Fomond?' he called, his voice a croak.

'Armestor,' was the faint reply. 'But Fomond is here.'

'We fell—?'

'The earth collapsed. Tree roots,' said Armestor, hazarding a guess.

'Perhaps the forest heard us,' came Fomond's voice. 'I can tell you I was praying pretty hard!'

'Are you all right, Armestor?'

'He'll live,' rejoined Fomond. 'Like us, he's worn out. Gods, that wind! Like an army of madmen.'

'Will it ever give up?' said Armestor. 'Listen to it!'

'Windwraiths,' said Fomond. 'So they are real.'

'We dare not go back up there,' said Ussemitus, trying to peer into the darkness, but only the vaguest of shapes were visible.

'I could sleep for a week,' said Armestor.

'Yes, and never wake up,' said Fomond. 'No, that's too dangerous. We have to move on, somehow.'

'The windwraiths will tear their way down into the forest eventually,' said Ussemitus. 'We have to get as far from them as we can.'

Fomond had started to move around in the dark, like some animal in its lair. Armestor struggled to sit up.

'Anything broken?' Ussemitus asked him, but he grunted a negative.

'We're in some sort of natural channel,' said Fomond. 'Almost like a tunnel. I can't smell anything animal, so I don't think it's inhabited. Shall we see if we can move along it?'

There was no other choice. Armestor appeared to have recovered some of his strength, and in a while the three youths moved ahead on all fours, winding through the narrow gully. Above them its sides closed in, though the wind yet tore through the trees, and high above it the snarling of the invisible windwraiths went on unabated.

As they moved on, agonisingly slowly, they at least had the satisfaction of getting out of the wind and its cold. The worst of it did not reach down to this channel, and some of their body warmth returned. The darkness closed up so that they could see absolutely nothing, guided by their hands, the rich smell of the earth a blessing. No one spoke for an hour, but they knew they were close together, aware of each others' bodies as they crawled on.

Eventually, unable to go further because of the tightness of the walls, they huddled up as one and allowed sleep to claim them.

When they woke, a faint stream of light behind them showed them that they had crawled into a fissure in the earth, its sides supported by thick roots that seemed to have prized it open for them like huge hands. The wind yet howled on incessantly outside, dust and leaves dancing. They opened their provisions and ate what they could spare.

'How far have we come?' said Armestor, his face drawn.

'Far enough, I hope,' said Ussemitus, 'to get away from the centre of the hunt. The windwraiths are still above the forest, worrying at it like hounds at a bone.'

'Can we elude them?' said Armestor, his own doubts clear.

'There may be a way,' nodded Ussemitus. 'Kuraal sent them, of that I am sure. He knows we are heading north to the mountains. If we branch away to the west–'

'But the lands are full of terrors there,' protested Armestor, eyes widening in the light. 'There are tales of strange beings–'

'In the remote west, maybe,' said Ussemitus. 'Yet we've not come far. We dare not go north. The windwraiths will be waiting.'

'What about the horses?' said Armestor.

Fomond put a hand on his shoulder. 'Already dead for certain, my friend. They left the forest, fearing its darkness. The windwraiths will have taken them. They'll not be seen again.'

They fell silent in recognition of the truth of Fomond's words, but at last resigned themselves to the journey west. The tunnel which they were in stretched like a river gulley this way and that, jagged as lightning, and a branch of it moved, as if by coincidence, to the west. Although they could still hear the wind above, the madness of the storm decreased as they went on, the search concentrated, it seemed, on the area where they had gone to ground.

Eventually the gully ended, rising sharply upwards. The air beyond was not still, but it was not as gusty as the air they had left in the night. Ussemitus clambered up and gazed about at the forest floor. It was thicker with vegetation here, light creating a mottled effect as the rising sun penetrated the high branches.

Like worms they crawled through the bushes, using their wooden knives to cut a passage in places. When at last they were able to stand, under some low boughs, they listened to the wind in the distance. They had come several miles.

'Kuraal cannot control the windwraiths all day, can he?' said Armestor.

'I doubt if even he can do that,' said Fomond. 'But he may well keep trying.'

'One day is all we need,' said Ussemitus. 'If we travel quickly.'

'I could do with some water,' said Armestor. 'Otherwise I'm fine. I owe you two my life,' he added, with an embarrassed grin.

'Nonsense!' laughed Fomond. 'We're all lucky to be alive.'

'It's the forest we should thank,' said Ussemitus, and the others saw a strange look in his eye, as though in some way he had communicated with the vast stretches of trees about them. 'The forest knows that what has been sent is evil. The Windmaster has no right to take the raw power of Innasmorn and bend it in such a way. It is not how Innasmorn would treat her children.'

Fomond frowned. 'No, you are right. Perhaps the Mother spoke to the forest for us, intervening.'

Ussemitus glanced at him, as if he had struck upon a deep, vital truth. 'Yes.' He looked away again, thoughtful for a moment, but then stirring himself. 'Well, we do thank the forest. And we must keep our wits about us in these parts.'

In better spirits they moved on, still cautious, using the undergrowth to mask their progress. They found a stream and drank thirstily, and Armestor used his uncanny skill as a bowman to bring down two rabbits. But Ussemitus would not allow them to cook them.

'Eat them raw, or wait another day to cook them,' he said. 'Smoke will carry on the wind.' Neither of the others argued seriously, though they both grunted their disappointment.

All that day they travelled, moving westwards as Ussemitus had suggested. They were deep in the forest, but in lands with which they were not familiar. Such tales as there were about them, Ussemitus said were put about by the hunters, jealous of their hunting territories. But there were no hunters' trackways here, and for all they knew, the forests had not been visited by their people before. Ussemitus was anxious that they should turn northwards eventually, knowing that the promised rendezvous with Aru and her people must not be missed, but at the same time he dare not get caught by the windwraiths. All hint of the storm had gone, but he knew it would come again as Kuraal attempted to find their scent.

The following day they were enjoying cooked meat, their spirits high, feeling safer as there was no further suggestion of a storm. Armestor was watching the forest around them, keeping a lookout as they could never be sure the lands were uninhabited. A silence had settled on the trees, and Armestor felt his stomach knot as he thought of the silence that had preceded the storm. Yet he was sure there would be no storm here. The sky was cloudless and there was no wind.

Something moved among the trees, up on a ridge, a flash of colour. A bird? He thought not. He moved from his post, keeping low to the ground. Fifty yards on he hid behind a boulder and looked beyond it. To his amazement he saw men approaching, but such strange people! They were almost naked, their brown skins daubed with bright scarlet and orange paint, their long hair tied with feathers of equally gaudy hues. Round their necks they wore necklaces made up of small bones, and in their hands they carried sharp weapons, also made from bone, while others carried bone clubs. They looked to Armestor as though they went armed not for the hunt, but for war.

Armestor turned, about to dash back to the camp, only to find himself surrounded by a dozen more of the warriors. All carried short spears, the points of which were levelled at his chest.

Their spokesman came forward and said something harsh, but Armestor could not understand. He replied in his own tongue, but the bone warrior merely grunted dismissively. His men jabbed at Armestor and he had no alternative but to march, terrified for his companions.

The warriors led him up a rough-cut pathway to the ridge, and among its many boulders they forced him to his knees. He tried to reason with them, but they took the wind from his body by thumping their spear butts into him.

To his horror, a short time later he saw Ussemitus and Fomond being brought up to join him. There were at least fifty of the bone warriors here now, and they moved like spectres through the forest.

'Forgive me,' breathed Armestor as Ussemitus was forced to kneel beside him.

'No, we were all careless. And these people move like cats,' Ussemitus said, but an immediate cuff across the head almost sent him to the ground.

Fomond snarled something, but three spear points

jabbed at his chest. The three youths were forced to wait, knowing that a single wrong move would mean death at the hands of these savages.

'Who are they?' Fomond asked Ussemitus softly when the bone warriors seemed to be ignoring them, preparing to turn this hilltop into what seemed to be a camp.

'I've heard the same tales as you,' whispered Ussemitus. 'Hunters' yarns about wild men of the forest. Primitives. Everything is made from bone.'

Armestor had gone white. 'We are exposed here,' he gasped. 'If a storm should come—'

But the others did not answer him. Instead they watched the bone warriors as they moved some of the larger boulders, ringing the hilltop, scooping out other parts of it. They brought heaps of brushwood and after a while ignited it. They later brought freshly cut stakes and sharpened them, digging them into the ground before sharpening the top ends.

Ussemitus felt the crawling horror of knowing what they intended, but he did not share it with his companions. Fomond's face was expressionless, but Armestor had shut his eyes tightly, his lips moving in a constant stream of prayer.

For hours she had flown the gliderboat out over the mountains, still numbed by what she had seen back in the Sculpted City on the rooftops. For all her years of bitterness, her loathing of her father, she had felt an agony of remorse at seeing him fling himself from the roof to save her. In that one act of sacrifice he had wiped away the years of suffering, the contempt, and for a moment she had seen him as he had once been, a father whom she had loved, a man not weakened by his passion for the mother she could not even remember, who had died when she was an infant. But it had come too late. And Mannaston would not have survived that leap.

The long hours of night had worn her down; she had

cried, finding it doubly hard to control her craft, which sensed her mental anguish and was confused by it. She had to use her skill at controlling to shut out her pain, and only the fear of losing control of the gliderboat, crashing it into one of the countless rock walls, kept her aloft. She had taken the gliderboat in a direct line into the mountains, pushing it to maximum speed, though it had protested. Her eyes were blurred by tears at first, and if there was a pursuit, she had given it no thought. There was only sorrow to engulf her, that and a vacuum beyond. They were all gone now, her knights, her friends, her family. The Sculpted City had nothing more to give her, unless it could be a target for her fury.

The day died again, but still she flew on, through the night towards another dawn. Locked at the controls, ignoring the anxiety of the gliderboat, she had no intention of stopping. Her past was dead, her hopes with it. Denandys and his loyal knights, who fought the corruption of that riddled city, were dead. The future was like a wall. Let her hit it. Let Innasmorn claw her from the sky as she had done to the other craft. Ussemitus and his people she had almost forgotten.

It was the wind that brought her out of her reverie. Shaking herself, she took her first proper look at the landscape below. She was passing the last of the mountains, heading out over a vast stretch of green forest. But the winds were growing in strength, whining about her like dogs, and for a moment she thought she had caught a trace of wild laughter in them, a flash of face. She ought to rest; the journey had exhausted her mind, and the craft sensed it, again anxious for its own safety. But where could she land? Down in the forest? There was nowhere safe there to land a gliderboat.

Another gust of wind shook the craft and she was forced to adjust its flight as it dropped. She could feel the terror growing in it, and it served to snap her out of her own self-pity. Again the winds gathered, laughing at her efforts.

Innasmorn, she thought. Mother of Storms. Are these your children?

There was no spoken answer, but now she was convinced that something was wrong. The air took on form, a fist, a swirl of energy that indeed seemed intent on hostility. Something flew by her head, shrieking, demonic.

Hallucinations, her mind told her. But the gliderboat veered dangerously, shaken as a child might have been. She had to struggle with it to keep it from stalling, bringing its nose up into yet another buffet of wind.

Again she dived down, suddenly finding herself just above the level of the trees, avoiding a crash by mere feet. The gliderboat levelled out but was becoming increasingly difficult to control, her emotions twisted out of true by this strange storm. She would have to land. The danger was that she might have to make it a crash landing, and the gliderboat knew it. It would be disastrous.

With a great effort she calmed herself and brought the nose of the craft up and began to gain height, though the anger of the wind slapped at her, its invisible hands turning to claws. The gliderboat rolled and she clung on, cursing aloud. Another twist righted the craft and she had to force it upward fiercely to avoid trees. Beyond her there were ridges and low hills poking up from the sea of green, but they, too, were tree-lined and where there were any open areas they were peppered with large boulders.

The bone warriors were calmly watching the skies, their attention hooked by the sudden squall that had blown up.

Armestor's face was glistening with sweat. 'The windwraiths?'

'I can't tell,' said Ussemitus.

'These apes don't seem ready to flee,' said Fomond. 'Do they worship the winds? If they do, they'll get a shock.' But a jab in the back from one of the guards' spears made him wince and he fell silent.

A huge gust of wind swirled about the hill like a wave

breaking, though as yet the prisoners could see no evidence of the windwraiths. This could be just a local squall. The bone warriors raised their weapons skyward, calling out their approval. Whatever rites they were intent on performing, they wanted the wind gods to witness them.

'There's something in the sky!' called Armestor. 'I cannot see what it is.'

Ussemitus followed his line of vision and he, too, caught a glimpse of a dark object, spinning and shooting forward, like a smooth branch caught in the fast flow of a stream. Something about it was familiar, but he could not be sure. As it came closer, the bone warriors saw it and danced up and down as though their gods had sent them a visitation.

The wind screamed about the hill top, the trees below it bending to its voice, and the gliderboat came racing in, straight past, but banking, returning in a wide curve. The bone warriors fell to their faces, all of them, making sounds of obeisance.

Armestor and Fomond stared in wide-eyed amazement, but Ussemitus was grinning. 'It's one of the craft used by Aru's people! She said it could fly. See! Someone is inside it.'

Fomond gazed at it as if dreaming. 'Are they controlling it?'

'The wind is trying to bring it down,' said Ussemitus. It was true, for Aru was desperately trying to master the craft. She had seen figures on the hill and banked again, slowly forcing the gliderboat in, hoping for a landing.

Ussemitus snatched up a fallen spear. 'Run! While these fools are praying, get clear of the hill. Unless you want to end up in their bellies!'

The others obeyed him at once, for the bone warriors would not move from their supine positions while the gliderboat circled. Ussemitus led his fellows down the slope, then watched as the gliderboat suddenly dipped. It was going to hit the hill unless its pilot could do something to avert a crash.

As the three youths ran for the trees, they caught a

glimpse of someone leaping from the spinning craft over-head, a body plummeting down into the uppermost branches of the trees beyond them. The gliderboat shot downwards and hit the side of the hill with a deafening roar. Earth and stone flew skywards to embrace the winds, and the gale roared as if in triumph. Within moments it had raced away as if satisfied with its kill.

There were screams from the top of the hill, and several stones rolled downward, moved by the explosion. Usse-mitus and his companions held their spears ready for an attack, expecting to be pursued, but they were not.

Armestor pointed to the trees where the pilot had fallen. They could hear branches snapping. Ussemitus raced forward to investigate.

'I wonder if these warriors have horses,' said Fomond.

'I think not,' said Armestor glumly. 'They're deep forest dwellers.'

'The craft in the sky,' mused Fomond, anxiously looking to see where Ussemitus had gone. 'It must have been destroyed.'

'We must get away at once,' nodded Armestor furiously. 'Either it's killed the bone warriors, or some of them must still be prone. Others may come. What is Ussemitus think-ing of! We must flee!'

They found a rough pathway that seemed to lead west-wards, but waited for Ussemitus. In the sudden silence that seemed to have closed in, they heard a distant groan, a deep murmur of pain, and stared at each other, confused by it.

'What beast is that?' said Fomond.

But before Armestor could reply, Ussemitus staggered out of the trees with a woman in his arms, helping her to walk. She was obviously shaken badly, though her legs had not been broken by the fall.

'It's the girl!' gasped Fomond. 'Aru, the girl from the city of the intruders.'

Armestor gaped as Ussemitus guided her to them.

'Was that her cry of agony?' said Fomond, though he guessed it could not have been.

Ussemitus looked up sharply. 'You heard it, too?'

Fomond and Armestor nodded, their faces troubled.

'The craft,' Ussemitus said softly.

The girl looked up groggily, but managed a smile. 'Ussemitus?' she said, but collapsed before she could say anything else. Fomond helped Ussemitus bear her weight and together they carried the girl along the narrow path. Armestor brought up the rear, his face a mask of anxiety as he watched the hill for signs of pursuit, imagining an army of bone warriors rushing down upon them.

Gradually the forest swallowed them, and though they moved into its cool, silent embrace, they heard nothing more from the bone warriors. And if there were further sounds of pain from beyond them, they were blotted out by the verdure.

14

DISTANT POWERS

Aru was stretched out on a bed of leaves. Ussemitus was wiping her brow with a strip of shirt soaked in a nearby stream. They had been travelling away from the hill where the gliderboat had crashed for over an hour and in that time there had been no signs of pursuit. Here in this open glade they rested, Armestor and Fomond keeping a close watch on the surrounding forest.

'Aru,' whispered Ussemitus. They had had to carry her, as she had not regained consciousness, and they all marvelled that she had not been killed or seriously injured in her fall. The trees must have cushioned it, and they took this to be a good omen, a sign that the forest had looked on her with favour, as it had them.

The girl stirred at last and Fomond handed Ussemitus some broth he had been cooking on a small fire. The group was wary of using fire, but the girl needed something inside her. She opened her eyes dazedly, but was able to take some of the broth. In a while she sat, arms crossed over her knees, huddled up now like a child, a contrast to the commanding woman that they had first met at the foot of the mountains.

'The gliderboat,' she murmured.

'If you mean your craft,' said Ussemitus, 'it is no more.'

She looked at him, closing her eyes and shuddering. I had no time to share its pain, she thought. Though its terror at the end had been almost overwhelming.

Ussemitus felt a sudden urge to put an arm around her, to comfort her, but he glanced up at Fomond guiltily.

His friend grinned hugely. 'Kuraal would not approve,' he said with a wink.

Ussemitus did not respond. But he was pleased that

192

neither Fomond nor Armestor had objected to his bringing the girl with them.

She opened her eyes again. 'I'll have some more of that broth,' she said. 'It's good.' Once she had started on it, she ate avidly, and Fomond handed her some dried strips of meat.

'It's no banquet,' he said. 'But you'll have to get used to it.' He could see, however, that she was glad of the food, and bit into it as any Innasmornian girl of the forests would have.

'Where are we?' she said, chewing.

'In the forest lands,' Ussemitus told her. 'My companions and I owe you our lives. The bone warriors had taken us.'

'They were about to eat us, I suspect,' said Fomond.

'I saw the hill,' Aru recalled. 'And many painted men.'

'Your craft sent them to their bellies,' said Ussemitus. 'You came on the wind. They thought you its servant.'

She laughed gently, and it seemed to put strength into her. Ussemitus saw again the warrior. 'Goddess of the wind! But it was the wind that brought me down. It was like a wild thing, tearing at me. I could not control the gliderboat. I lost contact with it. You must have seen – '

'Contact?' said Fomond suspiciously.

Aru looked saddened. 'Yes. A Controller speaks to his or her craft.' She touched her head. 'Here. All I could feel was the gliderboat's terror. It had never been sure of me, and not confident.'

The youths looked at each other, puzzled by her words, but they thought better of asking more of this mystery. 'It was fortunate for us that you came,' said Ussemitus. 'Your fall won us our freedom. How are you feeling? Can you move your legs?'

She stood up groggily, using his arm to help her, nodding. His powerful grip surprised her. 'Stiff, but nothing's broken. And my head is pounding.'

'We'll have to move soon. We have to find a safe place for the night. The bone warriors may come again.'

'Are we near your own people? I must speak to them as soon as I can.'

Ussemitus shook his head. 'We will explain things to you as we go. But my friends and I are outcasts. Much has happened since we last met.'

She nodded sadly, in her eyes a distant look. 'And to me.'

Once she had moved about the glade, testing her limbs, assuring Ussemitus that she was able to walk in relative comfort, the party moved on towards the west. They talked a little, Ussemitus explaining what had happened in his village on his return. Fomond also commented, drawn to the girl by her openness, her anxiety to understand the Innasmornians. Armestor said little, preferring the role of scout, as though unsure of the girl, her foreignness. Her strength came back gradually, but Fomond understood that she was far hardier than he had realised, and well used to exertion and an existence that made her the equal of her fellow warriors.

By nightfall they were rising up out of the forest, an expanse of open moorland stretching before them. They decided to camp in the forest for the night and move on into the open in the morning. Selecting a group of trees, they quickly cut stakes and erected a platform above the ground on which they would be safe from any prowling predators, or bone warriors. They used foliage to disguise their hiding place and Aru was amazed at the speed and dexterity with which the Innasmornians worked. No one would have seen the platform from below, and yet it was as safe and secure as any house might have been. She threw herself into the work, using it to push from her mind the events in the Sculpted City, the death of Mannaston, and she was conscious of the eyes upon her, knowing that her new companions were surprised to see a woman displaying skill at woodcraft. But she sensed no resentment in them, although Armestor was wary of her, a nervous youth who seemed to hear disaster in every creaking twig. Still, it made him an invaluable guard.

They had eaten some time before building the refuge, anxious that if they had to make a fire it should be before darkness fell. Up on the platform they got as comfortable as they could, Armestor taking the first watch, higher up in the trees, though he seemed as at home there as on the ground.

'Your people are a mystery to us, Aru,' said Fomond, the most open of the three men. 'Where are you from? We have heard tales, rumours, most of them about how evil you are.' He chuckled, his face crinkling, his eyes sparkling even though the light was fast fading. 'The Windmasters say you are here to conquer and enslave us.'

She sighed, shaking her head. Warrior she may be, but there was no denying her beauty, Fomond and Ussemitus thought together. 'I should tell you something of the history of my people.'

Ussemitus watched her avidly, and Fomond tried not to grin, wondering if his friend could be developing a real infatuation for the dark haired girl. But his interest in her story wiped the thought away and he leaned forward to catch every word.

'I suppose it begins over two thousand years ago,' Aru began. 'With a war that has lasted all that time. It is why we are here. Not to conquer, but to escape. It is Man who is slowly being wiped out. Our enemy is bent on genocide.

'My people are not from Innasmorn. Our own circle of worlds is – well, in honesty I do not know where it is in relation to Innasmorn. It is part of the mystery I will try to unravel for you. I'm from another world, or chain of worlds, if you like, for in our Empire there are many such worlds. It is possible to travel between them easily, for there are Pathways, corridors which allow us to move freely.'

'I don't understand,' said Fomond.

'You see the moors above us. Imagine that there is a gateway built on top of one of them. By entering it you could emerge not on the moor, but far away, in the mountains.'

'But surely that is sorcery!' exclaimed Ussemitus.

Aru shook her head, smiling patiently. 'I don't understand such powers. They are in the keeping of certain men. But they exist. Although our worlds are separated by great distances, as Innasmorn if from its moon, still we were able to move between them. The gates were places of great power, their mysteries ancient but understood by the wisest of us. Our sorcerers, if you will.

'All those years ago, and no one knows the true history of it, Man stumbled through a gate into a world ruled by another species. A cruel, barbaric race which thrived on war and conquest. They were stronger and faster than Man, and it was the beginning of the great war. They were the Csendook, and they soon discovered the mysteries of the gates for themselves. The Empire came under threat. What had become a peaceful chain of worlds became a vast battleground, as Swarm upon Swarm (that's what they call their battle legions) came forth to make war.

'There was no mercy, no respite. And the Csendook do not understand peace or consultation. They mean to destroy Man utterly. And soon they would have achieved that goal.

'We have an overall ruler, the Imperator Elect, and his government is comprised of the Consulate, which controls the armies and all the worlds of Empire. Not long ago, the Consulate knew that defeat loomed very large. In a few years we would be no more. If the Imperator Elect fell, the Csendook would triumph. The last citadel of Man's rebellious spirit would be breached.'

As she spoke, Ussemitus looked up at the stars. It was a clear night, and he wondered what remote eyes fastened on this world. Fomond, too, glanced at the heavens.

'Our Prime Consul is called Zellorian. Like the mages of old, he is party to great knowledge, staggering power. He sought ways in which to escape the Csendook. He used whatever dark powers were at his disposal.'

'Dark?' said Ussemitus. 'Evil powers?'

'Yes. Anything that could save the Imperator Elect. I don't know the real truth of matters, but there's no doubt that Zellorian used powers that other men would have shunned. One day he went to the Consulate and told them he had found a possible way. A gamble, he said, but with the Swarms of the Csendook about to crush us, there was nothing else to do.

'His intention was to open a gate of a different kind. Break out from the circle of worlds. Perhaps to another. If we achieved our goal, he said, the Csendook would never find us. We would be free to begin again, though our worlds would be lost to us forever.

'The Imperator Elect, his Consulate, and all the high officials and their families, together with the principals of the army, builders, traders, gathered together. Zellorian began the release of power. Darkness fell, unlike any other darkness you can imagine. On the world of Eannor. There was a storm, a storm of immense proportions that seemed set to tear the world apart. We fell into a sort of dream, a long sleep plagued by fractured nightmares, the pangs of a world.

'But at the end of it all, we were here. In your mountains.'

A long silence followed her revelation. It was broken at last by Fomond. 'What of these Csendook?'

She shook her head. 'They have not found a way to follow us. Zellorian says they cannot. It is as if the past had never been, he told us.'

Ussemitus rubbed at his chin. 'An amazing tale. If what you say is true, you should be thankful to have escaped such enemies. Innasmorn must seem like a haven to you. And I can imagine that the last thing your people want is another war!'

She nodded, tired. 'Yes. Most of us are ready to settle here. We want to try and begin a new life.'

'Most of you?' said Ussemitus.

Her face clouded. 'It is not that simple.'

Fomond grunted. 'There are always those who seek war. Even among your people, I suspect.'

She nodded again. 'Yes. Zellorian himself is never satisfied. He holds the Imperator Elect in the palm of his hand. Whatever he desires, he has.'

'And what does this sorcerer desire now?' asked Ussemitus.

She drew in a deep breath, controlling other emotions. 'To control Innasmorn.'

Fomond and Ussemitus glanced at each other and up at the face of Armestor, who had heard most of what had been said.

'There is more to this,' Aru went on. 'He uses power, as I said. Whatever power he can find. And he seeks power here.'

'Innasmorn is a world rich in power,' Ussemitus told her. 'As you discovered when you took to our skies.'

She nodded. She could see the image of her father before her, recalling the night she had found him drunk, babbling about powers, a lost place, a place that Zellorian sought.

Quickly she went on to tell them of her own position, her involvment in the affairs of the Sculpted City and of her father and Zellorian's intentions. At the end of it she sat back, tired, drained by the reliving of her grim flight. 'So you see,' she grinned weakly, 'I'm an outcast, too. I cannot go back, not alone. My friends, my knights, have either been discredited or murdered. Gannatyne is as good as imprisoned, and Pyramors has been fooled into believing falsities about me. Zellorian has triumphed. Soon his control will be total.'

Ussemitus gazed out at the night in anger. 'We thought to turn our people away from war, but perhaps we should let them converge on your city and its sorcerer.'

She sat up at once. 'No! Ussemitus, it would be disastrous. My people have powers they can draw on. They are dangerous. I would fear for your own people. We must seek peace.'

Ussemitus shook his head. 'Perhaps you are right. But anything we attempt will be difficult.'

Fomond was nodding thoughtfully. They all fell silent

for a time, each choosing his own image from the strange history Aru had described.

'Tell me about Innasmorn,' she said eventually. 'Tell me about its history. My people know very little about it. Even Zellorian has not been able to learn much from the ones he has captured.'

Armestor had come down from his perch, and Ussemitus nodded to him to sit with them. He looked dubious about imparting information to an outsider, but Ussemitus's expression warned him against arguing. 'My companions are naturally suspicious,' he told Aru with a grin.

'Surely you don't think me dangerous?'

Fomond laughed. 'Why not? Once you have learned our secrets, who's to say you won't take to the skies like a great bird?'

Aru returned his grin. 'If I did that, I suspect Armestor would put a dozen arrows in me. You've told me what an excellent archer he is.'

'The best,' chuckled Fomond, and Armestor looked embarrassed.

Aru's expression became more serious. 'You have to trust me. As I trust you. If not, nothing can prevent the disasters that will overtake this world.'

'She's right,' said Ussemitus firmly. 'We have to trust each other.'

Fomond shrugged. 'It is why we're here and not asleep comfortably in our village. Then you speak of our history, Ussemitus. Armestor and I are, as you know, men of deeds, and clumsy with words.'

Ussemitus snorted. 'Is that so?' But he let the banter pass, relieved that the mood was better than it had been, although he was still unsure of his course in the morning. Where were they to go now?

'Our own remote past is lost in mystery, even more so than yours,' he told Aru. 'There are fables of the beginning, but most of them refer to a time of power. A time when our ancestors used machines and things of metal.'

'They do not use metal now?'

'Metal artefacts are almost totally forbidden. It is said that the metals of old brought with them a curse, a plague that began to destroy the people of Innasmorn. So virulent was this plague that metal was forbidden, except for certain things. Swords, though only men of esteem have them, even now. But there are no machines, and those who use them would be considered evil. Thus when your own people were discovered, Aru, they were branded as evil. Your sky ships.'

Aru would have challenged him on this, but waited, waiting to hear more of his strange history.

'But we had no need of metal artefacts. Instead we had the elements, for Innasmorn is the Mother of Storms. Her gods, her wind elementals, favoured us, and gave us their powers to use, and to shape our destiny. We are one with them.'

He seemed to have finished, and Aru listened to the silence of the night, which itself seemed an audience, the still air listening to his words.

After a while Ussemitus went on. 'There are many lands in Innasmorn. My people, the Vaza, are not widely travelled, but our ruler, the clan chief, is Vittargattus. It is said he lives a nomadic life and that a number of large cities serve him. The biggest of these is Amerandabad in the west. He has his own circle of power, just as your Imperator Elect has his Consulate. They are the Windmasters, callers of the elements, and the most powerful of them are the Blue Hairs.

'They seek your blood, Aru. To them you are intruders who have brought the Curse with you. You must be destroyed. Already Vittargattus is mobilising his armies, forging new alliances, and his force will be huge.'

'What?' she gasped. 'Where?'

'All our villages have been warned to prepare. It will take a year, but Vittargattus will gather his armies and send them upon your city. But first there will be a sending.'

She frowned. 'What is that?'

'Storms,' said Fomond, leaning forward. 'Terrible storms. The earth will shake. The walls of your city will fall. Then the armies will flood in. Your people may have powers, Aru, but so do ours. It would be a mighty conflict.'

She closed her eyes. 'We must stop this,' she breathed. 'It is sheer madness.'

Ussemitus could see her genuine distress. He prayed that his companions would see it for what it was. The knowledge they had given her was dangerous. In the hands of an enemy it would undo his people. He turned to Fomond. 'Our position is difficult. We dare not go to her city, and if we go back to our own, Kuraal would have us killed.'

Fomond scratched his head, for once unable to smile about matters. 'Perhaps we should try to find our way to Amerandabad itself. Perhaps we should go to Vittargattus and let him hear Aru's tale.'

'Vittargattus!' yelped Armestor, as if he had been pinched. 'They say he's hungry for more land. Eager to conquer. Why should he listen to us when his Blue Hair has condemned us?'

Ussemitus swore under his breath. He chewed at his lip. Their position seemed hopeless, and the war unavoidable.

Aru frowned. 'Are there no men in this city who would oppose war? You have been sensible enough to see the futility of it. There must be other Innasmornians like you.'

'Unfortunately,' said Ussemitus, 'my friends and I have never been near any of our cities. We've spent our lives in the forests. We know very little of Innasmorn. No doubt there would be men who would oppose war, and there are always those who would wish to bring down the clan chief.'

Aru thought back over the events of the last few days, since her return to the Sculpted City. Her father's words came back to her, and she recalled some of the things Gannatyne had said before his fall. 'There is something else,' she said. 'Something that Zellorian seeks here. A place of power.'

At once she had their rapt attention.

'Gannatyne wondered why Zellorian had chosen this world. It could not have been done by chance. Zellorian must have known of it, though we have no idea how. He

201

came here to flee the Csendook, but he came here for another reason, too. Gannatyne is convinced that Zellorian wants to find a way to return to our old Empire, with some kind of power that he can turn on the Csendook. And defeat them.'

'But you speak of colossal power,' said Ussemitus.

'Yes. What place of power could Zellorian seek?'

Ussemitus looked at Fomond, but he shrugged. Neither of them were aware of anything that fitted Aru's description. Armestor, who had fallen very silent, drew closer to them.

'I remember my father talking once. He had friends with him one night. He would have thought me asleep. They spoke of a place in the far west.'

Aru nodded. 'The west, yes. Ganatyne said it was in the west.'

Armestor sniffed. 'I don't remember much, but there was talk of a haunted land. A place where no one ever goes because of the demons and storms that guard it. It was ravaged by the plagues of old. The Curse had taken root deeply there.'

'Because of artefacts?' said Ussemitus.

Armestor nodded. 'And a fire from the sky. I think my father and his friends were drunk. They embellished the tale liberally.'

'Yes, I've heard something of such a place,' agreed Fomond.

'There are many legends,' said Ussemitus.

Fomond pulled a face. 'A land of ghosts. Swamps. Artefacts long buried. When we were children, our mothers used to threaten us with such things.'

'Is the place in the west real?' said Aru.

Fomond laughed. 'I never really thought so.'

'Did the legends say it was far?' Aru asked Armestor.

But he shrugged. 'I was very young.'

'If it exists,' said Aru, 'Zellorian will be searching for it. You say we have a year before Vittargattus unleashes his armies?'

'You want to go to the far west?' said Ussemitus incredulously.

'If Zellorian finds this land of power, and uses it, it will be the worse for us all. My people, Innasmorn. We *have* to prevent him. Don't ask me how. But if we can find this place — '

Fomond rose up, stretching and again chuckling. 'Well, there's nothing else we can do, is there? We can't go to the mountains, nor back, nor south. Why not go westward?'

Ussemitus was forced to share the grin. 'I agree. For the moment we seem to have no other choice. Don't you agree, Armestor?'

Armestor looked white, shaken, regretting that he had mentioned the haunted land. He shrugged, then turned and climbed back to his post.

The following morning, by dawn's light, they began the journey up on to the moors. A strong breeze had sprung up in the night, though they were relieved that there was still no sign of the bone warriors. They assumed that Aru's dramatic arrival had filled them with terror.

As they climbed into the open, the wind grew more fierce, so that they wondered if this could be a hint of yet more pursuit by Kuraal's windwraiths, but from their high vantage point they could overlook the forest, and the lands below them seemed free of the creatures of the storm. The sky was overcast, broken now and then by patches of blue, without the threat of rain. Aru was intrigued by her companions, who seemed able to taste the very air and by so doing know what the weather would do.

Armestor grumbled nervously to himself about leaving the forest, saying it was unwise to expose themselves, but Ussemitus calmed him by explaining that if they could reach high and open ground they would at least be able to see the nature of the land that awaited them in the west.

Shortly after midday they topped one of the tors and sat amongst the heaped stone, sheltering from the wind. They could see the land beyond the moors clearly from here, spread like a map in the distance. There was a gleam of water, a possible barrier to their direct progress, and to its south a wall of mountains rose up, steep and sheer.

Fomond pointed to these. 'The way directly ahead would bring us to the feet of those mountains, but I think we would be wise to keep away from them. And if that's a lake, it spreads right to their feet.'

'It could be the sea,' said Armestor. 'Some of the huntsmen who travel northwest of our villages talk of a wide, northern sea, with a lesser one that runs from it, inland to mountains. If that is it, we'll have to cross it.'

'How?' said Ussemitus.

'There's a small city on the coast I've heard of,' said Armestor. 'Kendara.'

'Kendara!' Fomond laughed. 'The haunt of pirates?'

'A childhood story,' said Armestor. 'It's loyal to the Vaza.'

'What could we achieve there?' said Fomond. 'What could we barter with?'

Ussemitus smiled, looking north. 'Barter?'

Aru looked askance at him. Ussemitus clapped Armestor on the shoulder. 'We've our wits, that's all. And we need a boat. Or passage. Unless you want to chance the mountain route?'

Armestor shook his head. 'I've heard tales about those mountains – '

Fomond guffawed and Aru was startled by his amusement. 'I imagine,' said Fomond, 'that the primitive tribes who infest those mountains are far more savage than the bone warriors.'

'You know of tribes?' said Armestor.

'Haven't you heard? They hunt for heads, and having taken them, stuff them and hold them high on poles, their villages thick with them, like a forest.'

'I've never heard of any such legend,' snorted Armestor, turning his attention elsewhere, though he could not resist a covert glance or two at the mountains.

'You should be careful, Fomond,' said Ussemitus. 'Who know what lurks in such places?' He turned to Aru, who seemed lost in thoughts of her own. 'How far do you think this place is? Did Zellorian know?'

She shook her head. There seemed to be a sadness on her, but he could think of no way to console her. He sat close beside her, gazing at the distances. As he did so, he felt the wind swirl about him, almost as if it sang to him. His hands began to tingle faintly and he looked down at them, opening them and studying the lines in his palm, which were like the many lines on a map. He had not noticed Aru's expression as she, too, watched.

Without thinking, he stood up and put his hands into the air. He felt the coldness of it, the abrupt bite, as though he had put his hands into a fast flowing river. Fomond jumped back, his face surprised.

Ussemitus saw the air spark about his hands and then a great warmth came into them, not of fire, but of something else. It spread down his arms and into his upper body. In the space between his hands there was now a bright light, dazzling him for a moment. But it became subdued, a gentle haze, and through it he caught a glimpse of something distant, a strange shape rearing up out of the mist, though what it was he could not begin to know. Something spoke in his mind, the lost voice of the wind, but he could not understand it. In a moment it had gone, as had the vision. He dropped his hands.

Both Fomond and Aru were beside him and it seemed that he had been about to swoon.

'What is it?' said Fomond. 'Your hands.'

Ussemitus looked at them, but they were perfectly normal. The heat had gone, as had the strange glow.

'Power,' said Armestor, who had come behind them. 'Ussemitus has the power.'

'What is it?' said Aru.

'We all have it,' said Ussemitus. 'All Innasmornians. We are children of the wind gods. Sometimes, in such a high place as this, we feel the power of the sky. Our birthright.'

Armestor had thrust his own hands under his shirt, as though he were afraid of them.

'What did you see?' asked Fomond.

'You?'

'Light, no more,' said Fomond.

Aru sensed the mystery between them. 'Has this happened before?'

'Not like this,' said Ussemitus. 'Not to me. But it is not unusual.'

Aru turned to Fomond, but he would not look at her. This was Innasmornian, a profound truth, not yet for sharing with an outsider.

Ussemitus suddenly smiled. 'Come on, we've spent enough time up here. Let's get down out of the wind. Too much of it can make a man drunk. Armestor, where will we find the road to Kendara?'

Relieved that a choice had been made, Armestor pointed almost directly north. 'There, I think. It will mean a detour, but if we're to cross the sea, we'll need that boat.'

They moved on swiftly, and Ussemitus said no more of the incident, though Aru could sense it was in the minds of them all for many miles afterwards.

15

ARENA

Auganzar watched in silence as the first of the gladiators marched into the arena, turning in a line and bowing to those of the Garazenda who had come to view this exhibition of skills. These warriors had been chosen by the Garazenda from their own crack Zemoks, put forward as the best material they had, ideal, they said, for the forces of the Supreme Sanguinary's own newly forming elite. Auganzar would have the final say, and the gladiators would, undoubtedly, perform to the very best of their capabilities, short of killing each other, in order to impress him. He was looking forward to viewing the fighting, though it was not evident from his calm expression.

Among the Garazenda was, to Auganzar's mild surprise, Horzumar. The renowned member of the Marozul sat next to Auganzar above the arena, bowing to him. Auganzar knew that Horzumar had never been one of Xeltagar's admirers and had been instrumental in wanting the Crusade ended. It seemed to Auganzar that Horzumar should have preferred not to be involved in the new Supreme Sanguinary's work: once the post had been filled it seemed more likely that he would have let Xeltagar and others deal with the niceties of supplying the Zemok elite for it. Yet here Horzumar sat, a polite smile on his broad face. Auganzar was certain that he must have been one of the Garazenda behind the plot to conceal the escape of the Imperator Elect. Thought of that escape had tormented Auganzar regularly since the interview with Gannorzol. How many others here were close supporters of Horzumar? And why was he here?

'An impressive array,' said Horzumar, nodding at the

line up of hardened Zemoks, who had now begun exercising in final preparation.

Auganzar nodded. 'We shall see, Marozul. I am looking for a little more than muscle.'

If Horzumar was affronted, he made no show of it. 'Good. I'm sure the task ahead of you will require a degree of subtlety. Not really work for mad beasts any more.'

Auganzar knew this was a reference to Xeltagar, a tenacious warrior, but whose direct and violent methods had clearly fallen out of favour with the ruling Marozul. They were not methods he necessarily favoured himself, though such things had a place.

'I have a few further tests for prospective Zemoks in my new Swarm. Perhaps later on you'd care to see them, Marozul?'

Horzumar inclined his head. 'Excellent, Supreme Sanguinary.'

The arena below them was a large ovoid, some twenty yards across. Its walls curved upwards, leaning in at the top, constructed of stone that had been polished until it shone. No one would be able to climb it without a rope. The floor of the arena was of earth, beaten down, though not too heavily packed. It could be filled with water, or mud, or other hazards, depending on the nature of the demonstration, and Csendook Zemoks were trained in all aspects of combat on such ground. Up in the tiered seats, some two score watchers looked down, although a hundred could have been accommodated. There were numerous such arenas in the Warhive, and the largest of them, where the Great Games were held, were capable of seating thousands.

Auganzar had been given control of the morning's events, and he was satisfied that the gladiators were ready. They formed their ranks again and looked up at him. He stood up.

'Individual combat,' he called. 'Pair off. First ten.' He sat, not watching Horzumar or any of the others in the seats.

In the arena, ten of the warriors paired off and the rest, a score of them, returned to the waiting area beyond the arena, closing the portal behind them, sealing the arena. The ten remaining spaced themselves around the arena in five pairs, tipped their vizors down and stood ready to begin.

Auganzar nodded. The combat began.

'Have you chosen many yet?' said Horzumar. Below him two gladiators circled each other, making a few preliminary stabs with their weapons: each had a short sword and a small shield, both of them wearing traditional Csendook war armour. It rang as blows were landed around the arena.

'A good many of my own regulars will make up the core of my Swarm,' replied Auganzar, his eyes never leaving the fighting below. 'But I have discarded a good many of them. Otherwise I have singled out a few that the Garazenda have recommended. Apart from that, Marozul, these are the first of many groups that I will be inspecting.'

'How many Zemoks do you think you'll need to police our new empire?'

It was an interesting question, Auganzar reflected. He knew that the Garazenda, especially those who were loyal to Zuldamar, would not permit him to control a large force. In fact he suspected that they would gradually seek to reduce it. 'A thousand was what I had in mind, Marozul.'

Horzumar's surprise was genuine. 'A thousand? Is that all?'

'A thousand Csendook. But if we use Men as has been suggested, it will be enough.'

Horzumar sat back, nodding, considering this. To himself, he thought this must be a diplomatic answer. It could surely not be an honest one. The Empire was very large. Could a thousand Csendook police it?

'Each of the thousand,' said Auganzar, still not looking up from the fighting, 'would control a small force of Men. They'll serve us, Marozul. They will find glory in our arenas. Those of their kind who do not will be hunted. And

Men will do the hunting with us, under us. I shall call my Csendook, Auganzar's Thousand. Every Zemok in our race will hear of them and desire to become one.'

Horzumar laughed gently, aware that colleagues were listening to the conversation, as Auganzar was aware of it. 'Admirable. And what will be the battlecry of this Swarm of yours?'

'I have yet to think of something appropriate.'

'I'm sure you will,' said Horzumar, turning to the fighting.

The gladiators were superb, very fast and powerful, and extremely well matched. Auganzar dismissed first one group and then another, permitting them only to bruise each other and show enough of their skills, satisfied that he had indeed been presented with as fine a selection of Csendook Zemoks as was available. Xeltagar, who rarely missed a chance to watch such battles, gazed avidly at the spectacle: he seemed disappointed that there were no kills. In his view the only way to find true weakness among the Zemoks was to allow them to fight to the death, thus rooting out such weakness before it could be exposed later, when most unlooked for. But Auganzar had been allowed to set the rules of the day and wanted no deaths. These Zemoks were, to him, far too valuable. If they could be as loyal to him as they were to their training, then he would have the best Swarm in the Empire. The Thousand would be the ultimate elite. Everyone would fear them, including the Garazenda who had unwittingly fashioned them.

Near the end of the morning, when most of the Zemoks on display had been through their paces, there was a commotion at the back of the seating gallery. Horzumar looked up, disturbed by the noise as a number of Csendook swaggered down the steep incline between two rows of seats.

Auganzar did not frown, though he was annoyed. He had not expected any such intrusion. He glanced across at two of his guards, his eyes enough to question. Both looked surprised and they got up at once, as if to challenge the three newcomers.

'So these are the best on offer?' called one of them. Auganzar turned slowly and looked up at him, recognising him as Durrozol, a senior Zolutar under one of the Garazenda, reputedly a fine warrior and victor of a number of significant battles with the Imperator Elect's forces. With him were two of his own senior warriors, Uldarzol and Foruzol. They sounded as though they had been drinking, and were certainly far less respectful than they should have been in the presence of Garazenda. Some of the latter murmured among themselves, though this was Auganzar's day and they preferred to let the Supreme Sanguinary handle it his way.

Auganzar did not get up. 'I don't seem to have been sent any Zemoks from your own Swarm,' he said to Durrozol.

'An obvious oversight,' snorted the latter. 'That is, if you're trying to pull out the best, Supreme Sanguinary.' There was a note of scorn in his voice as he spoke the title. He was a huge fellow, his face scarred, his eyes cold, his mouth cruel, as though he cared for nothing other than the pain of battle.

Horzumar looked directly at Auganzar, attempting to read his reaction to the taunt, but he could detect none. The Supreme Sanguinary was every bit as cool as he was said to be.

'You think, perhaps,' said Auganzar, 'you have Zemoks capable of matching the skills of those below us?'

'This rabble?' Durrozol laughed, hands on his hips. No one laughed with him. 'What action have they seen?'

Horzumar stood up, his face calm. 'You do not seem to be acquainted with our requirements, Zolutar,' he said mildly.

Durrozol bowed. 'My apologies, Marozul,' he said, far too loudly. 'I forgot that you are looking for a new breed of Csendook. Zemoks with paper swords and no teeth.' This was a direct affront to Horzumar, and to his colleagues who had voted to discontinue the Crusade. Although there must be countless thousands of Csendook who were appalled at the ending of the war, none of them would have dared to speak his mind so openly before one of the Garazenda, and certainly not before a member of the Marozul.

'I think this Zolutar must be a little confused,' said Auganzar.

Every head turned to him. The fighting below had stopped. A strange silence fell, as though the Zemoks expected a conflict of another kind to begin.

Auganzar still did not rise. But he turned and looked directly at Durrozol. 'I am looking for Zemoks with intelligence. Perhaps that is why none of your own were sent to me.'

Durrozol was very still. For a moment he said nothing. Then he took a step closer to the sitting Auganzar. He laughed. 'Intelligence, strength of arm, skill in combat. My Zemoks have all that.'

'Someone does not share your faith,' said Auganzar.

The onlookers murmured. This was very promising. Like dogs, they scented blood here, possible conflict. Such insults! Surely Horzumar would interrupt, though. Did he not find Durrozol's rudeness intolerable? Or was this a test of Auganzar's mettle?

Durrozol leaned forward belligerently. 'I trained my crack Zemoks myself. With Uldarzol and Foruzol here.'

Auganzar turned to them again. 'Then, with respect, I have no desire to see any of them. I have all that I require.' He turned away.

Durrozol was getting the worst of these exchanges and the onlookers delighted in it, impressed with Auganzar. Most of their kind would have had a sword out by now, calling for blood.

'If your chosen Zemoks are so good,' said Durrozol through his teeth, 'you must have every confidence in them. You imply they are far superior to my own.'

'I see no reason to withdraw my observations,' said Auganzar.

Durrozol straightened as if he had been slapped. He

turned to Horzumar. 'I feel, Marozul, that this is an insufferable slight not just on my Zemoks, but on myself.'

'One that you invited,' said Horzumar. 'But how do you suggest this, ah, insufferable slight, be put right?'

Auganzar stood up, his movements slow, no hint of panic in them. 'I trust, Marozul, you are not going to request a demonstration? I am sure it is not necessary. I am perfectly capable of choosing the Zemoks I require – '

Durrozol pointed at him, his thick finger jabbing the air. 'Then pick your best!' he snapped. 'And I'll fight! *I'll* show you what real ability is.'

Horzumar turned to Auganzar. He did not seem to be intent on forcing the issue, respecting Auganzar. 'This is entirely up to you, Supreme Sanguinary. The Zolutar is quite out of order here – '

'Marozul – ' Durrozol began to protest.

'Be silent!' snarled Horzumar suddenly, taking the entire company aback. Horzumar watched Auganzar, who alone seemed unmoved. 'Supreme Sanguinary, I am quite prepared to have this Zolutar reprimanded. But this is your day. What do you wish?'

Auganzar had been thinking deeply through the exchange, although it had been short. What was behind this? It was no accident, no sudden spur. How had Durrozol come here and begun this? He was risking far too much with his insulting behaviour. It was true that there was much resentment in the empire about the new peace. But would it have goaded a Zolutar like Durrozol to this fever?

Whatever was behind it, there would be dishonour for them both if he dismissed Durrozol's challenge. And resentment. A Csendook back down from a challenge? Unheard of. It is what the people would say. And Auganzar's Thousand would be a laughing stock. Whoever had planned this, knew that.

'Thank you for your judgement,' Auganzar told Horzumar. Horzumar, who was an unexpected guest here. 'Durrozol is, in my opinion, out of order. But he is a Csendook. And I am well aware of his record.'

'I'm not interested in your opinion of me,' snapped Durrozol.

'I have none. But I have good opinions of my own Zemoks, and of those who have demonstrated their skills below us.' Auganzar went to the lip of the arena and waved to three of the Zemoks below. They came forward and bowed, carrying their war helms. Auganzar turned back to Durrozol.

'If you'd care to test your skill, choose a Zemok.'

Durrozol grinned, showing his yellowing teeth. He nodded. 'Very well.' He glanced back at his companions. 'And what about these two? Let them join me. Three by three. Or would you rather your Zemoks had a few of their Zolutars swell their ranks?'

The Garazenda murmured. This was unnecessary bravado. Durrozol was very good, they knew that much, but he would be a fool to take on too many.

Auganzar shook his head. 'Three by three will be acceptable.'

Durrozol bowed, still grinning, and Auganzar had his guards lead him and his grinning companions down to the changing areas to prepare.

Horzumar stood beside the Supreme Sanguinary, watching the Zemoks in the arena as they drew on their war helms. 'Have you considered the implications if your three Zemoks are beaten?'

'There is no room in my Swarm for him, nor for those with him,' said Auganzar.

'He's an excellent fighter, as are Uldarzol and Foruzol. Perhaps it would have been better if you'd permitted me to reprimand them.'

'I thought of the consequences of that, Marozul,' said Auganzar without emotion.

'But if your warriors are beaten – '

'We shall see.'

Moments later Durrozol came out into the arena with his companions. All three had donned armour and carried the familiar short swords and shields. Auganzar nodded to his Zemoks and they spaced themselves out, each one selecting an opponent. The Thousand were being tested here, Auganzar knew. This was the plan. Horzumar wanted them discredited.

Durrozol raised his sword. 'To a secure empire!' he called, and the Garazenda above him saluted him in return. Then he swung round, crouching, ready to begin.

Auganzar sat, his face a mask, and Horzumar watched, his own thoughts secret, his face suggesting indifference, though beneath it his mind raced. The trap was closing. Would it be this easy?

The three individual contests began slowly but simultaneously speeded up. Durrozol harried his opponent, preferring an offensive tactic, jabbing and swerving, his body remarkably agile for such a big warrior. Often Man found the Csendook build completely misleading: they were not slow and cumbersome, but deadly fast, far faster than a Man. The speed of their sword arms was beyond any human defence. And Durrozol was as fast as any that Horzumar had seen. It was why he had selected him for this particular assignment. At the moment it went very well. Auganzar had not, it seemed, recognised the trap. It had almost reached the point where he would be unable to escape its jaws.

Horzumar watched as Durrozol began to wear down his opponent, testing his defences, looking for a sign of weakness, preparing the attack that would exploit it fully. Beside him the other Zolutars fought almost as well, both of them deadly, extremely fast, and in truth, that much superior to the gladiators they fought, who had not had the degree of battle experience. But the three gladiators knew what was at stake here. All of them were trained to the peak of their own skill, and to be defeated here would be unthinkable. It would disgrace Auganzar, make a mockery of his elite troops.

Xeltagar had sat down beside Horzumar, his face a picture of pleasure as he avidly watched the fighting. Horzumar smiled at him, though the warrior Garazenda did

215

not notice. He, too, was falling neatly into the trap that had been laid.

'Excellent skills,' said Horzumar. 'Your Supreme Sanguinary chose well.'

'I sent him those warriors,' said Xeltagar. 'None better.'

Horzumar wanted to grin smugly but did not. This was better than he could have hoped. 'You did? I trust they can win this affair. If not, Auganzar will be made to look a little foolish.'

Xeltagar turned an unpleasant gaze on him, but bit back any retort. He knew the Marozul was correct.

'It is interesting, is it not?' went on Horzumar, aware that Auganzar must be able to hear him. 'We have appointed a Supreme Sanguinary so that our warriors have a new way to follow, a way of stealth and diplomacy instead of sheer, brute force. Yet we are witnessing a test of strength. Unless your warriors, Auganzar, have something else to teach us?'

Auganzar had no opportunity to reply. Durrozol had found a gap in his opponent's defence. He thrust deftly with his sword and must have broken a bone, for his opponent leapt back nimbly, one arm hanging limply, the shield falling into the dust. At once Durrozol was at him, intent on more harm.

Xeltagar scowled. 'Is this to the death?' It went against his instincts to question it, but it would be bad for Auganzar if his Zemoks died.

Horzumar looked unmoved. 'It is not for me to say. Auganzar?'

There was yet no hint of emotion in the Supreme Sanguinary's face. He said nothing. Below him Durrozol moved inexorably towards the moment when he would deliver the killing blow, his opponent backing, backing, knowing that unless the conflict was called off, he was about to die. The other two Zemoks were being pushed back around the arena, but as yet they were unmarked, their defences excellent, their resolve firm.

Finally Auganzar spoke, though quietly so that only the

two Garazenda beside him heard him. 'I want only the best.'

A moment late Durrozol delivered a telling stroke that caught the side of his opponent's helm, staggering him. As he dropped to one knee, Durrozol leapt in, using his weapon to chop down fiercely. Twice more he aimed blows at his opponent's head, and the warrior toppled, twitching in the last spastic motions of life before lying very still. There could be no doubt that he was dead.

Durrozol ignored the sounds from above. He turned to where his companions were yet exchanging blows with their own opponents. It was clear what he intended.

Xeltagar stood up, his face livid. 'No!' he snarled. 'The contest is three by three. Durrozol should retire until the others have ended their individual contests.'

Horzumar turned to Auganzar. 'You had better call him off. It is your privilege to do so.'

But to Xeltagar's amazement, Auganzar said nothing, merely watching events below. Durrozol joined Uldarzol and between them they cornered the latter's opponent. Again it was Durrozol who delivered the blows to the head that killed him.

'He favours the head,' said Auganzar as though looking at a painting and expressing an opinion on the style of the artist.

Horzumar's mind was racing. Why did he not stop this? Would he permit the death of the third warrior? Already the three others were hunting him down. Ah, did he think it would make heroes of them, his warrior elite? Impossible! This was defeat, disgrace for Auganzar.

Xeltagar stared open-mouthed at Auganzar, almost towering over him. This was ignominy! 'Auganzar!' he hissed. 'Stop this! You do your cause no good – '

But still he was ignored as the Supreme Sanguinary watched. It was not long before the last of his gladiators was despatched. For the third time, Durrozol administered the killing, again going for the head. At the end of it he

217

came below the Garazenda, bowing. He removed his helmet, his ugly head dripping with sweat.

'As you promised, Surpreme Sanguinary, they were very good. But no match for true warriors.'

Xeltagar sank down into his seat, trying hopelessly to mask his fury and his shame. Auganzar would be discredited! And so would he for having selected him. Confused, incapable of understanding what was happening, he gazed at the bodies in the arena, his eyes fixed.

Auganzar bowed slightly, acknowledging the victory of the Zolutars. 'An excellent performance,' he said flatly.

Horzumar coughed, as though the events had embarrassed him. Now the moment had come to close the trap, before any of the onlookers left to report what they had seen. 'If you have gambled, Supreme Sanguinary, you have lost.'

'Lost, Marozul?'

'I had assumed when you let this combat go on, that you must be sure of success. As it is, I'm not sure how you can possibly redeem yourself. In a while word of this will have spread to all the Garazenda. Your position is extremely difficult.'

Auganzar looked into his eyes. He understood it clearly. Horzumar knew everything. Somehow he had discovered how Gannorzol had died. Not in an accident with his family, in a fire that had consumed them all. But indirectly by Auganzar's hand. And Horzumar knew why they had been killed. He knew that Auganzar had found out about the Imperator Elect, that he was probably still alive, somewhere in an unknown darkness. Horzumar and Zuldamar did not want him pursued, wanted Man forgotten, or tamed. And they had found out that Auganzar meant to use his new position to find the Imperator. So they had set this up, this disgrace, as a first step to Auganzar's downfall.

Auganzar smiled for the first time that day. 'The matter can be resolved,' he said.

Horzumar, who up till that moment had been feeling delighted with the way things had gone, almost too perfectly, felt a stab of cold in his gut. The smile was as effective as a blade. What could he possibly have overlooked?

'Durrozol and his companions have shown themselves to be warriors of the highest order,' said Auganzar.

Durrozol bowed, though in mockery of the Supreme Sanguinary. 'But my Thousand will be the supreme force.' Horzumar was about to interrupt, but Auganzar lightly touched him on the arm. 'With your permission, Marozul, I will demonstrate. The combat is not quite at an end.'

Horzumar tried to fathom this, but there was no clear explanation. He looked at Xeltagar, but still the Garazenda scowled out at the dead. Horzumar nodded. 'Very well.'

Auganzar walked up through the seats. No one had left. They sensed there was more to come. Word had already begun to spread out to the Warhive, for others were arriving, Garazenda, Zaru and officials, until in a while the galleries were almost full.

Durrozol looked askance at Horzumar, but he waved him out into the arena. 'It appears you have another test,' was all he could think of to say. But the three Zolutars in the arena were not concerned. By now they had recovered their wind. If there was to be more fighting, it was all the same to them.

When at last the single figure emerged from the portal to the waiting arena, they turned to meet it, puzzled looks on their faces. A huge warrior, face concealed by the war helm, stepped towards them. Like them, it was armed with a short sword and a shield, though its armour appeared to be far thinner than their own battle gear. On the breast plate there were two scarlet circles, new symbols that represented Auganzar's elite, the Thousand. Already the Zemoks jokingly called the circles the Eyes of Auganzar.

The crowd fell silent. One warrior?

Without any further comment from Horzumar or the baffled Xeltagar, the conflict began. No other warriors had emerged.

Horzumar leaned over to Xeltagar, a sheen of perspiration on his brow. 'Who is this?'

Xeltagar had gone very cold. 'I surmise, Marozul, that Auganzar has decided on the only possible course that can redeem his honour.'

'Auganzar?' whispered Horzumar, but as he studied the helmeted figure in the arena, he realised what Xeltagar meant. The Supreme Sanguinary himself had donned the mantle of battle. He moved forward, not in the least defensively. Of course! Horzumar cried within. The only way to restore his honour. He had lost, and so would perish with glory, rather than face further shame. His insufferable ambitions, which the Marozul had so misjudged, would end here. Horzumar looked around the galleries. They knew!

Durrozol's fellows spread out, circling their single opponent. They thought nothing of the uneven odds. They had been called by Auganzar. His champion, whoever he was, must pay the penalty for that.

Uldarzol suddenly made a lunge for the legs of his opponent, but his sword glanced off the calf metal. Almost in the same instant the weapon of the defender came down, crushing through armour and bone alike, snapping the arm. Uldarzol howled in agony and staggered back as if he had been scorched, his sword spinning away. Both Foruzol and Durrozol moved in with deadly thrusts that would have slipped through the defence of any normal opponent. But their blows did not kill. Auganzar ducked Durrozol's thrust as easily as a breeze might have, and his shield clashed with Foruzol's weapon. To the amazement of the latter, he could not pull his sword away.

Auganzar was particularly powerful and he swung his shield arm so that the trapped Foruzol was hauled off balance. As he tried to right himself and wrench free, the weapon of his opponent crashed into his midriff, splitting his armour like a huge nut. He tumbled away, but had to release his weapon. It fell to the ground at Auganzar's feet. The audience gasped, scarcely able to believe what they had seen. Xeltagar leapt up and called out encouragement, his fists shaking.

Durrozol kept his head, almost distracted, but he backed off to safety. He could see that Uldarzol would be useless without his sword arm. How had it been *broken*? Surely his armour should have taken such a blow. But it had been superbly timed. This warrior was exceptional.

His own weapon rang against Auganzar's shield, held by the magnetic field. He released it instantly, ducking back. At once Auganzar pressed forward. Suddenly he had become the complete antagonist, facing three opponents who were without weapons. There was no possibility of their retrieving their fallen swords. Instead all three of them held their shields before them, searching for a different kind of opening. But Auganzar stood over their fallen blades.

He waited. Above him the crowd was aghast, knowing that within a few minutes this warrior had made a mockery of the three deadly opponents he had faced. And there were to be a Thousand of these?

Auganzar bent down and carefully picked up each of the swords, and somehow they disappeared from view behind his shield. It was done so smoothly and confidently that none of the three Csendook had a chance to rush him, as they had hoped to do.

Then, without any hint of warning, Auganzar rushed forward, straight for Foruzol. He ignored the other two as they swung their shield edges at him, using them as weapons. They glanced harmlessly off his thin armour, and both Durrozol and Uldarzol jumped back. Foruzol was not so fortunate. He could not get out of his assailant's path, and when he at last took a blow from Auganzar, it was across the chest.

In horror, the audience watched as it seemed to cave in, as if hit by an impossible force. Foruzol crumpled up as though all the bones had been sucked out of him. As he fell, Uldarzol screamed defiance and raced in, trying again to use the cutting edge of his shield. Auganzar ducked down and chopped sideways with his sword, aiming for the

221

thighs. Blood gushed as the weapon sliced clean through the first leg and bit deep into the second. Uldarzol gasped in agony as he toppled, hand clutching at air.

Durrozol stood rooted, hardly able to credit what had happened. What weapon could do this? Like one in shock, he watched as Auganzar neatly killed Uldarzol with a single downward stroke. Then the black-clad warrior turned to him. The twin circles seemed to blaze at him. Above there was absolute silence.

Horzumar's mouth opened. He could not believe the speed of the deaths, nor their manner. Was that Auganzar? Was he really in that suit?

Auganzar strode towards Durrozol, who breathed deeply, seeing his death coming, immobile as a warrior waiting for the executioner's blow.

'You favour the head when you kill,' said a voice that he recognised.

He almost croaked a reply. He was too slow to prevent what happened next. Auganzar swung his weapon and the air hummed as it struck through armour, flesh and bone, and Durrozol's head leapt, arching across the arena like a tossed ball. His torso stood for a moment, ridiculously, then gently wavered before folding up.

Auganzar turned his back on the three dead warriors and walked towards the galleries where Horzumar and Xeltagar sat. The latter was on his feet again, face beaming, his sword drawn.

'Superb!' he roared. 'Beyond description!'

Horzumar's mouth had gone dry. 'There had better be an explanation,' he began, but the words trailed away as the warrior pulled off his helm. As he had feared, it was Auganzar who stood before him.

At once there was a howl from the audience and they began cheering wildly. Auganzar's name was shouted back and forth, and Horzumar knew that within minutes the halls of the immediate Warhive would be ringing with the news.

'You asked me for a warcry,' called Auganzar. 'I'll give you one. *Only the strongest and the fastest.*'

It was taken up quickly, and it rebounded back a dozen times from the gathered onlookers, including the Garazenda, who revelled in bloodshed.

Horzumar was the only Csendook who did not shout out Auganzar's battlecry. He was thinking of the attempt to descredit the Supreme Sanguinary, to bring him down only a short time after he had taken office. And it had failed. For now, here among the dead, a new monster had arisen. Auganzar had brilliantly sacrificed three of his best Zemoks so that he himself could show the Warhive the mettle of his Thousand. He was a champion among champions, turning disaster into absolute victory. The Warhive would worship him.

Only the strongest and fastest, thought Horzumar. The plan to dispense with the Crusade and turn it into something else, a mastery of Man instead of genocide. Auganzar was not content with it. How much more did he desire?

Horzumar at last called out with his fellows, masking his horror and nodding at Auganzar as if in congratulations. But they both knew that this day marked the beginning of a new conflict between them. And the balance of power had shifted significantly.

BOOK FOUR

AMERANDABAD

16

JUBAIA

They travelled roughly north for three days, skirting the edge of the moors, preferring not to the enter the deep woodland below them. Although Ussemitus and his companions were of the woods, they were now a considerable distance from their home territory and could not be sure how the forests here would react to them. They did, however, pause to cut fresh saplings from which they made excellent bows, stringing them with twine, and cutting arrows for themselves. Their craftsmanship at this amazed Aru, who knew that her own people could not fashion better. She began to appreciate how important their relationship with the forest was, as if they saw in it a divine presence, or spirits that could be easily offended, and somehow she could not mock such an idea any more, not here, and not after the gliderboat had been so humiliated by the air of Innasmorn. The other concern of the group seemed to be the skies: Ussemitus had talked to Aru about Kuraal and his sending of the windwraiths, but he explained that as they got further from the shaman, Kuraal would have to exercise greater control over the winds. He would, Ussemitus felt certain, rather expend his energy driving a force northwards, expecting to cut off Aru's people, not knowing their fate.

They were still several days out from Kendara when they heard a commotion down in the trees below them. There were voices, shouts and the clash of weapons, which they took to be steel, something which alerted them. Ussemitus motioned them all behind cover, for there were many rocks about them, and they were able to conceal themselves and watch for signs of movement. It was not long before a figure burst out of the trees and scampered up on to the edge of the moor, pursued by six others.

The first of the figures appeared to be a youth, but as it skipped and hopped nearer to the onlookers, they saw that it was a man, though smaller than any of them. He had a hooked nose and thick black hair tied in a curling knot that swung half way down his back. There were bright rings in his ears – metal! – and he wore a thick belt that was also studded with metal. In his hand was a short sword, also of metal, and on his curiously bent back was a pack, strapped up tightly.

His pursuers were less extraordinary. These were evidently warriors, Innasmornians of normal stature, some carrying spears and some with shorter weapons, cut from wood and without metal tips, which would have been unusual for warriors who were not close to someone of high rank, like Vittargattus. The warriors wore leather scaled armour and leather caps, their faces far more tanned than those of the forest people, their features slightly bolder, harder. Aru still felt that they had a fragile look compared to the men of her own race, but it was clear that they were far more robust than the little being they were chasing. They were shouting and cursing in a dialect that she could not understand, and she glanced at Ussemitus, but he shook his head, unable to understand either. However, it needed no words to explain what was about to happen: the pursuit intended to catch up with and cut down the single figure. Aru wondered if they wanted to steal his metal, although she had learned from Ussemitus that Innasmornians went in fear of metal.

The figure turned by a large boulder and held out its sword, hissing like a trapped cat, and the warriors began to circle. Again they spoke, laughing and taunting, sure of an easy kill.

Ussemitus felt a sudden stab of anger, fury almost, at this unequal combat. He acted without a hint of warning to his fellows, fitting an arrow to his bow and letting fly all in one smooth motion. The arrow had barely lodged in the neck of one of the pursuers, when he had another fitted. Fomond and Armestor also let fly, and three of the pursuers fell, their legs kicking horribly as they died. Aru's eyes bulged as she saw this sudden destruction, shocked by the merciless efficiency of the Innasmornian woodsmen.

The Innasmornian who had been pursued glared at his fallen enemies, sneering at them. Then he turned to see who had come to his rescue. The other three pursuers had dropped flat to the ground, crawling to cover. As they hid themselves, their erstwhile victim hopped up and down, cursing them, laughing, his face an extraordinary mask, his nose like the hooked beak of a bird of prey.

Aru turned to Ussemitus. 'You've killed them,' she said softly, though she felt slightly ridiculous saying it.

Ussemitus looked momentarily puzzled, as if his own sudden impulse had surprised him. 'We've evened up the odds. They would have cut him to pieces.'

Suddenly the little being turned and began to run up the moor. One of his pursuers shouted, bobbing up and flinging a spear. It was enough for Armestor, who had been waiting for a hint of movement. He released another arrow and there was a scream, a thrashing in the undergrowth. Moments later the other two warriors had scuttled off down along the lower rocks and into the trees. The sound of their flight could be heard for several minutes as they crashed through the bushes and away into the distance.

Up in the higher rocks, the little figure turned, sitting down and trying to see who had saved him from a bloody death. Neither Ussemitus nor his companions had yet showed themselves. Ussemitus waved Armestor round to higher ground, and he circled the being from above. Ussemitus and Fomond began the climb, keeping out of sight. Aru, still stunned by the speed of the entire incident, followed Ussemitus. Her own knights had been excellent warriors, but these Innasmornians were unbelievable archers! Their accuracy deceived the eye.

The lonely figure called out, guessing that someone else was tracking him. He seemed to be trying several dialects,

229

until at last he hit one which Aru and the others understood. He had an unusual accent, as if used to speaking an altogether different language, and his voice was shrill, the words tumbling out of him rapidly.

'No need to split me with your arrows!' he called, face lined with anxiety. 'I'm grateful beyond words for your intervention. Surely you don't want my ugly head. You've four down in the bushes to pick from.'

Ussemitus stood up slowly, no more than ten yards from the little figure, who was startled to see him so near. 'Heads? Why should we want heads?'

Fomond grinned at Aru, then stood up. 'We're not hill folk,' he said. Ussemitus glanced at him, a warning look, and Fomond realised he would have done better to say nothing.

Aru stood up and the little man gasped audibly. 'No, I can see you are not,' he said, his face breaking into a smile. 'This lady with you is far too beautiful a creature to lurk among the hill demons.' He slipped his sword into his belt and hopped down from the rock, coming forward with sudden confidence, apparently having had his fears dispelled. He bowed before Aru, taking in her odd attire: she wore the robe that she had stolen in the Sculpted City, though she had cut away its arms and had slashed it at mid-thigh to make it easier for her to move in the forests. 'I am your servant,' said the little being, beaming.

His accent was very strange, but Aru understood him well enough. And the expression on his alien face was one she knew. At court she would have treated it with scorn, but here in this wild place she felt exposed by it, embarrassed. She felt angry with herself. Stupid to behave like a young girl! She was a warrior, and had commanded knights. Even so, she moved a little closer to Ussemitus.

'Who are you?' she said. Behind the figure she could see Armestor, who had taken up a position to cover the stranger's back, his bow ready, though it seemed unlikely he would need it now.

'I am Jubaia.'

'From where?' said Ussemitus, openly studying the man, his curious metal trinkets. Amazingly his baggy shirt was also studded with them and he wore a long necklace of linked chain, the work intricate, minute.

'From far away,' Jubaia laughed, and his amusement was genuine, his smile infectious. Fomond was grinning at him, ignoring Ussemitus's own rather stern expression. 'But these days,' Jubaia went on, 'I have become something of a wanderer. No city is my home any more. And you?'

Ussemitus glanced at Fomond, another warning to be silent.

Jubaia tapped his great nose and winked. 'Oh, oh. Yes, tact. Quite. I expect too much. Already you have been extraordinarily generous.'

'The contest seemed unequal,' said Ussemitus a little too hurriedly. 'You would have been cut to pieces. Why?'

'Why, for food, of course!' laughed Jubaia. 'I'm not very big, as you can see, but there's enough meat in me yet to –'

Fomond said something crude in his own dialect, though his smile had not dissolved. 'The men we killed were not cannibals.'

'How do you know that?' snorted Jubaia.

Ussemitus suddenly laughed, and in doing so seemed to step out of the cloud of doubt that had been enveloping him. Aru sensed a sudden relaxation in him. Perhaps he had come to terms with his almost irrational action in killing the warriors. 'Oh, we know, friend. We know. Now, who were they?'

Jubaia looked sheepish.'Villains, sir. You see the metal I wear? They coveted it. As·you probably do. No matter! It's yours, in payment. Spare my life and I'll get you more, much more.'

Ussemitus and Fomond drew back slightly. 'We're Innasmornian,' said Ussemitus. 'We do not covet metal.' He looked quickly at Aru as he said it, realising that perhaps he had insulted her.

But she did not react. 'We're not going to kill you,' she told Jubaia.

Ussemitus could see that her face was set, and in her manner was the bearing of the warrior he had first seen in the mountains. Whatever she had suffered back in her own city, she was quickly closing out, the strength of command growing in her.

'We are not common thieves,' he told the little man.

Jubaia looked oddly stung by the word. But then he brightened. 'Of course not, sirs! You are far too skilful with the bow. May I ask you where you are from?'

'First tell us why they pursued you. For the metal, perhaps. But what else? Where were they from?' said Ussemitus, his voice hardening.

Aru sensed in him something she had not understood before. He was no mere youth, and not typical of his kind, who seemed to be typified by Fomond, with his easy manner and relaxed nature, or Armestor, who saw danger in every tree. But Ussemitus was able to see beyond his surroundings, his fears. She would have vied with him for the leadership of this band, but already she was accustoming herself to the idea that he was the leader, and with good reason.

Jubaia appeared to be uncomfortable. 'I'm willing to explain everything, of course I am. How could I do otherwise when you have been so kind? But I am a wanderer, as I have said – '

Fomond grunted. 'You're tongue has taken a lesson from your feet. Come to the point!'

Jubaia bowed. 'Of course. I do not have your eloquence. You are right.' Fomond threw his hands up in the air and sat down on one of the rocks.

'I am not from these lands. Consequently I am concerned that the men of your race may look upon me – as they often do – with some hostility. While you have shown me none, I am, nevertheless, not a compatriot. Whereas the men you have killed are of your own race, evil though they were.'

232

'Who were they?' said Ussemitus, trying not to smile.

Aru chuckled. 'He's afraid that if he tells you why they were after him, you'd regret having killed them and cut off his own head.'

Jubaia gaped, and he swallowed hard. 'You have a great mind as well as great beauty, lady,' he said at length.

'Never mind that,' she said. 'Just tell your story and accept the consequences. You've no choice.'

He shrugged. 'Well, well. So be it. But tell me this – you are not from Kendara by any chance?'

Aru felt Ussemitus's fingers lightly touch her arm. Another warning: *say nothing*.

'Kendara?' said Fomond. 'That's a port, isn't it?' He looked quizzically at Ussemitus, who feigned confusion.

'I am sure I've heard the name. But isn't he a clan chief?'

Jubaia looked relieved. 'Ah. Just so. A port. Several days to the north of this place. Since you are clearly not natives of that wicked city – '

'Wicked?' said Fomond. 'Are its inhabitants cannibals?'

Jubaia smirked. 'Ah, sir, you saw through my pathetic deceit so easily! No, of course not. It was simply my fear that perhaps you were also of Kendara.'

Fomond frowned, glancing across at Ussemitus, who turned to look back at the corpses. 'Are you saying these men were of Kendara?'

'Indeed they were!' growled Jubaia. 'And typical of that verminous race! You see how they treat an innocent wanderer and attempt to rob him of his paltry valuables.'

Ussemitus groaned. This was the worst possible news.

'Jubaia,' said Fomond patiently. 'I can see that the metal you wear must have value. I am sure one as glib-tongued as you would make a nonsense of its true value, but even so, I find it hard to believe that six warriors of Kendara would hunt you through these forests for it.'

'Ah! You moor people are shrewd, eh?'

Ussemitus came in quickly. 'That's as may be. Answer the question.'

'Why did they hunt me? Well, in truth, it was not for

233

my trinkets, though had they killed me, they would have stripped me of them. They don't fear metal in Kendara. They're pirates. I was in Kendara a few days ago. I had been there, in fact, for two months. It is not the prettiest city I have ever visited, but there is trade there and many ships that come and go, opening up paths for someone like me. I enjoy travel, you see. I am incapable of remaining in one place for more than a few days at a time –'

'Yet you remained in Kendara for two months!' said Fomond.

Jubaia thought about it, but nodded. 'Yes, you see, I am not very good at deceit. It is true that I like to move on quickly. But in Kendara I lingered longer than I usually would. There was a lady there –'

'Ah,' nodded Fomond. 'Now we are coming to the truth of the matter.'

'Such a woman!' Jubaia said, lifting both eyes and hands to the skies in a way that made them all grin, even Aru, who could just about follow his rapid speech.

'I courted her ardently, sirs, having been smitten. Being a wanderer, I have known many women. Your pardon, lady, but it has not been my fate to remain with any of them. They tire of me so easily.'

'Such poor judgement,' said Aru, smiling.

'But this lady was exceptional and did seem to care for me.'

'Yet she threw you out –' said Ussemitus, enjoying the tale.

'Not at all! She swore her undying love to me. Night after night we –'

'Do we need to have the intimate details?' said Aru.

Jubaia coughed. 'Ah, no. How indiscreet of me. My apologies. Let us just say that the sweet lady and I were very content. Alas, her husband was not. Inevitably he found out about us.'

'Yes, and we can guess the rest,' said Ussemitus. 'So he paid these thugs to carve you into little pieces.'

'Not quite,' said Jubaia. He had begun to pace about as

234

he told his story, preening himself like a great bird as he did so, apparently proud of his exploits, though Aru was not the only one to wonder how much of this elaborate tale was actually true. 'You see, the lady in question was the wife of one of the port officials. An important man in Kendara. The warriors who harried me on his behalf were no ordinary cutpurses. They were garrisoned at the harbour.'

'*Soldiers*?' gasped Ussemitus. 'We have killed Kendaran soldiers?'

Jubaia took a deep breath, nodding. 'Yes, indeed.' But he turned to them with a sly grin. 'Ah, but they're a rabble. Pirates! Who cares?'

Ussemitus went back through the rocks to the corpses. He examined them, finding nothing of value, nothing to identify the men. Their weapons, however, were well crafted, and each had a small crest cut into its wooden haft, a sailing ship with waving lines underneath, signifying the sea. 'Soldiers,' he murmured. Why ever had he been so quick to kill them?

Aru and Fomond joined him. Beyond them Jubaia was sauntering down to them, and his shadow that he had not seen, Armestor, came after him.

'You seem disturbed,' said the little man, going to one of the corpses and giving it a hard kick.

'So much for our visit to Kendara,' said Fomond. 'The ones who fled us will be there long before us.'

'Wait,' said Aru. 'They never saw us. You killed their companions before they knew what was happening. They'll not have any reason to suspect us if we go there.'

Ussemitus and Fomond exchanged brief glances. 'She's right,' said Fomond. He turned to Jubaia. 'Where are you going now, wanderer?'

Jubaia shrugged. 'South, I think. As far from these lands as I can.'

'So you'll not meet any Kendarans, eh?' said Fomond.

'I've a better idea,' said Aru, and they all looked at her. 'Why don't we simply truss him up and take him with us to Kendara? He'll be our coin for a boat. The official he

235

has insulted will be delighted to have him back and is sure to reward us well.'

Ussemitus's eyes widened and Fomond guffawed. Jubaia looked as though he could not believe the evidence of his own ears. He let out a yelp and turning, leapt off among the rocks. But he ran straight into Armestor, who aimed an arrow at his chest, the point unwavering. Jubaia pulled up and fell over. He scrambled back to the others as Armestor advanced, his face serious, devoid of the humour of his companions.

'An interesting story,' he said. 'But Aru has a good point.'

'Mercy!' gasped Jubaia. 'This is intolerable. Please, kill me now! You cannot take me back. Not to that awful woman!'

There was a sudden silence. Jubaia stopped kicking and went very still. The others were all staring at him as if he had said something sacrilegious.

'That is,' he croaked, 'that awful *man*.'

Fomond had to smother another guffaw. 'So that's it! It's the wife who's after your skin! You made advances to her and she was not impressed – '

'No, no,' gasped Jubaia. Armestor let him stand. 'No, the truth is, sirs, that she was so taken with my courtship, she would not let me go. She was insatiable, sirs! I could not visit her as often as she demanded. I had to escape her! I made a terrible mistake. I hid in the inn of another woman that I happened to know – '

'You were exhausted,' said Fomond, 'so you took to the bed of another woman?'

'Not exactly. But I did dally with one of the wenches at the inn. I was discovered by a spy of my mistress. And for that she sought my hide. For that trivial incident, she set these hounds on me.' Again he aimed a kick at one of the fallen soldiers.

'I find all this incredible,' said Ussemitus. 'But Aru's idea seems best suited to our purposes. That we take you back to the port official's *wife*. And we're careful not to let him know.'

'You wouldn't!' cried Jubaia, squirming like a fish.

Aru waited until they had all had their fill of amusement at Jubaia's discomfort. 'I think perhaps we should avoid Kendara after all.'

'Oh?' said Fomond.

'Much as it would delight me to hand this oversexed brute over to his former mistress, for whom I have some sympathy, I think Kendara will be dangerous for us.'

'Why is that?' said Ussemitus. 'Have your own people been there?'

She shook her head. 'No. It's your weapons. The men who escaped will know that bowmen killed their fellows.'

Ussemitus nodded thoughtfully.

'You can't go into Kendara with your bows,' Aru went on.

'But we can't leave them behind!' protested Armestor. 'We'd be defenceless. I'd rather lose an arm than give up my bow.'

'You may lose more than an arm if you enter Kendara,' said Aru.

'Pardon me,' said Jubaia. 'But why are you good people thinking of going to Kendara at all? What could possibly interest you in that sink-hole?'

'It's a port,' said Aru, but then remembered herself and followed the policy Ussemitus had adopted of being guarded.

'Oh yes,' nodded Jubaia. 'And you want to sell me for a boat! A poor exchange! I am worth far more to you alive. Of course I am!'

'I was thinking,' said Fomond, 'that if we did exchange you for a boat, the boat would be of dubious merit.'

'Kill him and have done with it,' said Armestor.

The others looked at him. Ussemitus frowned. 'You would do that?'

Armestor looked at his feet, shuffling uncomfortably. 'Well, perhaps it would be somewhat unfair.'

Ussemitus studied the little man, whose fear was written plainly on his dark features. 'We cannot go safely to Kendara.'

'Why do you need a boat?' said Jubaia, suddenly brightening.

'That's not for you to know,' said Ussemitus.

'Boats are useful, of course,' Jubaia went on. 'But not indispensable.'

Aru took Ussemitus to one side. 'I think we should tell him that we mean to go west. There's no need to say much more than that. Perhaps in some way he can help to get us across. There may be other ports he knows of, as a traveller. He may not honour his word – '

'That's very unlikely,' Ussemitus grinned.

'He's our prisoner, though. He will have to earn his freedom. He knows that. And he's nothing to gain from betraying us.'

Ussemitus gave this some thought, but it was clear he could think of no other way west than by sea. Jubaia was indeed the only source of information open to them. 'Very well,' he nodded.

They hid the bodies among the rocks, covering them as best they could and then moved on along the forest edge, selecting a safe place to camp and eat. Jubaia had provisions with him and ate heartily. Afterwards they discussed how they should move on.

'We need to get to the western lands,' Ussemitus told Jubaia at last. Jubaia looked down at the forests that stretched westward, with an almost wistful look in his eye. 'Ah, the west,' he nodded. 'I've been there.'

'The mountain way is too dangerous,' Ussemitus went on. 'Which leaves the sea. A barrier that must be crossed.'

'Then go to the south,' said Jubaia at once. 'Through the forests and then turn west beyond the last mountains. It's a long route, but the northern seas are rough, even in summer. Many ships are lost.'

'If we went south, we'd walk straight into the armies of

238

Vittargattus,' said Fomond. 'They're coming north by that route.'

'Vittargattus,' muttered Jubaia. 'I've no great desire to meet him.'

'Oh, have you been bedding one of his wives?' said Aru. The others laughed, even Armestor, though his hand rested on his bow even as he ate.

Jubaia allowed them their humour, then scowled. 'No, sirs, but I know his clansmen, his Vaza. And I know his cities, especially Amerandabad.' He shook his head. 'A place of restless ghosts. Not for me. But why do you go west? You're moor people — well, I know that you are not. You are of the forests, surely.' No one answered him. 'Who else could use bows the way you do? And you must be Vaza, too. Have you done something to earn the wrath of Vittargattus? Is he marching on your lands?'

'Never mind that,' said Ussemitus.

'We are going to the west,' said Aru. 'So we need a boat. Or do we?'

Jubaia grinned at her, tossing back his long lock of hair. 'You, of course, are not from the forests. You are the strangest Innasmornian I have ever seen, lady. And one of the most beautiful — '

'Look, forget the compliments. I'm immune to flattery.'

'No flattery, lady. But where are you from? I should like to visit your lands.'

'You forget yourself,' cut in Ussemitus.

Jubaia nodded slowly. 'You want to go west? The sea is quickest, but it lies directly in your path. A ship from Kendara to Tollavar would be the surest way to cross it, but if you cannot go to Kendara, then there is no other port.'

'Then it's the mountains,' said Fomond.

'There is another way across,' said Jubaia. He bent down and picked up a stick, marking lines on the earthen floor of the forest, a crude map. 'See, here is the coastline . . . Here is Kendara. To the west of where we are — ' he jabbed at his map, ' — the sea breaks through a band of hard rock and opens out beyond it into a wide bay, like a huge lake.'

He pointed to the narrow opening that led out into the wider sea beyond. 'At it's narrowest, this is only a quarter of a mile across.'

Ussemitus and the others studied the map for a moment. Aru was thinking how easy it would have been if they had had a gliderboat.

'And what do we do?' said Fomond. 'Spread our arms and fly over?'

Jubaia looked hurt for a moment, but then smiled indulgently. 'There are strange legends about the place. The pirates in Kendara spoke in very veiled terms of them. I've not been there. But there are said to be ways to cross it. Dangerous, no doubt. Cliffs, pounding seas. Very inhospitable.'

'The alternative is Kendara,' said Ussemitus. 'Without weapons. Very well, we must go to this place and see it. If it is impassable, we'll have to try our fortune in Kendara.'

'But if you force me to go with you, I'll be killed!' protested Jubaia.

'In that case, Jubaia, you had better be sure of finding us a way across the neck of sea.' He leaned over him to bring home his point.

'And if I find such a way?'

Ussemitus frowned. He had not given it much thought. 'If we pass over in safety, then you'll be free to go wherever you please.'

Jubaia nodded, then rubbed out the map, scuffling the earth with his feet. 'To be honest,' he said, 'I no longer have the appetite to go southwards if I am to meet up with warriors of the clan chief. I'd not mind another trip to the west – '

'With us?' said Fomond.

'You don't trust him?' said Armestor.

'Hardly,' said Fomond.

'We'll see,' nodded Ussemitus. 'If you know the western lands, Jubaia, you may yet be useful to us.'

'If I *know* the west! Why, I was *weaned* in the west – '

'In which case,' said Aru, with a wry grin, 'we may be at some disadvantage.'

240

17

THE SPIDERWAY

They came to the lowlands beyond the forest within a few days and moved north, the coast dropping away in a range of cliffs that rose as the party followed them. Across the blue waters they could see the outline of land beyond as the coast in the west swept in to join their own eastern coast to form the narrow channel that Jubaia had spoken of. As they climbed upward, nearing the place where the narrows pinched in to their shortest distance, the skies were overcast, promising rain, and sea mist shifted restlessly about the cliffs, blurring them.

'How much further?' grumbled Armestor. He hated the exposure up here. The forest lands were behind and below them in the east, and although the open land was not barren, it was dotted with scrub and rocks, offering poor cover. It would be a bad place to be caught in a storm, especially if Kuraal still hunted them.

'Not much,' said Jubaia, who had been leading them. He seemed tireless for one so small, his thin legs far sturdier than Aru would have supposed, and he seemed in good spirits, as though there was nothing he would rather have been doing than leading this party westward. But the Innasmornians, she thought, were restless, as if they could feel a presence about them. Often she would find them, Ussemitus in particular, straining to catch a distant sound, or looking around as if he had heard something close by. She herself felt comfortable with the journey, the shadows of the Sculpted City not forgotten, but pushed back by the freshness of the land about her, the close murmurs of the sea.

'Have you crossed by this route before?' Ussemitus asked Jubaia.

'No, but I recall something about a way. It's coming back to me. The terrain is familiar, at least from the description I have heard.' He looked away and Aru glanced suspiciously at him. It was far too soon to be sure of him and whatever it was that motivated him.

'What's on his mind?' she whispered to Ussemitus.

She meant the comment innocently enough, but Ussemitus gave her a strange look. 'Only a Windmaster could read his thoughts,' he said with a frown, almost a hint of anger, though not at Aru. But she was surprised enough to back off, wondering if there was something in his remark that she had missed.

To their left, where the rocks sloped away to the cliff edge, there were a number of cracked gulleys where the land was gradually being eroded, the edge of the cliffs slowly working inward, the channel widening over a period of centuries. Jubaia took particular interest in these, as though looking for a specific one, a road perhaps. At last he led the party to the crest of a valley that crossed their path, sloping away toward the cliffs, cutting through their heights at a right angle to them. There were trees in the bottom of the valley, a deep slash of green, and the foresters all felt a sense of relief at sight of them. Overhead the clouds were conspiring, drawing together in immense grey banks.

Jubaia pointed. 'Down there,' he said. 'If this is the place I think it is, there should be a path.'

'To where?' said Fomond.

'Through the cliffs.'

But he had moved on before they could ask any more, the wind rising, making conversation out in the open difficult. Following Jubaia, they went downward towards the first of the low trees. They were twisted, bent by prevailing winds off the sea, their gnarled branches pointing inland in a bizzare uniformity that almost suggested a warning to go back. But Aru shook the ideas from her mind. There was a winding stream in the valley bottom, its sound muffled by the undergrowth, the boulders coated with moss. Birds

242

took to the air noisily, disturbed by their coming, and something larger crashed away through the bushes up the opposite bank, but otherwise the place seemed deserted.

Once into the cool embrace of the trees, the foresters felt much happier, though Aru hugged herself, colder than she would like to have been. They found the stream and drank, the water icy but pure, and there were a few strips of dried rabbit left to eat, so they paused to rest.

Armestor, who had disappeared into the bushes, emerged with a low call. He had found a narrow pathway, though it was overgrown and obviously had not been used for many years. By the time the party had assembled on it, ready to move on, Jubaia had begun to look a little less confident. Aru had been watching his face closely, aware that something was bothering him. What did he know about this place that he had not told them?

'Who made this path?' said Ussemitus.

Jubaia shrugged. 'All that is left to us is myth.'

Fomond put a hand on his shoulder, and though Fomond was not of a particularly large build, his fingers seemed thick on the little man. 'You had better enlighten us. Where does that path lead?'

'From here on, I can only guess,' mumbled Jubaia. 'But what else can I do for you? This is the path to the west. Am I free now?' This last he gabbled quickly, eyes roving the trees.

Ussemitus scowled. 'Free? You no longer wish to come with us?'

Jubaia made an effort to smile. It did not hide his unease. 'You don't want to be burdened by me. I think, after all, our paths should uncross – '

'Why this sudden change of heart?' Ussemitus insisted.

'No particular reason, I just – '

'You're frightened,' said Aru.

Jubaia tried to look indignant. 'My dear lady! Of what?' But he still looked around him as though expecting to see any number of savages burst from the cover.

'Oh, let him go,' said Fomond, his face serious for a

moment. The others looked at him, puzzled. But he grinned. 'That is, once we're across the channel. That was the bargain.'

'But the way is before you!' protested Jubaia. 'Just follow the path.'

Fomond's grip tightened. 'Lead on, little friend. Take us across, as you promised.'

Jubaia realised they meant it, and nodded, trying to brighten. He moved ahead again, but a little more cautiously, head darting from side to side. As they went further down into the narrowing valley, they found other paths, which seemed to radiate from the bottom of the valley, all joined there, and most of them quite wide, though all were overgrown. If people had once used them, it had not been for many years. The brows of the cliffs rose up over the back of the forest, drawn together in a disapproving frown. The little stream flowed faster, cutting steeply downward, the valley becoming a gorge.

'Perhaps it drops down to sea level,' said Fomond to Ussemitus. 'With a similar gorge on the other side.'

Ussemitus nodded, but Jubaia's attitude disturbed him. He could not read the little being's mind, but he knew that something dark lurked there, an unspoken fear. And the clouds overhead were like inquisitive demigods, looking down without favour on the mortals beneath. Shadows closed around the party. They left the last of the trees and were now in a deep rock cleft, a tall bar of light ahead of them where it opened to the channel and the sea. The walk downward was steep and slippery, the reek of the sea very strong, as if the tide swept in here at the flood.

Armestor was bringing up the rear. They all heard his stifled gasp and turned together in the cramped space. The far end of the cleft from which they had entered was no longer visible. Armestor could hardly be seen, like a ghost trapped in the light filtering down from above where the rocks almost fused.

'What is it?' called Ussemitus, voice muffled by the rocks.

'Something has closed the tunnel behind us,' Armestor

whispered. 'I was looking back at the trees, when suddenly a shadow took them.'

Fomond snorted. 'Did you hear anything?'

Armestor shook his head.

'The light plays tricks here,' said Jubaia. 'Soon we'll be out in the daylight.' But he moved forward so slowly that Ussemitus and Aru kept bumping into him, cursing as they did so.

Armestor again emitted a gasp and again everyone froze. He was holding up his hand in front of him. Something shimmered in the growing light from the end of the cleft.

'What is it?' said Fomond.

'Some kind of plant, I think. I can't see it clearly. Sticky. I can't get it off my hands.' There was more than a hint of panic in Armestor's voice.

They moved on, mindful of anything falling on them, but no one else experienced any difficulty. Jubaia reached the end of the cleft, and beyond him were the steep cliffs of the far wall, below him the swirl of the sea as it swept in towards the inner sea to the south. Beside him Ussemitus was the first to emerge. They were on a narrow ledge, some two hundred feet above the sea's race. Aru gasped as she came out on to the dizzy perch. But it was not the drop that stunned her, nor the sudden surprise of being confronted by the sheer wall opposite and its closeness.

Stretching between this ledge and a similar one across the far side of the gorge was some kind of swaying bridge, if bridge it was. It was made of a rope of which she had not seen the like before, almost translucent, shimmering, twisted into a fine line that threw off reflected light like pearls. It did not seem to have been fashioned in a way that would be suitable for men to use, its lines and weavings being too erratic.

Armestor came out into the light, shielding his eyes for a moment. As he studied the plant that had partially draped itself over him, he grimaced. 'This is no plant.'

Fomond looked at it, but did not touch it. 'It's web.'

Jubaia shuddered. 'As I feared,' he muttered.

Ussemitus leaned closer to him. One push would have sent the little being over the edge to his doom on the fangs of rock below, where the stream gushed out of the cleft and tumbled in a sparkle of spray to meet the sea. 'Where have you brought us?'

Aru had been looking up and down the gorge. There were numerous other bridges, strung haphazardly from one side to another, most of them below the height of the ledge. Some of them were overgrown, or seemed to be, with clumps of peculiar vegetation, possibly weed, clinging to them. They shimmered in the light, dancing in a slow way that suggested a fineness so delicate that the wind could snap them, but they had evidently held for an inestimable time. It was as though some gigantic planner had tried to weave the two sides of the gorge together, the glittering strands preventing the two land masses from drifting away from each other.

Jubaia shrugged uneasily. 'To be honest, I thought this place only existed in legends.'

'Where are we?' Ussemitus hissed.

'It's the Spiderway.'

None of the others had heard the name. Aru began to understand what some of the vegetation really was, swinging from the cables of webbing. It was a number of cocoons, things that had been trapped in the web. But by what?

'Explain,' Ussemitus demanded of Jubaia, who had flattened himself against the rock wall in real fear, fear that bordered on terror.

'It's spoken of in very old legends. Once there were creatures here, long ago, which wove the webs. See, they bind the two sides of the gorge. They were strange beings, cast out by the powers of Innasmorn because they used power to trap the first people – '

'First people?' said Fomond, leaning forward. 'Our ancestors?'

Jubaia shook his head. 'Before they came. When Innasmorn had her own races. Those who were lost when our ancestors came, with the curse that destroyed the first people.'

'Your ancestors,' said Aru, trying to catch at the deep implications. 'They came here? *To* Innasmorn? From where?'

Jubaia shrugged. 'I can only tell you so much. Must I recite the entire mythology of Innasmorn?'

'What of the creatures who dwelt here?' said Ussemitus.

'Banished here by the gods, who protected the first people. The creatures who made the Spiderway died out centuries ago. Afterwards, our ancestors found this place and used the Spiderway. In the days when there was more trade between the east and west. Until sea trade established itself, I suppose. In time this place became abandoned. Almost forgotten.' Jubaia spoke quietly, as though in a dream. But his fear had not deserted him, and the others could feel it.

Fomond gestured to the swaying webbing. 'So it's a way over. But if we are to take it, we'd better be quick. The wind is rising.'

'There's something else,' said Jubaia.

Ussemitus gave him a look that suggested he was thinking about throttling him, but he nodded.

'The gods cursed the creatures who hid here. It is said they put elementals here to protect the gorge from their abuse of it. The elementals guarded the gorge, preventing people from coming here and falling prey to the creatures. When our own ancestors came here and used the Spiderway, the winds came and made it impassable, finally driving them away.'

Fomond looked skywards. It was as though the clouds and wind gathered in answer to Jubaia, punctuating what he was saying with a fierce gust, a smatter of rain.

'Yes, the Spiderway is jealously guarded,' nodded Jubaia.

'And you brought us here,' said Aru. 'Rather than risk going back to Kendara?'

247

'Pah, it's just a legend!' Jubaia snorted, but his face was a mask of anxiety.

Fomond laughed softly. 'Yes, I'm sure it is.'

Ussemitus eyed the swinging webs. They looked extremely dangerous in the wind. He turned to Fomond. 'Dare we try this?'

Again Fomond looked to the skies. They grew darker. 'If the storm breaks, we'll have a long wait.'

'We can't go back,' said Armestor behind them. 'That is, we cannot go through the gorge until after the storm – '

'Aru?' said Ussemitus.

She had been scowling at the strange bridge. She put her hand on it, the translucent web smooth to her touch, but not sticky. She ventured out on to it, calling out that it felt strong.

Ussemitus nudged Jubaia. 'Lead on. We're going. Quickly, or I'll feed you to the sea.'

Jubaia followed Aru out on to the precarious Spiderway with alacrity. He began mumbling to himself, as if in incantation, but Aru ignored him, concentrating on the dangerous footing.

One by one they all moved out from the ledge, swaying as they went, the webbing bending as they swung out. It was not entirely smooth, in some places tacky, but this gave each of the party a little confidence. Around them the wind swirled, eddying, moaning gently to itself like a great beast in its sleep. More spots of rain fell, but as yet no squall.

As they moved further out from the cliff wall, they were aware of the sea below them, foaming about the rocks, waves thundering upward in great surges of spume and spray. Aru noticed the dark patches on the far wall, some hundred yards across from them: they were caves or openings, and from the mouths of each of them more of the webbing stretched. The entire gorge here was laced with the Spiderway, which was very fine, in places glistening and iridescent, as if woven from flexible ice. It seemed staggering that it could have lasted for such an age.

Armestor moved slowly, gritting his teeth against the fear that engulfed him, while Fomond and Ussemitus closed with Aru, Jubaia ahead of them. The little figure was conscious of them at his back, but he seemed to have closed his mind to everything but holding on to the swaying web, agile as an ant. In places he could stand on one strand only, in others a number of them interlaced, and it was equally as difficult to get a grip with the hands. The distance between the strands varied, sometimes making it hard to hold on and have a footing too. Yet Jubaia was acrobatic and light, almost as though, once he had overcome his fears, he could cross the web naturally like a fly on a wall.

They had almost reached half way when they noticed the first movements. Aru thought it must be the growing wind, tugging at the moorings of the strands, but there was a rhythmic pulsation to the movement, a hint of life in the strands themselves. She jerked her head round to face Ussemitus, whose own expression betrayed a fresh fear.

'Keep moving!' he had to shout, the wind snatching at his voice. Below them the sea seemed to heave upwards, a live thing, the waves blasting at the rocks in renewed fury, as if by their efforts they could dislodge those above them.

Armestor yelled something, trying to point. Below them, emerging from one of the caves opposite, was a glistening shape, stretching out a number of elongated limbs. They were as transparent as the webbing, while the bulbous bodies of the creatures they supported were like glass, opaque and shot through with pink veins and dark patches that were organs.

Jubaia almost lost his grip on the web, his eyes widening in horror. Other creatures were beginning to emerge, their hairless bodies pulsing like sacs of air, the light shining through them, almost as if it shone from within them. There were a dozen of them, and each of them tested the webbing as if interpreting its movements, listening to messages in the vibrations. They lifted the upper end of their bodies, where a globular, head-like section faced the intruders, the head made even more horrifying by the fact that it had no features, no eyes, only a mouth which gaped, revealing a slippery gullet down into the heart of the monster's interior.

'Some of those legends are not that old,' Fomond shouted to Jubaia, but the words were torn away as the wind began to rise.

Armestor had unslung his bow, and Fomond also did so. They let fly an arrow apiece, and both found their targets, sinking into the flesh of the gross bodies, where they could be seen far within it. But they did not seem to affect the creatures, which hopped forward, silent as ghosts, and equally as spectre-like to look upon. The raging waters below them could be seen through their bodies: it gave them futher awesomeness, as though they were fashioned by the elements, supernatural and indestructible. More arrows dug into them, but to no avail. They had the scent of blood.

'We can't go back!' Fomond yelled to Ussemitus. 'Keep moving.'

Ussemitus nodded, urging Aru onward, though from below they could see one of the creatures pulling itself slowly upwards. To their horror they saw that its front limbs were like swollen *human* arms, ending in soft claws. They did not move fast as a true spider would have, and in that there was some hope of survival.

Jubaia had no alternative but to go on, prodded and pushed by Aru, though she could feel her entire body shaking with terror. The wind was howling about them now, shaking the webbing with its own talons, but although it shook wildly, swinging up and down, it held. The creatures below seemed oblivious to the frantic movement, adjusting themselves with ease. Aru could see that she and the others would be cut off from the wall if the creatures could not be halted. Jubaia realised this at the same moment and froze, unable to move.

'You'll have to stop that monster,' Aru told Ussemitus as the first of the creatures lumbered up on to the Spiderway.

Ussemitus and his companions levelled their bows, hanging on to them as they tried to grip the strands of web with their knees. Together they released their arrows and watched as all four of them struck their mark, the gut of the creature. The arrows went in deep, dark stains within, and for a moment the creature lurched, but quickly adjusted itself, coming up on a level with them. Clearly it could not be stopped by arrows.

'Cut the strands!' cried Jubaia, panic overcoming him. 'It's the only way.'

'And fall into the sea?' replied Ussemitus.

'There are three more coming up under us,' shouted Armestor.

'Better to drop into the sea!' said Fomond.

Ussemitus cursed bitterly. They could not escape otherwise. But could they swim in those frightful waters? He faced Aru, whose own eyes were on him. But he could only look helplessly.

'Look!' shouted Armestor. Beyond them the creature was lurching, and it seemed that a fist of wind had come roaring down the gorge, punching at it.

Instinctively Ussemitus prayed to the skies, mentally shouting at them, invoking them to aid him. It was blind intuition that drove him now, a reaching out for the dark mysteries of his people. The air seemed to howl, eager to serve. The wind tore this way and that, savage as a wolf pack, swirling, unbridled. Ussemitus understood that it had not come to attack him and his companions, for all its volcanic anger.

'The wind gods!' cried Jubaia. 'They are coming!'

'Storm elementals?' gasped Fomond.

'They hear us,' Ussemitus bawled above the din. 'All of you! Use your minds to call them. Together we might make them hear us. They have no love for these abominations.'

The others, swaying precariously, exhausted by the movements that had become terribly erratic, held their heads as if voices shouted within them. Ussemitus yelled like a madman at the sky, meaningless words, shouting at whatever powers gathered there, challenging them to come down, to unleash their full fury.

A crack of thunder sounded directly overhead and forks

251

of white light struck down, dazzling the eye. One of them blasted a huge chunk of rock from the cliffs behind them, and it fell, taking with it a number of strands of the Spiderway, netting as they went two of the creatures. Encouraged, Ussemitus shouted again, but his voice was lost in the sudden din of fresh thunder. The skies were almost as dark as the night, full of rain, bursting to let it fall in thick drops. The creatures shuddered in the deluge as if brutally damaged by it. They turned away from the torrential rain, scrambling back as quickly as they could for the shelter of the caves. One of them stumbled, and the wind took it in triumph, picking it up like a bundle of leaves and pulping it against the rock wall, smearing it with the force of the impact.

Somehow the companions held on to the webbing, bounced up and down like flies, but they would not let go. Under them the sea was as grey as the sky, sucking at the lower web as though it must pull it down into it.

Ussemitus watched his fellows in the dripping rain. Even Aru had her eyes closed, praying. Bolts of energy seemed to dance about them, fuelled by the wind. Like a dozen wild beasts it howled, more rain tumbling from the sky, drenching the companions, its blows like tiny fists. They must get across soon, or be swatted away.

It took them an age to reach the far side of the Spiderway, and in that time neither the wind nor the rain abated. More thunder rocked the cliffs, and still the walls shook, releasing tons of rock and earth which were hungrily gobbled by the sea. But Ussemitus lost all fear: it was replaced by a sense of wild power, of unique fusion with the madness of the heavens, as if somehow its bolts of power had drilled into him and forged him, his will into a weapon of its own devising. He felt his reason slipping as the strength of the power struck him, forced to grapple with it as he crossed over.

The far walls closed around the company as it hopped off the Spiderway and into another high crevice in the cliff face. The rain did not beat so fiercely, and they were able to shelter under an overhang, watching the webbing behind them as it danced maniacally to the tune of the wind. Huddled together, arms wrapped about each other, they waited, too spent to do anything more. If there were any of the creatures here, they did not appear, themselves eager to escape the iron fist of the storm.

By the time the last of the rain had abated, they had recovered something of their strength. The passageway ahead was dark, dripping with rain, and the air remained thick with drizzle. Ussemitus moved them on, prodding Jubaia. He had no desire to go back, quickening his step into the waterlogged passage. He felt his heartbeat subside, the spell that had gripped him releasing him again, though it hovered in the air about him.

Fomond and Armestor exchanged glances, knowing that something strange, beyond their usual world, had occurred back on the Spiderway. Their combined pleas to the skies had coincided with the storm, almost as if they had brought it to fruition. But such thoughts were almost heretic. It was for Windmasters to do such things.

Ussemitus was also thinking of the storm. He did not speak as they moved on, climbing steadily up a steep incline that brought them at length to a way out of the passage towards more trees. Once among them they took shelter, finding a mercifully dry area protected by the thick spread of leaves above. They slumped down, glad of the chance to rest properly.

Aru sat with Ussemitus, though she was watching the bedraggled Jubaia, who quickly fell asleep. Armestor seemed to have taken up his customary post of guard: of all of them he seemed to be the one who least needed sleep, probably, she thought, because he lived on his nerves.

'What are you thinking?' Ussemitus asked her. He smiled, but there seemed to be weight on his mind.

'That we're lucky to have got out alive. What were those things?'

'Who knows?' he shrugged. 'Innasmorn spawns many

legends, some based on truth. It is said there are lands where stranger creatures roam.'

'Ussemitus,' she said, drawing closer to him so that Fomond could not hear her. He found himself surprised by her beauty, her alienness. She did not have that elemental force that coursed in the blood of all of his people, and yet she had a power of her own, a decided strength, which matched her looks. But he guarded himself against her attractiveness, seeing in his mind the amusement of Fomond, which in a way was a gentle warning.

'What about the storm?' she said. 'What happened?'

'I don't understand – '

'I think you do. It was like the moors. You called on the sky gods – '

He shook his head, not wanting to be drawn into that. 'We all did. Any Innasmornian would do. And even your voice must have helped us.'

'They answered us,' she said with a wry grin. 'I can't believe it was pure coincidence. Did we *summon* the storm?'

'We did. It is in us – '

'In you – '

'Only the Windmasters have individual control.'

She could read the concern and self-doubt in his face. 'Does it trouble you? That you may have powers you were not aware of?'

He drew back, alarmed. 'Don't say it,' he whispered, looking across at Fomond, but he had not heard. 'I am just a forester. Why should I have power?'

She had no desire to anger him. 'I meant no harm. But it came as a shock.'

He nodded, but turned away, masking his thoughts, and like Jubaia, he fell asleep. Aru looked at him for a while longer, fascinated by him, by more than the dormant power in him. Then she too, tried to sleep.

Fomond pretended not to watch her as he sat beside Armestor. 'What do you think happened?' he said softly. 'You must have sensed it.'

Armestor studied the patterns of the mist as it wreathed

the trees. 'Oh yes. Did we do that together? Or was it Ussemitus? Like on the moor – '

'I felt something reach inside of me,' said Fomond. 'But who drew it out, that power?'

Armestor looked at him grimly. 'It is him, isn't it? The gods have spoken through him. We would have died, fodder for those –'

For once Fomond remained serious. 'It must happen sometimes. It must be how the shamen are found. Ones with certain gifts. They go to the circle and are taught how to sharpen them.'

'You think he has that power?'

At last Fomond's face broke into a grin. 'Let us hope so, eh? We will need it on our strange quest.'

Armestor nodded towards Aru, who seemed to be asleep, stretched out beside Ussemitus. 'And the girl?'

'I don't know,' said Fomond, chewing his lip. 'But I think that Ussemitus is much taken with her. And with him, it is not just lust. You know he does not have it in him to abuse a woman in that way.'

'It would be dangerous if he thought too much of her.'

Fomond shrugged. 'The further we go into this business, the more confused it becomes. There is the little one, too.'

'I think we should rid ourselves of him as soon as we can.'

'You think so? If he truly knows the west – '

'As he knew this place!'

Fomond grinned. 'Hm. A mistake. And yet, we are safely across.'

Armestor got to his feet. 'I cannot sleep, not yet. I'll hunt. The crossing has made me hungry.'

'You won't catch anything in this,' Fomond began to protest, but his friend had already slipped into the mist. 'But no doubt you will prove me wrong,' he added good-naturedly to himself. 'You have your own brand of magic, Armestor. An enchanted bow that charms your prey out of the deepest places.' He smiled to himself, the terrors of the day beginning to subside. He looked about him, then

255

frowned. He got up and walked softly about the camp, half-expecting to catch a glimpse of something, a silent watcher. He had the feeling that for a while now, the party had been under observation, yet nothing had shown itself. Even so, a shadow remained, like a figure at the edge of vision.

18

QUAREEM

The following morning, after the company had managed to dry themselves under the clear skies, they felt their spirits rejuvenated, almost as if the events of the day of the crossing had been a dream. Armestor had brought several rabbits, proving Fomond's prediction to be correct, and the company ate them avidly, roasting them over a fire, no longer afraid of bringing attention to themselves. Aru had never enjoyed a meal so much, even in her own city, and a fresh part of her woke to the rawness of this world, with its peculiar storms and powers. There were moments when, deep within her, she felt an echo, a remote hint of a response to the Innasmornian elements. Perhaps, she told herself, it will come out of its darkness and surprise me as time goes on. She was no longer afraid of such a response, and somehow looked ahead to another taste of the wind's power.

Jubaia woke the day after the crossing, uncurling like an animal coming out of hibernation. He gratefully accepted some food. Once he had eaten it, he leaped up, splashed cold water from a stream in his face and pronounced himself ready to be of service in whatever way he could.

Ussemitus laughed. 'Well, you've earned your freedom, though we were lucky to survive.'

Jubaia gave him a quizzical look. 'Lucky? Perhaps. But anyway, I have no desire to wander off alone in this wilderness. Besides, you want to go west.'

'So you still want to remain with us?'

'Why not?' Jubaia grinned.

'What lies ahead?' said Fomond. 'How far do the forests extend? And are we to stumble into more of your myths? Will they be long dead, as was the Spiderway?' They had come up from the valley, which duplicated the one on the other side of the sea passage, and found themselves moving into a dense forest, tall pines rising up majestically in endless battalions, rustling in a gentle breeze.

'This is the forest of Spellavar. It spreads from here down along the coast of the northern sea to the mountains south of it. It also spreads across to the west, its fringes turning north of the city of Amerandabad. To the further north there are more mountains, wild, inhospitable places. The Dhumvald. And to the west runs a long spine of mountains, the Thunderreach Range, which we must cross.' As he spoke, he scratched in the dirt with a broken twig, making another of his crude maps.

'How do we cross?' said Aru.

Jubaia shrugged as if to say it would be an easy enough task. 'There are passes. Caravans use them. We could join one. Amerandabad trades with other cities beyond the Range. And caravans don't mind company. We can earn our passage by lending them our arms. Bowmen such as you will be a great boon to any caravan.'

'Why?' said Armestor suspiciously. 'Are they in danger?'

Jubaia grinned. 'To some extent. Amerandabad has become a major city of trade.' He drew more lines on his map. 'Running through it and on to the south is the Fulgor River, which later widens quickly through its flood plain to the sea. Ships travel up the Fulgor laden with all manner of things. And here in Thunderreach, with so many passes, Amerandabad has ideal routes for trade with the cities of the west. There have been a good few wars between the westerners and the southerners, so Amerandabad sits prettily in the middle, acting as an agent for trade between them. The westerners need the silk and cloth of the south, and the wheat of the south east, while the southerners need the oil and sea harvest of the west. Amerandabad does very well out of both.' He laughed again. 'And of course, there are always those who try to plunder a small caravan for its riches. Sometimes there are items brought across from the west of great value, to both the south and Amerandabad. Brigands take a chance on this when attacking a caravan.

258

So you see, we would be welcome on a crossing, provided we could convince the caravaneers we are not the agents of brigands, setting the caravan up for an attack.'

Fomond chuckled. 'I see. Then we had better leave that to you, glib tongue.'

'What of the western cities?' said Aru.

Jubaia's eyes narrowed. 'Well, good sirs, if you were to tell me what it is you seek in the west – '

Ussemitus shook his head. 'In time, we may tell you. But this is not yet a time for trust, Jubaia. You have to earn that.'

Jubaia screwed up his face, but nodded. 'Yes, I suppose it is only reasonable. But I'm curious, of course. You seem to know nothing of the west, yet seek it avidly.'

No one answered him and the conversation came to an end. After that they began the march once more, going deeper into the rising forests. These lands were like their own in many ways, though the trees were younger, less packed and without the banks of undergrowth that tangled those of the east. They could hear sounds from great distances, the columns of trees sending far messages to them, the movements of animals, birds in flight, and occasionally a moan of wind or a chuckle of water where another stream ran away to join the rivers that met with the Fulgor. The tranquillity of the forest held them, soothing them in its way, a welcome contrast to the bedlam of the Spiderway, and for several days they said very little.

One evening Aru jerked up from dozing. She had almost been asleep in a bank of dried needles when she thought she heard something above them. She was used to all the sounds the birds made and had become able to tell which was which, the hawks, the pigeons, even errant seagulls. But this had been a more familiar sound.

Ussemitus rolled over, eyes blinking in the faint glow of the fire. 'What was it?'

'Did you hear it, too? I thought it must have been a dream.'

He nodded, looking for the others. Armestor was sound

259

asleep, as was Jubaia, who seemed capable of sleeping at any time. Fomond was out among the trees, keeping watch.

'It was no bird,' said Ussemitus.

'The wind?'

'Possibly.'

They listened for a while longer, but there was no repetition of the sound, and soon afterwards they both dropped into a light sleep.

Fomond, meanwhile, had also heard something above him. He was quick to slip through the trees, going upwards to higher ground. As he came to the crest of a ridge, there was an open area, and he skirted it, looking for an outcrop that might give him a better view over the forest. Although it was night, it was clear, and his night vision was very good. Most of the foresters had this skill, and as long as the skies did not bring mist or low cloud, they could see for many miles.

Fomond saw nothing unusual below, but going beyond the ridge, he saw lights in the forest. They were low down among the trees in a dip, subdued. But it was no camp fire: he would have recognised its pattern. And there were no torches. Just a steady, roseate glow. Curious, he moved down the slope, keeping well hidden. He moved with absolute silence, a master of his craft. Even an animal would not have noticed his movement. There was a faint breeze, but it was from west to east, while he was going south, so no one would catch his scent, even an expert woodsman.

Down in the forest he came to a jumble of rocks, softened with a cover of moss and lichen. He slid among them, looking beyond the source of light. His eyes widened at what he saw.

A Blue Hair! And with him were three solid-looking warriors in the accoutrements of Vittargatus. They stood on guard over a single brand, though it was no firebrand that jutted from the centre of the little clearing. It seemed to be a rod, the tip of which glowed. The Blue Hair was watching the skies as if he had summoned elementals to help him in whatever ritual he was about to perform.

Fomond decided it would be better not to remain. Discovery would be the end of him. He was about to twist back through the rocks, when he heard again the sound from the sky, a gentle hiss of air as if something passed. Looking up, he saw the shadow, a stain on the sky. It was a craft, similar to the one he had seen Aru crash. A glider-boat, she had called it. In the glow, three faces peered down. Moments later the craft turned gently, coming down to land before the Blue Hair and his wide-eyed warriors as gently and delicately as a leaf.

The three intruders got out of the craft, picked out by the glow. They were all dressed in thin armour, made, Fomond was sure of it, of metal, and he recognised them as being similar to the warriors who had originally accompanied Aru. Men, and obviously from the Sculpted City in the far eastern mountains. But what did they seek here? With a Blue Hair! Fomond edged as close as he dared.

The voice of the Windmaster came to him clearly on the silent night air. 'I am Quareem,' said the shaman. 'The one you were to meet. You see, as it was promised, your craft has come this far without harm. I have spoken to the winds, who have not molested you.' He took from his robes a packet of something, Fomond could not see what, and handed it to the leader of the Men. The latter opened it, read something and nodded. He slipped the packet inside his tunic and handed something in return to the Blue Hair. It sparkled in the glow of the rod, metallic.

Quareem studied the metal object, turning it over and over, himself nodding.

'I am Vymark,' said the warrior to him. 'Zellorian told me you would be here. There is business we must conduct.'

The Blue Hair, Fomond now saw, was far less tall than Kuraal, and much older. His shoulders hunched and his face had a twist of cruelty that was unmistakable. Although his mane of hair spread down his back in the manner of his kind, it was thinning, revealing the pale skin of his skull, and his face and hands were almost white, as if he had contracted some illness. His features were drawn, lined and scarred, but his eyes were bright, and in them was a greed that almost burned. Fomond knew it instinctively.

'I have conducted business with your master before,' said Quareem. 'As he will have told you. But where is Urtbrand? I usually speak to him.'

The warrior who called himself Vymark stiffened as if a cold wind had brushed him. 'I knew him as a friend. But he is unable to come.'

Quareem stepped forward. Fomond could see that he was not in the least afraid of the Man before him, though Vymark appeared to be a formidable warrior and must surely be extremely dangerous. Fomond wondered if the Blue Hair could reach into the minds of Men as he did his own kind.

'He is dead?' said Quareem, looking into the eyes of the other.

Vymark looked angry, but held it in check. 'Murdered by our enemies.'

'They escaped you?'

Vymark looked out at the forest and Fomond felt the edge of hate in the Man's voice. 'One of them is here somewhere. Lost in your lands. But we will find her.'

'Here? Then we shall indeed find her. She will not go far on Innasmorn.'

Vymark suddenly snapped out of his black thoughts. 'Never mind that for now. What news do you have for Zellorian?'

Quareem grinned, but there was no warmth in that smile. 'Vittargattus is fully mobilised. He has called upon warriors from the south lands, and new alliances have been struck. Soon he will begin the first of his troop movements.'

Vymark nodded. 'The details?'

'They are in the papers I have given you, and with a map.'

'Tell me anyway,' said Vymark. Behind him the soldiers were listening attentively.

'Very well,' Quareem nodded. 'Vittargattus will send one

of his armies north, through these forests to the mountains beyond them, turning east for the coast and the city of Tollavar. From there the army will sail for Kendara. Vittargattus has agents there who have already prepared the city for the arrival of the army. He will himself travel with his main force to the south, joining with his southern allies under King Ondrabal, and they will move south and east. When the time comes, both armies will close in on your city, one from its north, and the other from its south.'

Vymark grunted. 'Are these warriors with you loyal to you?'

Quareem turned to his men. Their faces were locked, their emotions hidden, as if torture would not release them. 'Oh yes, indeed. I have not gathered many to me, but those that I have, I assure you, would put a knife into Vittargattus tomorrow had they the chance, or any of his Vaza scum.'

'Why?' said Vymark, going to the men and inspecting them as if they were on parade. They did not flinch under his gaze.

'Why?' repeated Quareem. 'Like me, they are ambitious.'

'Zellorian expects loyalty. The rewards will be very high.'

'I am sure.'

Vymark turned to him again, deliberately showing his back to the warriors. His own Men were motionless, but Fomond could sense their power, their strength. They were far more muscular than the Innasmornians, coiled with energy. In a fight, they would be very difficult to better for strength.

'Zellorian has promised you much,' he told Quareem.

'It is no little thing that I do for him. I am giving him the key to powers he has only guessed at.'

'Instead of taking them for yourself?' said Vymark sceptically.

Did he not feel the anger of the Blue Hair? Fomond wondered. Even from here it was apparent.

'Perhaps Zellorian did not tell you my circumstances.'

'Explain them to me.'

Quareem nodded, his eyes slitting. 'As you are aware, I am a shaman. A Blue Hair, which means that I am party to particular powers on Innasmorn. There is a circle of power, an inner circle, to which all Blue Hairs attain. I have been refused admission to it, in spite of my gifts. Unless I can become a member of the circle, I cannot move on. I cannot enhance my powers. Not unless I have help from another source.'

'Zellorian?'

'Yes. Zellorian has promised me power of another kind. Power within his new regime. With his own success will come the opening of other, greater doors.'

Fomond felt himself going cold, his arms gripping the rock tightly. Should he unsling his bow and kill the shaman now? And Vymark? Yes, he must do this. Slowly he slid the bow from his shoulders and took two arrows from their quiver.

'The door to the west?' said Vymark.

'Yes. The door to the west,' answered Quareem, eyes sparkling in the glow of the rod, which seemed to brighten as he echoed the words. Fomond felt his hands shaking. The west? He paused, waiting.

'What is this power in the west?' said Vymark.

'Very little is known of it,' said Quareem. 'Few Innasmornians have dared to search for it. It destroys. Legends say it is locked in a cursed land, a land pervaded by plagues and fire, and by other abominations. Only the insane would search it out.'

Vymark suddenly grinned, his face transformed. Fomond saw that he was surprisingly handsome, not the demon he had first thought him. 'Then my master is insane?'

Quareem chuckled, indulging the young man his humour. 'I am sure he is not. He merely taps powers that exist. He has powers of his own that no Innasmornian has.'

'You know the way to this land, this power?'

'I can find it.'

'Good.'

'But there is to be a testing first. A sharing.'

Vymark nodded. 'You have decided where it shall be?'

'Again, it is in the papers you have. I have suggested to Zellorian that we meet in the northern mountains. We will intercept Vittargattus's army there.' He stopped for a moment, looking out at the forest, seeing perhaps, the downfall of the clan chief.

Fomond lifted his bow, the arrow nocked. Should I kill him now? But if he knows the way to the place of power, we should save him. Capture him. Yet this seemed a hopeless idea.

'Zellorian is anxious to try out his new powers,' Quareem went on. 'His mastery of the magic of Innasmorn.'

Vymark nodded slowly. How much did this gnarled shaman know?

'With my help, he will blast the northern army to nothing. Between us we will summon up a storm that will wipe it from the face of the world. It will be a storm such as has not been seen on Innasmorn for centuries.'

'How many?' said Vymark.

Quareem turned to him, coming out of his frightful reverie of destruction. 'What?'

'How many will perish?'

'Vittargattus is sending ten thousand warriors north. Fodder for Zellorian's power. He will be content, I think?'

Vymark looked away, and for a moment Fomond wondered if he was appalled by the thought of the act. But when he turned back, Vymark was smiling.

'It is a beginning only,' said Quareem softly. His skeletal hand gripped Vymark's arm. 'When we have mastered the deathstorm, the storm-of-the-dark, then nothing will bar our way forward. With the deathstorm, we go to the west, to the forbidden lands, and open the gate to true power.'

Fomond felt the trickle of sweat down his back, and another that ran into his eyes. His entire body shook at the thought of the supernatural horrors that the renegade shaman was prepared to unleash. Combined with the powers of Zellorian, they would be frightful beyond imagin-

265

ing. Innasmorn stood on the very brink of annihilation. He must kill Quareem now!

Again he raised his bow, but his muscles seemed locked, his mind gripped by a powerful force. Had he been discovered! But the others made no show of knowing he was here. He could not release the arrow. A spell? Protection sown by the Windmaster?

Vymark moved, his body inadvertently shielding the shaman. He was speaking again, but his words had become muffled. A wind had sprung up, typically abrupt, and it bent the tops of the pines as it swirled around the camp.

Fomond caught a glimpse of movement beyond the rim of the clearing. Quareem's henchmen were leaving. Moments later Vymark turned to his own warriors, and to Fomond's horror he saw that Quareem himself had gone. Like the very air, he had vanished into the night. The meeting was ended. Vymark and his men were back inside the gliderboat. Fomond's arm sagged. The moment for the kill was gone.

The gliderboat hummed, rising. Minutes later it was above the trees and then away. Fomond sank down, exhausted.

Some time later, Fomond got to his feet and sped back up the ridge and beyond it. He slipped back to the camp of his companions. Armestor woke at once, the lightest sleeper of them all, and Fomond shook Ussemitus. Before long they were all awake, even Jubaia, who usually slept through anything. They gathered around Fomond, who did not raise his voice for fear that the very air would hear him and pass his words on.

He explained what he had seen, and what he had heard.

Aru shrank back, aghast, horrified at the thought of what Zellorian intended. None of them spoke for a long time, each picturing the dreadful destruction that was to be released in the north.

Jubaia shook his head, his face creased with anger. 'The deathstorm,' he said to himself, over and over. 'The deathstorm.'

'What do you know about it?' Ussemitus asked him.

Jubaia snorted. 'Only a madman like Quareem would attempt to summon such a thing.' He sat cross-legged by the last embers of the fire, gazing into them, into his own past perhaps. 'It is no secret that Quareem was rejected by the inner circle of the Blue Hairs. He has tried too often to tamper with powers that he should not. Dark powers.

'You all know, and even you, good lady, have learned something of the elemental forces of Innasmorn, how we worship them, how we communicate with them.' He looked across at Ussemitus, though his face was in shadow. 'Well, there are forces on Innasmorn that are never touched, forces beyond the limits of our normal world.'

Ussemitus leaned forward. 'How do you know so much of these things?'

'I have lived in Amerandabad and in other cities. Believe me, I have heard of such darkness. From long ago, centuries gone by. But not dead. Like those monsters we found, dormant. Waiting for a fool such as Quareem to come along—'

'But why should he do it?' said Armestor.

Jubaia shrugged. 'As Fomond told us, he sees no other way to win power. And he must think this Zellorian you spoke of can help him master the storm-of-the-dark. They are equally as foolish if they do.'

The company fell silent, considering Jubaia's words.

Aru touched Ussemitus gently. 'I think it is time we told Jubaia who I am and why we are here.'

Ussemitus glanced at the little being. Fomond had not thought to be guarded in his report, but Aru was right. Jubaia could not be an enemy. He was no fool, but what was his purpose? Was he the wanderer he claimed to be? Or was he an agent of the clan chief?

Ussemitus nodded. 'Yes. We have to trust you, Jubaia.'

Jubaia grinned, the expression they knew better. 'Ah, you forest folk! Every bit as suspicious as I had heard.'

'You knew where we were from the moment you met us,' said Fomond.

Jubaia chuckled. 'But of course! Anyone would have done. But please, this is no insult. In Amerandabad, people like you are thought of as rather special. Elementals, creatures of the trees. Even Vittargattus thinks there are demons in the far forests. His dreams are filled with such imaginings.'

They all smiled at this, though Armestor remained nervous. 'All the more reason to avoid the city,' he said.

'Ah,' sighed Jubaia, sitting back, stroking his chin. He looked like something carved from wood, a dwarf in the shadows. 'Perhaps.' He turned to Aru. 'But, lady, your story. I am avid to hear it.'

Aru looked to Ussemitus, and he nodded. 'Yes, he should be told.'

She went over her own story again, leaving out nothing, even about her father, and it was with an effort that she kept the tears from her eyes, her fingers digging into the soft earth, finding a strange comfort in it, as if Innasmorn understood her sorrow.

Jubaia listened as avidly as he had promised, and the others were also taken with the tale, understanding it better.

'And you saw Vymark,' she said to Fomond at the end of it, shaking her head. 'I have a debt to settle with him. Denandys and the knights were the best. Our hopes rested with them. What hope now for the Sculpted City?' She looked away, her eyes moist.

'Was he your lover?' Ussemitus asked her softly.

She shook her head, not speaking.

Jubaia looked upon her with a kind of reverence. 'My lady, I had guessed you to be of special origin. But from another realm! A place of wonders—'

'And of horrors,' she replied at once. 'You cannot know what we have left behind us. The Csendook.'

They all felt the bitterness in her voice. She repeated the hated name.

'They sound terrible beyond belief,' said Jubaia. 'You

268

did better to come to Innasmorn. The Csendook make our humble world sound civilised.'

'But don't you see! Zellorian can only be seeking power for one reason. Not to rule your world. He cares nothing for Innasmorn. To him it is a rock, a bare moon. Though he wants its power. And when he has it, he'll go back and turn it on the Csendook. *That's* what he wants.'

No one spoke. She knew best what this meant, though Jubaia looked appalled. 'He must be stopped. Whatever the cost. We must do everything we can to prevent this catastrophe in the north.'

'But how, Jubaia?' said Ussemitus. 'Should we go there in search of Quareem?'

Jubaia frowned, then covered his face with his hands, thinking. At last he looked up. 'No. We would get lost up there. I don't know the terrain, and Quareem has other allies. What of these flying craft?'

'Gliderboats,' said Aru.

'Yes, lady, gliderboats. If he has access to them, we would be like cripples trying to find him. Time becomes precious.'

Aru looked uneasily at the heavens. 'If the gliderboat came this far over the forests, Quareem must have prevented Innasmorn from harming it. Could he do this?'

Jubaia nodded. 'I think he could.'

Fomond snorted. 'It seems to me that we'll find it difficult to achieve anything in the far west, if the land is so evil.'

'I have a suggestion,' said Jubaia.

No one demurred: they had nothing to offer themselves.

'Go to Vittargattus. He is yet at Amerandabad. Tell him what you know.'

Armestor paled and Fomond looked dubious.

'It would be dangerous,' said Ussemitus in a tired voice.

'He knows Quareem, though not as well as the Blue Hairs do,' said Jubaia. 'They know he's a malcontent. And the Lady Aru can confirm your story. What else is open to us?'

Fomond nodded slowly. 'Yes, Vittargattus should be told. Think of his warriors marching to a slaughter.'

'It will be easy enough getting into Amerandabad,' said Jubaia. 'I have friends there. I can get you clothes. Everyone is going there, all eager to join the armies and serve.'

'Are they so hungry for war?' said Armestor.

Jubaia shook his head. 'It is fear that moves them. Fear of the Lady Aru's people. Tales of the sky falling. The curse from beyond Innasmorn. It is how the Blue Hairs have spoken of these things, filling the air with poison.'

'Then Aru will be in grave danger,' said Ussemitus. 'We cannot allow her to—'

'We'll disguise her,' said Jubaia. 'Until she is brought before Vittargattus. Then he can hardly fail to be charmed by her—'

Aru snorted. 'Spare me your flattery. You'll need your quick talking for Amerandabad.'

'You would go?' said Ussemitus.

'There's no other way. He must be warned,' she nodded.

Ussemitus glanced at Jubaia. How well did this suit the little being? Had he planned this? Ussemitus would have preferred another path, but there was none. They had to risk the wrath of the clan chief, otherwise his warriors would be annihilated.

19

VITTARGATTUS

Several days after Fomond had seen Quareem and Vymark, the company followed the banks of a narrow river that wound southwards. Jubaia said there would be villages and that they could probably ride by boat down to Amerandabad. He tapped one of his many pouches with a grin, telling them he had a few coins he could spare, though Ussemitus and his friends knew little about currency. They did know, however, that the little man had become indispensable. The uncertainty seemed to ease and they could not bring themselves to harbour misgivings about him.

'There are parts of the city where I have friends,' Jubaia told them. 'And places where we can stay. I'm good for credit, although there are other parts of Amerandabad where I'd be nailed to a door if I were seen.'

'Your amorous past?' said Fomond.

Jubaia laughed. 'Not that so much. No, it's my trade.'

'Which is?' said Aru.

'It can't hurt to tell you now. I'm a thief.'

The others looked surprised, but Jubaia laughed again.

'Then Amerandabad is even more dangerous for us, if you're wanted,' said Ussemitus. 'Why didn't you tell us before?'

'You'd have cast me out, I suspect. Don't worry, I've not stolen anything of yours. And thieving is a common enough trade in Amerandabad. It's a way of life. Mostly petty, though there are a few rogues who employ companies of thieves for their business. But mostly they operate further afield, in the southern lands where newer cities have sprung up.

'I'll find you a safe place to stay, trust me. And as you are my friends, you'll be trusted.'

271

Ussemitus and his companions wondered even more about the wisdom of visiting the city, but they could think of no better alternative. Armestor in particular grew increasingly alarmed, and would gladly have gone back into Spellavar, but Fomond kept his spirits up, talking him round.

When they came to the first of the villages, Jubaia spoke for them as he had promised and there were no problems getting a seat on the next boat downriver. The craft was not large, enough to take a dozen warriors, and a few individuals were already on board, men of the local forests by the look of them, who kept their thoughts to themselves. Aru wore a hood to cover her hair and part of her face, devised by Jubaia, who thought that in these parts she might attract attention to herself as the women of the river were of slight build, their features far narrower than Aru's.

They assembled in the prow of the boat, watching the river ahead where trees crowded its banks, obscuring the view of anything in the forest. Ussemitus was intrigued by the boat itself. It was thirty feet long, flat with a central deck raised above the others, and on this the pilot stood, turning a wheel this way and that as he negotiated the countless bends of the river. He was a swarthy-skinned fellow, his face vacant, as though he paid no attention to the passengers he carried. Above him the sail flapped, though there was little wind.

Jubaia saw Ussemitus's confusion. 'Kezrel has worked the river for years. The elements understand him well. I think he must have sealed a pact with the wind currents as well as those of the river.'

'What do you mean?' said Aru, who had overheard.

'Well,' said Jubaia, enjoying the gossip, 'when there's no discernible wind, it's time to get out the oars. But Kezrel's boat has none. He never needs them, no matter how calm it is. Be thankful, for it's no fun pulling at an oar, I can tell you.'

They sailed on downriver for many miles, sleeping where they sat at night. Eventually they came to the confluence with the Fulgor, and Kezrel moored his craft at a landing stage that led to another village. Jubaia thanked him, exchanging a few words with him in private, and the pilot seemed quite content. Already a small number of passengers were preparing to board his craft for the journey back upriver.

Jubaia led his companions along the landing stage, and they were intrigued by the activity there. There were mounds of pots, nets strewn about and people working busily, men, women and children, all shouting at each other and gesticulating, ignoring the travellers.

'Fisherfolk mostly,' said Jubaia, nodding cheerfully to several of them. Some acknowledged him, though they were not concerned about the foresters. 'There have been so many comings and goings of late, they're used to strangers.'

He led them to one of the many wooden huts and went inside. Ussemitus and the others waited, feeling conspicuous, but apart from the people working on the nets and scores of other small boats, there was no one about, and certainly no one that they needed to fear. Eventually Jubaia beckoned them inside and they were glad to go into the shadows of the hut.

Jubaia stood beside an old woman who was no bigger than he was. She bowed as the others came in, her face incredibly wrinkled, her back bent almost double. 'Come along,' she called, and they wondered if she could see them at all. 'There's plenty to suit you.' She had a marked accent, but Ussemitus caught her words.

Looking round the hut, which seemed extraordinarily large inside, he realised that it was a small warehouse of clothes. There were pelts, hides, bundles of sheepskin and various other materials, most of which he did not recognise, some in marvellous colours. All in all there must be considerable wealth here, and he commented on it softly to Jubaia.

'Urug has been collecting and bartering for years, haven't you, my darling?' Jubaia said to the old crone and she laughed pleasantly. 'She'll find you clothes to suit you, never fear.'

Urug inspected Aru, showing surprise at her build, though she said nothing. The robe that Aru had adapted fascinated the old woman, who kept feeling its material, sniffing at it like a hound. But she shuffled away amongst the piles of clothes and came back with a number of outfits. Aru chose a plain one that had a hood and enough play in the skirt to disguise her build.

'You want warriors' gear?' Urug said to the others.

'Nothing conspicuous,' Jubaia chided her. 'They aren't going to war. Not yet anyway. Just something to get by in Amerandabad.'

'For thieving?' said Urug matter-of-factly, as if discussing any other occupation.

Jubaia chuckled. 'She means that if you were to follow my trade, you'd want something special. In the clothes. Pockets and so on.'

They found what they needed and changed, leaving their old clothes with Urug as part payment, although she tried to haggle for the bows, which she obviously thought valuable. Jubaia took care of her, finally reaching an agreement that seemed to satisfy her. When the company was again in the sunlight, Jubaia told them he had known Urug for as long as he could remember. 'I've taken her many a gift in the past. She'll say nothing of our being here. There's a saying in Amerandabad: as tight as Urug's lips.'

Aru felt more comfortable as they boarded a larger craft that would take them out along the wide Fulgor to Amerandabad. She felt warm with the hood up, but if anyone asked, said Jubaia, she was to say she was unwell. But he did not think anyone would bother them. Amerandabad was a city of secrets, riddled with intrigues. Ussemitus and Fomond sat with Aru and a number of other youths, all of whom talked excitedly about the prospects of going south to the city. The ship moved sluggishly, but once it was in the main current, its prow cut a furrow through the waves and the wind whipped at the twin sails.

'Bound for Amerandabad?' said one of the young warriors. He wore a cracked leather harness of which he was obviously proud. 'Me and my friends are to join the army. Going to join the troops with King Ondrabal. Going to be a war soon. You with Vittargattus?'

'Surely,' nodded Fomond. 'News travels far.'

'Aye,' nodded the youth. 'Your friend looks ill. Not used to the river?' He was indicating Armestor, whose face was white.

Fomond clapped him on the shoulder. 'Well, we're far from home. In the western forests we don't have ships like this.'

'Oh, the west. We're from east. Quarries. But there aren't many of us left in our villages. Vittargattus is recruiting heavily. Same in the west?'

'Yes. Quite an army he's gathering.'

Aru turned to Ussemitus. 'Vittargattus must be gathering every available man for the armies. This is terrible, Ussemitus. If he sends them into Quareem's trap, this part of Innasmorn will be decimated. We have to succeed.'

He did not reply, nodding slowly. Beside him, Jubaia was talking animatedly to other potential soldiers, all of whom seemed excited about the prospects of battle.

'They don't understand what war is,' said Jubaia to Ussemitus and Aru. For once his face looked grave. 'I've seen such things, though far from here. If these youths knew.' He said no more for a while, and the company sat quietly among the travellers, who themselves grew more boisterous and noisy.

It was afternoon when they saw Amerandabad. Its walls rose up steeply, and above them there were numerous towers and blocks of stone, roofs stretching back into a cliff face, for the city backed on to the overhang of a mountain. Other peaks spread in lines to the north and south, the high Thunderreach, which dwarfed anything Ussemitus and his companions had ever seen before. The city came as a shock to them, for they could never have imagined anything so big, and for a while they gazed at it in bewilderment. Aru was surprised for a different reason. The city was no more spectacular than those of her own race, though it was primitive in many ways, but it spoke of a far more complex civilisation than she had expected on Innasmorn. How old was it?

Jubaia was amazed by his companions' fascination, explaining what the various buildings were, where the stone had come from to build them, and how the city had stood for many generations, since long before the time of Vittargattus. 'It was built originally by a race that is now long dead. Then it became deserted. That was another war. The two armies that fought almost wiped each other out. In the end no one won and they dissipated. Amerandabad became the home of anyone who could make a home there. They say it was the golden age of thievery!

'Vittargattus, like the Vaza he is, is nomadic, but in order to unite the clans he needed a base, so he chose Amerandabad. Since he has been here, some attempts have been made to restore parts of it. Ah, but what must the city have been like in its prime!'

The ship docked along a stone wharf, and scores of stevedores worked noisily, hauling supplies on shore, loading up carts that came and went in an endless array. Somewhat dizzied, Ussemitus and the others stepped on to the quay, only to be hustled away swiftly by Jubaia. 'Don't wait about here,' he said. 'You'll be stripped by the wharf thieves, or accosted by the whores while the urchins empty your pockets. On a bad day you'd be dragged off to serve on one of the southern galleys. They're always on the lookout for someone to man the oars.'

Aru was even more stunned than her companions. Innasmorn was more thickly populated than her people had known. And they were nothing like as primitive as Zellorian had said. The Imperator Elect was a complete fool if he thought he could dismiss these nations as vermin.

Inside the walls of the city the air was stifling, thick with shadows, for the buildings were piled one on top of another like hastily constructed towers, almost shutting out the bright sunlight. Jubaia seemed to know every inch of the place, the mazes of streets. Here and there he would call to someone, and they would wave or laugh, their insults friendly.

He took his charges to what must have been the most unsavoury part of the entire city. It was dirty, the minute streets full of rubble and rubbish; the people wore ragged clothes and looked as though they had never seen water. Beggars called out for food, stray cats and dogs prowled along the alleys nervously, scuttling from sight when Jubaia came near them. Harsh voices called down from above, sometimes haranguing those below. Ussemitus found himself wishing he had never left the forests. How could people live in such squalor! Did they know of the elements? Did they have shrines to them? He must ask Jubaia later. But here they were far from the sun. The buildings were crammed together, built on top of ruins, and though they rose almost desperately to the sunlight and open skies, the canyons they made were where the people scurried, like rodents in their lairs.

To Ussemitus's horror, the little man led them down some steps to yet another level of the city that went below it. They crossed over narrow bridges that spanned dark wells where waters gurgled. The walls here stank of the river and worse, dripping and slime-coated. But Jubaia insisted the company follow him through a number of rotting doors and over more chasms. At length they went through a compound and up some wooden stairs to a house which Jubaia promised them would be safe. He knocked softly a number of times and was at last admitted.

The place was bare inside, though there were a few ancient divans. It looked as if the rats enjoyed a home here.

'What a hovel!' exclaimed Fomond.

Jubaia ignored him. 'I'll get food and drink.' Without another word he left them and Aru was glad to toss back her hood, though she wrinkled her nose at their surroundings.

'Is your city as impoverished as this one? So far from the

light?' Ussemitus asked her. In the shadows he and his fellows looked fragile, as if the darkness diminished them.

'In the past, in my own world, there must have been such places.' She sat down, suddenly tired. Armestor slumped, looking like a man in a dream, his nerves rubbed raw by what he had seen in the last few days. He should never have come out of the forest, Aru knew. Too much of this and he would break. She had seen such things.

Jubaia returned and for a moment their spirits rose. He carried a large tray and on it were goblets and a pitcher of clear water. There was also bread but no meat. 'Give me time and I'll do better for us,' said Jubaia apologetically. 'Wine and meat. But for now — '

'This is perfect,' said Ussemitus and the others were glad of the food. 'And you can forget the wine, Jubaia. While we are here, we can do without it.'

Jubaia nodded. 'Very sensible. But when you live in this accursed city, you begin to appreciate strong wine, no matter now poor it is.'

'It has been arranged,' said Jubaia.

Ussemitus and the others had been waiting through the long evening for his return, trying to get a little sleep, although they were not at ease in the room they had been given. Although they heard voices in the house, they had seen no one, but Jubaia had promised them no one would trouble them. There were no enemies here, he had said.

'He has a surprising amount of influence,' Fomond had commented.

Now that he had returned, Ussemitus was relieved that he might at last be able to accomplish his mission. 'Vittargattus will see me?'

'I think so. I spoke to a friend, who spoke to an accomplice, who spoke to one of the guards, who in turn — '

'Spare us the details,' groaned Fomond. 'What do we do?'

'I am to take Ussemitus to meet another guard. If he

goes alone it will be best. Then when he has given his story, hopefully to the clan chief himself, Aru can be called to substantiate it.'

'I'd prefer to go with him,' said Fomond.

'And I,' nodded Armestor.

'In time, in time. We must tread very carefully here,' said Jubaia. 'The clan chief is a busy man. And far more powerful than you realise. If you all try and see him, he'll dismiss you without seeing any of you. One man has a better chance. Ussemitus?'

Ussemitus considered, but nodded. 'Very well.'

There was more protest, but at the end of it, Ussemitus left with Jubaia, who promised to be back with word as soon as he had it. He led Ussemitus on another tortuous route through the lower levels of the city, though at last they came to more salubrious quarters, where the streets were less confined and far cleaner, and where the quality of the shops was better and where there seemed to be no ragamuffins and beggars. They entered a courtyard where there were a number of uniformed guards, and Ussemitus recognised the livery of Vittargattus.

'This is the man you were told of,' Jubaia said to an officer at another gate. He turned to Ussemitus. 'This is Curubos, one of the inner guards. He is to take you into the fortress. Trust him,' he whispered.

'Wait here,' said Curubos to Jubaia, indicating a small room that led off from the gate arch. He was taller than Ussemitus, lean and angular, and although he had a short wooden knife in his belt, he also carried a sword that was cast from metal. His gaze was cool, non-commital, as though he perhaps acted against his better judgement, but Jubaia nodded encouragement to Ussemitus.

'Come with me,' said Curubos stiffly, and then said nothing else. Ussemitus left Jubaia, his heart hammering. They went under the arch and deep into the fortress, under more archways and through thick wooden doors that were opened on Curubos's command. Finally they climbed some wide steps and went into a building that seemed to be at

279

the heart of the fortress, rising to the sky as if, at last, there was a place where the winds could be met and worshipped. Inside this place it was bare, the walls and floors grey, little light admitted so that brands had been lit. The air hung with smoke and Ussemitus found himself coughing a number of times. Curubos ignored him as though he was not there.

He stopped outside a smaller door, one that had something stamped on it, words that Ussemitus did not recognise. Curubos knocked and in a moment was admitted. He nodded to Ussemitus for him to enter.

Within there was a bare table, several candles lighting the room where a single figure sat. This man, also a soldier, ran his fingers through his long hair tiredly, then waved Curubos away. The door closed and Ussemitus felt penned, trapped by the stone, for which he had no great love. The elements seemed as far away as his forest home.

The man before him yawned, bored. He had a face that was fuller than most of the other soldiers Ussemitus had seen, and he looked as though he took far less exercise than his subordinates. He got up slowly and stretched, studying the forester as if he had little interest in him. Perhaps, Ussemitus thought, this was a test.

'I am told you seek an audience with Vittargattus. Why is that?' He sat on the edge of the table, arms folded. He might have been interviewing one of his fresh recruits, one of the youths from off the ship.

Ussemitus had to clear his throat. 'I'm from the forests in the far east. My people live near the mountains in the shadow of the Falling Sky.'

If he thought he would impress the man with this, he was mistaken. The soldier picked at his fingernails, then scratched the side of his face. 'Seems a fanciful name. What about it?'

Ussemitus marshalled his thoughts. Should he attempt to convince this oaf that the war would end in disaster? He could see how difficult it would be. 'My words are for Vittargattus. No one else.'

The man grunted, his attention moving from his finger-nails to his teeth. He shook his head. 'Then you're a fool. No one speaks to Vitargattus. Except his advisers maybe.'

Ussemitus moved closer to him and the man's hand shot to the dagger in his belt. He was surprisingly quick.

'If you send me away,' Ussemitus told him coldly, 'you'll regret this day.'

The man studied Ussemitus properly. It seemed as if he would dismiss him, but he lowered his eyes and turned to another door. 'Wait here,' he said and left.

It was a long time before the door opened, and mercifully it was not the guard. Instead another warrior had come, but one who looked at Ussemitus with far more interest. He was sharp-eyed, his gaze fully appraising, and he nodded as though in recognition of the forester.

'What's your name?' he said.

Ussemitus gave it without thinking. Then he wondered if he would have done better to give a false name. But the warrior nodded as if it did not matter.

'Come with me. If you have important news, you'd better let us have it. I am Glaukan, clan commander.' He led the way through other stone passageways until they reached yet another room. It was larger, and from its conical ceiling hung a wooden ring set with small torches. Below this sat three men, drinking mead. They had finished a huge meal and a number of young girls were clearing up the dishes and bones that were strewn across the oak table.

Ussemitus was instantly struck by the central figure. He was not tall, but very large for an Innasmornian; he had a thick, matted beard and a crown of hair that spread out over his shoulders. Wooden ornaments adorned his thick arms and chest, and his eyes were tiny slits in the great face. His chest was bared, marked with tattoos. He swigged at his mead, belched, and regarded Ussemitus as he might have done an errant child.

'Well, boy? What brings you to the court of Vittargattus?'

'Answer the clan chief,' said the warrior who had brought him.

Ussemitus looked briefly at the other two seated men. Like Vittargattus they were large, both taller, and they wore similar ornaments, signifying, he assumed, their rank. Their hair was braided, tied with coloured beads, and they had long moustaches that were also braided. In battle they must have looked ferocious.

'I have important news, sire,' said Ussemitus, recovering his wits. It seemed incredible that he actually stood in the presence of the legendary warlord. But he would have been less daunted if they could have had their meeting in the open, under a clear sky. How could Vittargattus enjoy the confines of this dark and smoking citadel?

'From the land of the Falling Sky, they tell me,' rumbled Vittargattus. 'So what is happening there?'

'Sire, I know of your plans to send an army to the south to meet with King Ondrabal and to enter the forest lands of my people. And I know that another army is preparing to go north, to the port of Tollavar.'

The three figures looked surprised, exchanging deep scowls. Vittargattus banged down his goblet. 'And do you now! What else?'

'From Tollavar it will go across the sea to Kendara —'

'Where did you hear this! The word has not yet been given to the captains! Who has spoken out of turn!' he was evidently incensed by the news.

Ussemitus spoke hurriedly of the night Fomond had seen Quareem in the forest of Spellavar, his exchange with Vymark and Zellorian's men. 'They will be waiting for your army in the mountains, sire,' he finished.

Vittargattus and the others stared at Ussemitus for a long time. Then the clan chief nodded to Glaukan and he exited hurriedly.

'Sire,' Ussemitus went on, emboldened by their silence, 'there are things you must hear about the intruders in the mountains.'

'So it seems.'

'They are not all bent on destruction. Those who serve

282

Zellorian are your enemies, and dangerous ones. But there are those among them who would be our allies.'

'The intruders?' said the warrior on Vittargattus's right, face like thunder. 'But they have brought the old powers with them. Forbidden things. All manner of evil. How else should we deal with them but unleash the storm gods upon them?'

'I believe we should communicate with them first – '

The door opened. One of the Windmasters stood there. He entered in silence, his long blue mane flowing out behind him like a train. He turned his hawk-like eyes upon Ussemitus, his face a mask of annoyance and distaste. 'You are Ussemitus?' he said, without a hint of deference to the clan chief and his warriors.

Ussemitus nodded, feeling his throat constrict.

'You are known to us.'

'What of it?' snapped Vittargattus, leaning forward, fist clenching around his goblet. 'Come, Azrand, enough of your whisperings! You spend more time talking to the sky than you do to me! What is going on in my lands? This youth speaks of treachery.'

'If you opened yourself to the winds more often, sire – '

Vittargattus sat back with a snort. 'They torment me enough. I cannot sleep for the visions they send me – '

The Blue Hair's eyes blazed, as though in a warning, but Vittargattus flung a contemptuous glance at Ussemitus. 'What does it matter to him if I have nightmares to contend with? I've not abandoned the storm gods. But I have a campaign to plan, armies to muster. You and your Windmasters are my spokesmen where the gods are concerned. And one of your colleagues has dared to betray us.'

The Blue Hair sucked in his breath, his muscles clenching in his neck, his head poised, Ussemitus thought, like that of a serpent about to strike. 'Who might that be?'

'Quareem!' snarled Vittargattus.

'That scum,' hissed Azrand. 'He has violated our codes all too often. We have cast him out from among us. He should be shorn, divested of his powers.'

'If what the youth says is true, he should be fixed upon a stake and paraded through the city. He plots our ruin in the north.'

Azrand seemed to regain a little of his composure. 'But I am not surprised by the news, sire.'

'Plotting with the intruders,' Vitargattus stormed on. 'With their very leader, Zellorian!' He thumped the table once more so that the goblets danced.

'The intruders,' said Azrand quietly, 'have found a number of allies among the Vaza.'

Vittargattus scowled more deeply. 'Then your Blue Hairs had better find them.'

'I have received a number of reports from the east, sire. You will recall we sent Kuraal there, to prepare the tribesmen for war, the thrust from their lands.'

'What of it?'

'He speaks of a Ussemitus in his reports.'

Ussemitus felt the ground move under him as if he would topple into it. The hatred of the Windmaster could be felt as those reptilian eyes fixed on him.

'This is the same youth?' said Vittargattus.

'I think it must be, sire,' nodded Azrand slowly.

'What does Kuraal say of him?'

'That a number of youths led by Ussemitus met and trafficked with intruders. That Ussemitus was bewitched by one of their women, and that he fled into the mountains to meet her. To plot with her.'

Ussemitus shook his head, trying to keep calm. 'It is a lie.'

'Where is the girl? Where did you meet her soldiers?'

'There are none,' said Ussemitus. 'Just the girl. She taught me that not all her people are against us. Zellorian killed her father, and would kill her because she wishes to be an ally to us — '

'She has taught you these things!' hissed Azrand. 'When? Where?'

The story tumbled out of Ussemitus, but he was aware

284

as he spoke that none of the men who listened to it had any sympathy for Aru, nor for what she had tried to do.

'Where is she now?' said Vittargattus ominously.

'Sire, she is here, in the city. Of her own free will. She wishes to speak to you, as I have, openly, to warn you –'

'Here?' said Azrand. 'You dared bring her into Amerandabad?'

'Enough!' growled the clan chief. 'I'll have her brought before me. Take this youth away and rope him up.' He was on his feet, towering over them, but in a moment he had left the room.

Ussemitus would have protested, but it was useless. The warriors had gone. Azrand glared at him.

'You must trust me, and the girl,' Ussemitus told him, but the Blue Hair looked unreachable.

'Take him below,' he said to Glaukan and his warriors.

It was done quickly. Ussemitus could do nothing to prevent himself being taken down under the fortress. He was tossed roughly into a cell, the door banging shut, bolts slamming. The gamble had failed, and he was as far from the open skies as he had ever been in his life. He doubted now if he would see them again.

20

THE PHUNG

Ussemitus did not waste his energy in trying to persuade
his captors to listen to him. They returned and roped him
to the wall of his cell and left him in the damp silence.
After a while he felt the urge to scream in frustration, both
at the stubbornness of the clan chief and at his incarcer-
ation. There was barely enough light to see by; the cell was
large, cold, and there were no sounds from beyond it as
though he had been put deep under the earth and forgotten.
Briefly he contemplated trying to call out to the powers in
the skies above the city, but he knew it would be a waste
of effort: nothing could hear him so far from the sun.

He closed his mind to the nightmare of being there,
consoling himself with the thought that at least they had
not killed him. But if Kuraal should return, he would surely
want his head.

When his cell door thumped open, he thought perhaps
the Blue Hair, Azrand, had come for him, but someone
was thrust roughly inwards. The figure fell to its knees and
in a moment another was pushed in. Armestor and
Fomond. They saw Ussemitus and groaned. The guards
roped them to the wall in the same way they had their
leader, saying nothing as they worked. They left, and for a
while there was silence behind them.

Fomond turned to his companion. 'So much for the hospitality of this stinking city!'

'Were you betrayed?' said Ussemitus. 'Where is Aru?
And Jubaia?'

'We were resting in the house where Jubaia had put us,'
replied Fomond. 'We heard footsteps on the stair, but
before we could do anything, the door burst in and there

must have been a score of them. Soldiers. They didn't say much. But they knew what they were looking for.'

'We could have fought,' said Armestor, 'but if we had, we would likely have been chopped up.'

'And Aru?' said Ussemitus. His fear for her safety was like a cold pulse in his gut.

'They've taken her somewhere else,' said Fomond. 'Ussemitus, I am sorry. There was nothing we could do.'

Ussemitus nodded. 'No, I can see that. But I cannot believe this was a trap. Why should Jubaia have gone to such lengths if it was?'

'After he left you at the fortress, he came back to us and said he was going to seek information. He did not return. But who knows what was in his mind?' said Fomond.

'He must have been greatly rewarded for his part in our abduction,' said Armestor. 'I never trusted him.'

'Then you should have spoken more openly!' snapped Ussemitus.

Armestor looked away, but did not reply.

'You think he betrayed us?' said Fomond.

Ussemitus shook his head. 'No. I cannot read minds, Fomond, but I swear I saw enough concern in Jubaia to know that he shares our own fears for Innasmorn.'

'Well, if he does, it may be of little help to us now.'

Not far from the deep cell where Ussemitus and his companions languished, Aru was sitting in her own silent field of thoughts, though her chamber was far more comfortable than that of her erstwhile fellows. It was not a large room, but it was excellently decorated, having silk curtains, a large divan and priceless carpets on the floor and walls. The brickwork was exquisite, inlaid with bright tiles, the craftsmanship something she had not seen previously on Innasmorn. She wondered at such extravagance: a prerogative of the clan chief, she imagined. There was an anteroom with a sunken bath in it, and the water that flowed from a duct beside it was warm. By turning a curious wooden device, she saw that she could deflect the current into the bath, itself made from wood that had been treated with some kind of tough resin. When she was satisfied that no one was likely to visit her, and that she had indeed been imprisoned, she gave way to temptation and took a bath, luxuriating in the warmth. There were unguents beside the bath, and though they were nothing like the ones she was accustomed to in the Sculpted City, she found them a relief after the rigours of the forest and the journey.

Afterwards she was able to think more clearly. Her first thought was that Jubaia must have betrayed them, though she did not want to accept it. And yet it had been his idea to bring them here. They had placed themselves in his hands. The thought tormented her for a long time, and though she was very tired, she did not sleep. Strange how Jubaia had·influenced their lives since they had first found him. The impulsive killing of his assailants, the journey over the Spiderway, and then on to Amerandabad. She thought of her Casruel training. Would her knights have so openly accepted the little man? But what choice had there been?

When the door opened, she imagined it must be morning, though there was only lamplight in her chamber. Two guards had come for her and their presence reminded her that she was hungry. They merely gestured for her to go with them, using their swords to emphasise the point. She noticed that these weapons were made of wood. The fear of metal still ran through the Vaza, even here, though certain things were exempt.

She went with the guards down a long corridor and through a number of very small rooms, some of which contained weapons, all of wood, and others which seemed to be stores. She was then led downwards to a larger chamber, circular with a long table. She was told to stand and wait, and though there were crude wooden chairs along one side of the table, she ignored them. The guards, surprisingly, left her. She studied the chamber, but it was almost bare, though kept immaculately clean. A single frame for the lamps hung from overhead, the ceiling conical, the point lost in darkness.

At last a door opposite her opened. She did not recognise the strange being who came in, though from the descriptions she had been given by Ussemitus of the Blue Hairs, this was one of them, as were those who followed him in. A dozen of the robed Windmasters entered and took their places at the table, and when their leader sat, they did so as one. Aru looked directly into the face of the leading Blue Hair, and his sharp eyes met hers, his face sheathed in contempt, which he made no attempt to hide. His fellows looked more blank, as if awaiting a cue to which they could respond.

'Your name?' said the leading Blue Hair. Before him on the table he had spread some papers, and he took a quill from inside his voluminous robe and dipped it in a glass phial that was sunk into the tabletop.

'Aru Casruel,' she said mechanically. She looked at the others, but none of them met her gaze. 'Why am I here?' she snapped.

'I am Azrand,' said the leading Blue Hair. 'And you see before you the principals of the inner ring of Windmasters. We advise the clan chief on all matters. We are his senses. There is nothing that happens in the lands of the Vaza, or beyond them, that is not of interest to us. Especially the intrusion of people who have no business in Innasmorn, let alone the lands of our race.'

'Is that a reason to persecute me?'

'Have you been harmed?' said Azrand, his brows raising as if she had surprised him, though it was merely a pose, she knew that.

'I have not. But I resent the treatment I have received. And where are my companions?'

'You will all be given an opportunity to speak to us. What do you know of the forester, Ussemitus?'

'He has vital news for Vittargattus.'

'This concerns the rebel, Quareem?'

His reply took her by surprise, but she straightened. 'Yes. Do you know what he intends? How dangerous – '

'We have been searching Amerandabad for him, but as yet we have not found him here, nor beyond the city. You wish to confirm the story of Ussemitus? That he is in allegiance with your own people?'

She could see the trap easily enough. 'My own people are divided. They are controlled against their will by Zellorian, who intends to bleed power from Innasmorn.'

'What power?' said Azrand suspiciously and Aru felt them all watching her closely, as if a mental ripple had run through them.

'Whatever power he can find. Quareem will teach him about the use of his own powers–'

'That accursed charlatan! His power is paltry–'

'But he knows of the western lands, where there is said to be a source of vast power. Zellorian seeks that, and will stop at nothing to find it. My people are not united. They would bring Zellorian down if they could. They would gladly give him into your hands.'

'Why are your people here at all?' said another of the Blue Hairs.

She could see how avid they were for an answer. She began to tell them something of her history, and as they listened, Azrand's face was impassive, his own thoughts perfectly shrouded. From time to time he wrote something down, and Aru's smooth dialogue was interrupted only occasionally as the Blue Hairs put questions to her. They were amazed by the things she told them, that much was not shrouded.

Jubaia swigged at the ale he had been given and nodded to the man at the bar, who took his mug and poured him another. 'You must be a fool coming back to Amerandabad, Jubaia,' grunted the man. 'What have you brought to sell? Mut be worth a lot to tempt you into this poxy hole again.'

Jubaia grinned, but he looked over his shoulder. This

inn was about as safe a place as any he knew in the city, but he could not be too careful. The cramped room was choked with bodies, the air thick with fumes, both from the fire and from the strange things that many of the occupants smoked. Most of the men and women here were thieves or rogues of one kind or another, and not likely to give Jubaia away, although for the proper price they would be tempted. It was their code, and his. There were, as the man at the bar had implied, a good few people in Amerandabad who would pay handsomely for Jubaia's hide.

'A fleeting visit,' Jubaia grunted, accepting the ale.

'A lady, perhaps?'

Jubaia was about to make an appropriately facetious remark, when a figure shuffled out of the fug and gripped his arm. For a moment he froze, but then recognised the old man as a friend.

'Come to the alley,' croaked the fellow. 'Someone to speak to you. Urgent.' He melted back into the press of bodies.

Jubaia shrugged at the man at the bar, but pushed his laborious way through the company to a side door. He squeezed through it, a knife in his hand, and peered into the night's gloom. It was suddenly cold, the silence like a pool.

Someone hissed his name. 'It is Dyasor. News of your friends.'

Jubaia looked up and down the alley. There was no one in sight. He moved toward the voice, knife hidden. The man was well concealed in a doorway but Jubaia found him, nestling in beside him, still watching the alley. Many a careless thief had died in a doorway in Amerandabad.

'What news?'

'You must leave at once.'

'What has happened?'

The eyes regarded him from a swarthy face. The little, rat-like man, no bigger than himself, swathed in dark cloth, was a ragged bundle, leaking fear. 'I've word from the guard, Curubos. Vittargattus knows about you. He's taken all your companions and imprisoned them.'

'The girl, too?'

'Aye. For questioning. Curubos was forced to tell the Blue Hairs that it was you who led Ussemitus to him. Now there are patrols out looking for you. There's blood in the air tonight, and it's yours, Jubaia.'

'Nonsense! But I'm glad of the news. How did they find the house?'

'Don't know. But someone spies for the Blue Hairs. Their network is wide. Trust no one. You should not have come back.'

Jubaia grinned, but quickly sobered. 'My thanks, Dyasor.' He pushed some coins, far too many, into the man's hands and the eyes lit up.

'I'd never betray you – '

'Of course you would. But go and find a bolt-hole. Lie low for a few days. Speak to no one.'

'What will you do?'

'Where will I find Spetweng and his cronies?'

Dyasor's eyes widened, white blobs in the dark of the doorway. 'You don't want to get mixed up with those vermin – '

'Where are they?'

'With the whores. Work is scarce for their kind.'

Jubaia nodded, and moments later he was threading through the narrow alleys, hood pulled up. He heard shouts from some of the streets and the barked commands of guards. They were indeed out in force tonight, and if he was their prey, he would have to move very quickly. Ussemitus and the others prisoners! The thought galvanised him.

He found the men he sought at the third attempt. Having barely managed to extricate himself from two houses of ill repute, Jubaia discovered Spetweng and a number of his obnoxious associates in another place near the harbour. The huge, one-eyed giant who looked after the house, Baraganda, almost scooped Jubaia up with one hand.

'What, little man? Lost your skill with the fair ladies? You never used to resort to my house. Or is it that you have no coins left? Fallen on hard times?'

'It's not a woman I want, you oaf, it's one of your clients.'

'Spetweng?' Baraganda frowned, his face a terrifying sight with its one great moon of an eye. 'He'll want good money. Mind you, he has little enough of it at present.'

'He'll earn his wages. But is he sober?'

'Sober enough,' laughed Baraganda. 'You don't want him cold sober, or he couldn't skewer a rat without wine in his belly. I'll drag him away from whichever bed he's in. He won't like it, but the little worm owes me money. He can earn his pleasures and pay me for 'em!'

Baraganda was as good as his word, thumping up the creaking stair with a bellow. There were shouts upstairs, a scream and the sound of bodies tumbling about. Jubaia doubted that anyone would quarrel with Baraganda, who had the strength of six men and the temper of a wind elemental. It was not long before someone came crashing down the stairs, to land in an untidy sprawl at the feet of Jubaia. Three other men followed, and by the time they had all struggled to their knees, Baraganda was glaring down at them from the top of the stair.

'Go out and earn your credit,' he boomed. 'There's work for you, so don't grizzle that you can't get any.'

'What in the pits is wrong?' snarled the first of the four bruised men. He wore clothes that looked as if they had been painted on him they were so tight, his body skeletal, his bones poking through his skin as if he had not eaten for weeks. But there was colour in his cheeks and fire in his eyes. His hair was long, tied in a greasy tail, black as the night, and his fists, bunched at Baraganda, were like balls of stone.

'Peace, Spetweng,' said Jubaia.

For the first time, the other noticed him. 'Are *you* responsible for this, you crooked little worm?'

Jubaia bowed. 'Regrettably, I am. I need something in a hurry.'

Spetweng put his hands on his bony hips, nodding to himself. 'Graves give up their ghosts, it seems.'

'You didn't think I was dead?' said Jubaia, pretending surprise.

Spetweng snorted. 'I should have guessed not. Slippery little bugger. I bet you took valuables as well. But why in the wind are you dragging me away from my bed at this time? Couldn't you have waited?'

'No time. But there's good money in it for you and your men.'

Spetweng turned to the other three, who were as thin as he was. They had a look of starved dogs about them. 'Ah, do I hear the voice of restraint? A calming wind.' He grinned, showing almost as many gaps in his teeth as he had teeth. His companions appeared to be suitably mollified.

'Come on,' said Jubaia. He called up to Baraganda. 'Sorry to trouble you, old friend. But it'll be worth it. This rable will have plenty to spend on your delectable delicacies when they return.'

'You mind your hide,' Baraganda called. 'There's a whisper going round that the Blue Hairs want your balls!'

Jubaia waved and led his fresh company out into the alleyways. Soon they were beyond the wharfs and had climbed like cats up among the chimneys where they knew they would not be disturbed. Spetweng and his fellows were as agile as spiders, and Jubaia no less so. In the darkness they were almost invisible, a requirement of their trade, for Spetweng was considered to be one of the city's most efficient assassins. Although Jubaia did not know the three men with him, he knew they must be good at their work, for Spetweng chose only the most capable to work with him.

'Word was,' said Spetweng, 'that you left without anything. So let's see your money.'

Jubaia pulled from his pouches a small bag and opened it to reveal a number of tiny jewels, each worth a small fortune.

Spetweng's eyes were like moons as he saw the sparkle.

Jubaia knew that they could kill him and make off with this loot, but they based their trade on a strange kind of honour. 'More than you earn in a good year,' Jubaia told them, which he knew to be true.

'I won't deny it. But what do you want, old friend? The head of Vittargattus?'

Jubaia chuckled. 'Not quite. But he does have something of mine. In his fortress. Friends of mine. I want them out.'

'In the fortress? *Prisoners*? Do you think we are mad?'

'No. It will take a Phung.'

Spetweng glowered, falling silent. An unease spread immediately to his companions. Spetweng shook his head. 'You have the wrong team, Jubaia. I have no contact with the Phung.'

Jubaia swore. 'I know better. Come on, there's a lot of money in this. And I'm not without funds. I need a Phung.'

'The fortress,' murmured Spetweng, gazing over the roofs to the mass of buildings that rose up into the night. 'I've been over it. Did that when I was a boy. Part of our training was to get in over the roofs and go down as far as you could without being seen.'

'Have you been inside it?' said Jubaia.

Spetweng screwed his face up. 'Never.'

'I came to you because you are the best. So they tell me. Or have I been away too long? And you've worked with the Phung before.'

Spetweng scratched himself, sitting cross-legged. 'Well, lads? Want to try this one out? It's a lot of money. Enough to take us south. Maybe to set us up down there. Good pickings in the south, if you can pay the guild your rent.'

The others nodded one by one. The temptation to them was great. 'What's the kill?' said one of them.

Jubaia explained. 'There are four of them. I want them all out, alive.'

'Alive?' growled Spetweng. 'Can't we just go in and kill them? We could probably manage that without being seen.'

'Alive,' insisted Jubaia. 'But you may have to kill anyone who stands in your way. Anyone.'

'Hence the Phung,' nodded Spetweng.

'If you do it,' said Jubaia, 'there'll be another bag like this one.' He handed the bag to the assassin.

Spetweng took it slowly and huddled together with his companions. They took a long time to talk it over, but in the end agreed. 'But we'll need time to plan. And I'll have to contact the Phung.'

'I have no time,' said Jubaia. 'For all I know, the Blue Hairs will execute my friends at dawn.'

Spetweng grimaced. 'I need a week at least! You are asking us to commit suicide as it is. Give us some hope, Jubaia!'

'You will have the Phung.'

They argued for a time, but in the end Jubaia had to bite back his impatience and agree to letting them have time to plan, to find out what they could about the precise whereabouts of the prisoners.

'When you have them,' said Jubaia, 'bring them to the Zone of Echoes. In the old city.'

Spetweng groaned. 'Jubaia, are you mad? No one in their right mind enters that place.'

'That's where I'll be. With enough money to set you up in the south. A new life, with all the prospects you desire.'

Spetweng snorted. 'The Zone of Echoes. A Phung. Mother of Storms! Very well.'

The guards who brought Ussemitus and his companions their food and water said very little when they came. They merely cleared away the platters and mugs, faces empty. They untied their prisoners and allowed them brief exercise periods each day, though never outside the chamber, and permitted them to use the closet beyond where the toilet was sited. It was a while before the foresters got used to it, but its system intrigued them, flushed as it was by regular flows of water through an internal piping.

'There are drains below us which carry everything to the Fulgor,' said one of the guards, amused by Ussemitus's interest.

'Who built this city? It could not have been the Vaza.'

The guard shook his head. 'No. We occupied it when it was deserted, except for a few beggars. Parts of it go back before history began, so they say.'

Seeing that this guard, who was the oldest of those who watched over the prisoners, was more inclined to talk than usual, Ussemitus pressed him gently for more information. 'This is Vittargattus's capital?'

'In a way, but he is a true nomad and likes to keep moving. He thinks if he stays in one place too long, there'll be rebellion somewhere else.' The guard grinned. 'I daresay you'd know more about that than me.'

'He thinks we're rebels?'

The guard shrugged. 'They say he never sleeps properly. Too many bad dreams. Thinks everyone is plotting his downfall. And he doesn't even trust the wind gods. Hardly ever goes up on to the towers.'

Ussemitus frowned. 'I only wish there was some way we could convince him that we are his allies. If he goes north, it will be to disaster.'

'I wouldn't worry about it. Too late.'

'What do you mean?'

'The army's already left. Gone north. Other one south east. The invasion has started.' After this, the guard would say nothing, as if annoyed with himself for already having said too much. Ussemitus relayed the news to his companions and they cursed, but there was nothing that could be done. They were trapped, and they could see no way out of the chamber. Even if they had broken free, the fortress was full of guards.

Time dragged on, the days and nights one long shadow.

Fomond nudged Ussemitus awake, crawling over to him at

the limit of the rope that bound his wrists. 'Ussemitus!' he hissed.

Ussemitus opened his eyes, shocked out of a dream of the forest. He saw Fomond leaning over him, fear in his eyes.

'A disturbance. Beyond the door.'

Ussemitus listened. He could hear someone struggling, then there was a strangled gasp. The door bumped, then there was silence. For a long time nothing happened. Armestor was awake, on his feet, flat against the wall, watching intently, though afraid that death awaited him beyond the door.

The door slowly opened and figures that were almost entirely composed of shadows entered. They moved in utter silence, and as they came to the prisoners they drew back their hands. Ussemitus gasped, seeing the slick metal. He tried to twist away, expecting to be gutted.

'Be still,' hissed a voice from the invisible face. 'We're here to cut you loose. Jubaia sent us.'

As the shadow cut his bonds, Ussemitus felt his heart leap. Jubaia! So he had not betrayed them. Fomond rubbed his wrists, freed, and in a moment they were all free.

'Keep tight behind us as we go,' said the shadow man. 'Where is the girl?'

'Aru?'

The shadow nodded, only his eyes visible, body clad in black material. Like ghosts his companions slipped out into the corridor, blades before them.

'She's never been kept with us,' whispered Ussemitus as they left the chamber. 'We haven't seen her since we came.'

The leader motioned for silence. It came down like a blanket. Two dead guards sprawled on the stone floor, blood seeping from their throats, glazed eyes looking up in horror and accusation. Their assassins stripped them of weapons and handed them to Ussemitus and the others. They took them and followed, up into the fortress.

There were torches to light the way, but few guards. Ussemitus felt the nape hairs on his neck rising. Something else was here with them, a presence, something that spoke of death and of blood, of the assassin's tools. Outside it must be night, for no one was about. However, voices ahead made him stop dead in his tracks. Another shadow swept forward along the corridor, too fast to discern clearly. Spetweng held Ussemitus back. They waited. The voices ceased. The silence that followed was funereal.

Again Ussemitus caught a glimpse of the loping shadow ahead, but Spetweng waited until it had moved on. They slipped up a stairway until they came to an antechamber. Spetweng peered around its doorway. There was light within. He saw two Blue Hairs, talking in soft tones, the words unclear. He turned back and pressed Ussemitus and the others to the wall. While they waited, a tall shape detached itself from the very stones opposite, blocking the doorway before it went in.

Something snapped in the room, and one of the Blue Hairs fell, gurgling. The other had rushed for the door, but Spetweng was ready for him. He put an arm around his neck and placed a needle-like dagger point to his ear. His fingers clamped down on the Blue Hair's windpipe and the man's eyes bulged. Behind him something dark and terrible was happening to his companion. Blood trickled from the doorway.

Spetweng leaned close to the Blue Hair's ear. 'The girl, Aru Casruel. Quickly, or I'll pierce your brain.'

The Blue Hair could not conceal his terror. He had no time to call upon his powers. With his eyes he indicated a direction. Spetweng forced him along the corridor, a shield. One of his assassins covered his back, and behind him Ussemitus, Armestor and Fomond followed. Something came out of the room, tall and cloaked, like a huge bird of prey with wings folded up over it so that no face, no hands were visible. None of the foresters could speak as it slid by them and went on ahead of the assassins. But it reeked of blood and carnage.

It seemed as though the Blue Hair would lead them around inside the fortress for an eternity. They were almost discovered a number of times, but each time the frightful messenger of death took another victim, the complete silence of its kill making the act progressively more terrifying. Ussemitus was desperate to ask what this horror could be, but the spell of silence froze his throat.

The Blue Hair used his eyes to indicate directions, as well as his utter terror, as if he had already seen his own death. At length he led the party to the door of another room and nodded at it.

'Open it,' hissed Spetweng.

The Blue Hair shook his head, trying to say that he had no key.

'Open it,' said Spetweng again, pressing the knife point into flesh.

The Blue Hair closed his eyes, and the air trembled, a breeze gusting down the corridor. It struck the door almost like a fist and there was a splintering as the thick wooden bolt gave.

Spetweng pushed the door with his foot. It swung slowly in, leaning.

'Someone's coming,' called Fomond softly.

'He's summoned help,' said an assassin.

Spetweng swung the Blue Hair around and pushed him hard up the corridor. He sprawled, turning to protest about something, but the dark shadow of the destroyer took him, dragging him away in one swift motion. The Blue Hair died in silence.

'Inside,' Spetweng whispered, ignoring the slaughter, and the entire party slipped into the chamber.

Ussemitus's eyes lit up; Aru was beyond, pressed to a wall by her fear. He went over to her and she gasped, but threw her arms about him and laughed.

'Say nothing,' he cautioned her. 'We aren't outside yet.'

Fomond beamed, but his smile faded as Spetweng pulled him back to the door, knowing they had found the girl they sought. As they all began to move down the corridor once more, they heard footsteps and voices. Guards were coming, alarmed by something.

They turned back up the corridor to some stairs. Spetweng took the lead and they sped upwards, rising higher and higher. They heard a scream from below and shouting. Above them there was a window set in the wall. One of the assassins leapt up, gripping the sill. He peered out, then nodded to the people below. With his knife he worked at the frame of the window. In a moment he had it open. He jumped down just as more guards appeared on the landing.

Spetweng threw something that flashed. One of the guards gasped and fell, clutching at his face.

'Up!' Spetweng snapped at Ussemitus. 'On to the roof.'

Ussemitus pointed to Armestor and he shinned up the wall to the sill, pulling himself through the window. Fomond followed him. The guards were yelling for reinforcements, closing in, swords waving. The assassins were preparing to meet them, their own swords cutting deadly slashes through the darkness.

'Here, bring a torch!' a guard called, but the words died in his throat as Spetweng pierced it.

Ussemitus helped Aru up and Fomond hauled her to him, disappearing into the night. Ussemitus followed. Behind him the assassins were engaged in a furious struggle, but their skills would prevail as long as no more guards reached them. On the rooftop, Ussemitus was not sure what to do. Should they abandon the men who had saved them?

'Someone's coming!' said Aru, pointing to another rooftop that was sloping away below them. A single figure bounded over it, carrying something wrapped in darkness. They prepared to defend themselves, Aru getting behind Ussemitus, furious at not having a sword of her own. Below them they heard the cries of the dying, but could not tell who was killing who. The assassins must climb up here soon if they were to avoid the closing trap.

BOOK FIVE

STORM CREATURES

21

ZONE OF ECHOES

'Keep down!' called Ussemitus, though there was no need to say it, for the others were ducking as low as they could on the roof. Their attention was split between the window from which they had emerged and the shadowy figure that was closing with them. It reached a tall chimney stack no more than a few yards away and called out something. Aru recognised the voice and waved.

'Jubaia! This way.'

Moments later the little figure was upon them, arms clutching a dark bundle. He dropped it to the tiles. 'Here. Not as good as your own weapons, but they'll do.'

Armestor gasped with pleasure. They were bows. He picked one up, weighing it. His face creased in a brief frown, but he nodded. There were arrows, too, and he scooped up a handful, sighting along them.

'What of Spetweng?' said Jubaia, trying to see beyond the window.

'He may need help,' said Ussemitus. 'Come on.' Taking a bow for himself, he led them to the window. Peering down, he could see that one of the assassins had been killed, as well as a number of guards. Bodies were packed in the corridor, but something else moved down there, and there was a smell of spilt blood that made Ussemitus draw back. But he released an arrow and it took one of the warriors in the neck. He ducked back and Armestor took his place in an instant, also felling a warrior. Fomond loosed an arrow quickly, and it was enough to force the guards back out of range.

'Climb!' Ussemitus called down to the assassins. 'How many are there?'

Someone shouted, but it was lost in the awful din beyond.

One of the assassins turned and leapt upwards, sword gripped in his teeth through his black mask. Ussemitus gave him a hand and pulled him through and out on to the roof. Ussemitus balanced precariously on the window ledge, Fomond gripping his waist.

The second assassin leapt for the sill and Ussemitus got him to safety. Spetweng was the last of them below, but none of the guards rushed him. They were engaged in a murderous battle with the other dark intruder. Spetweng paused for a last glance at the confusion then turned and leapt up the wall like a cat, his fingers reaching out and gripping those of Ussemitus. In a matter of seconds they were all outside.

'One is missing,' said Jubaia.

Spetweng glared at him. 'What are you doing here? I thought you were to meet us in the Zone of Echoes.'

'Just be glad I came with the bows,' said Jubaia. 'Otherwise you'd be dog meat by now.'

Spetweng snorted, eyes narrowing. 'You reckon without the Phung. Don't think you can wriggle your way out of paying us.' He held up his thin blade.

'Let's just get out of here,' interrupted Aru, taking a sword gratefully from Jubaia.

'Good idea,' nodded Jubaia. 'And as it happens, the Zone of Echoes is the best place to hide. In fact, the only place in this accursed city.'

'We'll take our pay now, if you don't mind,' said Spetweng, watching the window. Something moved there, silhouetted in its light. The great shadow slipped out on to the roof, pulling shut the window, though there seemed to be no further pursuit.

Ussemitus tried to see a face, but the darkness covered what he took to be the creature's head. Whatever it was, it wore darkness like a cloak, head and shoulders covered, its body wrapped around in the billowing robe. He could hear it breathe, sense eyes upon him, and he felt himself shudder. Aru was beside him, trembling involuntarily. Was it beast or man?

'Not so fast,' Jubaia told Spetweng, though his eyes never left the swaying shape of the Phung. 'You haven't got us out of this fortress yet. Once we're safe beyond it – '

Armestor pointed across the roofs. 'We must hurry! There are more of the guards. We've kicked over a hornet's nest of them.'

Spetweng said something to the Phung and like a bird of the night it swooped over the roof and merged with another of the stacks.

'Very well, to the Zone of Echoes,' said the assassin. 'I'll settle with the Phung afterwards.'

There were no more words wasted in argument. They moved on across the many roofs, weaving in and out of the many stacks that were like a bizarre brick forest above the sleeping fortress. There were sounds of pursuit, shouts and then lights, then a frightful scream. Spetweng, who knew the roof as he knew the streets, wove a way over it, moving with a speed that was not easy to match, but with the thought of the Phung behind them, the party went quickly away from the scene of their imprisonment.

'The army has gone north,' Ussemitus told Aru when they paused for breath. 'We're too late to stop it.'

'They wouldn't listen to me,' she said. 'Or if they did, they showed no sympathy. What do we do now?'

'Let's get out of Amerandabad if we can.'

Spetweng's knowledge of the roof complex saved them from capture, though they had to swing down the outer walls like flies on the ropes he had placed there earlier. There were guards below, patrolling as they usually did at night, but thankfully they had not yet heard of events within the fortress. They were not expecting the shadows from above them, and the assassins fell upon them, despatching them swiftly. Spetweng's men pulled the bodies into the dark shadows of the wall as Ussemitus dropped down with the others.

Jubaia led the way through the streets, and though they saw other patrols, they kept out of sight until they came to an area of the city that seemed to be composed entirely of

307

ruins. Stepping through the remains of a crumbling wall, they suddenly felt themselves cut off from Amerandabad, as though they had entered a gate into another time, another far realm. Silence closed over them more completely.

Jubaia turned to his companions, about to whisper something, but his eyes widened as he saw Spetweng. The assassin had taken hold of Fomond and had a hand over his mouth, his blade to his throat.

'This is far enough for us,' he hissed. 'We've done all the killing we're doing for you tonight, Jubaia. We'll take the rest of our wage, if you please.'

Ussemitus would have made for him, but the other two assassins barred his way, their eyes like slits, their weapons ready. He had seen how swift they were with them.

'He won't harm Fomond,' said Jubaia. 'Very well, Spetweng. You've earned this.' He tossed another pouch to the assassins. One of them caught it and examined its contents. They sparkled, even in this dim light, and he nodded to Spetweng, who instantly released Fomond and pushed him into Ussemitus.

'There is hardly any need for this drama,' said Jubaia, trying to smoothe the fury of the foresters.

Spetweng chuckled softly. 'No hard feelings, eh? It was a good kill. And thanks to this, it will be our last in Amerandabad.' He tapped the pouch of jewels. 'One day we'll meet again, Jubaia, and you must tell me how you came to win them.' He motioned to his men and they went back out through the wall, making no sound.

Ussemitus scowled after them, but Aru put a restraining arm on him. 'Let them go.'

He grunted and turned to Jubaia. 'We owe you our lives – '

Jubaia snorted dismissively. 'Yes, and you've cost me a king's ransom! But no matter. We've far more work to do yet – '

'Before we go on,' said Aru, 'tell me, what was that creature?'

Jubaia frowned. 'Forget that you saw it.'

'What was it?' said Ussemitus. Fomond and Armestor also looked questioningly at the little figure.

Jubaia sighed. 'It was a Phung. There are a few left under the city. They are the remnants of a race of Innasmornians from the dawn of time. Little is known about them, except that they are an elemental creature, quite different from us. Created from the forces of Innasmorn, perhaps.'

'Was it the servant of the assassins?' said Aru incredulously.

Jubaia nodded. 'For a price, the Phung will serve. Spetweng, who led the assassins, belongs to an ancient cult which worships the darker side of the Mother's power. The Phung are the servants of this power. Spetweng and other disciples like him can call upon the Phung in times of need. But I knew Spetweng to be greedy. The riches I offered him were enough to bribe him to summon the Phung. The powers that the Phung serves will not be pleased at the use that Spetweng has made of the Phung. But Spetweng is a gambler. He will be gone by dawn, and if the Phung is sent to hunt him, it may never find him. But then again, perhaps it will.'

He turned and scrambled over the rubble into the ruins, leading the party on yet another journey through mazes of old alleys and fallen bridges, houses that had collapsed and roads that were cracked and gaping, the way underfoot treacherous. They came to a sudden gulf, a black emptiness that fell away before them. Beyond it, the walls of the Thunderreach range rose up. A single bridge curved over the chasm, reaching a ledge opposite that was at the mouth of a tall slash in the cliff wall, a narrow canyon that led back into more darkness, a darkness peppered with the broken towers of more buildings.

Jubaia put a finger across his lips. 'Always whisper,' he said softly. 'We are entering the Zone of Echoes. Once it was sacred to the wind gods, worshipped by those who

309

built it, long before Amerandabad was even thought of. But the builders passed on many years ago.'

'Who were they?' said Fomond as they began the crossing of the single span, keeping close to one another as if afraid the bridge might crumble.

'They sought to control the wind through their dark magics, but it is said that the wind gods were angered by them and set a curse upon them. The winds came and broke this citadel, and even now there are ghosts set to guard it. An echo, it is said, will travel throughout the Zone and with it will carry a trail of destruction, bringing madness to anyone caught in it. So whisper softly, my friends, whisper very softly.'

Fomond's eyes widened. 'I begin to wonder if you take a particular delight in bringing us to such charming places, Jubaia. We may have been safer back in the cell.'

Jubaia grinned. 'Legends,' he snorted, though he kept his voice very low. 'But they serve us well. No one dares to come here. Even Spetweng refused. Here we can take time to plan.'

Beyond the bridge they went through yet more tortuous mazes of ruins, walking for a mile into the heart of this most ancient of places. They stopped at length at the edge of an open area where a score of statues leaned over them, broken at the waist. Alien faces looked up in silent comtemplation of the tall cliffs, the night sky beyond them.

Jubaia sat among the fallen columns as though they were old friends. He pulled from his shirt another bundle.

Aru grinned. 'How many more items have you got stuffed in that shirt of yours? Can you not conjure up horses for us?'

Jubaia snorted, but unwrapped the bundle to show them food. They had forgotten their hunger and gladly took what the little man offered, eating in silence.

Ussemitus put an arm across the shoulders of the chewing Jubaia. 'We owe you our lives, and an apology. I should tell you, we thought you had betrayed us.'

Jubaia shrugged. 'I would have thought the same.'

'Even so, I'm sorry we thought ill of you. But now, as you say, we are very much in your debt. Those jewels – '

'Forget them;' Jubaia smiled, as if embarrassed. 'They were stolen, so I had no right to them. I told you, I'm a thief. There'll be opportunities for me to take other such spoils. Sometimes I take more pleasure in the act of thieving than I do from the spending. If I were a rich man, still I would thieve.'

The others had gathered around to catch the soft words, to enjoy the warmth of his humour. 'We owe you our lives,' said Fomond. 'And we'll not forget it.'

Armestor shuffled, looking away. 'Aye. We owe you much.'

Aru bent and kissed Jubaia on the cheek, and the little man's eyes lit up. 'My lady,' he laughed. 'That is all the reward I could want.'

'But we have to think about tomorrow,' said Ussemitus after a pause. 'Since Vittargattus has not listened to us, what can we do? Do you think he would have warned his generals as they march north?'

'He would be a fool,' said Armestor, 'if he has not at least told them. And the Blue Hairs should have listened to Aru.'

Jubaia nodded. 'If we could reach the army to warn it, we may yet turn it back from Quareem's trap. But how?'

'I know we demand much of you,' Ussemitus told him. 'But is there any way you can get us horses?'

Jubaia screwed up his face. 'I've nothing left with which to barter. There are those who trust me, but if I ask for horses on credit, they'll assume I want to ride off and never return. By morning the entire city will be after my blood, and yours. The rewards for our capture will be very high. And I dare not go back yet. The Blue Hairs will undoubtedly send out their wind crawlers tonight. There will be a storm in Amerandabad. Another reason why we should stay here.'

'Will the Blue Hairs send the storm here?' asked Ussemitus.

'No. It would stir up the ghosts. The Windmasters fear the echoes of such a conflict. It could damage Amerandabad, even destroy it.'

Fomond looked suddenly grave. 'Did you know, Jubaia, that two of the Blue Hairs were killed tonight. By the Phung.'

'What!' gasped the little man, hopping up. 'They *killed* Blue Hairs?'

Fomond nodded. 'To find Aru.'

Jubaia's reaction had stirred the dust and a whisper of sound went around the courtyard. Across the way from them a statue groaned in its bed and a ripple of echoes spread around it, thankfully dying down quickly. The company froze, no one moving nor speaking for long moments.

'I must be careful,' said Jubaia at last. 'But what you have said shocks me. Now we are in dire peril. The Blue Hairs are of the inner circle. They will devote every energy to their revenge. Azrand will insist that you, Aru, are an agent of the intruders, here on Innasmorn to pave the way for our conquest.'

'Is there a way out of the Zone of Echoes and the city?' said Fomond.

Before Jubaia could ponder an answer, there came a sound of rubble shifting and again a stir of echoes around it. They fell flat to the ground, feeling it quiver as if it were alive. Armestor, always watchful, slithered forward, serpent-like, making his way towards the source of the noise. He disappeared around the edge of a stone block.

Jubaia's eyes widened. 'Has he already lost his mind?' he whispered to Ussemitus.

The latter smiled. 'He's the best scout you could want. Whatever he has heard was not an echo of our own movements. Someone else is here.'

Armestor came back to them from another direction, his face pale. 'A single warrior, a guard. He is making his way through the maze,' he said.

'Let us follow him,' said Jubaia. 'And kill him.'

'Is he looking for us?' said Ussemitus.

'The Blue Hairs — ' began Jubaia.

But Armestor shook his head. 'I don't think so. He carries scrolls with him and has some other purpose.'

It was enough to convince them they should follow and they began the tracking of the stranger. Some distance on through the ruins they saw him below them, in one of the leaning roadways. He was walking slowly into the centre of the citadel, and clearly not searching for the runaways. Under his arm he carried a bundle of rolled parchments.

Aru turned to Ussemitus. 'Yet another secret meeting. Could Zellorian have agents here? Where safer from the eyes of Amerandabad?'

Ussemitus nodded. Some distance further on, the man turned into a wide courtyard, the buildings of which had not been completely ruined. Jubaia led the company up inside one of them, treading the stone stairs lightly until they came to the first floor. They went over to one of the open windows and looked down.

Below them a group of three figures had gathered. From their harness, Aru recognised them as Zellorian's men, and to her utter surprise, she saw beyond them a gliderboat.

'How did they bring it here?' she whispered.

Jubaia shrugged. 'Quareem has helped them placate the winds. But if its sound did not bring the watchers of these ruins, then the myths are unfounded.' Yet he did not raise his voice above a whisper.

The man they had been following handed over to the men of Zellorian his parchments and they began to read them eagerly. One of them took a container from his pocket and drank from it, offering it to the spy. They looked about them occasionally, but did not seem concerned about their eerie sourroundings.

'Surround them,' said Aru, the knight in her exercising control of her nerve.

'You wish to kill them?' gasped Jubaia.

'I want that craft,' she said, the tone of her command irresistible.

Fomond and Armestor glanced at Ussemitus, their looks

313

implying that they ought to take commands from him, but he was grinning wolfishly. He nodded, and for once Armestor managed a smile.

Slowly they went back down the stairs, Jubaia keeping very close to Aru, unsure of himself, not knowing what sort of enemies these were. Did they have weapons he had not seen, like those of the Blue Hairs?

Ussemitus and his companions fanned out, moving through the rubble like the very ghosts they feared, and in a short time had encircled the unsuspecting men in the courtyard. They could not hear the words of the intruders, for the latter spoke in whispers, evidently paying some respect to the legends about this place.

Ussemitus watched, knowing that he could not be seen by his fellows, but that they would be waiting for him to make the first move. They had enacted this particular hunt many times together in their native forests, though the prey had never been human.

The men finished reading the parchments, pleased with what they contained. More information from Quareem's conspirators, Ussemitus guessed.

Four of them to deal with. Ussemitus knew that Aru would attack also, so there were five of them to finish it. He fitted an arrow to his bow. It would be the signal. Choosing his target, he released the arrow, and in spite of the poor light, it struck home, under the breast plate of one of Zellorian's soldiers. The man gasped, falling in agony, as arrows sped from the night at the other men. Two of them were lucky, for the arrows glanced off their harness, but the spy from the city toppled over, dead before he hit the ground.

Ussemitus pulled out his stolen sword and leapt over the stones. Fomond and Armestor were already moving with him. One of the soldiers saw them and turned, running for the gliderboat. The other panicked and ran across the courtyard. He found himself confronted by Aru, and Ussemitus almost cried out a warning to her. But if he had thought her in danger, he was mistaken. She swerved to

314

avoid the wild lunge of the warrior and cut at him with the slim blade she had been given by Jubaia. It glanced off the harness, but the warrior went down. He scrambled up quickly, showing in his movements at last that he was no fool and a skilful opponent. But he had reckoned without Jubaia, who hurled himself at his back, knocking him from his feet.

The two of them rolled end over end, Jubaia hanging on grimly like a hound. Aru picked her moment and sank her weapon into the warrior's throat.

The last of them was in the gliderboat, about to attempt its raising, but Armestor sent an arrow into his arm that had him tumbling over the side of the craft into the dust. He rolled over agilely, only to find Fomond standing over him.

'Who are you?' he hissed.

There was no answer. Fomond prepared to kill him, and as the warrior realised there was no mercy, he let out a piercing scream. It was cut off as the sword took his life, but Ussemitus went very still, waiting. He could see both Aru and Jubaia in the darkness, also standing and watching, like wolves with ears back.

The echoes of that frightful shriek rang out again and again in the enclosed courtyard, seemingly growing and not diminishing. There were other echoes beyond, as if a dozen, then a score of other warriors were calling out as they died.

Jubaia tried to say something, but in the awful din the words were lost. Aru ducked down to avoid the sudden swirl of dust and ran as fast as she could towards the gliderboat. She called something, the words muffled, but Ussemitus could see her intention. They could fly out of here! He waved at his companions and they converged on the craft, though wary of it.

Around them the walls of the court began to groan, and the ground heaved gently, the echoes still sounding, now like a chorus of a thousand screaming warriors. Huge cracks appeared in the ground and a wall fell with a

315

resounding crash, ominous as thunder. It set up still more echoes and a storm of dust that spun round in a cloud. Jubaia could see faces in the cloud, leering down in triumph, and he imagined that great talons reached for him. He ran, swallowed by the dust that obscured everything. Other buildings fell, the noise so loud that he had to press his hands over his ears.

His eyes smarted from the sting of sand and dust and he leapt and dodged the masonry. Again the ground lurched and he was flung to his knees, scrambling away for the shelter of some huge blocks. For a moment flight would have to wait.

Aru reached the gliderboat and leapt over its side, waving to Ussemitus. He saw her through the clouds of dust, and the others; he shouted at them, though his voice was engulfed in the wave of noise that now roared over them all. He reached the gliderboat and got in, and there was just enough room for Armestor and Fomond to follow.

They ducked down as more dust clouds rolled over them, almost choking them. They were forced to bend and close their eyes, half expecting the walls to squeeze in on them.

'Where's Jubaia?' shouted Aru, but again her voice was snatched away. She could see nothing, not even sure if Ussemitus sat beside her. It would be madness to attempt to raise the gliderboat until this bedlam died down. She did not even attempt to close with its mind, knowing it would be closed up, cocooned from this terrifying conflict of elements.

On and on the din roared, and somewhere above it there were huge shapes swirling, the ghosts of a forgotten past, as terrible as the storm elementals that had pursued Ussemitus in the forests. But the billowing clouds obscured him and his companions from those searching eyes.

As they huddled in the gliderboat, Jubaia rolled further under the cover of the stone blocks. He could feel them move, but as long as they did not roll with him, he would be relatively safe. The fury of the echoing storm resounded around him, endless. He held his ears, trying to shut out the noise, and as he pressed himself into the ground, a rat burying itself, a crack opened for him and he rolled into it; then there was nothing and he was falling. Darkness took him, the sounds receding above him and he hit something soft. It took the breath from him and he opened his eyes, unable to move. He was in a bed of sand, somewhere below the courtyard. The night sky was far above, dust colouring it. But the darkness grew and his head rang to the diminishing echoes. He passed out.

Aru could stand the noise no longer. She spoke to the gliderboat and at last felt it shudder, as if it had been in a cold sleep. Slowly she talked it to lifting from the rocking floor of the courtyard and it inched forward, protesting at her intrusion. She kept its belly down, close to the ground. She coaxed it to accelerate gently, but a wall rose up before her and she had to back off. Swinging the craft round, she found an opening out of the courtyard and took the craft through it. It was not responding well, its mind fogged by fear, its body weighed down with the intruders. But she talked to it, trying to convince it that it would not be harmed.

Aru dare not climb, not with this wind, which would gladly pulp the craft on the masonry below. But she moved it away from the buildings out to more open terrain. When she felt less threatened, she dropped the craft and allowed it to rest. They waited.

It was not until dawn that the reverberations died down. Behind them a whole section of the Zone of Echoes had collapsed, and the clouds of dust were a thick haze over it. Aru and the others looked back at it, dazed by events, their heads ringing as if they had been beaten unconscious.

'Jubaia!' said Fomond. 'He's not with us.'

At once Aru woke the gliderboat and took it gently back to the ruins, though she could feel its reluctance. She passed back and forth, the craft as silent as a gliding bird, but there was no sign of the little man. The courtyard they had been in was unrecognisable, flattened and covered in

317

mounds of dust. The bodies of the men they had killed were buried.

In despair, they were forced to the conclusion that Jubaia had also died.

'We'll have to leave,' said Ussemitus.

The others would have argued, but they knew it was hopeless.

'If he did survive,' said Fomond, 'he'll wriggle to safety.'

But they did not smile, fearing the worst.

'I'll try once more,' said Aru, but another sweep proved fruitless.

Afterwards they moved towards the outer ring of the Zone, following a canyon that led back to the cliffs beyond Amerandabad's north. Aru satisfied herself that the storm of the night had ended, and seeing the skies overhead had cleared somewhat, she took the craft upwards in a gradual spiral that had her passengers gasping. They ducked down, hiding their eyes, though Ussemitus was able to look down at the ruins, wondering if, after all, Jubaia could have made it to safety.

The object of his thoughts was at that moment opening his eyes. A shaft of sunlight fell across him as Jubaia tested his arms. Nothing broken, though his back ached abominably. He struggled on to his side, then to his knees. His mouth was as dry as the desert, but he was intact. Cursing, he moved forward, trying to find a way out of the chasm into which he had fallen. There was none. It was not a cellar, nor any part of a building as he had hoped, but a fissure opened up by the storm. He could hear that it had abated, but had his companions survived it?

Carefully he climbed up to the daylight. It took him several hours, and by the time he emerged from his erstwhile prison, it was midday. The sun scorched down, and he swore at it silently, but it ignored him. The scene that met his eyes was one of utter devastation. Buildings had fallen, dust was heaped up into small hills, and there was

318

no sign of his companions. He could not tell whether they had lived or died.

He turned and tried to find a path that would lead him back into Amerandabad, though he knew he must cross the stone bridge first. It was a weary trudge, and by the time he had softly wound through the ruins to the span, dusk was beginning to fall.

He staggered across the bridge and through the ruins beyond to another old part of the city, which he recognised from events long in his past. Pausing only to drink from a small fountain, he moved on, finding an old house that looked familiar.

A crone opened the door for him and after peering at him for an age, clapped her hands and cackled as if a long lost son had come home. She took him in and prepared him some food, chortling and wheezing to herself, talking about old times that he had almost forgotten. He was too tired to say much himself, glad of the bed she gave him.

'I'll tell you everything I've been doing after I've slept,' he promised her.

She cackled again, covering him with a filthy blanket, fussing over him, and he was asleep within moments.

When he woke, he found a number of unfamiliar faces staring down at him, like unwanted visitors in a dream. But this was no dream. They were Vittargattus's men. They smiled at him, though he knew there was nothing friendly about them.

'Ah, the little thief wakes,' said one of them. 'You have been a busy fellow.'

Jubaia groaned. The old crone had sold him. But then again, they would have paid her an excellent fee for this prize.

From behind the warriors, in the doorway, she nodded, smiling, as if to say, what choice did I have?

319

22

THE DHUMVALD

Quareem watched the lower slopes of the mountains from his lofty perch high up over the pass. The floor of the valley was open ground, dotted here and there with a few clumps of shrub, a jutting boulder fallen from above. The torrent that gushed through the pass in the winter months was a stream now, tame and almost silent, so that the movements of the army when it came would be heard clearly, voices carrying up to the watchers far above.

The Blue Hair made out his servants as they came scurrying up the sloping path that wound here to the heights. There were three of them. They met and conferred, two of them going back down the slope, the third coming on. It was a long, arduous climb, but the figure moved steadily. Quareem waited patiently. Today would be a great day, a day he had waited for for so long. The day of his power. The preparations were made. When the army came, it would be met, oh how it would be met!

When the solitary climber finally reached the upper crags of the deep valley, he looked about him for the signs that had been promised him, and saw them with a shiver. Paint had been daubed over many of the rocks, a bizarre mix of bright colours, with blue dominating. The hieroglyphs that had been meticulously painted were not visible from below, but would have been easily seen from the skies. Beyond them there were other things that made the climber's heart judder. Birds had been staked out, their wings pinned to the ground, their eyes glassy, and further on there were other creatures, all ritually sacrificed and spread out as offerings to the sky. The climber looked upwards, watching the clouds as they gathered. But he saw nothing yet in their hifting expressions. The wind was gentle: the mountains that rose on all sides were silent, clear of cloud.

A hand gripped him while he watched the sky and he let out an inadvertent cry which rang back at him from the rocks. He turned to look into the cold gaze of the Blue Hair, his master.

'Where are they?' said Quareem.

The man bowed low. 'Lord, they will be in the pass by midday.'

'How many?'

'Lord, there must be ten thousand.'

'Is there news of the others?'

'Word has come from Amerandabad. Vittargattus is almost ready to leave. He has another ten thousand and will meet King Ondrabal south of the flood plain with another huge force.'

'Then Amerandabad will be defenceless,' breathed Quareem, looking south over the peaks.

The climber bowed again, eager to be away from this terrible eyrie.

'See that the army is watched. But when midday comes, leave the mountains quickly. Tell your fellows. If you value your lives.' Quareem turned from him and went beyond the place of the sacrifices. The climber looked to the sky once more, shuddering. Then he raced away, clambering downwards as though the spirits of the sky were already close behind him.

Quareem reached a narrow defile and went through it to a wide ledge that made a natural platform overlooking the pass. There were other sacrifices here, and blood had been daubed on the walls of rock, drying thickly in the sun. There were also heaped bones, many of them human, as well as skulls, the gaping sockets of which were turned skyward.

Two warriors stood to attention as the Blue Hair came to them, their faces expressionless.

'Midday,' said Quareem. 'Is there no word of the others?' The warriors shook their heads.

Quareem cursed. 'Then I'll begin without them. I dare not abort the ritual now. But they should be *here*!' he snarled, looking over his shoulder to the northern reach of the pass. This entire event had been prepared for the new powers in the east. So that they could witness Quareem's strength, his worthiness.

As he studied the far peaks, he caught a glimpse of movement in the sky, the flash of the sun on something that could not have been a bird. Something metallic. A gliderboat! It had to be. They came.

'Go up above,' he told the warriors. 'Guide our allies to us. They are coming.'

Not long afterwards Quareem was relieved to see Vymark stepping through the defile towards him. There were a dozen of his warriors with him, all armed and armoured. Vymark bowed.

'I am honoured to have you with us,' said the Blue Hair. 'Today is the day I promised to deliver your enemy into your hands.'

'Are they coming?' said Vymark, his keen eyes searching the valley below. He could see it winding towards them from the south.

'Soon.'

'You have chosen a fine setting,' said a voice behind him.

The Blue Hair swung round. The Man who faced him looked even more calculating and icy than Vymark, and Quareem knew at once that this was the intruder with whom he had been dealing for so long, yet whom he had never met. Zellorian.

He wore an enveloping grey cloak that merged well with the terrain, and his hands were hidden within it, only his face visible. Though he was tall, as most of his kind were to Innasmornians, Zellorian looked thin, his features drawn though not from age. And there was no mistaking the look of the eagle in his eyes, the bird of prey, the hunter. Quareem read it in him at once as surely as he felt the vibration of power about him, the current as strong as that in the Windmasters, though it was of a strange nature.

322

Quareem smiled. 'It is an honour and a pleasure to meet you, Zellorian.'

Zellorian inclined his head. 'I have awaited today eagerly.' He indicated the walls daubed with blood. 'I have seen something of your preparations. You have given life to set your stage.'

'Every detail has been attended to, I assure you. Rituals that have been forbidden for millennia, almost forgotten, have been undertaken to ensure our success. Blood is life. Life feeds life. From this high place, you will witness everything.'

'How many?'

Quareem smiled into those probing eyes. He knew how vital numbers were to this intruder, who understood sacrifice better than any other. 'Ten thousand.'

'And the – elements?' said Zellorian, watching the clouds, which continued to gather, crowding out the sun and lowering over the peaks across the pass.

'Those that I summon will serve us well. You will feel their power. You will hold it.'

Zellorian nodded. Behind him Vymark and the warriors from the east took up their positions. As one the company watched the southern end of the valley, waiting for the emergence of the army, their supreme sacrifice.

Jubaia pretended to be baffled by the appearance of so many warriors. 'Sirs, you honour me! What could you possibly want with–'

A finger jabbed at his chest. 'Save your breath, turd!'

They gripped his arms and swung him easily off the bed. Outside in the street all was silent, as if no one wanted to witness this abduction. The old woman had disappeared too. She had her money, Jubaia imagined, but would be too ashamed to show her face again. Ah well, such was life among the thieves.

'Where are you taking me?' he asked.

The warriors grinned. 'Pray to the wind gods, little thief. You've stolen your last trinket.'

'Am I not entitled to an explanation?' he said as indignantly as he could.

They pushed him along the narrow streets. 'Of course you are. And I'm sure Azrand will furnish you with one.' The soldiers laughed, and there was still no one in the streets to watch.

Azrand! Jubaia thought. How much could he know? 'Ah, the noblest of Blue Hairs. Of course. But why should he want me?'

The soldier holding him shrugged. 'Our orders were to find you and bring you to him personally. I have a feeling the clan chief wants words with you as well. What have you stolen? One of his women?'

The others laughed again, enjoying the discomfort of the little man.

'I've stolen nothing. But wait.' He pulled up short and the soldiers stopped, grinning down at him.

'Not going to bribe us, are you?' their leader laughed. 'You'd need a heap of jewels for that.'

'No. But there is something you must see. I have to show you before you take me to Azrand.'

One of the others laughed aloud. 'He really is trying to bribe us!'

'Or lead us into a trap. A dozen of his fellows await us—'

'Only a dozen?' chuckled another.

'I'm serious,' Jubaia frowned. 'There are traitors in the city.'

The warriors studied him, but could not refrain from laughing anew.

'*Really?*' said their leader. 'Jubaia, you amaze us. Can this be so?'

'Not me, you fool! Agents from the east.'

The laughter subsided, though the humour did not die. 'The east? In this land we have heard of where the sky falls?'

Jubaia nodded furiously. 'Just so. Last night I was with friends—'

'What friends?' The man's grip tightened. His eyes narrowed.

Jubaia flinched. 'Give me a moment and I'll explain.'

'Where are these friends?'

'We were not far from here—'

'What friends?' They pinned him to a wall like a moth. There was an anger in them now.

'Just a few friends. Loyal to Vittargattus.'

'Your kind are loyal only to themselves,' said the warrior.

'That's not so,' protested Jubaia, squirming. 'But we saw these agents. They were in the Zone of Echoes.'

Now the warriors had fallen very quiet. Their leader released Jubaia, who rubbed at his shoulder.

'There were great disturbances reported there last night. Had you anything to do with that?'

Jubaia nodded. 'Yes. My friends and I came across agents of the east. They consorted with a man of Amerandabad. A man in the employ of one of the Blue Hairs. Quareem, the traitor.'

'Quareem?' echoed the leader. He turned to his companions. 'It could explain the murders in the fortress. The use of power.'

There were nods of assent.

'What did these agents intend?' the leader asked Jubaia.

'They plot the destruction of the northern army. Quareem is there, with warriors from the eastern city.'

'Where are your friends?'

Jubaia described the fight in the Zone of Echoes, the killing of the agents, but he did not speak of his companions by name. 'If we can get back there,' he ended, 'I should be able to find the bodies of the agents.'

'And from the collapse of the buildings you described,' said the warrior, 'the bodies of your friends as well, maybe.'

Jubaia nodded glumly. 'Maybe.'

The soldiers frowned at each other, trying to decide whether they ought to follow up Jubaia's story. If they did and they found the bodies he spoke of, Azrand and Vittargattus would have to know at once. If there was nothing to see, then only a little time would have been lost. The army was not due to go south until tomorrow.

'We'd better look,' said the leader.

'In the Zone of Echoes?' said another. 'After the upheavals of last night?'

'You must find the bodies,' said Jubaia. 'Otherwise Azrand will never believe me.'

'From what we hear, he is in a poor mood. I don't know what happened in the fortress last night, or why half the rogues in the city are being dragged in, but there were assassins at work. It's whispered that two Blue Hairs died.'

'*Blue Hairs?*' said Jubaia, as if horror-stricken. 'Assassins killed Blue Hairs? That's unbelievable—'

'Certain captives may have escaped,' said the warrior, looking with deep suspicion at Jubaia. 'Not these friends of yours?'

'Of mine! You jest—'

'I hear you entered Amerandabad with strangers. It wouldn't be their bodies we're looking for in the Zone of Echoes, would it? Their *live* bodies?'

'I don't understand—'

The warrior grunted. 'We'll look. But we'll take a few more of our men with us. Just in case there's a reception waiting for us, eh?'

'But won't you make a lot of noise?' said Jubaia innocently.

'We'll take that chance,' grinned the warrior, pushing Jubaia forward. He did not see the little man smile as he searched out the way back to the Zone of Echoes.

They were free of the city, high above it, and flying northwards. Aru had calmed the gliderboat, though she wondered how long she could keep it aloft without the interference of the powers of Innasmorn. Evidently Quareem had found a way to protect the flight of the craft, and it was true that there were parts of its mind she could not reach: perhaps Innasmorn could not reach them either, and so bring it down. It seemed a docile craft, once flown reconciled to flight without too much question. Gliderboats usually accustomed themselves to a single Controller, or at least regular ones. But it was as well that this one was obedient, Aru reflected.

Armestor and Fomond had almost overcome their fear of what had happened to them, gripping the edge of the gliderboat and gasping at the view of the world, spread out like a map below them.

Ussemitus sat beside Aru, utterly amazed by what she had done, lifting them into the air. The flight had been a stunning experience, though his stomach curdled and knotted as they rode on the eddies of the wind.

'I'll have to drop lower,' Aru said, once they were clear of Amerandabad. 'She seems to fly truly, but the last time I took to your skies, my craft came down. I never know how your winds will react.'

'You believe in the power of the winds?' he asked her.

'Once I would have doubted. Not any more. Not on Innasmorn.'

The answer seemed to satisfy him. They were silent for a time, both thinking of Jubaia, the pain of his loss. He had gone to amazing lengths to help them. Could he have survived somehow? They could not be sure.

Ussemitus looked at the controls of the craft. They were strange, not being all metal, nor flesh, nor wood. Aru placed her hands on a flat area, but only operated the craft by pressure of hand and finger. Was there a power in her she had not spoken of? Something that communicated itself to the craft? His own mind veered away from any contact.

'How does it work?' he asked her at last, overcome by curiosity.

She smiled, her hair streaming out behind her. Her beauty suddenly made him shiver, as though something in him responded to it more deeply than it had in the past.

Love? But again his mind veered away. Such thoughts were dangerous.

'The gliderboat is alive. Not a true machine. It senses the mind of its pilot, or Controller. Between us there is an understanding. My hands guide it, but the control is from here.' She tapped her head and smiled.

'Symbiosis,' said Ussemitus. It was something he had heard of certain Windmasters, who claimed to be able to control the minds of animals, and some of them said, men.

Aru looked surprised. 'Why, yes, in a way. Though I am not dependent on the gliderboat.'

'But if it is alive, how does it feed?'

'Sunlight powers it.'

'As with a plant?'

She nodded. 'Exactly.'

'But how did such things evolve?'

Again she laughed. It was a good question. 'They did not evolve, Ussemitus. They were created. By my people. Though it is one of the many lost arts, I fear. Few have been made in recent times.'

'Because of the war?' he said, sensing her sudden sadness.

She nodded. 'So many things have been destroyed or forgotten.'

'Does the gliderboat have thoughts of its own?'

'I think so. But I cannot reach them. What we share is a brief touching in the dark.'

He studied her for a long moment, as though they were both somewhere else, safely on the ground, in the forest perhaps, and all the world about them was cut off from them. She looked at him, puzzled by his silence, then smiled.

'Look!' called out Fomond, breaking the spell. Ussemitus turned back to see his friend pointing to the north. Mountains rose up from the mist, greys and purples topped with cloud.

'That's our goal,' said Aru, again dropping the craft, though it had so far shown no signs of being confused by the Innasmornian sky.

328

Ussemitus nodded. 'The army. What shall we do?'

They had made no detailed plans since leaving Ameran-dabad. Fomond crawled towards them and Ussemitus chuckled as he saw him acting so nervously. Flight was not that appealing to him, for all its marvels.

'Want to land?' he grinned.

Fomond nodded. 'For all our sakes. But what are we to do about the army? Do you think it has been warned? Was anything you said to Vittargattus and Azrand taken seriously?'

'If it had been, the army would not have left Amerandabad.'

'If we go directly to its leaders—'

Ussemitus shook his head. 'I don't know. They may just ignore us. Or try to kill us.'

'There is a way,' said Aru. 'Though it'll be hazardous.'

'Yes?'

'I'll take the gliderboat down as close as I dare to them. We can warn them from the air. If they get hostile, we can move away.'

Ussemitus considered. He saw Fomond's uncharacteristi-cally glum expression and burst out laughing and Aru joined him.

'What is it?' gaped Fomond.

'Nothing,' said Ussemitus. 'Aru's right. We fly close to them.'

'And if they won't turn back?' said Fomond.

Ussemitus looked ahead to the mountains as they drew closer. 'Then we must find the Blue Hair, Quareem. And Zellorian's agents.'

No one argued. The gliderboat sped on, over the rising foothills and to the first of the mountains. Aru searched for a pass, and though there were a number of possibilities, one of them stood out like a great gash. There was a distinct road leading out from it, a white band that twisted through the hills.

The gliderboat dropped, barely out of arrow range of the land, and still the craft moved on smoothly, though Aru was alert for the slightest hint that the skies worked against it.

They all looked for signs of life below, but apart from the birds and occasional wildlife, they saw nothing. The army had passed beyond here and was in the mountains. Overhead the skies were beginning to change, the sun disappearing, the clouds swirling slowly, stirring themselves like gigantic warriors preparing for what was to come.

'Storm,' said Fomond. 'I can feel it.'

No one needed to reply. Armestor was huddled in a corner of the craft, while Ussemitus studied the heavens, trying to read them, searching for signs of immediate danger. He could taste the breath of Innasmorn as it drew it in, gathering energy to itself.

The craft flew into the pass, the walls rising up on either side of it, swallowing it, and the silence closed in. For a long time the pass wound this way and that, through the rock outcrops. An eagle swooped away from the craft, and hunting hawks rose up in awe of it.

It was close to noon when Aru saw the first signs of the army. There were a number of men below, bringing up the rear, keeping an eye out for anyone who might be tracking the army. But they did not look up at the heights, where the gliderboat moved like a silent, black ghost. Further on, beyond another twist of the deep pass, the body of the army moved forward at its own fast pace to where the pass opened out into a wider valley, through the main spine of the mountains before its slow drop down to the northern plain. This was the very heart of the Dhumvald.

Aru sped over the army; many of the heads turned upwards, though it was not easy for the massed ranks to see anything clearly. The gliderboat was not noticed until it had passed over the army and swung round to meet its vanguard. Immediately the foremost archers bent down, notching arrows, shields going up like a wall to screen them. Several of the leaders were mounted, and they held their lines in place steadily.

Aru brought the craft to within a short height of them,

hovering. But she could feel its unease as if it were a horse beneath her.

Ussemitus stood up and cupped his hands. His appearance caused a stir below and he could hear the murmurs like great ripples running back through the ranks. The army was like a sea before him. So many! his mind cried. 'Who commands here?' he shouted, his voice ringing out clearly in the still air.

Three riders edged forward, the first of them lifting his bearded face to the skies. Ussemitus knew him at once. He had sat beside Vittargattus and listened to him before. 'I am Telemorgas, commander of the north. Wulfhorn and Skaggeric are beside me, my generals. I know your face, boy. What is your business with us?'

The riders controlled their restless mounts with difficulty, for the steeds sensed the thing in the sky and were uneasy. Telemorgas shook his sword at the gliderboat.

'We come to warn you again,' called Ussemitus. 'Your army is in grave danger. There is a trap awaiting you here in the Dhumvald.'

'Whose trap?' bawled Telemorgas.

'The rebel, Quareem. He plans to unleash a storm on you. And it will be the deathstorm, the storm-of-the-dark.'

Some voices murmured at this, but Telemorgas glowered back at his troops as if he would charge them. He spoke to his generals. 'Come down from your perch,' he called at last. 'Let us discuss the matter properly.'

'We cannot land,' said Ussemitus.

But the riders below him were filled with evident suspicion. Aru whispered that they probably assumed them to be a part of any trap.

'Then if you will not land,' shouted Telemorgas, 'we will not debate with you. But we will be vigilant. We have protection from storms.'

'Windmasters?'

'We have protection,' repeated Telemorgas cagily.

Ussemitus turned to the others. 'It's no use. Unless we land—'

Aru shook her head. 'No. They'll kill us.'

'An army such as this,' said Fomond, 'must have Windmasters with it.'

'But they did not come to fight,' said Ussemitus. 'Only to move to the base in Kendara.'

'If they move on,' said Aru, 'we'd better do as we said. Search for the Blue Hair.'

'In this maze?' said Fomond.

She grinned. 'He can't be far away. I can't imagine he'd unleash something and not stay to watch.'

'If he truly intends to unleash the deathstorm,' said Fomond, 'he'd be wise to be a hundred miles away.'

Aru swung the gliderboat upwards away from the host, and Ussemitus watched as the leaders waited to see what would happen. But they must have dismissed the intrusion, for soon the army moved forward again, though from its formation it at least looked as if it was on its guard. It seemed that Telemorgas was more concerned about an attack from the ground than any from the sky.

The gliderboat rose way up above the valley until the army was a small dark snake below it. Ussemitus looked this way and that, but the crags and bare outcrops revealed nothing. Quareem could be anywhere. They moved back and forth until it was Armestor who shouted that he had seen something.

They squinted down to a place among the peaks, an overhanging ledge. Around it there were strange markings, bright hieroglyphs that combined to form a larger design, a great face, with a wide mouth and bulbous eyes. At first they thought it must be something that had been there, hidden from sight, for many years, but then they saw movement, the face crawling with life.

'Warriors!' said Fomond.

'Quareem's lair?' said Aru.

'Don't go in too close,' warned Ussemitus. 'He'll try to bring this craft down.'

'There must be two score of them,' said Fomond. 'How

332

are we to lead Telemorgas's men up here? There must be a pathway.'

A yell from Armestor made them turn. Behind them the skies were opening up, huge banks of swollen black cloud churning to release yet more cloud, a mass of writhing shapes and forms, moulded from the very wind.

The sun was at its zenith. The storm-of-the-dark had begun.

23

THE THIEF'S TALE

As the company moved across the Zone of Echoes, mindful of every step, Jubaia listened for the slightest sound, the merest hint of ground movement. Having been almost buried alive once, he had no desire to repeat the experience. The warriors who followed him, all two dozen of them, were equally as cautious, their weapons drawn against any attack. Though they were wary of an ambush, their real fears were of the Zone, which as far as they knew was filled with demons and powerful evil spirits. Most of them were typically suspicious. Jubaia realised that the death of the Blue Hairs and subsequent fury of Azrand was the only thing that could have goaded them into coming here with him.

He could see that last night's destruction had wrought much havoc, bringing down many buildings and clogging roads and pathways so that it was very difficult to tell which way he should be going. But he persevered. Ussemitus and the others must have escaped in the gliderboat, he told himself repeatedly. If they had not, their chances of survival were small.

At last he came to an area he recognised, and soon reached the ruins of the square where the confrontation had taken place. But he knew at once how difficult it was going to be to find the dead agents. The entire square had collapsed in on itself.

'We'll have to dig,' he whispered.

'Where precisely?' replied the captain.

Jubaia marked out an area. 'They must be under here.'

The captain threw him a glance that would have cracked rock, but he gathered his men and they began to work, mindful of the noise. Jubaia could see the terror they held in check. All of them worked quickly but jerkily, constantly watching the surroundings, listening for sounds, waiting for the devil wind. Jubaia dug, too, but to no avail. The devastation was absolute. It was impossible to tell how deep the rubble was. It could take an army weeks to move it all.

'We have no more time to waste,' said the captain to him softly. 'We've indulged you, but there's no further point.'

Jubaia began to argue, but before he could say more than a few words, he was gagged. They did not trust him and feared he would start shouting, bringing destruction down on them all. Wriggling and kicking, Jubaia was carried away from the only place that could have proved his case. With great relief the company returned to the streets of the city. In a small square they cleaned themselves in water troughs, dumping Jubaia in one with shouts of amusement, their relief at being away from the Zone of Echoes plain.

They marched him, dripping, back into the fortress. He did not have long to wait before he was taken before the Blue Hairs. Azrand himself had been summoned.

In the long chamber, Jubaia felt very small. When the Blue Hair entered with his principals, together with a number of leading Vaza warriors, he felt himself shuddering, knowing that there would be no mercy here. Another door to the chamber opened and he was horrified to see Vittargattus himself come in, his face like thunder, his eyes bloodshot, filled with hatred.

He sat heavily in a huge wooden chair, flanked by two of his commanders, and they looked no less angry than their clan chief.

'What do you know about the deaths in the fortress last night?' said Vittargattus icily, looking directly at Jubaia, as if with his gaze he could crush him to the wall.

335

Jubaia flinched, bowing low. 'Master, I know nothing of these things.'

'You're lying!' snarled Vittargattus, banging his fist down on the arm of his chair. 'Tomorrow I leave for the east, and in my fortress there is murder. Spies at my back. I'll have the truth, little man, or I'll have your body pulled apart, piece by piece and I'll use the pieces to decorate every tower in Amerandabad.'

Jubaia swallowed. All morning he had been trying desperately to think of a way to tell the truth of the matter without inviting personal disaster. But nothing would justify the deaths of the Blue Hairs, not to Vittargattus, nor to Azrand.

The latter had remained far cooler than the clan chief, but he spoke now, his own voice cold, better controlled. 'I think we should go back a little in time if we are to get at the truth of what is happening around us.'

Vittargattus glowered at him, stroking his thick moustache, but he growled an assent. 'Then get on with it.' He alone seemed unafraid of the Windmasters.

Azrand ignored the rudeness, turning his attention to Jubaia. 'I have reliable reports that you came from upriver, with a number of companions. Do you deny it, or must we pull the truth out of you with steel? Or if you have no fear of steel, then we have at our disposal far more painful tools—'

'I assure you, sire, I am most anxious to assist you in any way I can. I am only a poor tradesman—'

'You are a common thief!' snapped Azrand.

Jubaia almost retorted at that. Common indeed!

Vittargattus grunted his annoyance. 'Who exactly is this creature? What is his name? Where is he from? Whom does he serve?'

'Well?' said Azrand.

Jubaia bowed again. 'I am Jubaia, sire. From the far western lands, over the sea. I left my homelands in favour of an adventurer's life.'

'Get on with it,' prompted Azrand.

336

'But since coming to your lands, I serve only yourself.'

Azrand turned to Vittargattus with a sneer. 'I think we may be wasting time—'

'Let him finish,' said Vittargattus. 'Elaborate, thief.'

Jubaia bowed again. 'While I was in the forests of the north east, sire, I met a strange company. There were three men, foresters, and a girl.'

'What girl?' said Vittargattus.

'I knew there was something strange about her, but I could not place it. But I let it pass at first, for Innasmorn is a large world, as I have discovered. There is so much of it I have yet to see. But the company and I shared a few tales. Sire, they spoke of very strange things. They professed to be much concerned for the safety of Innasmorn, made anxious by what they had seen in their lands.'

Vittargattus would have fired off more questions, but he could see that Azrand wanted the little man to continue, whether this was deceit or not.

'They convinced me, sire, that you and all of Innasmorn are in grave danger.'

'From what?' said Azrand.

'From certain eastern powers.'

'The same intruders I am preparing to wipe from the face of our world?' said Vittargattus, unable to remain silent.

'Yes, sire. But the girl, whose name is Aru Casruel, told me it was not a simple matter. You see, I had not realised this at first, but then I agreed to help them—'

'In what way help them?' said Azrand.

'Didn't I say? Oh, to bring them to you. They did not know the way to Amerandabad, being foresters. They said they had urgent messages for the clan chief. I would have continued my own wanderings to the far east, where I have heard there are other wonders to see, but my duty, I felt, was to you, sire. That is, to lead these people to you with their urgent news.'

'You said you had not realised,' prompted Azrand. 'What?'

337

'Why, sire, the girl. She herself was one of the intruders.'

'You admit that?' said Vittargattus. 'You brought one of them here?'

'At first, lord, I had no idea who she was. I thought her from some eastern race. But I could not doubt her genuine fear for Innasmorn. It was only much later, when we were almost here, that I found out the truth. That she was from the mountain city.'

'Yet even then you did not give her up to me?' said Vittargattus.

'With every respect, sire, I brought her to you. Not as a prisoner, though, for I believed her story.'

'Which was what?' said Azrand.

'She spoke of her own people. How they had come from another realm, beyond Innasmorn, meaning only to dwell here in peace, escaping a war that had almost destroyed them. But she spoke of a leader, Zellorian, who is greedy for power. He has killed his own kind to win power, and now he seeks power here. He is the true enemy, but not all of Aru Casruel's people are your enemies. They would gladly fight alongside you.'

'So much she told you,' said Azrand sceptically.

'I brought them all here so they could warn you of Zellorian's intentions. Did they not do so? Did they not warn you?'

Vittargattus would have spoken, but Azrand deftly deflected him with a question of his own. 'Remind us of what they were to say.'

'Zellorian, who serves the Imperator Elect of Aru's people (though he is a puppet ruler) seeks power in two ways. The first is through the renegade, Quareem.' Jubaia watched the faces of the Blue Hairs, but they were blank. 'Quareem, whom I understand was cast out for some reason–' Still no one prompted him. 'Quareem also seeks power. He has sold himself to Zellorian. Together they intend to perform forbidden rituals for the summoning of power, power that they will control and forge into a dangerous element. The storm-of-the-dark.'

338

'Only a madman would attempt to raise the forces of nightmare,' said Azrand.

'Quareem could not achieve it, so they felt. But Zellorian is powerful. He created a gate between his world and Innasmorn. A man with such power can achieve many things if he is given the key. And Quareem has given him just such a key.'

Azrand's voice had dropped. 'And where is this to be done?'

'In the north, sire. In the passes of the Dhumvald, as your army marches to Tollavar. It is in grave danger. But the evil does not end there. Zellorian seeks greater power than that. He seeks to drain as much power from Innasmorn as he can, in order that he can go back to his own world and use it to destroy his enemies there.'

'What power is this?' said Azrand, and Jubaia could feel the coldness in him, the suppressed fury.

He turned to the clan chief, whose brow was still clouded. 'Sire, I am from the far west. There are legends there of a land, a forbidden place, where terrible evil dwells. A land where once artefacts of old almost destroyed Innasmorn. It is said that there is power there, unimaginable power. But the price for its taking is life itself. Aru Casruel is sure that Zellorian seeks this power. It is what he desires most. To unlock that ultimate secret. Aru was so afraid of his intentions that she came to you. Zellorian must be stopped.'

Vittargattus was nodding slowly, as though trying to piece something together. 'So you say,' he murmured, but Jubaia could not tell whether he had spoken in scorn or not.

Azrand stood up, moving slowly and silently around the table. He faced Jubaia, looking down at him. 'You have a gifted way with words, little thief. It helps you in your work, no doubt.' He turned to Vittargattus. 'This is only part of the tale. If it were all, perhaps even the deaths of my colleagues could be better tolerated.' He said this last with some bitterness, but went to one of the doors and opened it.

339

Another man came through it. Jubaia's eyes betrayed his shock, which Azrand had been watching for. But Jubaia pretended calmness. The man who had entered was fat for an Innasmornian, dressed in preposterously rich robes, his jowls quivering as he walked to the centre of the room.

'I am Scorrupus, from the city of Kendara,' he said in a high-pitched voice which eloquently indicated his nervousness.

Azrand pointed at Jubaia. 'You know this man?'

Scorrupus eyed Jubaia with disgust, snorting as he spoke. 'Indeed I do, your worthiness. He is a thief. A scoundrel. A liar and a degenerate. A fornicator–'

'Could you be more precise?' said Azrand patiently. Vittargattus was not amused by any of this, and neither were the two warriors on either side of him.

'Sire, I am a humble merchant of Kendara. During the course of a year, many items of merchandise pass through my warehouses, and the ships that dock at my wharfs bring valuables of rare qualities. When you enter Kendara–'

'Be more precise,' said Vittargattus, who had little time for fat traders who grew fatter while his warriors fell in the field.

'This creature came to Kendara some time ago, and at once he began to ply his trade. Using the women of my city, who for some reason seem to fall under his spell–'

'He uses power to seduce women?' said Azrand, and the question was not intended as a jest.

'I am sure of it,' said Scorrupus petulantly. 'Otherwise my own wife, a woman of rare beauty, rare beauty–'

'Be more precise,' said Vittargattus again, his tone ominous.

'Sire. This thief seduced her, using his black arts, I am sure. And with her unwitting co-operation, he stole certain items . . .' He paused as he saw the look in Vittargattus's eyes grow colder yet. 'In fact, some valuable jewels.'

'This is relevant?' said the clan chief to Azrand.

The Blue Hair nodded gently. 'With your indulgence, sire. Go on, Scorrupus. The jewels. Describe them.'

'They were garrols, elvor and zarrilli. Brought to me from the far north by a trader who had no use for them, but to whom I gave weapons and other valuables more to his liking. It needed three ships to bear away what I gave him, so the exchange was scrupulously fair. I pride myself on my honesty.'

Jubaia would have spat in scorn at this, but he was very still. He knew the jewels were worth far more than Scorrupus had paid for them.

'I prized the jewels for their rare beauty.'

'And this man stole them?' said Azrand.

'I had him pursued. Once my wife came out from the spell that he had woven, she was able to tell me everything. She was terribly distressed.'

'Tell us about the pursuit,' said Azrand.

'I hired six good men. Warriors of the city who were prepared to earn a little extra. I asked them to bring Jubaia back to me. I had no idea that he had other accomplices.'

Jubaia looked up at that. The shadows began to gather about him as he saw what Scorrupus implied.

'What happened?' said Azrand. He could see that at last Vittargattus was beginning to take an interest in this complex tale.

'Only two of the men returned to me. They gave me the woeful report. Jubaia had eluded them for a few days, but they hunted him down into the northern fringes of the forests. But it was a trap. Foresters were waiting, and when the warriors thought they had cornered the thief, archers shot them down, killing four of them with no warning. The other two escaped and came back to me.'

'Did they describe these assailants?'

Jubaia's hopes rose for a moment: he knew the men who had escaped had not seen their attackers.

'Foresters, they said. And there was a woman with them. A woman unlike any Innasmornian they had seen.'

Jubaia opened his mouth to refute this, but closed it as Azrand came over to him. 'And these were people you met by chance in the forest?'

'They saved me from death!' Jubaia protested. 'Those warriors were not going to take me back alive, I promise you. They would have hacked me to pieces. It is because of that that the girl and the others took pity on me.'

'They were accomplices!' squealed Scorrupus. 'Where are my jewels?' he added, forgetting himself. Azrand waved him away and the merchant thought better of arguing, bowing to the clan chief before making a hurried exit.

Azrand leaned very close to Jubaia. 'Two of my Blue Hairs died last night. In excessively unpleasant circumstances.'

'Sire?'

'Do you know how they died?'

'How could I?'

'Assassins. The very best. Amerandabad has a good many hired killers. We have used them in foreign parts ourselves. But some of them are very, very expensive. Most of them are looking for well paid work so that they can move on. It is said that in Ondrabal's lands, where there are more cities, the work is even better. Whoever paid the assassins last night, paid them well. They employed a Phung.' Azrand let the word hover like poison between them.

'But such things, sire, are for legends . . .'

'No. Windmasters do not use such powers, and yet if we had to, we could bring one before us. Perhaps you need convincing of the existence of such a thing?'

'Not at all, master. Have the assassins been apprehended?'

Azrand shook his head. 'One of them was killed. But it is unlikely that the others will be found. We have searched the roofs for any sign of them. We did find something.' He snapped his fingers and to Jubaia the sound was like the snapping of his own neck.

One of the Blue Hairs rose and came forward. He held out an object that sparkled in the torchlight.

'I don't understand,' said Jubaia.

Azrand picked up the jewel and held it up to the light,

admiring its flawlessness. 'It is quite rare. And very valuable. It is an elvor. They are found in the far north. But we found this one on the roof. The assassins must have dropped it. Very careless of them to drop an item of such value. But perhaps they had many more and did not miss this trifle.'

Jubaia tried to swallow, his throat constricted.

'It must be a little like the jewels you stole from Scorrupus. May we see them?'

Jubaia coughed. 'Ah, but sire, I did not dare hold on to them. Such a fortune! I got rid of them as soon as I came here.'

'To whom? And for what?' said Azrand, his voice very low, though everyone in the chamber heard him.

'I— uh, sire, this is very difficult for me. I am a thief, I won't deny it, but to reveal—'

'Who did you give the jewels to?' snarled Vittargattus, rising and coming over. 'Tell me now, or I'll have your head on a pole! Who?'

Jubaia cowered back.

'Isn't it true,' said Azrand, still calmly, 'that you were searching for assassins last night? Making enquiries?'

Jubaia paled. They had him. But what of Spetweng? Was he taken? The assassin who had died, had he been identified, under torture? He had been at Baraganda's.

Vittargattus suddenly gripped Jubaia by the scruff of his shirt and pulled him towards him. 'You paid assassins to kill my men? You brought a *Phung* to my fortress! *A Phung*!' There was madness in his eyes, as if he looked out on the nightmares that haunted his sleep.

'Something had to be done,' gasped Jubaia. 'The prisoners had to be freed.'

Slowly Vittargattus released his grip. 'Then you admit it,' he breathed.

'Blue Hairs were murdered,' said Azrand incredulously. 'Was that a fair price to pay for the freedom of your allies? Blue Hairs, protectors of the Mother? You brought a Phung to kill them?'

343

'It was not the intention. But I knew that if you imprisoned Ussemitus and Aru, you could not have believed them, their story of Quareem's plot with Zellorian. Aru is not an enemy—'

'*Where are they now*?' said Vittargattus in a voice that spoke only of retribution.

'They have gone to the north, to warn your army.'

Azrand shook his head. 'You still expect us to believe you? They are a week too late. How could they hope to catch Telemorgas?'

Jubaia dared hold back nothing. He had to be truthful now or his own lies would turn against him. 'They have a craft. A craft that flies.'

Azrand at last looked surprised, his eyes widening. He turned to the clan chief, but Vittargattus looked even more incensed.

'It is true, sire,' said Jubaia quickly. 'I have seen it. It belonged to the agents of Zellorian. Such things are used in his city. It glides through the air. Last night we discovered Zellorian's spies in the Zone of Echoes—'

'Last night?' said Vittargattus. 'You were with the fugitives last night?'

'I met them after their escape. But the enemy—'

'Where is this enemy? What happened to these spies?'

Jubaia explained about the battle, the sudden collapse of the buildings. And he spoke of the search that he had persuaded the warriors to make.

'But they found nothing?' said Azrand.

'Convenient,' snapped Vittargattus. 'Well, I cannot spare the men to search again.' He walked back to his chair and sat in it, his chin on his fist. 'This is a pretty concoction of lies. Flying craft! If your friend from this city can fly, then she uses an artefact to do it! They have brought the old Curse with them. And *you* have been party to it.'

'Sire, they have gone to try to save your northern army.'

'Ten thousand men!' snorted Vittargattus. 'What do they need to fear? What can Quareem and his new master do to them?'

344

Azrand did not seem to share his confidence. To him the storm-of-the-dark meant much more. He leaned towards Jubaia again. 'Tell us the whole truth, little thief. Why is the girl really here?'

'But it is the truth, sire. All of it.'

Azrand drew himself up. Again he went to the door and opened it, and yet another figure entered the room. This time Jubaia did not recognise the man. He was a Blue Hair, a tall being with eyes that, if anything, had more coldness and hatred in them than those of his fellows. He held himself very straight, pausing only to bow before Vittargattus.

Azrand introduced him. 'Sire, this is Kuraal. You recall him, I am sure. He has been in the lands of the east, preparing the Vaza there for your coming, telling them to gather themselves for the assault on the mountains in the north.'

'Is this creature known to you?' Vittargattus asked Kuraal bluntly.

Kuraal glowered at Jubaia, shaking his head. 'He is not, sire. But if he is in allegiance with the alien woman, Aru Casruel, and the forester, Ussemitus, then he is surely your enemy.'

Jubaia shook his head.

'What do you know of them?' Azrand asked Kuraal.

'Conspirators, sire,' said Kuraal simply. 'When I came to the village of Ussemitus in the eastern forests, some of the young men there had already made fools of themselves by going up into the northern mountains, the lands fringing the area we call the land of the Falling Sky. Ussemitus had met the woman, Aru Casruel, and had been bewitched by her. If you'll allow me, sire, I have a man with me—'

Vittargattus gestured impatiently for him to bring him in.

Kuraal went to the door and called to someone who was waiting beyond. One of his own warriors came in, escorting a dishevelled youth. The latter looked drawn, his face pale

345

in spite of the dust that coated it, and he seemed in need of sustenance, even more hollow-ribbed than his kind.

'An eastern forester,' said Kuraal. 'From the village of Ussemitus. His name is Gudrond.'

The youth's eyes were fixed on the floor, his gaze watery, his hands shaking.

'Well?' said Vittargattus.

Kuraal put his hand under the youth's chin and lifted it roughly. 'Speak up, boy. Tell the clan chief about your friend's meetings with the northern witch.'

Gudrond swallowed. 'It's true, sirs,' he said, voice trembling.

'Speak up!' snapped Kuraal.

'It's true!' Gudrond gasped. He began to babble about the forest, about a journey he had undertaken with Ussemitus and others. And about the way the woman, the intruder, had bewitched and beguiled Ussemitus, using sorcery to trap him, to make him her slave. At the end of it, Gudrond collapsed, almost in tears.

'What is wrong with the boy?' said Vittargattus suspiciously. He knew well enough how harsh the methods of the Blue Hairs could be.

'I have tried to ease things from him,' said Kuraal. 'But the evil used on his fellows spreads quickly. It has tainted him. But not enough to blind him to the truth. Ussemitus and his companions are the victims of the witch from the mountains. Whatever she has in mind, sire, they are a part of it.'

'How did these foresters escape you?' Vittargattus asked him.

Kuraal explained, and spoke of his search with the windwraiths, to no avail.

'They escaped windwraiths?' said Vittargattus. 'Using sorcery?'

'How else could a man evade them?'

'Then they came east,' said Azrand. 'To another rendezvous, with this creature.'

Vittargattus gazed even more balefully at Jubaia. 'This

346

woman is capable of great power, it seems. She can turn aside windwraiths, and it seems she is able to command the mind of a Phung. What else can she do that you have not spoken of?' he said to Jubaia. 'Can it be that she can put evil into the minds of men? Fill their nights with strange dreams?'

Azrand glanced at him as if to warn him of speaking further, but the clan chief had finished his speech.

'The meetings were chance,' said Jubaia.

Kuraal bowed once more, then with his warrior and Gudrond, he left the chamber.

'You must believe us,' said Jubaia, though he felt helpless under the eyes of his questioners. 'Your army is in grave danger, and if you go out against the city of Zellorian, you will be in greater danger still.'

Vittargattus stood up. 'I have given your explanation much thought, little thief. And I shall continue with my intent. I will not divert my northern army. It will cross the sea to Kendara. And I will go southwards to Ondrabal. When we are ready, *we* shall unleash a storm. A *cleansing* storm, not something from our black and forbidden past. A storm that will remove this threat of the Curse from Innasmorn. And with it all sorcerers and witches that stand in its path.

'And you, thief, will be the first. Today you will be executed. When I ride out of Amerandabad tomorrow, your body will be hung on the gates for us all to spit upon. Azrand! See that this is done!'

24

DEATHSTORM

'It begins,' said Quareem, eyes gloating over the impending slaughter of the army far below, Vaza who served the Blue Hairs who had cast him out. Let them all perish in the horrors to come!

Zellorian watched more calmly. This was a minor affair compared to the wars he had witnessed with the Csendook Swarms. But the use of the elements intrigued him. There was power here he could use, and there was no telling yet to what extent it could be tapped. Quareem's invocations had brought thunderheads, moulding the skies, and in them a whirling confusion of forces, living entities, wind elementals, he called them. Zellorian watched as the clouds billowed downward extraordinarily quickly like vast banks of fog spilling over from a mountain plateau. There was a roaring sound within them, as though each of the darting shapes carried with it its own fist of thunder. Bolts flickered out in the valley, the air crackling, alive. Already the army was beginning to dig itself in against the sudden storm.

In the gliderboat, Aru had to swerve to avoid a sudden gust of air and cloud that threatened to envelop the craft. Horrible faces leered at her, shaped from cloud; they broke up as quickly as they had formed only to reshape themselves into something as bad. The craft's terror was like a cold throb in her mind and she struggled to take it down into the valley once more.

'Can we not attack Quareem?' called Ussemitus, though he and his companions were flat to the bottom of the craft as it bucked and danced, like a boat caught in sudden seas.

'I dare not climb into this cloud. Not yet. It's alive with lightning.' And stars know what else, she thought. She said

348

no more, concentrating her efforts on avoiding a plunge that would break them up on the cliffs.

More thunder echoed around the valley, giant laughter. Rain fell in huge drops, increasing in volume, becoming torrential. The army below had formed a defensive circle, shields outward, the horses rearing in terror as the wind elementals tore backwards and forwards overhead. Aru was stunned by them: she had seen nothing like them, these flitting ghosts, too fast to view clearly.

Up on the ridge, Zellorian's expression of mild interest had not altered. 'It is interesting,' he told Quareem. 'But surely the army below us can be in little danger from a storm.'

Quareem darted him a glance that had scorn in it, but then remembered his precarious position with these outsiders. 'It will pin them down. The real storm is yet to come. The storm-of-the-dark.' He turned away and cupped his hands to his mouth. Moments later, in answer to his shout, shapes were forming in the sky above him. Great, writhing things, shot through with the greys and blacks of thunderclouds, they broke up and swirled into a host of smaller shapes, creatures that moved so quickly it was difficult to follow them. But a number of them swooped over the ledge, circling. They had faces of a kind, wide, staring faces, with eyes that were like beams of fury and hatred. Zellorian saw that Quareem spoke to them, ordering them on some course in a strange tongue. They listened avidly, like a starving crowd promised a feast.

Cries split the air and whether they were of delight or anger, Zellorian could not tell. His men drew back from the sounds and terrible visages of the wind beings. But Quareem motioned Zellorian forward. He stood beside the Blue Hair.

'They will go down and begin the killing. And they'll raise up the earth killers, the dhumhagga. Stand beside me, Zellorian. You and I will drink this power. The lives of the ten thousand will bring forward the forgotten powers, the lords of the deathstorm that were locked away millennia ago. The elementals will summon them for us as they sate themselves on blood, and when they come, all Innasmorn will shudder. The power will pass into your hands, for I cannot contain it. You will hold it. The lords of the death-storm will obey you, and only you can keep them here once they have materialised.'

'Through more sacrifice?'

'As long as you are able to feed them, they will do your bidding.'

Zellorian smiled. 'They will feed as they have never done before. But stand beside me, Quareem. You must share this divine power.'

Quareem nodded, though already his face was drawn, as if he would regret the terrible destruction he had unleashed. On the ledge behind him, his servants pressed back into the rock, hoping it would absorb them. Vymark and the other warriors also looked appalled, for the storm that now gripped the mountains and the valley was beyond anything they could have imagined. It lived, a feral thing, with a thousand eyes, a thousand claws, and as it launched itself downward, they felt the rejoicing in it, the hunger of the beast about to sate itself on flesh.

Aru saw the first wave of power tear into the front ranks of the army. Fire crackled in the air and there was an explosion of earth, bodies hurled this way and that like dolls. Scores of Telemorgas's warriors were cut down. His men fought, swinging their weapons, shouting, trying to oppose forces they could hardly see. Lights danced in the air, the skies falling upon the army, the heavens screaming.

'I must land the gliderboat!' shouted Aru above the awesome cacophony. 'If I don't, it'll be pulled to pieces.'

None of the others argued and she took the craft low to the ground, swerving to avoid knuckles of rock outcrop, heading back up the throat of the valley, away from the worst of the storm. Like an animal it had fallen on its prey, concentrating its energy on the army and its circle of defence. The gliderboat dropped behind a bank of rocks,

on to open ground that was partly sheltered under a looming wall of stone.

'What can we possibly do?' said Ussemitus. He felt sick-
ened, unable to prevent the destruction of the army. 'Unless
we go up in the gliderboat, we cannot reach Quareem and
the others.'

'It's pointless joining the army,' said Fomond. 'What can
we do that ten thousand cannot?'

'Quareem has called down the storm,' said Aru. 'Either
we get to him and kill him, or we resist the storm.'

'*Resist* it?' repeated Ussemitus. 'How in the gods do we
do that?'

She was looking at him in a strange way, and for a
moment he could not meet her gaze. 'When we were on
the Spiderway, the storm came. But not to harm us. It
helped us. It pushed back the monsters that threatened us.'

Fomond was looking at Armestor, then both watched
Ussemitus. 'Did we bring that storm?' said Fomond.

'You must have!' said Aru. 'We all prayed to the skies,
and they answered.'

'You want us to attempt to summon help – from above?'
gasped Ussemitus. 'But the skies are already ablaze with
fury –'

'This is not the storm you called,' insisted Aru.

'I did not call a storm,' said Ussemitus, the rain streaming from him. 'I am no Windmaster! I have no skill.'

'You have to try!' Aru shouted above the din of the
rain, which seemed to conspire to strengthen Ussemitus's
argument.

Thunder hammered overhead, as though the elementals
were searching for them.

'Fomond, tell her this is ridiculous,' said Ussemitus.

But Fomond was frowning, remembering his conversation with Armestor after they had survived the crossing
of the Spiderway. 'Perhaps we should try, my friend. What
else is there?'

'But we'll draw the attention of the elementals!'

'You're just making excuses!' cried Aru. 'Do it, Ussemitus! Use whatever you have. And you, Fomond. Armestor. I'm not an Innasmornian. I can't reach your gods. But Innasmorn needs your gods now. Call on them!'

Ussemitus stared at her in amazement, stunned by the intensity of her plea, her fierce desire to help their world. If only that fool Vittargattus could see her, he thought, he would realise that she was no enemy.

They crept up through the rocks and were able to see down into the valley through the sheets of rain. The army was still attempting to withstand the bolts of lightning that tore into the earth about it, the passing overhead of the elementals. Clouds of them swirled downwards, and even from this distance Ussemitus could hear the screams of the dying, the awful shouts of those in terror.

'Do it,' Aru called to him. Her hand reached out and took his and he nodded, though fear held him even more tightly. He closed his eyes, his mind, shutting out the fury of the storm. Beside him Fomond and Armestor did the same, shivering in the rain. They began trying to reach into the darkness.

Ussemitus felt himself floating, no longer wet and cold but adrift in an airless place, his body light, the dark a sudden, warm glow. He called out, though there was no sound. *Innasmorn. Mother of Storms. Hear me. Save your children.*

As he began the ritual, Fomond and Armestor felt themselves drawn to him, their own minds unable to penetrate the noise of the storm. Fomond opened his eyes, but Aru motioned for him to be still. He could see that Ussemitus was rigid, eyes wide, but not seeing the horrors below.

'What is it?' said Fomond softly.

'He has a power within him,' Aru answered. 'I've seen it more than once. You all have it. But in him it is the strongest.'

Fomond nodded. 'I have known this. I used to think it was luck. But then I wondered if Innasmorn favoured him.'

'I'm sure she does,' Aru grinned.

Her attention was snapped by Armestor, who pointed to the valley, a shout of fresh fear torn from his lips. 'Look!'

They followed the line of his arm. The ground before the army had begun to heave. A hundred elementals were dancing upon it, their insubstantial bodies drifting this way and that as the ground moved, bursting in a dozen places. Up from below came strange shapes, loamy and grotesque, and as they stood they began to form themselves into something more recognisable. The wind elementals were doing this, dragging up the earth and sculpting it into these forms, the dhumhagga. Like huge, shambling beings, the earth-things moved towards the army. Scores of them erupted from the ground, some so badly finished that they toppled forward, only to stand again and be worked on anew by the screaming aerial horrors.

Aru studied Ussemitus. He was still in the trance, the calling ritual. Despite the fact that the things from the earth filled her with dread, Aru managed to remain outwardly calm. 'We must not interrupt Ussemitus,' she warned the others.

Neither demurred, their eyes fixed on the terrible dhumhagga that now clashed with the front ranks of the army. The warriors beat at them with their weapons, clubbing, chopping, knocking many of the earth-things to the ground. But it was their source of power and they fed on it, rising again. They came on in wave after wave, dragging warriors down, killing and maiming remorselessly. The most badly damaged of the dhumhagga crawled away, only to be reformed by the elementals and sent back to wreak even more havoc. The air howled maniacally, countless voices screaming in glee, revelling in the carnage, the sickening breaking of bones, the spilling of blood. Fomond saw through the blur of rain the shapes from the skies flash down, enveloping warriors, the air pulsing with crimson as blood was drawn from the foe, warriors toppling like empty husks, drained. Horses reared, also sucked dry, crumpling, and warrior after warrior fell in the panic and was trampled, killed by his own companions.

High above all this pandemonium, Zellorian watched through a break in the clouds that never wavered, as if the elements were proud of their work and eager to show him their worst excesses. Though he did not control these powerful agents of the wind, he could sense the power coursing through Quareem as the Blue Hair conducted the whirling dance of death below. As the death toll rose quickly, Quareem turned to Zellorian, his face contorted with evil pleasure.

'The storm lords await your pleasure. They have tasted blood. Bring them out of their ancient dark.'

Zellorian felt the slightest tremor of uncertainty as he always did when standing on the brink of some new experience, the first step towards fresh power. But he had sacrificed before, recalling the unimaginable sacrifice he had made in order to create a gate from Eannor to Innasmorn, a world beyond the circle of existence that encompassed the worlds of his own lost empire. The giving of life was nothing, an essential part of creation, of building.

He held out his hands and called to the storm. He used words that came naturally to him, words of power, of evil, of the dark, of blood. Words that were, to him, beyond human definitions of pain and horror. Words that were part of another language, another being. Words that were without emotion, transcending it. From the depth of his own experiences he drew them, and they came effortlessly to him, spreading into the ether of Innasmorn as easily as they would have spread on any world in any realm. It was the language of the gods and it was as pure as life itself, and a thousand times more potent.

The storm-of-the-dark heard him.

Above the dying army, the elementals heard the remote thunder that signified the coming of their masters, masters who would gladly feed on the death and destruction they had wrought. With fresh glee they set to creating more mayhem, and the warriors below them closed ranks again in an effort to save themselves from annihilation.

Quareem sensed a change in the air, a growing darkness over the mountains, as if the very rocks were about to burst and produce monstrous children, gods that could walk

Zellorian knew that the sacrifices below fed this coming power. He reached out to it, probed it, and found his answer. His own blood sang, the song of ecstasy. They came.

Ussemitus gasped, his eyes still wide, fixed on nothing, but Aru could see that something had shaken him, as if he drew back from it. She put her arm around him, though he did not seem to notice. Fomond and Armestor watched in fear, anxious to help, but not knowing what to do. They waited like children.

Ussemitus had heard a distant roar in his vision, a deep, awesome sound that threatened to well up from immeasurable darkness under him and burst, filled with sickness and decay. He moved away from it swiftly, like an aerial spirit, still seeking help, a link with the storm gods. Whatever it was that moved, it was no ally, but a dire threat to Innasmorn.

Suddenly he shouted out, toppling back, so that Aru had to call to Fomond to help her keep Ussemitus on his feet. He felt oddly light, as if no more than a shadow.

'What does he say?' shouted Fomond, still having to raise his voice against the storm, for the rain had not ceased, nor the thunder overhead.

'He called on Azrand, the Blue Hair,' she told him.

'Their ruler?' gasped Armestor. 'In Amerandabad?'

'We need him,' said Aru. 'All the Windmasters must aid us now.'

Ussemitus called the name again. In his mind he saw the streets of Amerandabad, the people, the fortress. On its walls a group of figures appeared, looking skyward. Azrand was one of them.

'Azrand!' Ussemitus called again.

He saw the figure stiffen as if an arrow had pierced it. Azrand squinted against the sunlight. Over the city the skies were blue, cloudless. Azrand was looking to the north, to the Dhumvald. Beside him were a number of his fellow Blue Hairs. All looked puzzled. Abruptly, Azrand turned to them, as though he had made a sudden decision. They left the parapet, but Ussemitus followed them through the stone, down into the bowels of the fortress. They went through endless passageways and corridors, emerging at last into another place, a smaller fortress. As they came up into its towers, their numbers growing, Ussemitus saw that it had been built on an island beyond the city, out in the river Fulgor. The Blue Hairs went up to the tallest of the towers, a circular building with a wide, flat top. Here they quickly formed themselves into a circle, linking arms, their eyes raised to the heavens. Ussemitus could see their fear, could feel its breath.

Azrand stepped into the middle of the circle, an elaborately carved pike in his hand.

'Azrand! Hear me,' called Ussemitus across the gulf.

'But who are you?' came the soft reply in his mind.

'You were warned of the danger in the north,' Ussemitus told him. 'It is here. Quareem has summoned the death-storm. Your army will feed its monstrous power. We must have help!'

Ussemitus could see the Blue Hair stagger, clearly amazed by the voice that must have come to him from out of the sky, though he could see nothing.

'What must be done?'

'Wake Innasmorn's skies! Anything that can push back this storm.'

Aru held tightly to Ussemitus, who could hardly stand. She could hear him faintly, but had no idea whether he was reaching the distant Windmasters.

Ussemitus saw Azrand turn to the others, and they began their working at once, sensing that something was terribly wrong in the north. This was no idle warning.

Ussemitus slumped for a moment, then twisted, stumbling to his feet. He looked at Aru. The rain seemed to take him by surprise.

'What happened?' said Fomond. 'Are you all right?'

Ussemitus nodded, dazed. 'I saw Azrand and the Blue Hairs. They are helping. Combining their powers. They will send power. The storm-of-the-dark must be contained.

If it breaks, this entire valley will be swallowed by it. Nothing will survive.'

'And then what?' said Armestor, his eyes wild.

Aru answered. 'Zellorian will control it.'

'Impossible,' said Ussemitus.

Aru shook her head. 'Oh no. He will control it. Believe me.'

'Then we must get to him,' said Ussemitus. 'Listen, there will be a contest here, a colossal battle in the skies. Innasmorn will bring her powers to bear on this storm. I must help Azrand and the Blue Hairs. They will need my guidance. But we will create a way for you.'

'A way?' said Aru. 'What do you mean?'

'The gliderboat. You must use it. To find Zellorian. Kill him. You must! He cannot be allowed to master the deathstorm. The army feeds it, gives up its blood, its life, to bring it through. Stop the slaughter. Stop the flowing of blood.'

Aru looked up at the skies. They boiled, the lightning still licking out wildly. 'A way? Through that chaos?'

'Yes,' said Ussemitus. He leaned against the rocks. 'I must begin again.'

Within moments he had closed himself off from them, as though sure of his own power now. He sent out his mind in search of Azrand, and it was as though two forces met on the plains beyond Amerandabad. The Blue Hairs had summoned the forces of the world, drawing on Innasmorn's storms and elemental powers, but even so there was fear in them, a cold fear of the storm-of-the-dark. It was a force beyond knowing, and fed as it was on the countless lives in the pass, it became more powerful, vastly bloated.

'Can it be forced back?' said Ussemitus.

Azrand's voice was faint, uncertain. 'It has been held in check for so long. I fear for Innasmorn.'

'Then we must contain it long enough for those who summoned it to be destroyed.' He explained exactly what he needed.

A short while later the clouds above the valley churned

357

as though a fresh storm had clashed with them, alien to them, and the mountain peaks rocked to this new contest. The ground shook and the elementals above the army tore away from it, going upward to meet the new assault. For a moment the rain ceased, but there were numerous detonations of thunder and it came again, a solid wall that drove Fomond and Armestor for cover. Aru tried to move Ussemitus, but he was like a stone, and rooted to the earth.

Above her, Aru saw an opening in the clouds, a way that was clear of rain and the flickers of lightning. Fomond pointed to it and shouted something but it was lost in the din. He waved her to him. Reluctantly she left Ussemitus, but his face was turned skywards, his concentration intense.

Fomond grabbed the lurching Aru by the arm and pulled her towards the gliderboat. 'We have to go aloft,' he said, in spite of his terror.

She felt a shock of guilt. Fomond, she knew, was horrified by the prospect of flying again, but he recognised their only hope of success. Quickly she went with him to the gliderboat. Both turned to Armestor.

'Are you coming?' Fomond called. 'Stay here if you must.'

Armestor looked back at Ussemitus, but he unslung his bow and climbed aboard the craft.

Aru took a long time to penetrate the frightened mind of her craft, for the storm had driven it into an inner darkness that was like a thick fog. But she wrenched the craft free of its torpor and got it into the air, aiming it at the narrow corridor that Ussemitus had opened for them in the heavens. They caught a last glimpse of him below them, a bedraggled, pale figure, his face a white mask.

In his mind, Ussemitus could see the gliderboat, swirling up like a leaf caught in a whirlpool. He knew that the storm would lock with the darkness and that the confrontation could go on for days. In the pass, the elemental forces were amassing for a renewed assault on the army, knowing that without its blood the deathstorm would be reduced.

Above him the winds chased each other wildly to and

fro, seeking him out. Their dark masters knew he had betrayed them. They wanted him. Their lust for his pain was a tornado howl.

The gliderboat curled upward, around it the storm raging. Numerous hideous shapes materialised, clawing at the craft, unable to reach it, seared by the power the Blue Hairs were pouring into that corridor. Fire spat and thunder rolled deafeningly like the enraged shouting of gods. Armestor gripped the side of the craft until his knuckles were white, trying to force the bile of terror back. Fomond felt no less helpless, but he could read the determination of the girl, who held her course as though the gods themselves could not break it.

Up beyond the valley they soared at last, still following the unnatural break in the clouds. They swept across the upper crags, searching for the figures they had seen before. Again the attacks came, more persistent now. The skies were thick with elementals, their voices a lunatic choir, their innumerable claws raking the air, though yet ineffectually. They burned up in the corridor, and the skies burst, the wind shrieking in fury.

Aru ignored the madness. She forced the gliderboat to swallow its terror, held it on its course with the anger of her will. The deaths of all her allies rose before her and she heard their ghosts crying out to her, goading her on, strengthening her. She had seen the face of the mountain, the awful blood-drawn thing that Quareem had put there, a sign to the gods he called. She took the gliderboat down, dropping quickly so that Fomond and Armestor felt their stomachs flip over. But they held on, gasping for air, their faces like chalk. Aru swept over the ledge, seeing at once the enemies she had known were there.

Zellorian stood on the brink of the ledge, arms raised, while beside him Quareem laughed like an imbecile.

'Armestor!' Aru shouted. 'I'm going to pass them again. If you ever used your bow to good purpose, do it now!'

Armestor crawled to her, ignoring the screaming air, the

racing wind as the gliderboat banked and swung round. 'One arrow, mistress,' he called. 'Who shall I kill?'

'Zellorian!' she snarled. She filled the word with hatred, her fury as livid as that of the storm about them.

'I'll try for the Blue Hair,' said Fomond. 'Between us we'll douse this storm.' And this time I will not hestitate, he told himself.

'Don't miss,' Aru said through her teeth.

Fomond grinned, but he felt the doubt creeping in.

As they dropped down, he and Armestor raised their bows, both unsure of themselves, but saying nothing. At this speed, falling, with the winds howling at them like wolves, how could anyone be sure of accuracy?

They swept over the ledge. Fomond saw his target and released his arrow. It went through the storm quicker than the eyes could follow it, but on the ledge Quareem staggered back as if he had been smashed in the chest by a fist. Armestor let fly seconds after Fomond, but before he could see what had happened, the gliderboat rose upward and swerved away as Aru tried to keep it in safe air. Clouds shut out the skies, a great black pall filling the sky above them.

'We cannot go back!' Aru screamed, frightened. 'The path is going to close. The darkness – ' but her words were blanked out by fresh noise as more thunder exploded.

The craft seemed to scream, spinning. Fomond almost toppled headlong into space. He gripped the floor, but Armestor held him by the belt, his face ashen.

'Did we kill them?' Fomond called, but Armestor could not answer. The gliderboat plummeted, the valley floor racing up to meet it, while around the craft the elementals were screaming their jubilation.

On the ledge, Quareem toppled over. Agony seared his chest as though a heated metal rod had been plunged into it and he plucked at it, unable to believe what he found. Something had lodged there, smashing his ribs, tearing at his lungs like the talons of an eagle. It had been driven in by the hand of the storm, and blood congealed around it thickly. He tried to speak, but more blood frothed at his lips. He crawled from the stone to his men. One of them leaned over him, but the Blue Hair vomited blood, collapsing.

Vymark had rushed forward as soon as he saw the gliderboat in the sky. Gliderboat! his mind yelled. But whose? Again it had passed, flung by the hurricane winds, and as it did so, figures in it released arrows on the men below. Quareem was hit, the arrow almost passing through him. But Zellorian, who was still wrapped in the ritual of the storm, had not even seen the danger. As Vymark flung himself to his side, an arrow tore through his master's side, ploughing on and digging deep into Vymark's groin. He screamed with pain and fell, but he had done enough to push his master away from death.

Zellorian's concentration was broken. Above him there was a great blast of thunder and the ridge shook as though it must be torn loose. Zellorian clutched his side, surprised by the blood seeping into his robes. He swore.

Vymark tried to rise, his eyes filled with tears of acute pain. His men came to his aid, one of them snapping the arrow and pulling it out, ripping flesh to free it.

Zellorian ignored his fallen officer, moving quickly to the back of the ledge. He saw Quareem, knowing at once that he was dead. He studied the heavens. Like a maddened cur, the storm-of-the-dark raved and Zellorian felt the great surge of energy swelling before him like a tide, but suddenly no longer one he could control or direct at will. He felt it heave, threatening to pull loose from him, and with it his own deep powers. Desperately he fought to control those powers, knowing that the deathstorm hungered for them and focused on his pain, his relaxation of effort.

He had to let go.

He withdrew, closing mental doors upon that rapacious darkness. Crushed against the stone, thwarted, he laughed in spite of it. There was inestimable power on Innasmorn! Quareem had not exaggerated it at all. And it had been tapped. Zellorian continued to watch the storm, enjoying its wildness, its ferocity. He could feel it grope like a blind man for him, though it was unable to find him. Instead it raged on, shaking the mountain range. He exulted in its rawness.

At last he turned from it, still smiling. This did not end here. No, it had been but a taste. In time he would sate his hunger. And after the long search he had a weapon he could forge. How his enemies would feel it!

25

CONCLAVE

Aru brought the craft under control with a great effort: she could almost hear its inner scream. Eventually she took it down to the valley floor. Ussemitus was still where he had been, his back to a rock, his eyes gazing upwards, though seeing events far away. The thunder and the rain had mercifully ceased, the dark clouds rolling back, lifting as quickly as they had fallen.

But the havoc revealed in the valley was horrifying.

Fomond could see the army spread out along the pass, its numbers depleted, many of the dead sprawled out as though a pack of wild hounds had been at them. The earth was churned and furrowed, although there was no sign of the grim elemental dhumhagga that had been formed from it. The air whistled overhead, still filled with darting shapes, but the attack had ended. Somewhere in the mountains there was a deafening boom, followed by a series of others, getting slowly fainter, as if other forces had met the storm and vied with it for control of the Dhumvald.

Exhausted, Fomond turned to Armestor and Aru, who was watching Ussemitus closely. 'The storm-of-the-dark has gone. Something else has pushed it back.'

Surprisingly it was Ussemitus who answered. 'Yes, the Windmasters invoked Innasmorn and she answered them. But it was almost too late.' He closed his eyes, shuddered, then opened them again.

Aru grinned and hugged him. He laughed, but the sound died as he saw the destruction in the pass.

'Fomond must have killed Quareem,' said Armestor. 'The storm was focused through him. It broke his grip.'

'And Zellorian?' said Ussemitus.

Armestor looked away. 'I never saw where my arrow went.'

'I've never known you to miss yet!' Fomond smiled, putting an arm around Armestor, who smiled thinly.

'I fear this time—'

'If he does survive,' said Aru, 'he'll go back to the Sculpted City. And he'll search out this mythical land of power.'

'Then we have an advantage,' agreed Fomond. 'Let us go to the west at once—'

Ussemitus shook his head. 'No. We have to go back to Amerandabad. Jubaia is in grave trouble. I don't know how exactly, but we must find him.'

'He's alive?' grinned Fomond.

'Yes, he's alive. And I have to talk again to Vittargattus.'

Armestor groaned. 'But he'll only imprison us again!'

'We have the gliderboat,' said Aru.

Ussemitus nodded. 'We must make haste. But first we must try and find Telemorgas. If he survived the carnage.'

They boarded the gliderboat and this time rose more easily into the stilling air. As they drifted above the decimated army, they understood just how much damage it had suffered. Thousands must have died, and as many were wounded. It would be a long time before the survivors were ready to march again.

As the gliderboat dropped lower, heads turned and arrows were fitted to bows. But when the archers saw there was no hostile intent from above, they lowered their weary arms. Ussemitus called out to them, asking for Telemorgas, but he did not come forward. Neither did any of his captains. No one seemed to know who commanded now. Dazed and bewildered, the army began to prepare the pyres for its dead, for they would not be placed under this earth.

'Make for Tollavar!' Ussemitus called to them. 'There will be no more storms here.'

The gliderboat passed over them one last time, then swooped away up the pass, searching for the way back out of the Dhumvald.

364

As they sped back to the south, Fomond spoke privately to Ussemitus. 'What exactly happened?'

Ussemitus explained as best he could, his eyes widening as he did so, as though he still found it hard to understand the powers that had worked through him.

'Did the gods come into you?' whispered Fomond.

But Ussemitus was quick to deny it. 'Although they must have given me the power to guide them.'

'Then you are a Windmaster,' said Fomond, his eyes twinkling.

Again Ussemitus shook his head. 'No. I could not control such things. I called Azrand, and he heard me. His Blue Hairs cannot deny us now.'

After that they fell silent as the landscape beneath them sped by, thinking of the horrors they had seen and how close they had come to annihilation. They knew that if the storm-of-the-dark had come to the Dhumvald unhindered, it would have been beyond controlling, a power to shake the very foundations of their world.

It was early evening when the towers of Amerandabad came into view. The gliderboat dipped down, Aru wary of any aerial defences the Windmasters might have set up, though there seemed to be none. The gliderboat remained calm, as it had been when first she took it into the sky.

'Can you speak to the Blue Hairs as you did?' Aru asked Ussemitus.

He shook his head. Whatever power he had been granted during the storm was not with him here.

They swooped as low as they dared. Soldiers on the battlements and towers saw them and shouted out in alarm, scurrying like ants along the walls. It was twilight as Vittargattus appeared, Azrand beside him.

'You will not be harmed!' called the Blue Hair, his voice carrying. 'There is a tower to the east of us, on the island in the river. Take your craft to it and land. We will meet you there.'

The gliderboat moved over the city, over the roofs of the fortress where the company had fled with the assassins, going over the Fulgor to the island of the Windmasters. Aru set the craft down gently on the flat top of the tower at its heart. Ussemitus stepped from it first, insisting that he do so alone, but neither Fomond nor Aru would agree.

'And we'll keep our bows to hand,' said Fomond. 'Just to be sure.' Armestor nodded.

When Azrand arrived, he was unarmed, though there were soldiers accompanying Vittargattus. The clan chief looked haggard, his eyes bloodshot. He wore a look of deep suspicion, his tiredness evident, the anger that always seemed to simmer beneath his surface still there. The way he looked at Aru made it clear that he did not yet trust her, and hated anything to do with the intruders from beyond Innasmorn.

Ussemitus, however, spoke with a new confidence. 'Sire,' he said, addressing Vittargattus, 'we have witnessed the unleashing of the storm-of-the-dark, just as we promised you it would come.'

'The army,' breathed Vittargattus, stepping forward, his hand on the hilt of the long sword he wore at his side. 'I have had evil dreams about my army. What has happened to it?'

His warriors' faces were no less drawn than his, etched by the guttering torches that partly ringed the circular tower's battlements.

Ussemitus gave an account of events in the Dhumvald, of the destruction, and of the eventual defeat of the deathstorm.

'Quareem is dead?' said Vittargattus.

'We think so, but cannot be sure,' said Aru.

Azrand had said nothing thus far. He had watched the strangers with an odd fascination, particularly Ussemitus. He cleared his throat. 'Sire, I think you can be assured that he is. When a Blue Hair dies,' he added, with a pointed look at Aru, 'the brethren know of it. Your archer's arrow struck true. We are certain that Quareem is dead.'

366

Vittargattus nodded. 'And it seems that we are in your debt,' he told Ussemitus, though there was no trace of warmth in his voice.

'The power sent by the Windmasters broke up the storm, enough to help us,' said Ussemitus. 'I make no claim to being a Windmaster myself.'

'Then what are you?' said Azrand.

Ussemitus shrugged. 'I have been a vessel, no more than that.'

'And will you be so again?' said Vittargattus. 'Do you serve me?'

'If the need arises,' nodded Ussemitus. 'Of course. As will my companions.'

'What of the girl?' said Vittargattus, taking his hand from his sword haft and pointing to her. 'She who pilots this – thing.' He gestured to the gliderboat, voice thick with scorn.

'I told you her own people had been betrayed. They are not your enemies. Surely today's events make that clear to you?'

'Today makes nothing clear to me,' said Vittargattus bitterly. 'Except that I have lost many, many men.'

Azrand shifted uncomfortably. 'Yet had these people not helped us, sire, we would have lost the entire ten thousand. And the deathstorm would even now be let loose upon us.'

Vittargattus swung round to glare at him, almost as if the Blue Hair's words were a betrayal, but Azrand held his gaze. 'So what would you have me do?' said the clan chief. He turned back to Ussemitus and Aru. 'You seek asylum for your people in the mountains? Well, I cannot grant that. This evil that came upon the Vaza was nurtured by the traitor you call Zellorian. Until your people cast him out, I am still at war with them.'

Aru, infuriated by his stubbornness, would have retorted, but Ussemitus restrained her gently. 'We understand this, sire. We must assume Zellorian survived, though he may already be feeding the kites of the Dhumvald. If he returns to Aru's city, it will take time for his downfall to be engineered. He has power there and controls the armies. But he will be opposed.'

'In the meantime,' said Vittargattus, 'I will march upon his city. Azrand and the Blue Hairs will summon the storm that was promised. It will be unleashed. Tell your allies in this place to beware its coming. For I shall follow it with force.'

There was a momentary silence, broken only by the low moaning of the wind. Then Azrand spoke. 'Zellorian and his followers must be brought to justice.' He looked pointedly at Aru. 'Are you yourselves in pursuit of him?'

'We know his intention,' said Ussemitus. 'It lies in the west. We will go there before him.'

Azrand said something to Vittargattus that no one else heard. The clan chief looked at Ussemitus, grunting his approval.

'There is something else,' said Ussemitus.

'Name it,' said Azrand.

'There was another who came with us to Amerandabad. When we made our escape from the fortress, he was with us, though we feared him dead in the Zone of Echoes. But I know that he is alive.'

Vittargattus's eyes narrowed to thin slits, his hand again tightening on his sword as though it was a great effort for him not to drag it out and lay about him with it. 'The thief?' he said, voice like frost. 'You ask for him?'

'His name is Jubaia,' said Ussemitus.

Vittargattus snorted. 'I know his name! And he is alive. But there is very little time left to him.'

'Alive,' said Ussemitus, his pleasure clear.

'He is to be executed,' said Azrand. 'Two of my Blue Hairs died because of him.'

'Because of *us*,' corrected Aru. 'It was our escape.'

Ussemitus could see that Aru was prepared to argue, possibly to undo what he had done, and he put an arm on her. 'He was not responsible for that. But if we had remained in your prison, your army would not have been saved. We had no choice but to free ourselves.'

368

Vittargattus spat, his anger suddenly breaking. 'You dared to bring a *Phung* into my fortress! You unleashed that upon my men!'

'We had no powers of our own,' said Ussemitus calmly.

'And have none now,' said Azrand.

Fomond held his bow tightly as he heard this, knowing that Armestor had already singled out Azrand as his target if this business came to a fight.

Ussemitus smiled. 'That is so. But everything we have done, we have done in your service, and for Innasmorn. You cannot believe we seek your downfall.'

'We mourn our dead,' said Azrand.

'And I mourn my dead,' said Aru stiffly. 'My own father. My closest friends. All dead at the hands of these same enemies.'

'So you say,' said Vittargattus.

'The thief is to be executed this night,' said Azrand. 'The decree has already gone out.'

'Rescind it,' said Ussemitus.

'It is not possible,' said Vittargattus.

'Are you not the ruler here?' said Ussemitus.

Vittargattus's frown deepened, his brow like thunder. 'You add insult to your actions?'

Ussemitus shook his head. 'You mistake me. I seek only to unify our people.'

'You would make a hero of a common thief, a murderer?' said Azrand.

'And would you reward the one who spared your army with death?' countered Ussemitus.

Again there was a long silence. Vittargattus walked to the battlements and looked out into the night, his mind torn between avenging the stigma of the deaths in his fortress and allowing the strangers their request. The thief should be made an example of, and yet he had done Innasmorn a service. Last night, Vittargattus had slept badly, as he seemed to do these nights, and among his nightmares he heard the voice of his enemy, trying to beguile him to think no evil of these strangers from the forest lands. He imagined he heard that voice now, the voice of the thief, pleading for mercy. Annoyed at his imagination, he swung round.

'Very well,' he snapped. 'If it is not too late, you may have him.' He pointed at Aru. 'But you must leave us at once. Follow your destiny in the west. But mark this. You must never return here. If you are seen in Amerandabad, your lives are forfeit. All of you.'

'Where is Jubaia?' said Aru.

Vittargattus called one of his captains to him. He spoke to him and the man bowed.

'Go with this warrior. He has my instructions.' With that, the clan chief turned on his heels and left the tower, his warriors following him.

Azrand and the warrior remained, the latter waiting in silence for his next instructions. Azrand ignored him, walking forward.

'Perhaps you should have been better rewarded,' he said.

Ussemitus shrugged. 'We killed your brethren.'

Azrand nodded sourly. 'You did what you had to do. But it sits badly with us. You used a forbidden darkness to do it. We shall have to bear the weight of the consequences. You must exercise great care, Ussemitus, over the powers you have. Strange gifts.'

'I did not choose them.'

'None of us does. We do not control our destiny, not in the end. Windmasters are born, the gifts put into them by something greater than us all. The Mother of Storms has chosen you as her own. Only that spares you here, for you can see the hatred of Vittargattus, like a brand. Take the thief and leave us. But serve the Mother well.'

Ussemitus nodded, sensing something akin to envy in the eyes of the Blue Hair.

Azrand bowed and without another glance, left the tower.

'If you'll follow me,' said the warrior.

Aru and Armestor agreed to remain with the gliderboat, while Ussemitus and Fomond went with the warrior down into the tower, beyond its maze to the chambers of the fortress. The guard made a number of enquiries as they went, speaking to others, asking about the execution.

'Surely they have not killed him already,' whispered Fomond, but Ussemitus had no answer.

Jubaia was not in any of the cells, and their fears for him deepened. The warrior led them out into a small quadrangle, splashed by the rays of the moon. At its far end there was a stone dais, and upon it a group of figures. Ussemitus hurried over to it. Two strong guards held a third figure, bending it forward, its neck bared, ready to receive the blow of another guard who stood with an axe beside him.

Jubaia looked up, his eyes meeting those of Ussemitus. 'Master!' he croaked, but could manage no more.

'Put your axe away,' Ussemitus's warrior told the headsman, who scowled ferociously, disappointed.

'Eh? This is work for the clan chief—'

'I come from Vittargattus. The thief is to be spared.'

One of the men holding Jubaia released his arm. 'Ormus, you blockhead, it's the captain. Put the axe aside.' The guard turned to the warrior beside Ussemitus, recognising him with an oily smile.

'Apologies, sir. My eyesight leaves much to be desired.'

'So does the ale you fellows drink,' snorted the captain.

The guards laughed, though nervously. Jubaia was released and he hopped down off the dais with a low bow.

'Keep silent,' Ussemitus told him.

The captain led them back up through the fortress. A number of guards looked askance, but no one spoke or objected. Even so, Ussemitus and Fomond felt greatly relieved when they got back up on the battlements of the tower.

When Aru saw Jubaia, she ran to him and swept him off his feet, hugging him to her as if she had been reunited with a son. The little thief laughed, his face beaming.

The captain stared at them in amazement. 'You'd better leave at once,' he said, with an uneasy glance at the glider-

371

boat. 'If you're still here when dawn comes, my master may well have a change of heart.'

Ussemitus nodded, ushering the others into the glider-boat. Aru took the craft up into the skies, and although the warrior on the tower watched in fascination, his face was as pale as that of a ghost.

Ussemitus leaned over the little figure of Jubaia, who watched the land falling away in wonder. 'The Mother left it late to spare you,' he said softly to him.

Jubaia sniggered. 'I thought Vittargattus would never listen.'

'You pleaded with him?'

'All day,' said Jubaia, but suddenly clammed up as though he had said something indiscreet.

'You were locked away below and you pleaded with him all day?'

'I didn't mean that I was with him—'

Ussemitus gave him a sudden, knowing look. 'I think I understand, little thief. I have been meaning to ask you about our first meeting. How we acted so impulsively in killing those men of Kendara. Strange how such a thought entered our heads—'

'You are speaking in riddles,' protested Jubaia.

'I don't think so,' said Ussemitus. Before he could say more, however, Jubaia perched himself dangerously at the edge of the gliderboat, careless as a bird. The flight of the craft held no terrors for him at all.

'Hey! We've just pulled you out of the fire!' yelled Fomond. 'Get down before you topple to your doom.'

Jubaia threw back his head and laughed. He put his fingers to his scrawny neck and massaged it gently. 'Me? Fall? On a night like this, my friend, I feel that I could fly.'

'If you can fly,' called Armestor, still not used to the motion of the gliderboat, 'then perhaps you'd care to swoop down into the first forest we come to and catch us a few rabbits, or maybe a deer. If I don't eat soon, the flesh will fall off my bones.'

Jubaia laughed again. 'Ah, we can remedy that. Go north

west, dear lady Aru. I know a village there. There's an inn, and the girl who runs the place will provide us with all the comforts we could wish for. I am known there.'

'No doubt,' said Ussemitus, grinning.

They rose up, the moon huge before them, like the welcoming eye of a god.

Below them, in the city of Amerandabad, Vittargattus sat alone in his war chamber, studying the maps before him, though their detail seemed to blur. He shook himself, the events on the tower coming back to him again and again. He had freed them! Against his better judgement. But then again, were they his enemies? Would they serve Innasmorn and not the darker side of the Mother? They had used evil to escape him once.

He was so absorbed with his thoughts that he did not see the Blue Hair enter.

'You seem lost in your thoughts, Vittargattus,' said Azrand softly.

The clan chief gazed up at him. He seemed far less ferocious than he appeared to his vassals. And far more tired.

'You should sleep,' Azrand told him.

'Aye. Last night I slept better, though I dreamed.'

'Of what?'

'I forget most of it. There were nightmares, as is common enough. War. But something soothed me. Was it a sending of yours?'

Azrand glanced at the ceiling, thinking of the gliderboat and its strange occupants. 'I think not,' he said, but Vittargattus did not seem to hear him.

'Should I have killed them?' the clan chief asked.

'Before the storm, I would have said yes. But not now.'

'My fury said to do it. But something else warned me to spare them. Perhaps it was the Mother herself. Perhaps she does watch over them.'

Azrand masked his feelings by looking down at the maps. 'Will you ride south to meet Ondrabal?'

'At dawn.'

'Then sleep well again.'

Vittargattus grunted, but already his thoughts had sped ahead to the meeting with his ally.

That night he slept deeply, and for the first time in months there were no dreams to trouble him.

As Aru's gliderboat sped to the north western forests at the foot of the Thunderreach range, another craft slipped through the night skies, far to the east of them. It had travelled all day, bearing its occupants from the ill-fated storm-of-the-dark. Its Controller gritted his teeth, keeping the gliderboat moving on a direct course as fast as he could coax it, though he feared the sudden arrival of a squall. The weather on this world seemed set against anything that took to the air.

Behind him, two warriors sat in silence, exhausted. Zellorian had not moved for an hour, his eyes fixed on the darkness in the east as if his will alone would pilot the craft there. He had bound his wounded side, staunching the flow of blood that had been leaking alarmingly. But he would recover soon enough.

On the deck, Vymark did not fare so well. His wound was also bound up tightly, but even if the leg could be saved, he would never walk as a man should again, not for all the skills of Zellorian's surgeons in the city.

The warriors knew that even a soldier such as Vymark could be replaced. None of them were indispensable. They had seen how calmly and emotionlessly Zellorian had prepared to wipe away the ten thousand soldiers in the Dhumvald. He had seen the looks on the faces of his warriors.

'Think of them as Csendook,' was all he had said to them.

Vymark groaned in his sleep, as though he already fought a fresh war against the ancestral enemy. But unlike Vittargattus, his dreams were dark and feverish, filled with the sound of war, the screams of the dying.

374

EPILOGUE

EPILOGUE

Vorenzar entered the sumptuous apartments with an appreciative nod. His superior lived even more luxuriously than he had done at the time of his appointment. Vorenzar doubted that even the Marozul lived better than this.

When he saw Auganzar beside the fountain, he grinned.

'I hope your new-found power is not softening you, Zaru.'

The Supreme Sanguinary looked up. He also smiled, though there were very few of his colleagues who were favoured this way. 'I like to let the Garazenda think so.'

'It will be a long time before any of them think to bring about your downfall again.'

'I hope you are right.' But Auganzar knew that he had gained much power through his defeat of the Garazenda plot. All over the Warhive, the Csendook spoke his name with new reverence. There were few things that he pressed for with his superiors that he could not gain.

'You wanted to see me?'

Auganzar went to the long window and looked out over the gardens as if seeing them for the first time. 'Permission was granted this morning. You are to be the new Keeper on Eannor. You are prepared?'

Vorenzar's smile widened. 'Oh yes. I have already trained the warriors I need. They can be trusted implicitly. Give me the word and I will go to Eannor without delay.'

Auganzar turned to him. 'The Garazenda don't want us here, Vorenzar. They want our pass closed. But there is a gate there. A gate.' He looked angry for a fleeting moment, but it passed. He smiled again. 'Find it for me. The Imperator Elect is beyond it. Cowering somewhere. *Find him.*'

Vorenzar nodded. 'I will.'

Auganzar nodded. 'He's there.' After a moment he turned to study the gardens again. 'Yes, he's there.'

'I am ready.'

'Very well. Go now. At once.'

Vorenzar saluted, turning on his heel. His smile remained on his face until he reached his quarters. At last he could begin the work for which the Warhive had prepared him, the true service of all that he believed in.